PENGUIN TWENTIETH-CENTURY CLASSICS

THE LIME TWIG
SECOND SKIN
TRAVESTY

John Hawkes was born in Stamford, Connecticut in 1925, an only child and an asthmatic, and grew up in New England, Alaska, and New York. In 1943 he began six intermittent years at Harvard, for the most part writing poetry and, in 1944, taking time off to serve as an American Field Service ambulance driver in Italy and Germany, an experience that determined the often European settings of his fiction. In 1947 he married Sophie Tazewell, who became his lifelong literary collaborator, and also met his Harvard mentor, Albert J. Guerard. At that time, he turned to the writing of fiction, his first work establishing him as one of the earliest Postmodernists, known for his comic vision, his mastery as a prose stylist, and the range and power of his gifts as an innovative writer. His first novel, *The Cannibal*, recognized as a classic of World War II, was published by James Laughlin at New Directions in 1949.

Although he spent most of his professional life teaching at Brown University, Hawkes has been a constant traveler whose visits to various countries have been essential to the writing of his "landscapes of the imagination." Thus, of his major works, *The Lime Twig* (1961), an "English" novel written before he had been to England, derives from the voices of the British troops he worked with in the American Field Service; he wrote his "island" novel, *Second Skin* (1964), in the West Indies; four of his novels, including *Travesty* (1976), reflect his years in France and his passionate feelings for that country. *The Blood Oranges* (1971), his most controversial novel, made unmistakable the erotic qualities of his language and owes its mythical landscape to Greece. *Adventures in the Alaskan Skin Trade* (1985) and *Sweet William: A Memoir of Old Horse* (1993), both available from Penguin, are more personal than the rest of his work and refer back to Alaska and to his native New England boyhood.

John Hawkes is the author of fifteen novels, and has received Le Prix Medicis Étranger, one of France's most distinguished prizes, and has been supported by the Ford Foundation, the Guggenheim Foundation, the Lannon Foundation, and the Rockefeller Foundation. He is T. B. Stowell Professor Emeritus, Brown University and is a member of the American Academy of Arts and Letters. He has four children and lives in Providence, Rhode Island.

Patrick McGrath was born in London in 1950 and is the author of five books of fiction: *Blood and Water and Other Tales* and the novels *The Grotesque, Spider, Dr. Haggard's Disease,* and *Asylum.* He is coeditor with Bradford Morrow of an anthology, *The New Gothic.*

Robert Coover's novels include *The Public Burning, Gerald's Party,* and *John's Wife.*

BOOKS BY JOHN HAWKES

NOVELS

The Cannibal
The Beetle Leg
The Owl
The Lime Twig
Second Skin
The Blood Oranges
Death, Sleep & the Traveler
Travesty
The Passion Artist
Virginie: Her Two Lives
Adventures in the Alaskan Skin Trade
Innocence in Extremis
Whistlejacket
Sweet William
The Frog

PLAYS

The Innocent Party: Four Short Plays

COLLECTIONS

Humors of Blood & Skin: A John Hawkes Reader
Lunar Landscapes: Stories and Short Novels

Fn Julio. Fn Claudia
admiration!
Jack

THE LIME TWIG
SECOND SKIN
TRAVESTY

JOHN HAWKES

PREFACE BY
ROBERT COOVER

INTRODUCTION BY
PATRICK MCGRATH

PENGUIN BOOKS

Prov.

May 17, 1996

PENGUIN BOOKS
Published by the Penguin Group
Penguin Books USA Inc., 375 Hudson Street, New York, New York 10014, U.S.A.
Penguin Books Ltd, 27 Wrights Lane, London W8 5TZ, England
Penguin Books Australia Ltd, Ringwood, Victoria, Australia
Penguin Books Canada Ltd, 10 Alcorn Avenue, Toronto, Ontario, Canada M4V 3B2
Penguin Books (N.Z.) Ltd, 182–190 Wairau Road, Auckland 10, New Zealand

Penguin Books Ltd, Registered Offices: Harmondsworth, Middlesex, England

This volume published in Penguin Books 1996

1   3   5   7   9   10   8   6   4   2

PUBLISHER'S NOTE
These are works of fiction. Names, characters, places, and incidents either are the product of the
author's imagination or are used fictitiously, and any resemblance to actual persons, living or dead,
events, or locales is entirely coincidental.

LIBRARY OF CONGRESS CATALOGING IN PUBLICATION DATA
Hawkes, John, 1925–
[Novels. Selections]
The lime twig; Second skin; Travesty/John Hawkes; with an
introduction by Patrick McGrath.
p.   cm.
Includes bibliographical references.
ISBN 0 14 01.8982 3 (pbk.)
1. Psychological fiction, American.   2. Horror tales, American.
I. Title.   II. Title: Second skin.   III. Title: Travesty.
PS3558.A82A6   1996
813'.54—dc20   95–50538

Printed in the United States of America
Set in Sabon

Dearest Sophie
for you

CONTENTS

PREFACE

ONE OF THE GREAT PLEASURES granted the young writer (and there are many, this is not a bad life) is that of discovering, buried beneath the heaped-up overlauded drivel of the day, the authentic voice of the as-yet-unrecognized literary master. It now seems hard to believe, but writers like Borges, Nabokov, and Beckett were once just such underground icons, known only to a few, mostly other writers, and used, especially among the young, as a kind of recognition code. This was in the post–World War II years when established American fiction was (as it is yet, sad to say) tediously conventional, imitative of the past, trite in its forms and shallow in its ambitions—with a few startling exceptions, found mostly in the back corners of offbeat bookshops where works published by the likes of Grove Press and New Directions could be found: the young William Burroughs, for example. Young William Gaddis. Young John Hawkes.

Finding Hawkes was like finding, in a stifling lockup, a secret message of imminent liberation. Here was, truly, a writer after my own heart, one who was at once disruptive, luminous, daring, funny yet terrifying, and utterly devoted to the art of fiction, not as confession or entertainment, but as a form of artistic expression to be explored to its very depths. Wherein lay art's only conceivable morality. "I dislike autobiographical fiction," he said, "I don't write fiction in order to use my life up as its source." He called the prevailing realistic tradition "pedestrian," disdaining reflection or representation. "I want my fiction to destroy conventional morality and conventional attitudes," he said. He said: "I began to write fiction on the assumption that the true enemies of the novel were plot, character, setting, and theme." He said: "The problem is that people don't know that life is a kind of fiction that we create and we accept as 'real.' We need to challenge such realities all the time." Ah, how could I *not* love this writer, laboring as I was through my own early breakaway fictions, convinced only that the dreams we'd all dreamt needed somehow to be undreamt? "The writing of each fiction," he said, "is a taking of a psychic journey."

As it turned out, we were not traveling alone. The 1960s witnessed the rise of a new generation of American writers, as yet widely scattered and unrecognized as such, each on distinctive journeys of their own, but clearly sharing this iconoclastic spirit, a more or less spontaneous outburst of narrative innovation that has since come to be known as "postmodernism," or "metafiction," "surfiction," etc., a movement noted for its formal experiments, its bleak comedy, and its impassioned declarations of imaginative freedom. And at the very beginning of the decade, like gate-opening clarions, appeared the third and fourth novels of John Hawkes, the startlingly original masterpiece *The Lime Twig*, in 1961, and three years later, *Second Skin*, which, with its inventiveness, awesome intensity, savage comedy, and verbal brilliance, became a kind of centerpiece for that generation and its critics, cited by adherents and foes alike, one of those books which seems so to mark a moment in time that the moment itself comes to be identified by them.

Another dozen or so books have followed in the decades since, each of them at once grotesque and beautiful, cruel and loving, heart-wrenching and darkly comic, each celebrating—like Skipper, the desperate clown-narrator of *Second Skin*—the very powers of the imagination which terrorize him, and each of course richly phrased in the inimitable Hawkes style, with its unabashed eroticism, its fleshly tones and arousing textures, its impassioned verbs, its plump adjectives and prurient adverbs, its vulnerable innocent nouns.

If I were to attempt to capture the art of John Hawkes in a single phrase, I think it would be one he himself used as the title of a rare little volume published by Burning Deck Press in Providence in 1985: *Innocence in Extremis*. "Everything is dangerous," he has said, "everything is tentative, nothing is certain," and into such perilous circumstances is cast the artist, whose primary quality, for Hawkes, is innocence of heart and mind—not ignorance, not naive optimism or false illusion—but a naked appetite for life, a pure love for "the saving beauties of language" ("her shape was in itself a flaunting of her spirit," says the young narrator of *Innocence in Extremis*), and a willingness, like *Second Skin*'s Skipper, forced by his own daughter to suffer the humiliating ordeal of the tattooer's needles "burning their open pinprick way across my chest," to be written upon as much as to write.

—Robert Coover
November 1995

INTRODUCTION

JOHN HAWKES HAS BEEN CALLED A "DEMONIC ARTIFICER," and the three novels published here are prime examples of his unsettling art. These fictions are allegories of the mind, symbolic dramas about violent, chaotic forces of the unconscious that come surging up to batter the ego's defenses and launch assaults on rational order. The density and strangeness of the work, and also its beauty, are a function of Hawkes's employing in its design the structural properties and logic of the nightmare. He floods his books with the nightmare's grotesque imagery, and cloaks them in an atmosphere of constriction, obscurity, and dread.

Not surprisingly, this is fiction that has little in common with the conventionally plotted novel, and must be read with an ear and an eye to its poetic form. A poetic reading opens us to the strange, sensual ambience of a John Hawkes novel, and to the elegance and complexity of the patterns of meanings with which it is constructed, and most of all, to the intense beauty of its language. Hawkes's prose is music. Delicately accented and strongly rhythmic, it courses forward with a liquid grace that would seem to be at odds with its often macabre or uncanny content. But the effect, paradoxically, is to transform the nightmare; our pleasure in the almost erotic quality of the writing controls and redeems its horrors.

Two of the three novels published here, *The Lime Twig* and *Second Skin*, came out in the early sixties and share an atmosphere of menace and confusion, and also a certain impotence, or vulnerability, in their protagonists, each of whom is in various ways persecuted. The third, *Travesty*, published in 1976, differs from the earlier books in that its nightmare quality is more cerebral than sensual, and its narrator very much in control—if not of his reason then certainly of the two poor creatures he intends to take with him to a violent end.

This character, named only Papa, is in a way a reversed reflection of his creator. A frustrated artist obsessed by an insane idea, he is intent on destroying his own life and the lives of his daughter and her lover in a deliberate car wreck. Considerable irony therefore attaches to the claim he makes, late in the novel, to a penetrating night vision: "The night is to my eye as is the pair of goggles to the arc-welder. Through the thick green lens of the night I see only the brightest and most frightening light."

In a man of moral blindness and corrupted reason, such a peculiarity of vision only confirms that his perspective is skewed. Night vision, however, in the sense of the ability to detect form within darkness, is the particular quality of Hawkes's work. He discovers in the dark, disordered regions of the psyche an impulse of negation, or inversion, which he then weaves deep into the very fabric of the fiction, so that it infiltrates not only the visual field, the imagery, but the moral, rational, social, and natural orders of things as well. Everything is thus turned upside down. Corruption is revealed within innocence; sound structure rings hollow and collapses into ruin. For what Hawkes brings up into the light is the unspeakable: that which the psyche represses lest it disturb the ego's order.

The dominant themes encountered here include madness, deformity, suicide, mutiny, murder, mutilation, incest, and rape. Transgression is universal, and death figures larger than love.

The Lime Twig, Hawkes's fourth novel, was published in 1961. Set in a shabby postwar England of bad food, squalid lodging houses, and constant rain, it is the story of a young man called Michael Banks who is drawn into a crude racetrack scam with a gang of deeply unsavory underworld types. The man responsible for Michael's introduction to a life of crime, and thus—in a desperate escalation of negatives—to his involvement with the underworld, and eventually his death, is called Hencher, and it is with Hencher and his old mother that *The Lime Twig* begins. There is tenderness in their relationship, but that tenderness exists in an atmosphere of squalor and too-close contact with the organic world and hence decay. The description of Hencher's mother's leftovers from dinner—"cartilage, raw fat, cold and dusty peels and the mouthful—still warm—which she leaves on her plate"—has a particularly repulsive appeal.

The mood of mild comic disgust turns to one of blackest farce when Hencher, remembering an air raid on London during World War II, describes his mother's breast catching fire:

> On hands and knees she was trying to crawl back to me, hot sparks from the fire kept settling on her arms and on the thin silk of her gown. One strap was burned through suddenly, fell away, and then a handful of tissue in the bosom caught and, secured by

the edging of charred lace, puffed at its luminous peak as if a small forced fire, stoked inside her flesh, had burst a hole through the tender dry surface of my mother's breast.

It is in the depiction of the body that the impulse of negation is expressed most vividly in Hawkes's fiction. Any idea of wholeness, or integrity, is alien to a world in which order is disturbed at every level, and so fragmentation, incompletion, or, as here, bizarre injury, all conspire to make the body monstrous. In these three novels there are characters who possess false hands or false knees or false legs; who are missing a lung or an arm or a set of fingers or a head of hair; who wear tattoos or goggles or steel vests or brass knuckles; who are crushed or trampled or beaten or stabbed or raped or shot. A wife haunted by the sound of the gunshot with which her husband killed himself blocks it out forever by filling her ears with melted wax. And where physical beauty, or sexual perfection, occurs, a stain of impurity will always be revealed, and the deformity identified as an internal condition, a corruption of the soul. This is true of the young women, the daughters, in both *Second Skin* and *Travesty*.

Three major features of the Hawkesian world imbue it with its peculiar dreamlike atmosphere of dread. The first and most visible is this pervasive sense of disorder, of deformity, that works itself out not only in the bodies of the characters but in their architecture, their social formations, the flora and fauna around them.

The second feature is obscurity, both climatic and subjective. Gloom, steam, fog, darkness, incomprehension, drunkenness—all are forms of obscurity, which in *The Lime Twig* is the condition of almost all the key scenes. When Michael, after agreeing to go along with Hencher's proposal that he claim to be the owner of a stolen horse, then finds his involvement with the criminals deepening, Hawkes uses weather to point up his protagonist's uneasy plight:

Fog of course and he should have expected it, should have carried a torch. Yet, whatever was to come his way would come, he knew, like this—slowly and out of a thick fog. Accidents, meetings unexpected, a figure emerging to put its arms about him: where to discover everything he dreamed of except in a fog.

An illustration of a meeting unexpected occurs in this same scene, by the river, in the fog, at night, when a stolen horse is winched up from a barge onto the quay. It is an extraordinary image, the blindfolded animal dangling over the water in a sling of webbed canvas, an image that will be echoed in *Second Skin* when, in the early stages of a mutiny, a lifeboat is lowered over the side of a ship and blocks the light from the captain's porthole. The effect is the same, that of a huge object displaced, out of its element, unnaturally suspended, though here the horse is not strange merely because it is displaced. The violent potential of the horse has already been alluded to, and that violence is soon to be unleashed.

The third feature of the Hawkesian ambience is constriction. Transporting the stolen horse to the racetrack, five men are squeezed tightly into the cab of a truck. This is a situation Hawkes returns to again and again, too many people crowded into too small a space. After the claustrophobic drive, Hencher experiences an even more intense constriction when he goes into the horse's box and is promptly kicked to death.

This is what happens to men trapped in the wrong sort of tight spaces: their boxes turn into coffins. A little later, at the racetrack, we come upon a variation on the theme, when the social world, the racing community, is rendered thus:

> They were coming down from the stands, from the stable area, from amusement tents, tramping across the beds of flowers left crushed or covered with spittle. White faces, a hat or two, a hearing aid, all packed together, stranger against stranger, and making their voices shrill over winnings or poor luck.

This is what other people, in the mass, mean, in Hawkes's fiction: crowds of strangers packed together and heedlessly crushing flowers underfoot, covering them with spittle. This image of community informs not only *The Lime Twig* but much of *Second Skin* as well, with the exception there of an idyllic society of cows and willing women discovered on a floating island.

The climax of *The Lime Twig* takes place on a day of violent death at the racetrack, preceded by a night of sexual excess. On the last night of his life, Michael's moral descent is almost complete as he participates in a wild party with the criminals and their women. Between his first bout of sex, with a tarty one called Sybilline, and his second, with "the widow," he is fed an aphrodisiac meal of eggs and meat sauce. "Brown and broken yellow, thick and ovarian, his mouth was running with the eggs and sauce while the whiskey glasses of the women were leaving rings."

He is led upstairs shortly afterward.

> Then she took hold of him, and behind the door at the end of the hall he dropped his trousers in the widow's sleeping chamber, heard her quick footsteps round the bed and in his hands caught the plumpness of the hips. . . .
>
> "Go gently, Mr. Banks," fending, giggling, "go sweetly, please."

His night is far from over. On his way downstairs—"He was fierce now, fierce but dry"—he meets Annie, a girl about whom he has been entertaining sexual fantasies for some time. This night all dreams are fulfilled.

> He opened her coat directly and ran his hand inside, up lisle and tenderness until he found the seam, the tight rolled edge and drops of warmth against his fingertips, and said, ". . . You want me to, you really want me to?" She stood up then—he hadn't known that she could stand—and with fingers steadying on his shoulders lifted first one tiny knife-heeled slipper and then the other, bending each leg sharply at the knee, swinging alternate thin calves in an upward and silent dancing step, removed the undergarment and the slippers, and came down slowly, slowly, across his lap.
>
> "I want you to."

This is edgy, dirty sex, rendered all the more so because of the number of willing partners Michael finds, and the fact that it is the night before he dies. There are many forms the erotic can take. In *The Lime Twig* the sex is excessive, perfunctory, illicit, and quick, and marks the penultimate stage in a process of corruption that can end only in death.

Of these three novels, the greatest formal complexity is to be found in *Second Skin*. In both *Travesty* and *The Lime Twig* the narrative accelerates as it moves directly to its climax, which in both cases involves a collision at high speed resulting in violent death. *Second Skin*, by contrast, is languid and playful by design; it moves backward and forward, demanding the reader's participation in the organization of events. Its tone is often whimsical, wry, even joyful, and while the book includes a great many dark elements—rape, suicide, mutiny, and murder—there is a comic happy ending in which the gothic tone gives way to a sort of mock pastoral and the point is made that this story is as much about birth as it is about death.

The relationship in *Second Skin* of the narrator—variously known as "Skipper," "Edward," and "Papa Cue Ball" (because of his bald-ness)—and his daughter Cassandra is heavy with incestuous undercur-rents. When the story proper begins in the second chapter, the first words are, "She was in my arms"—he is dancing with his daughter in a seedy bar in San Francisco—and a little further on:

> And suddenly I was aware of the blind, meaningless, momentary
> presence of her little breast against my own and I . . . wished all
> at once to abandon rank, insignia, medal, bald head, good nature,
> everything, if only I might become for a moment an anonymous
> seaman second class, lanky and far from home and dancing with
> this girl."

What Skipper really wants to abandon is the incest taboo, and the fact that this is so plainly articulated is an indication that we are present once again in that dark disordered region of the mind where the re-pressed claws up into the light. The scene is quintessentially Hawkesian not only because of this hint of transgression, this sexual contact be-tween father and daughter, but also because there is a strong sense of *crowdedness*, of too many people crammed into too small a place, al-most as if to insist that *this* is the human condition, this is the banal horror of everyday life, this being pushed together with strangers, or with people vaguely hostile to oneself, in cramped spaces from which there is no escape.

This sort of deeply ironic vision of a distorted cosmos, with its gro-tesque exaggeration of mundane tribulation, is a feature of the pica-resque tradition in fiction, and it is here that we might pause to identify Hawkes's literary kinship. By his own account, the line begins with the Spanish picaresque writers and runs through Thomas Nashe to Lau-treamont, Céline, Nathanael West, Flannery O'Connor, Faulkner, Hel-ler, Purdy, and Nabokov. To this distinguished register one might add Freud, Kafka, and Poe.

Second Skin belongs squarely within this pedigree. It is a true pica-
resque in that it concerns the episodic adventures of a roguish protagonist. Skipper's journey takes him to two very different islands, one an
island of death, the other of life. The island of death is located somewhere off the northeast coast of North America and is remarkable for
the inhospitable character of both its people and its weather.

These elements conspire to humiliate Skipper one strange, cold night.
He and Cassandra are going to a dance in the high school gym in the
company of a group of locals including Captain Red and his two sons,
Jomo, who has a steel hand, and Bub. All three have lecherous designs
on Cassandra. The journey to the gym has a familiar awfulness: Bub at
first won't let Skipper into the car, and when at last he does, he makes
him sit on his knee.

> Steaming upholstery, six steaming people. Smells of gasoline,
> spilled whiskey, fading perfume, antifreeze. And Bub. With my
> head knocking against the roof of the car I knew him for what
> he was: a boy without underwear, holes in his socks, holes in his
> pockets, rancid navel, hair bunched and furrowed on the scrawny
> nape of his neck, and the mouth forever breathing off the tell-
> tale smell of sleep and half-eaten candy bars. This country boy,
> this island boy. Filled with fun. With hate. With smelly self-
> satisfaction.

Later Skipper leaves the dance and goes outside into the darkness
and is pelted by snowballs: "Malevolent missiles. From every corner of
the lot they came, and from the vicinity of the all-but-hidden cars—
lovers? could this be the activity of island lovers? nothing better to
do?—and even, I thought, from as far as the cemetery."

In these novels the world tends to become menacing when obscured
visibility, or obscured faculties, leave a character vulnerable to the assaults of an essentially hostile and malignant environment. In *Second
Skin* the sea is the central, all-enclosing feature of that environment, the
great fluid nothingness beneath all things, beneath the boats and the
islands and the people they contain. Here is the sea as it appears to
Skipper from that "black island" in the north Atlantic:

> The shoals were miles long and black and sharp, long serrated
> tentacles that began at the base of the promontory and radiated
> out to sea, mile after square mile of intricate useless channels and

breaking waves and sharp-backed lacerating shoals and spiny reefs. Mile after square mile of ocean cemetery that wasn't even true to its dead but kept flushing itself out on the flood tide. No wonder the poor devils wanted a lighthouse here. No wonder.

The sea, then, as an "ocean cemetery," a place of death. And the black island shares this identification with death, for Cassandra will die there after leaping from a ruined lighthouse.

But the equation is incomplete. In this novel Hawkes sets up a counterpoint to the island of death, giving us an island of birth, of life, where Skipper ends up with his trusty mess boy, Sonny. We may catch Hawkes's attitude to his island of life ("a wandering island, of course, unlocated in space and quite out of time") from the profession Skipper adopts there:

> And the work itself? Artificial insemination. Cows. In my flapping tennis shoes and naval cap and long puffy sun-bleached trousers, and accompanied by my assistant, Sonny, I am much esteemed as the man who inseminates the cows and causes these enormous soft animals to bring forth calves. Children and old people crowd around to see Sonny and me in action. And I am brown from walking to the cows in the sun, so brown that the green name tattooed on my breast has all but disappeared in a tangle of hair and in my darkening skin. An appealing sort of work, a happy life. The mere lowing of a herd, you see, has become my triumph.

This is the best sort of Hawkesian joke, a gloriously rich mockery of a certain arcadian romanticism that worships the state of nature. This island provokes laughter rather than any sense that the love, peace, redemption, and plenty that Skipper finds there—along with a corresponding absence of malice—could exist anywhere outside a fantasy. And Hawkes has by no means finished yet. For Skipper is not merely happy, he is in love—with a large black woman called Catalina Kate. "And this—Sonny and I both agree—this is love. Here I have only to drop my trousers—no shirt, no undershirt, no shorts—to awaken paradise itself, awaken it with the sympathetic sound of Catalina Kate's soft laughter."

With the mention of Catalina Kate it is impossible not to be reminded of another of those startling images at which Hawkes excels. Skipper goes down to the swamp: "Dark green tepid sludge of silent waters drifting inland among the ferns and roots and fuzzy pockets and pools of the infested swamp. Harem of veiled orchids, cells of death."

There he finds Catalina Kate, who is heavily pregnant.

> She was lying there and watching me. Must have been watching me all the time. Lying there on her stomach. Chin in her hands. Naked. Legs immersed halfway up the calves in the warm yellowish pea soup of that disgusting water. And stuck to her back, spread eagle on her broad soft naked back, an iguana with his claws dug in.

A big one, too.

> His head reached her shoulders, his tail dropped over her buttocks, and he might have been twenty or thirty pounds of sprawling bright green putty. Boneless. Eyes like shots in the dark. Gorgeous bright green feathery ruff running down the whole length of him. Thick and limp and weak, except for the oversized claws which were grips of steel. Kate was looking at me and smiling and the iguana was looking at me, and I heard the noise of locust or cricket or giant swamp fly strangling behind a nearby bush.
>
> "Hold on, Kate," I whispered, "don't move. Just leave him to me."

Hawkes creates his peculiar and unique effects in part through complex systems of symbols and elaborate networks of metaphor. *Second Skin*, with its opposed themes of death and birth, compresses the associated imagery: between leaving the West Coast and reaching the "black island," Skipper and Cassandra travel in a bus that is hijacked in the desert by three soldiers gone AWOL. In the course of the hijacking the leader of the soldiers tells the other two to bury their "eggs," that is, their hand grenades. This curious echo of reptilian reproduction occurring during the strangely inconclusive ambush will later come to mind as Catalina Kate lies in the sand on her swollen pregnant belly with the iguana clamped to her back. Juxtapose the two images and a vivid complex of meanings is aroused—connotations of life and death, violence and fertility, human and reptile. These uncanny chords of meaning set off unconscious patterns of evoked response, complex and contradictory, that underscore the more obvious climatic and psychic expressions of obscurity, constriction, and threat.

Also in *Second Skin* we find an event that perfectly illustrates this Hawkesian deployment of condensed, discordant imagery: the mutiny. Mutiny of course is a most potent manifestation of breakdown and inversion within a closed social community—the overthrowing of authority, its replacement by an illegitimate regime—and also, in the context of this novel, a further instance of our narrator's unending victimization. For Skipper is the actual skipper of the vessel in question.

The incident begins with that extraordinary image, a lifeboat being lowered over the side of the ship and blocking the light from Skipper's porthole. In the same lifeboat, that night, the ultimate transgression of authority is enacted, the rape of Skipper by the leader of the mutineers, a character called Tremlow, who is at the time wearing a grass skirt. The scene is not, however, undiluted with grace: the ship's chaplain, Mac, whom Skipper had earlier assisted in giving Holy Communion to the crew, saves Skipper's life by throwing him a rope just as the lifeboat is being cut loose. Elements of grace and abasement are thus conjoined in the context of the mutiny, as they are in the greater design of the book, with its two islands, one dark, one light, one portending death, the other fertility, perpetuation, birth, and life. Throughout *Second Skin* this running together of contradictory symbols is further complicated by irony and idiosyncrasy, so producing a still higher level of compression as the various oppositions are themselves undermined.

Perhaps this is best summed up in the striking simplicity and earthy humor of the book's last image: the joyful feast, the celebration of Catalina Kate's new baby, which takes place on the Night of All Saints—in the cemetery.

The vehicle in *Travesty* is roomier, more comfortable, more powerful, than the various vehicles in *The Lime Twig* and *Second Skin*; but the fate of those trapped within is grimmer by far, for this car is the ultimate coffin. And here Hawkes finds a fresh set of possibilities for constricted enclosure, for the speeding car in *Travesty* stands metaphorically for the enclosed space within the skull of our narrator, Papa. No other voice is heard, though there are two other people in the car with Papa. Both are controlled by his design, which is perhaps one of the most chillingly brilliant ideas in contemporary fiction.

The great challenge and paradox of all fiction, and in particular fiction that foregrounds the operations of consciousness *in extremis*, is managing, within the coherent formal organization of a narrative, the formlessness, the irrationality, the associative links and switches of mental experience. And it is precisely this conflict that Hawkes addresses in *Travesty*. Almost immediately we are aware of the frightening detachment of the narrator, his ability to see his own life—and the lives of others—purely as elements in an aesthetic design. Early on he calls the poet Henri a "banal moralist" when Henri, in his terror at what the madman at the wheel intends to do, accuses him of planning to murder them all.

> So you accuse me of planning murder. But with the very use of the word you reveal at last that you are only the most banal and predictable of poets. No libertine, no man of vision and hence suffering, but a banal moralist. Think of the connotations of "murder," that awful word: the loss of emotional control, the hate, the spite, the selfishness, the broken glass, the blood, the cry in the throat, the trembling blindness that results in the irrevocable act, the helpless blow. Murder is the most limited of gestures.

Murder, that awful word. No, what is being contemplated here is not murder, although it certainly looks like it to those who are about to die; it is a work of art. Bit by bit, insight by insight, Hawkes allows us access to the mind that would deny that what it contemplates is murder:

> What can you do? How in but a few minutes can you adjust yourself successfully to what for me is second nature: a nearly phobic yearning for the truest paradox, a thirst to lie at the center of this paradigm: one moment the car in perfect condition, without so much as a scratch on its curving surface, the next moment impact, sheer impact. Total destruction. In its own way it is a form of ecstasy, this utter harmony between design and debris.

The detachment of the artist from life, a necessary precondition of creation, is here taken to an absurd extreme, to an utter disregard for the lives of others, specifically Papa's own daughter and her lover. And he cannot see it! "I am," he tells Henri a little later, "the kindest man you will ever meet."

The structure of this novel, as of the other two, is built of corre-

spondence and displacement. Everything Papa observes and reflects on
during the death drive is in some way ruined or spoiled, from an empty
grave and a blasted tree to a heap of clothing that "might have been
stripped from dead bodies." Such evidence of physical decay echoes the
cloying decadence Papa reveals in his private life and even in his family
life. He talks of the time that Honorine and Chantal, his wife and
daughter, urged him into the arms of a prostitute. Then, late in the
book, comes the unforgettable description of how the young Chantal
was given over to a man called Lulu who then, with the parents' con-
nivance, involved her and two other young girls in a spectacle designed
to provoke salacious enjoyment of their nubile bodies by the adults. It
is no surprise to learn that Papa is a pathologically cold man who must
warm his hands before he touches his wife and requires that the temperature in the car be set uncomfortably high.

Papa is contemptuous of Henri's accusation that he is motivated by
jealousy. Instead he talks of what he and Henri share. His wife Honorine has told him, he tells Henri, that

> she thought you and I were both a little out of our heads. She said
> that we were selfish, that we were hurtful, and that she did not
> trust either one of us. But then she laughed and said that she loved
> us both, however, and was willing and capable of paying whatever
> price the gods, in return, might eventually demand of her for lov-
> ing us both.

And here at last the full monstrousness of the man's mind is revealed,
and the nature of the travesty he is contemplating. Henri has inscribed
his volumes of poetry to Honorine. Now Papa will pay his wife *his*
tribute; he will present her with his own work of art. And that work is
the destruction of the three people who comprise Honorine's world. She
will know, he says, "that just as she was the source of your poems, so
too was she the source of my private apocalypse."

What a wealth of pathology resides in this piece of logic! And yet so
blind is he that just a few pages earlier he brushed off the suggestion
that he suffered, as Henri does, from any mental illness.

> So you think that my brain is sewn with the sutures of your
> psychosis. . . . I am well aware that in that short time they so
> sutured the lobes of your brain with designs of fear and hopeless-
> ness that the threads themselves emerged from within your skull

to travel in terrible variety down the very flesh of your face, pinching, pulling, and scoring your hardened skin as if they, your attendants, had been engaged not in psychological but surgical disfigurement. I appreciate all this. I regret that you were so abused and that you took such dreadful pleasure in the line that cracked your eye, cleft your upper lip, stitched the unwholesome map of your brain to the mask of your face. But we must remember that we are talking not about me but you.

This is a brilliant passage, with its Faulknerian rhythms and its Frankenstein imagery, and it gathers together many Hawkesian motifs. But what it reveals most dramatically is the mechanism of a near-psychotic projection that accounts for the extraordinary moral blindness that so disfigures this narrator.

Despite my theory of likenesses, as I have called it, you are simply not to think that your former derangement has reappeared in me and, at present, is driving all three of us to what the authorities define as death by unnatural causes. I believe that if you have been listening you will have heard in my words the dying breath of your own irrationality, not mine.

It would be difficult to find a more startling instance of psychological disturbance in twentieth-century literature, nor one that more clearly demonstrates why, in his sustained exploration of the deep reaches of the libido, Hawkes's fiction is unique. His body of work now stretches to fifteen novels, plus collections of short stories and plays. He has developed fresh structures, locations, and constellations of characters with each new book, yet the work as a whole displays a remarkable coherence and continuity, driven as it is by the linked themes of passion, transgression, and violence. In his commitment to these themes, as in his formal inventiveness, his intelligence, and the sheer grace of his prose, John Hawkes remains the most consistently interesting and challenging writer at work in this country today.

PATRICK MCGRATH
October 1995

SUGGESTIONS FOR FURTHER READING

BOOKS

Ferrari, Rita. *Innocence and Power: The Novels of John Hawkes.* Philadelphia: University of Pennsylvania Press, 1996.

Gault, Pierre. *John Hawkes: La parole coupée: Anatomie d'une écriture romanesque.* Preface by Maurice Naudeau. Paris: Klincksieck, 1984.

Greiner, Donald J. *Comic Terror: The Novels of John Hawkes.* Memphis, Tenn.: Memphis State University Press, 1978.

———. *Understanding John Hawkes.* Columbia, S.C.: University of South Carolina Press, 1985.

Hryciw-Wing, Carol. *John Hawkes: A Research Guide.* New York: Garland Publishing, Inc., 1986.

Kuehl, John. *John Hawkes and the Craft of Conflict.* New Brunswick, N.J.: Rutgers University Press, 1975.

O'Donnell, Patrick. *John Hawkes.* Boston: Twayne, 1982.

Ziegler, Heide. *Ironie ist Pslicht: John Barth und John Hawkes.* Heidelberg: Universitätsverlag C. Winter, 1995.

ARTICLES

Chénetier, Marc. " 'The Pen & the Skin': Inscription and Cryptography in John Hawkes's *Second Skin.*" *Review of Contemporary Fiction* 3 (Fall 1983): 167–77.

Guerard, Albert J. "The Prose Style of John Hawkes." In *Critical Essays on John Hawkes*, edited by Stanley Trachtenberg, 87–95. Boston: G.K. Hall & Co., 1991.

Karl, Frederick R. *American Fictions, 1940–1980: A Comprehensive History and Critical Evaluation*, 215–23, 508–14, 526–29, and passim. New York: Harper & Row, 1983.

Laniel, Christine. "John Hawkes's Return to the Origin: A Genealogy of the Creative Process." In *Facing Texts: Encounters Between Contemporary Writers and Critics*, edited by Heide Ziegler, 215–46. Durham, N.C.: Duke University Press, 1988.

———. "The Rhetoric of Excess in John Hawkes's *Travesty.*" *Review of Contemporary Fiction* 3 (Fall 1983): 177–85.

Le Vot, André. "From the Zero Degree of Language to the H-Hour of

Fiction: or, Sex, Text, and Dramaturgy in *The Cannibal*." *Review of Contemporary Fiction* 3 (Fall 1983): 185–192.

O'Donnell, Patrick. "Self-Alignment in John Hawkes' *Travesty*." In *Passionate Doubts: Designs of Interpretation in Contemporary American Fiction*, 23–40. Iowa City: University of Iowa Press, 1986.

Rosenzweig, Paul. "Aesthetics and the Psychology of Control in John Hawkes's Triad." *Novel* 15 (Winter 1982): 146–62.

Scholes, Robert. "John Hawkes's Theory of Fiction" and "*The Lime Twig*." In *Fabulation and Metafiction*, 169–177; 178–179. Urbana, Ill.: University of Illinois Press, 1979.

Singer, Alan. "The Parody of Fate. *Second Skin* and the Death of the Novel." In *A Metaphorics of Fiction: Discontinuity and Discourse in the Modern Novel*, 79–114. Gainesville: University Presses of Florida, 1983.

Tanner, Tony. "Necessary Landscapes and Luminous Deteriorations." In *City of Words: American Fiction 1950–1970*, 202–29. New York: Harper & Row, 1971.

Thornton, Lawrence. " 'What Country, Friends, Is This?': The Inner Terrain of *The Blood Oranges*." In *Unbodied Hope: Narcissism and the Modern Novel*, 186–200. Lewisburg, Pa.: Bucknell University Press, 1984.

Unsworth, John M. "Practicing Post-Modernism: The Example of John Hawkes." *Contemporary Literature* 32, 1 (Spring 1991): 38–57.

Ziegler, Heide. "Love's Labours Won: The Erotics of Contemporary Parody." In *Intertextuality and Contemporary American Fiction*, edited by Patrick O'Donnell and Robert Con Davis, 58–71. Baltimore: Johns Hopkins University Press, 1989.

COLLECTIONS

Graham, John, ed. *The Merrill Studies in "Second Skin."* Columbus: Charles E. Merrill, 1971.

Santore, Anthony C., and Michael Pocalyko. *A John Hawkes Symposium: Design and Debris*. Insights-1: Working Papers in Contemporary Criticism. New York: New Directions, 1977.

Trachtenberg, Stanley, ed. *Critical Essays on John Hawkes*. Boston: G.K. Hall & Co., 1991.

INTERVIEWS

Enck, John. "John Hawkes: An Interview." In *Critical Essays on John Hawkes*, edited by Stanley Trachtenberg, 59–70. Boston: G.K. Hall & Co., 1991.

LeClair, Thomas. "A Dialogue: John Barth and John Hawkes." In *Anything*

Can Happen: Interviews with Contemporary American Novelists, edited by Thomas LeClair and Larry McCaffrey, 9–19. Chicago: University of Illinois Press, 1983.

O'Donnell, Patrick. "Life and Art: An Interview with John Hawkes." *Review of Contemporary Fiction* 3 (Fall 1983): 107–26.

Ziegler, Heide. "John Hawkes." In *The Radical Imagination and the Liberal Tradition: Interviews with English and American Novelists*, edited by Heide Ziegler and Christopher Bigsby, 169–87. London: Junction Books, 1982.

THE LIME TWIG

For Maclin Guerard

SIDNEY SLYTER SAYS

Dreary Station Severely Damaged During Night . . .

Bomber Crashes in Laundry Court . . .

Fires Burning Still in Violet Lane . . .

Last night Blood's End was quiet; there was some activity in
Highland Green; while Dreary Station took the worst of Jerry's
effort. And Sidney Slyter has this to say: a beautiful afternoon,
a lovely crowd, a taste of bitters, and light returning to the faces
of heroic stone—one day there will be amusements everywhere,
good fun for our mortality, and you'll whistle and flick your
cigarette into an old crater's lip and with your young woman go
off to a fancy flutter at the races. For Sidney Slyter was recognized last night. The man was in a litter, an old man propped
up in the shelter at Temple Place. I pushed my helmet back and
gave him a smoke and all at once he said: "You'll write about
the horses again, Sidney! You'll write about the nags again all
right. . . ." So keep a lookout for me. Because Sidney Slyter will
be looking out for you. . . .

HAVE YOU EVER LET LODGINGS in the winter? Was there a bed kept
waiting, a corner room kept waiting for a gentleman? And have you
ever hung a cardboard in the window and, just out of view yourself,
watched to see which man would stop and read the hand-lettering on
your sign, glance at the premises from roof to little sign—an awkward
piece of work—then step up suddenly and hold his finger on your bell?
What was it you saw from the window that made you let the bell continue ringing and the bed go empty another night? Something about the
eyes? The smooth white skin between the brim of the bowler hat and
the eyes?

Or perhaps you yourself were once the lonely lodger. Perhaps you
crossed the bridges with the night crowds, listened to the tooting of the
river boats and the sounds of shops closing on the far side. Perhaps the
moon was behind the cathedral. You walked in the cathedral's shadow
while the moon kept shining on three girls ahead. And you followed
the moonlit girls. Or followed a woman carrying a market sack, or
followed a slow bus high as a house with a saint's stone shadow on its
side and smoke coming out from between the tires. Then a turn in the
street and broken glass at the foot of a balustrade and you wiped your
forehead. And standing still, shoes making idle noise on the smashed

glass, you took the packet from inside your coat, unwrapped the oily paper, and far from the tall lamp raised the piece of hot white fish to your teeth.

You must have eaten with your fingers. And you were careful not to lick your lips when you stepped out into the light once more and felt against your face the air waves from the striking of the clock high in the cathedral's stone. The newspaper—it was folded to the listings of single rooms—fell from your coat pocket when you drank from the bottle. But no matter. No need for the rent per week, the names of streets. You were walking now, peering in the windows now, looking for the little signs. How bloody hard it is to read hand-lettering at night. And did your finger ever really touch the bell?

I wouldn't advise Violet Lane—there is no telling about the beds in Violet Lane—but perhaps in Dreary Station you have already found a lodging good as mine, if you were once the gentleman or if you ever took a tea kettle from a lady's hands. A fortnight is all you need. After a fortnight you will set up your burner, prepare hot water for the rubber bottle, warm the bottom of the bed with the bag that leaks round its collar. Or you will turn the table's broken leg to the wall, visit the lavatory in your robe, drive a nail or two with the heel of your boot. After a fortnight they don't evict a man. All those rooms—number twenty-eight, the one the incendiaries burned on Ash Wednesday, the final cubicle that had iron shutters with nymphs and swans and leaves —all those rooms were vacancies in which you started growing fat or first found yourself writing to the lady in the *Post* about salting breast of chicken or sherrying eggs. A lodger is a man who does not forget the cold drafts, the snow on the window ledge, the feel of his knees at night, the taste of a mutton chop in a room in which he held his head all night.

It was from Mother that I learned my cooking.

They were always turning Mother out onto the street. Our pots, our crockery, our undervests, these we kept in cardboard boxes, and from room to empty room we carried them until the strings wore out and her garters and medicines came through the holes. Our boxes lay in spring rains, they gathered snow. Troops, cabmen, bobbies passed them moldering and wet on the street. Once, dried out at last and piled high in a dusty hall, our boxes were set afire. Up narrow stairs and down we carried them, over steps with spikes that caught your boot heels and into small premises still rank with the smells of dead dog or cat. And out of her greasy bodice the old girl paid while I would be off to the unfamiliar lavatory to fetch a pull of tea water in our black pot.

"Here's home, Mother," I would say.

Then down with the skirt, down with the first chemise, off with the little boots. And, hands on the last limp bows: "You may manipulate the screen now, William." It was always behind the boxes, a screen like those standing in theater dressing rooms or in the wards of hospitals, except that it was horsehair brown and filled with holes from her cigarette. And each time we changed our rooms, whether in the morning or midday or dusk, I would set up the screen first thing and behind it Mother would finish stripping to the last scrap of girded rag—the obscene bits of makeshift garb poor old women carry next their skin—and after discarding that would wrap herself in the tawny dressing gown and lie straight upon the single bed while I worked at the burner's pale and rubbery flame. And beyond our door and before the tea was in the cup, we would hear the footsteps, the cheap bracelet tinkling a moment at the glass, would hear the cold fingers lifting down the sign.

Together we took our lodgings, together we went on the street. Fifteen years of circling Dreary Station, she and I, of discovering footprints in the bathtub or a necktie hanging from the toilet chain, or seeing flecks of blood in the shaving glass. Fifteen years with Mother, going from loft to loft in Highland Green, Pinky Road—twice in Violet Lane—and circling all that time the gilded cherubim big as horses that fly off the top of the Dreary Station itself.

If you live long enough with your mother you will learn to cook. Your flesh will know the feel of cabbage leaves, your bare hands will hold everything she eats. Out of the evening paper you will prepare each night your small and tidy wad of cartilage, raw fat, cold and dusty peels and the mouthful—still warm—which she leaves on her plate. And each night as softly as you can, wiping a little blood off the edge of the apron, you will carry your paper bundle down the corridor and into the coldness and falling snow where you will deposit it, soft and square, just under the lid of the landlady's great pail of slops. Mother wipes her lips with your handkerchief and you set the rest of the kidneys on the sooty and frozen window ledge. You cover the burner with its flowered cloth and put the paring knife, the spoon, the end of bread behind the little row of books. There is a place for the pot in the drawer beside the undervests.

In one of the alleys off Pinky Road I remember a little boy who wore black stockings, a shirt ripped off the shoulder, a French sailor's hat with a red pompom. The whipping marks were always fresh on his legs and one cheekbone was blue. A flying goose darkened the mornings in that alley off Pinky Road, the tar buildings were slick with gray goose slime. After the old men and apprentices had left for the high bridges and little shops the place was empty and wet and dead as a lonely dockyard. Then behind the water barrel you could see the boy and his dog.

Each morning when the steam locomotives began shrieking out of Dreary Station the boy knelt on the stones in the leakage from the barrel and caught the puppy by its jowls and rolled its fur and rubbed its ears between his fingers. Alone with the tar doors dripping and the petrol and horse water drifting down the gutters, the boy would waggle the animal's fat head, hide its slow shocked eyes in his hands, flop it upright and listen to its heart. His fingers were always feeling the black gums or the soft wormy little legs or quickly freeing and pulling open the eyes so that he, the thin boy, could stare into them. No fields, sunlight, larks—only the stoned alley like a footpath on a quay down which a black ship might come sailing if the wind held, and down beneath the mists coming off the dead steeplecocks the boy with the poor dog in his arms and loving his close scrutiny of the nicks in its ears, tiny channels over the dog's brain, pictures he could find on its purple tongue, pearls he could discover between the claws. Love is a long close scrutiny like that. I loved Mother in the same way.

I see her: it is just before the end; she is old; I see her through the red light of my glass of port. See the yellow hair, the eyes drying up in the corners. She laughs and jerks her head but the mouth is open, and that is what I see through the glass of port: the laughing lips drawn round a stopper of darkness and under the little wax chin a great silver fork with a slice of bleeding meat that rises slowly, slowly, over the dead dimple in the wax, past the sweat under the first lip, up to the level of her eyes so she can take a look at it before she eats. And I wait for the old girl to choke it down.

But there is a room waiting if you can find it, there is a joke somewhere if you can bring it to your lips. And my landlord, Mr. Banks, is not the sort to evict a man for saying a kind word to his wife or staying in the parlor past ten o'clock. His wife, Margaret, says I was a devoted son.

Yes, devoted. I remember fifteen years of sleeping, fifteen years of smelling cold shoes in the middle of the night and waiting, wondering whether I smelled smoke down the hallway to the toilet or smelled smoke coming from the parlor that would burn like hay. I think of the whipped boy and his dog abed with him and that's what devotion is:

sleeping with a wet dog beneath your pillow or humming some childish tune to your mother the whole night through while waiting for the plaster, the beams, the glass, the kidneys on the sill to catch fire. Margaret's estimation of my character is correct. Heavy men are most often affectionate. And I, William Hencher, was a large man even then.

"Don't worry about it, Hencher," the captain said. "We'll carry you out if we have to." On its cord the bulb was circling round his head, and across the taverns and walls and craters of Dreary Station came the sirens and engines of the night. Sometimes, at the height of it, the captain and his man—an ex-corporal with rotten legs who wore a red beret and was given to fainting in the hall—went out to walk in the streets, and I would watch them go and wait, watch the searchlights fix upon the wounded cherubim like giants caught naked in the sky, until I heard them swearing in the hall again and, from the top of the stair, an unfamiliar voice crying, "Shut the door. Oh, for the love of bleeding Hell, come shut the door."

We were so close to the old malevolent station that I could hear the shifting of the sandbags piled round it and could hear the locomotives shattering into bits of iron. And one night wouldn't a cherubim's hand or arm or curly head come flying down through our roof? Some dislodged ball of saintly brass palm or muscle or jagged neck find its target in Lily Eastchip's house? But I wasn't destined to die with a fat brass finger in my belly.

To think that Mr. and Mrs. Banks—Michael and Margaret—were only children then, as small and crouching and black-eyed as the boy with the French sailor's hat and the dog. It is a pity I did not know them then: somehow I would have cared for them.

Such things don't want forgetting. When they anchored a barrage balloon over number twenty-eight—how long it was since we had been evicted from that room—and when the loft in Highland Green had burned Ash Wednesday, and during those days when the water would curl a horse's lip and somebody's copy of *The Vicar of Wakefield* was run over by a fire truck outside my door, why then there was plenty of soot and scum the memory could not let go of.

There was Lily Eastchip with bird feathers round her throat and a dusty rag up the tiny pearl lacing of her sleeve; there was the captain dishonorably mustered from the forces; there was the front of our narrow lodging which the firemen kept hosing down for luck; there was the pink slipper left caught by its heel in the stairway rungs and hanging toe first into the dark of that dry plaster hall. And there were our boxes with broken strings, piled in the hallway and rising toward the slipper, all the cartons I had not the heart to drag to Mother's room. So I see the pasty corporal—Sparrow was his name—rubbing together the handles of his canes, I see Miss Eastchip serving soup, I see Mother's dead livid face. And I shall always see the bomber with its bulbous front gunner's nest flattened over the cistern in the laundry court.

Margaret remembers none of it and Mr. Banks, her husband, is not a talker. But Miss Eastchip's brother went down in his spotter's steeple, tin hat packed red with embers and both feet in the enormous boots burning with a gas-blue flame. Lily got word of it the eve he fell and with the duster hanging down her wrist and the tears on her cheek she looked as if someone had touched a candle to her nightdress in the dark of our teatime. She stood behind the captain's chair whispering, "That's the end for me, the end for me," while the bearer of the news merely sat for a moment, teacup rattling in the saucer and helmet gripped between his knees.

"Well, sorry to bring distressing information," the warden had said. "You'd better keep the curtains on good tonight. We're in for it, I'm afraid."

A pale snow was coming down when he passed my window—a black square-shouldered man—and I saw the dark shape of him and the gleam off the silvery whistle caught in his teeth. Somebody laid the cold table, and far-off we heard the first dull boom and breath, as if they had blown out a candle as tall as St. George's spire.

"Good night, Hencher. . . ."

"Good night, Captain. Mother gave you the salts for Lily, did she?"

"She did. And—Hencher—if anything uncommon occurs in the night, you can always give me a signal on the pipes."

"I'll just do that, Captain. It's good of you."

Mother got the covers to her chin and, lights off, blackout drawn aside, I sat watching to see the aircraft shoot out the eyes of the cherubim who, beyond sifting snow, and triangulated, now and then, by flooding white shafts of light, hugged each other atop the Dreary Station dome. I held my cheeks. I listened to the old girl's chamber pot—she had stuffed it with jewelry and glass buttons and an ostrich plume—that rolled about beneath the bed. Missing one front wheel, a tiny tar-painted lorry passed in dreadful crawl and the bare hub of its broken axle screeched and sent off sparks against the stones. And all through that blistering snowy night my hands were drenching the angora white yarn of a tasseled shawl, twisting it like a young girl's lock of hair.

When engines shook the night beyond the nymphs and apple leaves in the filigreed shutters of my window, I began suddenly to smell it: not the stench of rafters burning, not the vaporized rubber stench that stayed about the street for days after the hit on the garage of Autorank, Limited, but only a faint live smell of worn carpet or paper or tissue being singed within the lodging house itself. And I fancied it was coming round the edges of my door—the odor of smoke—and I held to the arms of my chair and slowly breathed into my lungs that smoke.

"Are you awake?" I said.

She sat up with the nightdress slanting down her flesh.

"You'd better put your wrapper on, old girl."

She sat there startled by the light of a flare that was plainly going to land in old John's chimney across the way. I could see her game face and I squeezed on the slippers and squeezed the shawl.

"Don't you smell the smoke? The house is going up," I said. "Do you want to burn?"

"It's only the kettle, William. . . ." And she was grinning, one foot was trying to escape the sheet. They were running with buckets across the way at John's.

"You look, William, you tell me what it is. . . ."

"Out of that bed now, and we'll just have a look together."

Then I pulled open the door and there was the hallway dry and dark as ever, the slipper still hooked on the stair, the one faint bulb swinging round and round on its cord. But our boxes were burning. The bottom of the pile was sunk in flame, hot crabbing flame orange and pale blue in the draft from the door and the sleeve of a coat of mine was crumbling and smoking out of a black pasty hole.

Mother began to cough and pull at my hand—the smoke was mostly hers and thick, and there is no smudge as black as that from burning velveteen and stays and packets of cheap face powder—and then she cried, "Oh, William, William." I saw the pile lean and dislodge a clump of cinders while at the same moment I heard a warden tapping on the outside door with his torch and heard him call through the door: "All right in there?"

I could taste my portion of the smoke; the banging on the door grew louder. Now they were flinging water on old John's roof, but mother and I were in an empty hall with only our own fire to care about.

"Can't you leave off tugging on me, can't you?" But before I could close my robe she was gone, three or four steps straight into the pile to snatch the stays and an old tortoise-shell fan from out of the fire.

"Mum!"

But she pulled, the boxes toppled about her, the flames shot high as the ceiling. While a pink flask of ammonia she had saved for years exploded and hissed with the rest of it.

From under the pall I heard her voice: "Look here, it's hardly singed at all, see now? Hardly singed . . ." Outside footfalls, and then the warden: "Charlie, you'd better give us a hand here, Charlie. . . ."

On hands and knees she was trying to crawl back to me, hot sparks from the fire kept settling on her arms and on the thin silk of her gown. One strap was burned through suddenly, fell away, and then a handful of tissue in the bosom caught and, secured by the edging of charred lace, puffed at its luminous peak as if a small forced fire, stoked inside her flesh, had burst a hole through the tender dry surface of my mother's breast.

"Give us your shoulder here, Charlie . . . lend a heave!"

And even while I grunted and went at her with robe outspread, she tried with one hand to pluck away her bosom's fire. "Mother," I shouted, "hold on now, Mother," and knelt and got the robe round her—mother and son in a single robe—and was slapping the embers and lifting her back toward the bed when I saw the warden's boot in the door and heard the tooting of his whistle. Then only the sound of dumping sand, water falling, and every few minutes the hurried crash of an ax head into our smothered pile.

At dawn I returned to the charcoal of the hall and met the captain in corduroy jacket and wearing a gun and holster next his ribs. For a moment we stood looking at the scorch marks on the lath and the high black reach of extinguished flames. The captain ran his toe through the ashes.

"How is your mother, Hencher? A bit hard on her, wasn't it?"

"She won't say, of course, though the pain must be considerable. . . ."

"Well, Hencher," rattling tin and glass in his pocket, "give me a call on the pipes if it gets worse. I happen to have a needle and a few drops in an ampule can relieve all that."

"Oh, she'll do quite nicely, I'm sure. . . ."

But the blisters did not go down. They were small, translucent, membranous and tough all over her body, and no matter how often I dressed them with marge from Lily's kitchen they retained their bulbous density. And even today I smell them: smell the skin, smell the damp sheets I wrapped her in, smell that room turned infirmary. I smell that house.

For after a decade it is the same house, a different landlord—Michael Banks now, not poor grieving Lily—but the same house, the one in the middle of Corking Street not five minutes east of the station. Refurbished, an electric buzzer at the door, three flats instead of beds for lodgers, and a spirit shop where John's house stood—from the peaked garret to the electric buzzer it is the exact same place. I know it well. A lodger is forever going back to the pictures in black bead frames, back to the lost slipper, or forever coming round to pay respects when you think you've seen the last of him, or to tell you—stranger as far as you know—that his was the cheek that left the bloody impression in your looking glass. "My old girl died on these premises, Mr. Banks," looking over his shoulder, feeling the wall, and he had to take me in. And then it was home again for William when I found the comforter with hearts on it across my bed. Now there are orange deck chairs in the laundry court, and sitting out with a sack of beans on my stomach and hearing the sounds of the wireless from Annie's window, still through half-shut eyes I see the shadow of the bomber that once filled the court.

Sometimes I wake in the night, very late in the still night, and go sit in the lavatory and run the water and smoke half a thin cigar until there is nothing to feel, nothing to hear except Margaret turning over or the cat pacing my step in the parlor. I see the cherubim safely lit, I wipe my hands, I sleep.

I waited three weeks before signaling the captain on the pipes, and then I beat at them with my slipper until I threw it across the room and found the warden's torch in the covers and, after the blow that smashed the glass, fetched the captain with loud strokes on first the hot water pipe and then the cold. Together they came, captain and corporal, while the pipes still shivered up the wall. I looked away when I saw the captain pulling out the plunger.

"You ain't going to give my stuff to her?" said Sparrow. "Not to the old woman, are you? I'd sooner you give a jab to this fat man here. . . ."

I trembled then.

"No use giving my stuff to her," said Sparrow, the corporal.

And then in the dark: "She'll do now, Hencher. I'd get a little sleep if I were you."

But it was not sleep I wanted. I fastened the robe, tied the white shawl round my throat. "Good night, old girl," I whispered and went out of the door, flinging an end of the shawl aside flier fashion. It was cold; I walked beneath the black supports and timbers of a burned city, and how often I had made passage through the length of Lily Eastchip's corridor, carried my neat square of dinner garbage past the parlor when Mother and I first joined that household and ate alone. No garbage now. Only the parlor with pinholes in the curtain across the window and a pile of clothing and several candles in the fireplace; only the hall-way growing more and more narrow at the end; only the thought that, behind the screen, I had left Mother comfortable and that tonight, this night, I was going to stand bareheaded in the laundry court and breathe, watch the sky, hear what I could of the cries coming from Violet Lane, from the oil-company docks, the Mall. When I found the bolt and pulled it, squeezed out of that black entrance with a hand to my throat, I expected to see the boy dancing with his dog.

The light snow fell, tracers went straight up from behind the garret that faced me across the court, I noticed a pink reflection in the sky west of the station. The airplanes were bombing Highland Green. I saw the humps of dead geraniums and a wooden case of old stout bottles black and glistening against a shed. I had not moved, I felt the snow wet on my shoulders and on the rims of my ears.

Large, brown, a lifeless airplane returning, it was one of our own and I saw it suddenly approach out of the snow perhaps a hundred feet above the garret and slow as a child's kite. Big and blackish-brown with streaks of ice across the nose, which was beginning to rise while the tail sank behind in the snow, it was simply there, enormous and without a trace of smoke, the engines dead and one aileron flapping in the wind. And ceasing to climb, ceasing to move, a vast and ugly shape stalled against the snow up there, the nose dropped and beneath the pilot's window I saw the figure of a naked woman painted against the bomber's pebbly surface. Her face was snow, something back of her thigh had sprung a leak and the thigh was sunk in oil. But her hair, her long white head of hair was shrieking in the wind as if the inboard engine was sucking the strands of it.

Her name was Reggie's Rose and she was sitting on the black pack of a parachute.

Dipped, shuddered, banged up and down for a moment—I could see the lifted rudder then, swinging to and fro above the tubular narrowing of its fuselage—and during that slapping glide the thick wings did not fall, no frenzied hand wiped the pilot's icy windscreen, no tiny torch switched on to prove this final and outrageous landfall. It made no sound, but steepened its glide, then slowed again with a kind of gigantic deranged and stubborn confidence and pushed on, shedding the snow, as if after the tedium of journey there would be a mere settling, rolling to silence, with a drink and hot sandwiches for her crew. And I myself fell down next to Lily Eastchip's garbage tin, in darkness drove my cheek among the roots of her dead bushes. Through the dressing robe and bedroom silks the heat of my body dissolved the snow. I was wet and waited for the blow of a flying gyroscopic compass or propeller blade.

Or to be brushed to death by a wing, caught beneath cold tons of the central fuselage, or surely sprayed by petrol and burned alive: tasting those hard white rubber roots I wondered whether the warden and his friend Charlie would hear the crash. And tightening, biting to the sour heart of the root, I saw the bomber in its first shapeless immensity and thought I could hold it off—monstrous, spread-winged, shadowy—hold it off with my outstretched arms eternally or at least until I should escape by Lily's door.

The warden must have heard the crash. His Charlie must have heard the crash.

Something small and round struck suddenly against my side. When again I made out the sounds from the far corner—the steady firing of the guns—I breathed, rolled, sat with my back to the wall. My fingers found the painful missile, only a hard tuft of wool blown loose from inside a pilot's boot or torn from the shaggy collar of his flying coat. The snow was falling, still the sky was pink from the bombing of Highland Green. But no whistles, no wardens running: a single window smashed on the other side of the court and a woman began shrieking for her husband. And again there was only silence and my belly trembling.

I took one step, another. Then there were the high dark sides of the intact bomber and the snow was melting on the iron. I reached the first three-bladed propeller—the two bottom sweeps of steel were doubled beneath the cowling—and for a moment I leaned against it and it was like touching your red cheek to a stranded whale's fluke when, in all your coastal graveyard, there was no witness, no one to see. I walked round the bubble of the nose—that small dome set on edge with a great crack down the middle—and stood beneath the artistry of Reggie's Rose. Her leg was long, she sat on her parachute with one knee raised. In the knee cap was a half-moon hole for a man's boot, above it another, and then a hand grip just under the pilot's door. So I climbed up poor

Rose, the airman's dream and big as one of the cherubim, and snatched at the high door which, sealed in the flight's vacuum, sucked against its fitting of rust and rubber and sprang open.

I should have had a visored cap, leather coat, gauntlets. But, glancing once at the ground, poised in the snow over Rose's hair, I tugged, entered head first the forward cabin.

The cabin roof as well as the front gunner's dome was cracked and a little snow fell steadily between the seats. In the dark I sat with my hands on the half wheel and slippers resting on the jammed pedals, my head turning to see the handles, rows of knobs, dials with needles all set at zero, boxes and buttons and toggle switches and loop of wire and insulated rings coming down from the roof. In this space I smelled resin and grease and lacquer and something fatty that made me groan.

I tried to work the pedals, turn the wheel. I could not breathe. When suddenly from a hook between two cylinders next to my right hand I saw a palm-shaped cone of steel and took it up, held it before my face—a metal kidney trimmed round the edges with a strip of fur—I looked at it, then lowered my head and pressed my nose and mouth into its drawn cup. My breath came free. The inhalation was pure and deep and sweet. I smelled tobacco and a cheap wine, was breathing out of the pilot's lungs.

Cold up here. Cold up here. Give a kiss to Rose.

Surely it was Reggie's breath—the tobacco he had got in an Egyptian NAAFI, his cheap wine—frozen on the slanting translucent glass of the forward cabin's windows. Layer overlapping icy layer of Reggie's breath. And I clapped the mask back on its hook, turned a wheel on the cylinder. Leaning far over, sweating, I thrust my hands down and pushed them back along the aluminum trough of floor and found the bottle. Then I found something else, something cool and round to the skin, something that had rested there behind my heels all this while. I set the bottle on top of the wireless box—I heard the sounds of some strange brass anthem coming from the earphones—and reached for that black round shape, carefully and painfully lifted it and cradled it in my lap.

The top of the flying helmet was a perfect dome. Hard, black, slippery. And the flaps were large. On the surface all the leather of that helmet was soft—if you rubbed it—and yet bone hard and firm beneath the hand's polishing. There were holes for wire plugs, bands for the elastic of a pair of goggles, some sort of worn insignia on the front. A heavy wet leather helmet large enough for me. I ran my fingernail across the insignia, picked at a blemish, and suddenly I leaned forward, turned the helmet over, looked inside. Then I lifted the helmet, gripped it steadily at arm's length—I was sitting upright now, upright and staring at the polished thing I held—and slowly raised it high and twisting it, hitching it down from side to side, settled the helmet securely on my own smooth head. I extended my hands again and took the wheel.

"How's the fit, old girl?" I whispered. "A pretty good fit, old girl?" And I turned my head as far to the right as I was able, so that she might see how I—William Hencher—looked with my bloody coronet in place at last.

Give a kiss to Rose.

Between 3 and 4 A.M. on the night she died—so many years ago—that's when I set out walking with my great black coat that made the small children laugh, walking alone or sometimes joining the crowds and waiting under the echoes of the dome and amid the girders and shattered skylight of Dreary Station to see another trainload of our troops return. So many years ago. And I had my dreams; I had my years of walking to the cathedral in the moonlight.

"My old girl died on these premises, Mr. Banks."

And then all the years were gone and I recognized that house, that hall, despite the paint and plaster and the cheap red carpet they had tacked on the parlor floor. I paid him in advance, I did, and he put the money in his trouser pocket while Margaret went to lift their awkward sign out of the window. Fresh paint, fresh window glass, new floorboards here and there: to think of the place not gutted after all but still standing, the house lived in now by those with hardly a recollection of the nightly fires. Cheery, new, her dresses in one of the closets and his hat by the door. But one of his four rooms was mine, surely mine, and I knew I'd smell the old dead odor of smoke if only I pushed my face close enough to those shabby walls.

Here's home, old girl, here's home.

So I spent my first long night in the renovated room, and I dared not spend that night in the lavatory but smoked my cigars in bed. Sitting up in bed, smoking, thinking of my mother all night long. And then there was the second night and I ventured into the hallway. There was the third night and in the darkened cubicle I listened to the far bells counting two, three, four o'clock in the morning and all that time—thinking now of comfort, tranquillity, and thinking also of their two clasped hands—I wondered what I might do for them. The bells were

slow in counting, the water dripped. And suddenly it was quite clear
what I could do for them, for Michael and his wife.

I hooked the lavatory door. Then I filled the porcelain sink, and in
darkness smelling of lavender and greasy razor blades I immersed my
hands up to the wrists, soaked them silently. I dried them on a stiff
towel, pushing the towel between my fingers again and again. I wiped
the top of my head until it burned. Then I used his talc, showed my
teeth in the glass, straightened the robe. I took up the pink-shelled hair
brush for a moment but replaced it. And off to the kitchen and then on
boards that made tiny sounds, walking with a heavy man's sore steps,
noticing a single lighted window across the court.

It grew cold and before dawn I left the kitchen once: only to pull the
comforter off my bed. Again in the kitchen and on Margaret's wooden
stool I sat with the comforter hooded round my head and shoulders,
sat waiting for the dawn to come fishing up across the chimney pots
and across that dirty gable in the apex of which a weathered muse's
face was carved. When I heard the dog barking in the flat upstairs, when
water started running in the pipes behind the wall, and a few river gulls
with icy feathers hovered outside the window, and light from a sun the
color of some guardsman's breast warmed my hooded head and arms
and knees—why then I got off the stool, began to move about. Wine
for the eggs, two pieces of buttered toast, two fried strips of mackerel,
a teapot small as an infant's head and made of iron and boiling—it was
a tasteful tray, in one corner decorated with a few pinched violet buds
I tore from the plant that has always grown on Margaret's window
shelf. I looked round, made certain the jets were off, thought to include
a saucer of red jam, covered the hot salted portions with folded table
napkins. Then I listened. I heard nothing but the iron clock beating next
to the stove and a boot landing near the dog upstairs.

The door was off the latch and they were sleeping. I turned and
touched it with my hip, my elbow, touched it with only a murmur. And
it swung away on smooth hinges while I watched and listened until it
came up sharply against the corner of a little cane chair. They lay beneath a single sheet and a single sand-colored blanket, and I saw that
on his thin icy cheeks Banks had grown a beard in the night and that
Margaret—the eyelids defined the eyes, her lips were dry and brown
and puffy—had been dreaming of a nice picnic in narrow St. George's
Park behind the station. Behind each silent face was the dream that
would collect slack shadows and tissues and muscles into some first
mood for the day. Could I not blow smiles onto their nameless lips,

could I not force apart those lips with kissing? One of the gulls came round from the kitchen and started beating the glass.

"Here's breakfast," I said, and pushed my knees against the footboard.

For a moment the vague restless dreams merely went faster beneath those two faces. Then stopped suddenly, quite fixed in pain. Then both at once they opened their eyes and Banks' were opalescent, quick, the eyes of a boy, and Margaret's eyes were brown.

"It's five and twenty past six," I said. "Take the tray now, one of you. Tea's getting cold. . . ."

Banks sat up and smiled. He was wearing an undervest, his arms were naked and he stretched them toward me. "You're not a bad sort, Hencher," he said. "Give us the tray!"

"Oh, Mr. Hencher," I heard the warm voice, the slow sounds in her mouth, "you shouldn't have gone to the trouble. . . ."

It was a small trouble. And not long after—a month or a fortnight perhaps—I urged them to take a picnic, not to the sooty park behind the station but farther away, farther away to Landingfield Battery, where they could sit under a dead tree and hold their poor hands. And while they were gone I prowled through the flat, softened my heart of introspection: I found her small tube of cosmetic for the lips and, in the lavatory, drew a red circle with it round each of my eyes. I had their bed to myself while they were gone. They came home laughing and brought a postal card of an old pocked cannon for me.

It was the devil getting the lipstick off.

But red circles, giving your landlord's bed a try, keeping his flat to yourself for a day—a man must take possession of a place if it is to be a home for the waiting out of dreams. So we lead our lives, keep our privacy in Dreary Station, spend our days grubbing at the rubber roots, pausing at each other's doors. I still fix them breakfast now and again and the cherubim are still my monument. I have my billet, my memories. How permanent some transients are at last. In a stall in Dreary Station there is a fellow with vocal cords damaged during the fire who sells me chocolates, and I like to talk to him; sometimes I come across a gagger lying out cold in the snow, and for him I have a word; I like to talk to all the unanswering children of Dreary Station. But home is best.

I hear Michael in the bath, I whet Margaret's knives. Or it is 3 or 4 A.M. and I turn the key, turn the knob, avoid the empty goldfish bowl that catches the glitter off the street, feel the skin of my shoes going down the hallway to their door. I stand whispering our history before that door and slowly, so slowly, I step behind the screen in my own dark room and then, on the edge of the bed and sighing, start peeling the elastic sleeves off my thighs. I hold my head awhile and then I rub my thighs until the sleep goes out of them and the blood returns. In my own dark room I hear a little bird trying to sing on the ledge where the kidneys used to freeze.

Smooth the pillow, pull down the sheets for me. Thinking of Reggie and the rest of them, can I help but smile?

I can get along without you, Mother.

1

SIDNEY SLYTER SAYS

Happy Throngs Arrive at Aldington for Golden Bowl . . .

Mystery Horse to Run in Classic Race . . .

Rock Castle: Dark Horse or Foul Play?

Gray toppers, gray gloves and polished walking sticks; elegant ladies and smart young girls; fellows in fedoras, and mothers, and wives—all your Cheapside crowd along with your own Sidney Slyter, naturally. Pure life is the only phrase that will do, life's pure anticipation. . . . So you won't want to show up here without a flower in your buttonhole, I can tell you that. . . . The horses are lovely. Sidney Slyter's choice? Marlowe's Pippet without a doubt—to win (I took a few pints last night with a young woman, a delightful Mrs. Sybilline Laval, who said that Candy Stripe looked very good. But you'll agree with Slyter. He knows his horses, eh?) . . . A puzzling late entry is Rock Castle, owned by one Mr. Michael Banks. But more of this . . .

IT IS WEDNESDAY DAWN. Margaret's day, once every fortnight, for shopping and looking in the windows. She is off already with mints in her pocket and a great empty crocheted bag on her arm, jacket pulled down nicely on her hips and a fresh tape on her injured finger. She smells of rose water and the dust that is always gathering in the four rooms. In one of the shops she will hold a plain dress against the length of her body, then return it to the racks; at a stand near the bridge she will buy him—Michael Banks—a tin of fifty, and for Hencher she will buy three cigars. She will ride the double-decker, look at dolls behind a glass, have a sandwich. And come home at last with a packet of cold fish in the bag.

Most Wednesdays—let her stay, let her walk out—Michael does not care, does not hold his breath, never listens for the soft voice that calls good-by. But this is no usual Wednesday dawn and he slips from room to room until she is finally gone. In front of the glass fixes his coat and hat, and smiles. For he intends not to be home when she returns.

Now he is standing next to their bed—the bed of ordinary down and ticking and body scent, with the course of dreams mapped on the coverlet—and not beside the door and not in the hall. Ready for street, departure, for some prearranged activity, he nonetheless is immobile this

moment and stares at the bed. His gold tooth is warm in the sun, his
rotting tooth begins to pain. From out the window the darting of a
black tiny bird makes him wish for its sound. He would like to hear it
or would like to hear sounds of a wireless through the open door or
sounds of tugs and double-deckers and boys crying the news. Perhaps
the smashing of a piece of furniture. Anything. Because he too has his
day to discover and it is more than pretty dresses and gandering at a
shiny steam iron and taking a quick cup of tea.

He can tell the world.

But in the silence of the flat's close and ordinary little bedroom he
hears again all the soft timid sounds she made before setting off to
market: the fall of the slippery soap bar into the empty tub, the limpid
sound of her running bath, the slough of three fingers in the cream pot,
the cry of bristles against her teeth, the fuzzy sound of straps drawing
up on the skin of her shoulders; poor sounds of her counting out the
change, click of the pocketbook. Then sounds of a safety pin closing
beneath the lifted skirt and of the comb setting up last-minute static in
the single wave of her hair.

He pulls at the clothes-closet door. He steps inside and embraces two
hanging and scratchy dresses and her winter coat pinned over with bits
of tissue. Something on a hook knocks his hat awry. Behind him, in the
room, the sunlight has burned past the chimes in St. George's belfry and
is now more than a searching shaft in that room: it comes diffused
and hot through the window glass, it lights the dry putty-colored walls
and ceiling, draws a steam from the damp lath behind the plaster,
warms the small unpainted tin clock which she always leaves secreted
and ticking under the pillow on her side of the bed. A good early-
morning sun, good for the cat or for the humming housewife. But the
cat is in the other room and his wife is out.

Inside the closet he is rummaging overhead to a shelf—reaching and
pushing among the dresses now, invading anew and for himself this
hiding place which he expects to keep from her. He stands on tiptoe,
an arm is angular at the crook, his unused hand is dragging one of the
dresses off its hanger by the shoulder; but the other set of high fingers
is pushing, working a way through the dusty folds toward what he
knows is resting behind the duster and pail near the wall. His hipbone
strikes the thin paneling of the door so that it squeaks and swings outward, casting a perfect black shadow across the foot of the bed. And
after a moment he steps out into the room, turns sideways, uncorks the
bottle, tilts it up, and puts the hot mouth of the bottle to his lips. He

drinks—until the queer mechanism of his throat can pass no more and his lips stop sucking and a little of it spills down his chin. Upstairs a breakfast kettle begins to shriek. He takes a step, holds the bottle against his breast, suddenly turns his face straight to the sun.

She'll wonder about me. She'll wonder where her hubby's at, rightly enough.

He left the flat door open. Throughout the day, whenever anyone moved inside the building, slammed a window or shouted a few words down the unlighted stair—"Why don't you leave off it? Why don't you just leave off it, you with your bloody kissing round the gas works"—the open door swung a hand's length to and fro, drifted its desolate and careless small arc in a house of shadow and brief argument. But no one took notice of the door, no one entered the four empty rooms beyond it, and only the abandoned cat followed with its turning head each swing of the door. Until at the end of the day Margaret came in smiling, walked the length of the hall with a felt hat over one ear, feet hot, market sack pulling from the straps in her hand and, stopping short, discovered the waiting animal in the door's crack. Stopped, backed off, went for help from a second-floor neighbor who had a heart large with comfort and all the cheer in the world, went for help as he knew she would.

Knowing how much she feared his dreams: knowing that her own worst dream was one day to find him gone, overdue minute by minute some late afternoon until the inexplicable absence of him became a certainty; knowing that his own worst dream, and best, was of a horse which was itself the flesh of all violent dreams; knowing this dream, that the horse was in their sitting room—he had left the flat door open as if he meant to return in a moment or meant never to return—seeing the room empty except for moonlight bright as day and, in the middle of the floor, the tall upright shape of the horse draped from head to tail in an enormous sheet that falls over the eyes and hangs down stiffly from the silver jaw; knowing the horse on sight and listening while it raises one shadowed hoof on the end of a silver thread of foreleg and drives down the hoof to splinter in a single crash one plank of that empty Dreary Station floor; knowing his own impurity and Hencher's guile; and knowing that Margaret's hand has nothing in the palm but a short life span (finding one of her hairpins in his pocket that Wednesday dawn when he walked out into the sunlight with nothing cupped in the lip of his knowledge except thoughts of the night and pleasure he was about to find)—knowing all this, he heard in Hencher's first question the sound of a dirty wind, a secret thought, the sudden crashing in of the plank and the crashing shut of that door.

"How's the missus, Mr. Banks? Got off to her marketing all right?"

Then: "No offense. No offense," said Hencher after Banks' pause and answer.

The *Artemis*—a small excursion boat—shivered and rolled now and again ever so slightly though it was moored fast to the quay. Banks heard the cries of dock hands who were fixing a boom's hook to a cargo net, the sound of a pump, and the sound, from the top deck, of a child shouting through cupped hands in the direction of the river's distant traffic of puffing tugs and barges. And also overhead there were the quick uncontrollable running footfalls of smaller children and, on the gangway, hidden beyond the white bulkhead of the refreshment saloon, there was the steady tramp of still more boarding passengers.

A bar, a dance floor—everyone was dancing—a row of salt-sealed windows, a small skylight drawn over with the shadow of a fat gull: here was Hencher's fun, and Banks could feel the crowd mounting the sides of the ship, feel the dance rhythm tingling through the greasy wood of the table top beneath his hand. For a moment and in a clear space past the open sea doors held back by small brass hooks, he saw hatless members of the crew dragging a mountain of battered life preservers forward in a great tar-stained shroud of canvas.

"No offense, eh, Mr. Banks? Too good a day for that. And tell me now, how's this for a bit of a good trip?"

The lodger's hand was putty round the bottom of the beer glass, the black-and-cream checkered cap was tight on the head—surely the fat man would sail away with the mothers and children and smart young girls when the whistle blew.

"No offense, Hencher. But you can leave off mentioning her, if you don't mind."

Perhaps he would sail away himself. That would be the laugh, he and Hencher, stowaways both, elbowing room at the ship's rail between lovers and old ladies, looking out themselves—the two of them—for a glimpse of the water or a great furnace burning far-off at the river's edge. Sail away out of the river's mouth and into the afternoons of an excursion life. Hear the laughter, feel the ship's beam wallow in the deep seas and lie down at night beneath a lifeboat's white spongy prow still hot to the hand. No luggage, no destination, helmsman tying the wheel—on any course—to have a smoke with a girl. This would be the laugh, with only the pimply barkeep who had never been to sea before drawing beer the night long. But there was better than this in wait for him, something much better than this.

In the crowd at the foot of the gangplank an officer had asked for their tickets, and Hencher had spoken to the man: "My old woman's on that boat, Captain, and me and my friend here will just see that she's got a proper deck chair and a robe round her legs."

And now the dawn was gone, the morning hours too were gone. He had found the crabbed address and come upon the doorway in which Hencher waited; had walked with him down all those streets until the squat ship, unseaworthy, just for pleasure, lay ahead of them in a berth between two tankers; had already seen the rigging, the smokestacks, the flesh-colored masts and rusty sirens and whistles in a blue sky above the rotting roof of the cargo sheds; had boarded the *Artemis,* which smelled of coke and rank canvas and sea animals and beer and boys looking for sport.

"We'll just have some drink and a little talk on this ship before she sails, Mr. Banks. . . ."

He leaned toward Hencher. His elbows were on the table and his wet glass was touching Hencher's frothy glass in the center of the table. Someone had dropped a mustard pot and beneath his shoe he felt the fragments of smashed china, the shape of a wooden spoon, the slick of the mustard on the dirty spoon. A woman with lunch packed in a box pushed through the crowd and bumped against him, paused and rested the box upon their table. Protruding from the top of the box and sealed with a string and paper was a tall jar filled with black bottled tea. The woman carried her own folding chair.

"Bloody slow in putting to sea, mates," she said, and laughed. She wore an old sweater, a man's muffler was knotted round her throat. "I could do with a breath of that sea air right now, I could."

Hencher lifted his glass. "Go on," he said, "have a sip. Been on the *Artemis* before?"

"Not me."

"I'll tell you then. Find a place for yourself in the bows. You get the breeze there, you see everything best from there."

She put her mouth to the foam, drank long, and when she took the glass away she was breathing quickly and a canker at the edge of her lip was wet. "Join me," she said. "Why don't you join me, mates?"

"We'll see you in the bows," said Hencher.

"Really?"

"Good as my word."

It was all noise of people wanting a look at the world and a smell of the sea, and the woman was midships with her basket; soon in the shadow of the bow anchor she would be trying to find a safe spot for her folding chair. Hencher was winking. A boy in a black suit danced by their table, and in his arms was a girl of about fourteen. Banks watched the way she held him and watched her hands in the white gloves shrunk small and tight below the girl's thin wrists. Music, laughter, smells of deck paint and tide and mustard, sight of the boy pulled along by the fierce white childish hands. And he himself was listening, touching his tongue to the beer, leaning close as he dared to Hencher, beginning to think of the black water widening between the sides of the holiday ship and the quay.

"What's that, Hencher? What's that you say?"

Hencher was looking him full in the face: ". . . to Rock Castle, here's to Rock Castle, Mr. Banks!"

He heard his own voice beneath the whistles and plash of bilge coming out of a pipe, "To Rock Castle, then. . . ."

The glasses touched, were empty, and the girl's leg was only the leg of a child and the woman would drink her black tea alone. He stood, moved his chair so that he sat not across from Hencher but beside him.

"He's old, Mr. Banks. Rock Castle has his age, he has. And what's his age? Why, it's the evolution of his bloody name, that's what it is. Just the evolution of a name—Apprentice out of Lithograph by Cobbler, Emperor's Hand by Apprentice out of Hand Maiden by Lord of the Land, Draftsman by Emperor's Hand out of Shallow Draft by Amulet, Castle Churl by Draftsman out of Likely Castle by Cold Masonry, Rock Castle by Castle Churl out of Words on Rock by Plebeian—and what's this name if not the very evolution of his life? You want to think of the life, Mr. Banks, think of the breeding. Consider the fiver bets, the cheers, the wreaths. Then forgotten, because he's taken off the turf and turned out into the gorse, far from the paddock, the swirl of torn ticket stubs, the soothing nights after a good win, far from the serpentine eyes and bowler hats. Do you see it, Mr. Banks? Do you see how it was for Rock Castle?"

He could only nod, but once again—the *Artemis* was rolling—once again he saw the silver jaw, the enormous sheet, the upright body of the horse that was crashing in the floor of the Dreary Station flat. And he could only keep his eyes down, clasp his hands.

". . . Back sways a little, you see, the color of the coat hardens and the legs grow stiff. Months, years, it's only the blue sky for him, occasionally put to stud and then back he goes to his shelter under an old oak at the edge of a field. Useless, you see. Do you see it? Until tonight when he's ours—yours—until tonight when we get our hands on him and tie him up in the van and drive him to stables I know of in Highland Green. Yours, you see, and he's got no recollection of the wreaths or seconds of speed, no knowledge at all of the prime younger horses sprung from his blood. But he'll run all right, on a long track he'll run better than the young ones good for nothing except a sprint. Power, endurance, a forgotten name—do you see it, Mr. Banks? He's ancient, Rock Castle is, an ancient horse and he's bloody well run beyond memory itself. . . ."

Flimsy frocks, dancing children, a boy with the face of a man, a girl whose body was still awkward; they were all about him and taking their pleasure while the feet tramped and the whistle tooted. But Hencher was talking, holding him by the brown coat just beneath the ribs, then fumbling and cupping in front of his eyes a tiny photograph and saying, "Go on, go on, take a gander at this lovely horse."

Then the pause, the voice less friendly and the question, and the sound of his own voice answering: "I'm game, Hencher. Naturally, I'm still game. . . ."

"Ah, like me you are. Good as your word. Well, come then, let's have a turn round the deck of this little tub. We've time yet for a turn at the rail."

He stood, trying to scrape the shards of the smashed mustard pot from his shoe, followed Hencher toward the white sea doors. The back of Hencher's neck was red, the checked cap was at an angle, they made their slow way together through the excursion crowd and the smells of soap and cotton underwear and scent behind the ears.

"We're going to do a polka," somebody called, "come dance with us. . . ."

"A bit of business first," Hencher said, and grinned over the heads at the woman. "A little business first—then we'll be the boys for you, never fear."

A broken bench with the name *Annie* carved into it, a bucket half-filled with sand, something made of brass and swinging, a discarded man's shirt snagged on the horn of a big cleat bolted to the deck and, overhead, high in a box on the wall of the pilot house, the running light flickering through the sea gloom. He felt the desertion, the wind, the coming of darkness as soon as he stepped from the saloon.

She's home now, she's thinking about her hubby now, she's asking the cat where's Michael off to, where's my Michael gone to?

He spat sharply over the rail, turned his jacket collar up, breathed on the dry bones of his hands.

Together, heads averted, going round the deck, coming abreast of the saloon and once more sheltered by a flapping canvas: Hencher lit a cigar while he himself stood grinning in through the lighted window at the crowd. He watched them kicking, twirling, holding hands, fitting their legs and feet to the steps of the dance; he grinned at the back of the girl too young to have a girdle to pull down, grinned at the boy in the black suit. He smelled the hot tobacco smell and Hencher was with him, Hencher who was fat and blowing smoke on the glass.

"You say you have a van, Hencher, a horse van. . . ."

"That's the ticket. Two streets over from this quay, parked in an alley by the ship-fitter's, as good a van as you'd want and with a full tank. And it's a van won't be recognized, I can tell you that. A little oil and sand over the name, you see. Like they did in the war. And we drive it wherever we please—you see—and no one's the wiser."

He nodded and for a moment, across the raven-blue and gold of the water, he saw the spires and smokestacks and tiny bridges of the city black as a row of needles burned and tipped with red. The tide had risen to its high mark and the gangway was nearly vertical; going down he burned his palm on the tarred rope, twice lost his footing. The engines were loud now. Except for Hencher and himself, except for the officer posted at the foot of the gangway and a seaman standing by each of the hawsers fore and aft, the quay was deserted, and when the sudden blasting of the ship's whistle commenced the timbers shook, the air was filled with steam, the noise of the whistle sounded through the quay's dark cargo shed. Then it stopped, except for the echoes in the shed and out on the water, and the man gave his head a shake as if he could not rid it of the whistling. He held up an unlighted cigarette and Hencher handed him the cigar.

"Oh," said the officer, "it's you two again. Find the lady in question all right?"

"We found her, Captain. She's comfy, thanks, good and comfy."

"Well, according to schedule we tie up here tomorrow morning at twenty past eight."

"My friend and me will come fetch her on the dot, Captain, good as my word. . . ."

Again the smothering whistle, again the sound of chain, and someone shouted through a megaphone and the gangway rose up on a cable; the seamen hoisted free the ropes, the bow of the *Artemis* began to swing, the officer stepped over the widening space between quay and ship and was gone.

"Come," said Hencher, and took hold of his arm, "we can watch from the shed."

They leaned against a crate under the low roof and there were rats and piles of dried shells and long dark empty spaces in the cargo shed. There were holes in the flooring: if he moved the toe of his shoe his foot would drop off into the water; if he moved his hand there would be the soft pinch of fur or the sudden burning of dirty teeth. Only Hencher and himself and the rats. Only scum, the greasy water and a punctured and sodden dory beneath them—filth for a man to fall into.

"There . . . she's got the current now. . . ."

He stared with Hencher toward the lights, small gallery of decks and silhouetted stacks that was the *Artemis* a quarter mile off on the river.

"They'll have their fun on that little ship tonight and with a moon, too, or I miss my guess. Another quarter hour," Hencher was twisting, trying for a look at his watch in the dark, "and I'll bring the lorry round."

Side by side, rigid against the packing crate, listening to the rats plop down, waiting, and all the while marking the disappearance of the excursion boat. Only the quay's single boom creaking in the wind and a view of the river across the now empty berth was left to them, while ahead of the *Artemis* lay a peaceful sea worn smooth by night and flotillas of landing boats forever beached. With beer and music in her saloon she was off there making for the short sea cliffs, for the moonlit coast and desolate windy promontories into which the batteries had once been built. At 3 A.M. her navigator discovering the cliffs, fixing location by sighting a flat tin helmet nailed to a stump on the tallest cliff's windy lip, and the *Artemis* would approach the shore, and all of them—boy, girl, lonely woman—would have a glimpse of ten miles of coast with an iron fleet half-sunk in the mud, a moonlit vision of windlasses, torpedo tubes, skein of rusted masts and the stripped hull of a destroyer rising stern first from that muddied coast under the cliffs.

Beside the rail the lonely woman at least, and perhaps the rest of them, would see the ten white coastal miles, the wreckage safe from tides and storms and snowy nights, the destroyer's superstructure rising respectable as a lighthouse keeper's station. All won, all lost, all over, and for half a crown they could have it now, this seawreck and abandon and breeze of the ocean surrounding them. And the boy at least would hear the moist unjoyful voice of his girl while the *Artemis* remained off shore, would feel the claspknife in the pocket of her skirt and, down on the excursion boat's hard deck, would know the comfort to be taken with a young girl worn to thinness and wiry and tough as the titlings above the cliffs.

Michael stood rigid against the packing crate, alone. He waited deep within the shed and watched, sniffed something that was not of rats or cargo at all. Then he saw it drifting along the edges of the quay, rising up through the rat holes round his shoes: fog, the inevitable white hair strands which every night looped out across the river as if once each night the river must grow old, clammy, and in its age and during these late hours only, produce the thick miles of old woman's hair within whose heaps and strands it might then hide all bodies, tankers, or fat iron shapes nodding to themselves out there.

Fog of course and he should have expected it, should have carried a torch. Yet, whatever was to come his way would come, he knew, like this—slowly and out of a thick fog. Accidents, meetings unexpected, a figure emerging to put its arms about him: where to discover everything he dreamed of except in a fog. And, thinking of slippery corners, skin suddenly bruised, grappling hooks going blindly through the water: where to lose it all if not in the same white fog.

Alone he waited until the great wooden shed was filled with the fog that caused the rotting along the water's edge. His shirt was flat, wet against his chest. The forked iron boom on the quay was gone, and as for the two tankers that marked the vacated berth of the excursion boat, he knew they were there only by the dead sounds they made. All about him was the visible texture and density of the expanding fog. He was listening for the lorry's engine, with the back of a hand kept trying to wipe his cheek.

An engine was nearby suddenly, and despite the fog he knew that it was not Hencher's lorry but was the river barge approaching on the lifting tide. And he was alone, shivering, helpless to give a signal. He had no torch, no packet of matches. No one trusted a man's voice in a fog.

All the bells and whistles in mid-river were going at once, and hearing the tones change, the strokes change, listening to the metallic or compressed-air sounds of sloops or ocean-going vessels protesting their identities and their vague shifting locations on the whole of this treacherous and fog-bound river's surface—a horrible noise, a confused warning, a frightening celebration—he knew that only his own barge, of all this night's drifting or anchored traffic, would come without lights and making no sound except for the soft and faltering sound of the engine itself. This he heard—surely someone was tinkering with it, nursing it, trying to stop the loss of oil with a bare hand—and each moment he waited for even these illicit sounds to go dead. But in the fog the barge engine was turning over and, all at once, a man out there cleared his throat.

So he stood away from the packing crate and slowly went down to his hands and knees and discovered that he could see a little distance now, and began to crawl. He feared that the rats would get his hands; he ran his fingers round the crumbling edges of the holes; his creeping knee came down on fragments of a smashed bottle. There was an entire white sea-world floating and swirling in that enormous open door, and he crawled out to it.

"You couldn't do nothing about the bleeding fog!"

He had crossed the width of the quay, had got a grip on the iron joint of the boom and was trying to rise when the voice spoke up directly beneath him and he knew that if he fell it would not be into the greasy and squid-blackened water but onto the deck of the barge itself. He was unable to look down yet, but it was clear that the man who had spoken up at him had done so with a laugh, casually, without needing to cup his hands.

Before the man had time to say it again—"You couldn't do nothing about the bleeding fog, eh, Hencher? I wouldn't ordinarily step out of the house on a night like this"—the quay had already shaken beneath the van's tires and the headlamp had flicked on, suddenly, and hurt his eyes where he hung from the boom, one hand thrown out for balance and the other stuck like a dead man's to the iron. Hencher, carrying two bright lanterns by wire loops, had come between himself and the lorry's yellow headlamps—"Lively now, Mr. Banks," he was saying without a smile—and had thrust one of the lanterns upon him in time to reach out his freed hand and catch the end of wet moving rope on the instant it came lashing up from the barge. So that the barge was docked, held safely by the rope turned twice round a piling, when he himself was finally able to look straight down and see it, the long and blunt-nosed barge riding high in a smooth bowl scooped out of the fog. Someone had shut off the engine.

"Take a smoke now, Cowles—just a drag, mind you—and we'll get on with it."

She ought to see her hubby now. She ought to see me now.

He had got his arm through the fork of the boom and was holding the lantern properly, away from his body and down, and the glare from its reflector lighted the figure of the man Cowles below him and in cold wet rivulets drifted sternward down the length of the barge. Midships were three hatches, two battened permanently shut, the third covered by a sagging canvas. Beside this last hatch and on a bale of hay sat a boy naked from the waist up and wearing twill riding britches. In the stern was a small cabin. On its roof, short booted legs dangling over the edge, a jockey in full racing dress sat with a cigarette now between his lips and hands clasped round one of his tiny knees.

"Cowles! I want off . . . I want off this bloody coop!" he shouted.

The cigarette popped into his mouth then. It was a trick he had. The lips were pursed round the hidden cigarette and the little man was staring up not at Cowles or Hencher but at himself, and even while Cowles was ordering the two of them, boy and jockey, to get a hop on and drag the tarpaulin off the hold, the jockey kept looking up at him, toe of one little boot twitching left and right but the large bright eyes remaining fixed on his own—until the cigarette popped out again and the dwarfed man allowed himself to be helped from his seat on the cabin roof by the stableboy whose arms, in the lantern light, were upraised and spattered with oil to the elbows.

"Get a hop on now, we want no coppers or watchman or dock inspectors catching us at this bit of game. . . ."

The fog was breaking, drifting away, once more sinking into the river. Long shreds of it were wrapped like rotted sails or remnants of a wet wash round the buttresses and hand-railings of the bridges, and humped outpourings of fog came rolling from within the cargo shed as if all the fuels of this cold fire were at last consumed. The wind had started up again, and now the moon was low, just overhead.

"Here, use my bleeding knife, why don't you?"

The water was slimy with moonlight, the barge itself was slimy—all black and gold, dripping—and Cowles, having flung his own cigarette behind him and over the side, held the blade extended and moved down the slippery deck toward the boy and booted figure at the hatch with the slow embarrassed step of a man who at any moment expects to walk upon eel or starfish and trip, lose his footing, sprawl heavily on a deck as unknown to him as this.

"Here it is now, Mr. Banks!" He felt one of Hencher's putty hands quick and soft and excited on his arm. "Now you'll see what there is to see. . . ."

He looked down upon the naked back, the jockey's nodding cap, the big man Cowles and the knife stabbing at the ropes, until Cowles grunted and the three of them pulled off the tarpaulin and he was staring down at all the barge carried in its hold: the black space, the echo of bilge and, without movement, snort, or pawing of hoof, the single white marble shape of the horse, whose neck (from where he leaned over, trembling, on the quay) was the fluted and tapering neck of some serpent, while the head was an elongated white skull with nostrils, eye sockets, uplifted gracefully in the barge's hold—*Draftsman by Emperor's Hand out of Shallow Draft by Amulet, Castle Churl by Draftsman out of Likely Castle by Cold Masonry, Rock Castle by Castle Churl out of Words on Rock by Plebeian . . . until tonight when he's ours, until tonight when he's ours. . . .*

"Didn't I tell you, Mr. Banks? Didn't I? Good as his word, that's Hencher."

The whistles died one by one on the river and it was not Wednesday at all, only a time slipped off its cycle with hours and darkness never to be accounted for. There was water viscous and warm that lapped the sides of the barge; a faint up and down motion of the barge which he could gauge against the purple rings of a piling; and below him the still crouched figures of the men and, in its moist alien pit, the silver horse with its ancient head, round which there buzzed a single fly as large as his own thumb and molded of shining blue wax.

He stared down at the lantern-lit blue fly and at the animal whose two ears were delicate and unfeeling, as unlikely to twitch as two pointed fern leaves etched on glass, and whose silver coat gleamed with the colorless fluid of some ghostly libation and whose decorous drained head smelled of a violence that was his own.

Even when he dropped the lantern—"No harm done, no harm done," Hencher said quickly—the horse did not shy or throw itself against the ribs of the barge, but remained immobile, fixed in the same standing posture of rigorous sleep that they had found it in at the moment the tarpaulin was first torn away. Though Cowles made his awkward lunge to the rail, saw what it was—lantern with cracked glass half sunk, still burning on the water, then abruptly turning dark and sinking from sight—and laughed through his nose, looked up at them: "Bleeding lot of help he is. . . ."

"No harm done," said Hencher again, sweating and by light of the van's dim headlamps swinging out the arm of the boom until the cable and hook were correctly positioned above the barge's hold. "Just catch the hook, Cowles, guide it down."

Without a word, hand that had gripped the lantern still trembling, he took his place with Hencher at the iron bar which, given the weight of Hencher and himself, would barely operate the cable drum. He got his fingers round the bar; he tried to think of himself straining at such a bar, but it was worse for Hencher, whose heart was sunk in fat. Yet Hencher too was ready—in tight shirtsleeves, his jacket removed and hanging from the tiny silver figure of a winged man that adorned the van's radiator cap—so that he himself determined not to let go of the bar as he had dropped the lantern but, instead, to carry his share of the horse's weight, to stay at the bar and drum until the horse could suffer this last transport. There was no talking on the barge. Only sounds of their working, plash of the boy's feet in the bilge, the tinkle of buckles and strap ends as the webbed bands were slid round the animal's belly and secured.

Hencher was whispering: "Ever see them lift the bombs out of the craters? Two or three lads with a tripod, some lengths of chain, a few red flags and a rope to keep the children away . . . then cranking up the unexploded bomb that would have bits of debris and dirt sticking peacefully as you please to that filthy big cylinder . . . something to see, men at a job like that and fishing up a live bomb big enough to blow a cathedral to the ground." Then, feeling a quiver: "But here now, lay into it gently, Mr. Banks, that's the ticket."

He pushed—Hencher was pushing also—until after a moment the drum stopped and the cable that stretched from the tip of the boom's arm down to the ring swiveling above the animal's webbed harness was taut.

"O.K." It was Cowles kneeling at the hold's edge, speaking softly and clearly on the late night air, "O.K. now . . . up he goes."

The barge, which could support ten tons of coal or gravel on the river's oily and slop-sullied tide, was hardly lightened when the horse's hoofs swung a few inches free of that planking hidden and awash. But drum, boom, cable and arms could lift not a pound more than this, and lifted this—the weight of the horse—only with strain and heat, pressure and rusted rigidity. Though his eyes were closed he knew when the boom swayed, could feel the horse beginning to sway off plumb. He heard the drum rasping round, heard the loops of rusted cable wrapping about the hot drum one after another, slowly.

"Steady now, steady . . . he's bloody well high enough."

Then, as Hencher with burned hands grasped the wheel that would turn the boom its quarter circle and position the horse over quay, not over barge, he felt a fresh wind on his cheek and tilted his head, opened his eyes, and saw his second vision of the horse: up near the very tip of the iron arm, rigid and captive in the sling of two webbed bands, legs stiff beneath it, tail blown out straight on the wind and head lifted—they had wrapped a towel round the eyes—so that high in the air it became the moonlit spectacle of some giant weather vane. And seeing one of the front legs begin to move, to lift, and the hoof—that destructive hoof—rising up and dipping beneath the slick shoulder, seeing this slow gesture of the horse preparing to paw suddenly at the empty air, and feeling the tremor through his fingers still lightly on the bar: "Let him down, Hencher, let him down!" he cried, and waved both hands at the blinded and hanging horse even as it began to descend.

Until the boom regained its spring and balance like a tree spared from a gale; until the drum, released, clattered and in its rusty mechanism grew still; until the four sharp hoofs touched wood of the quay. Cowles—first up the ladder and followed by Jimmy Needles the jockey and Lovely the stableboy—reached high and loosed the fluttering towel from round its eyes. The boy approached and snapped a lead-rope to the halter and the jockey, never glancing at the others or at the horse, stepped up behind him, whispering: "Got a fag for Needles, mister? Got a fag for Needles?" Not until this moment when he shouted, "Hencher, don't leave me, Hencher . . ." and saw the fat naked arm draw back and the second lantern sail in an arc over the water, and in a distance also saw the white hindquarters on the van's ramp and dark shapes running—not until this moment was he grateful for the little hard cleft of fingers round his arm and the touch of the bow-legged figure still begging for his fag but pulling and guiding him at last in the direction of the cab's half-open door. Cowles had turned the petcocks and behind them the barge was sinking.

These five rode crowded together on the broad seat, five white faces behind a rattling windscreen. Five men with elbows gnawing at elbows, hands and pairs of boots confused, men breathing hard and remaining silent except for Hencher who complained he hadn't room to drive. In labored first gear and with headlights off, they in the black van traveled the slow bumping distance down the length of the cargo shed, from plank to rotted plank moved slowly in the van burdened with their own weight and the weight of the horse until at the corner of the deserted building—straight ahead lay darkness that was water and all five, smelling sweat and river fumes and petrol, leaned forward together against the dim glass—they turned and drove through an old gate topped with a strand of barbed wire and felt at last hard rounded cobblestones beneath the tires.

"No one's the wiser now, lads," said Hencher, and laughed, shook the sweat from his eyes, took a hand off the wheel and slapped Cowles' knee. "We're just on a job if anyone wants to know," smiling, both fat hands once more white on the wheel. "So we've only to sit tight until we make Highland Green . . . eh, Cowles . . . eh, Needles . . . eh, Mr. Banks?"

But Michael himself, beneath the jockey and pressed between Cowles' thick flank and the unupholstered door, was tasting lime: smells of the men, smells of oil, lingering smells of the river and now, faint yet definite, seeping through the panel at his back, smells of the horse—all these mixed odors filled his mouth, his stomach, and some hard edge of heel or brake lever or metal that thrust down from the dash was cutting into his ankle, hurting the bone. Under his buttocks he felt the crooked shape of a spanner; from a shelf behind the thin cushions straw kept falling; already the motor was overheated and they were driving too fast in the darkness of empty shopping districts and areas of cheap lodgings with doorways and windows black except for one window, seven or eight streets ahead of them, in which a single light would be burning. And each time this unidentified black shabby van went round a corner he felt the horse—his horse—thump against one metal side or the other. Each time the faint sound and feel of the thumping made him sick.

"Hencher. I think you had better leave me off at the flat."

Then trying to breathe, trying to explain, trying to argue with

Hencher in the speeding overheated cab and twisting, seeing the fluted dark nostril at a little hole behind the driver's head. Until Hencher smiled his broad worried smile and in a loud voice said: "Oh well, Mr. Banks is a married man," speaking to Cowles, the jockey, the stableboy, nudging Cowles in the ribs. "And you must always make allowance for a married man. . . ."

Cowles yawned, and, as best he could, rubbed his great coatsleeves still wet from the spray. "Leave him off, Hencher, if he gives us a gander at the wife."

The flat door is open and the cat sleeps. Just inside the door, posted on a straight chair, market bag at her feet and the cat at her feet, sitting with the coat wrapped round her shoulders and the felt hat still on her head: there she waits, waits up for him. The neighbor on the chair next to her is sleeping—like the cat—and the mouth is half-open with the breath hissing through, and the eyes are buried under curls. But her own eyes are level, the lids red, the face smooth and white and soft as soap. Waiting up for him.

Without moving, without taking her eyes from the door: "Where's Michael off to? Where's my Michael gone?" she asks the cat. Then down the outer hall, in the dark of the one lamp burning, she hears the click of the house key, the sound of the loose floor board, and she thinks to raise a hand and dry her cheek. With the same hand she touches her neighbor's arm.

"It's all right, Mrs. Stickley," she whispers, "he's home now."

The engine is boiling over when the van reaches Highland Green. Water flows down the dented black hood, the grille, and a jet of steam bursting up from the radiator scalds the wings of the tiny silver figure of the man which, in attitude of pursuit, flies from the silver cap. Directly before the machine and in the light of the headlamps Hencher stands shielding his face from the steam. Then moves quickly, throws his belly against the hot grille, catches the winged figure in a rag and gives it a twist.

"Come along, cock, we haven't got all the bleeding night," says Cowles.

It is dark in Highland Green, dark in this public stable which lies so close to the tanks and towers of the gasworks that a man, if he wished, might call out to the old watchman there. Dark at 3 A.M. and quiet; no one tends the stables at night and only a few spiritless horses for hire are drowsing in a few of the endless stalls. Hardly used now, dead at night, with stray dogs and little starved birds making use of the stalls, and weeds choking the yard. Refuse fills the well, there is a dry petrol pump near a loft building intended for hay.

Hencher steps out of the headlamp's beam, drops the radiator cap, throws the rag to the ground, soothes his hand with his lips. "You needn't tell me to hurry, Cowles," he says, and kicks the tiny winged man away from him into the dead potash and weeds.

Hencher hears the whistles then—two long, a short—and all at once straightens his cap, gives a last word to Cowles: "Leave the animal in the van until I return. And no noise now, mind you. . . ." From beneath the musty seat in the cab he takes a long torch and walks quickly across the rutted yard. Behind him the jockey is puffing on a fresh cigarette, the stableboy—thinking of a girl he once saw bare to the flesh—is resting his head against a side of the van, and Cowles in the dark is frowning and moving his stubby fingers across the watch chain that is a dull gold weight on his vest.

Once in the loft building Hencher lights the torch. Presses the switch with his thumb but keeps the torch down, is careful not to shine the beam toward the exact spot where he knows the man is standing. Rather lights himself with the torch and walks ahead into the dark. He is smiling though he feels sweat on his cheeks and in the folds of his neck. The loft building smells of creosote, the dead pollen of straw, and petrol. He cannot see it, but he knows that to his left there is a double door, closed, and beside it, hidden and waiting within the darkness, a passenger car stately with black lacquer and a radiator cap identical to that on the van. If he swings the torch, flashes it suddenly and recklessly to the left, he knows the light will be dashed back in his face from the car's thick squares of polished window glass. But he keeps the beam at his heel, walks more and more slowly until at last he stops.

"You managed to get here, Hencher," the man says.

"I thought I was on the dot, Larry . . . good as my word, you know."

"Yes, always good as your word. But you've forgotten to take off your cap."

Hencher takes it off, feels his whole head exposed and hot and ugly. At last he allows himself to look, and it is only the softest glow that his torch sheds on the man before him.

"We got the horse, right outside in the van . . . I told you, right outside."

"But you stopped. You did not come here directly."

"I did my best. I did my bloody best, but if he wants to knock it off, if he wants to stop at home and have a word with the wife, why that's just unfortunate . . . but no fault of mine, is it, Larry?"

And then, listening in the direction of the car, waiting for a sound —scratch of the ignition key, oiled suck of gear-lever—he sees the hand extended in front of him and is forced to take hold of it. One boot moves, the other moves, the trenchcoat makes a harsh rubbing noise. And the hand lets go of his, the man fades out of the light and yet— Hencher wipes his face and listens—once in the darkness the footsteps ring back to him like those of an officer on parade.

He keeps his own feet quiet until he reaches the yard and sees the open night sky beginning to change and grow milky like chemicals in a vat, and until he sniffs a faint odor of dung and tobacco smoke. Then he trudges loudly as he can and suddenly, calling the name, shines the bright torch on Cowles.

"Pissed off, was he," says Cowles, and does not blink.

But in the cab Hencher already braces the steering wheel against his belly; the driver's open door swings to the movement of the van. Cowles and the jockey and stableboy walk in slow procession behind the van, which is not too wide for the overgrown passage between the row of stalls, the long dark space between the low stable buildings, but which is high so that now and again the roof of the van brushes then scrapes against the rotted eaves. The tires are wet from the dampness of tangled and prickly weeds. Once, the van stops and Hencher climbs down, drags a bale of molded hay from its path. Then they move—horse van, walking men—and exhaust fumes fill empty bins, water troughs, empty stalls. In darkness they pass a shovel in an iron wheelbarrow, a saddle pad covered with inert black flies, a whip leaning against a whited post. Round a corner they come upon a red lantern burning beside an open and freshly whitewashed box stall. The hay rack has been mended, clean hard silken straw covers the floor, a red horse blanket lies folded on a weathered cane chair near the lantern.

"Lovely will fetch him down for you, Hencher," says Cowles.

"I will fetch him down myself, if you please."

And Lovely the stableboy grins and walks into the stall; the jockey pushes the horse blanket off the chair, sits down heavily; Cowles takes one end of the chain while Hencher works with the other.

They pry up the ends of the chain, allow it to fall link upon ringing link into bright iron pools at their feet until the raised and padded ramp swings loose, opens wider and wider from the top of the van as Cowles and Hencher lower it slowly down. Two gray men who stand with hands on hips and look up into the interior of the van. It is dark in there, steam of the horse drifts out; it appears that between the impacted bright silver flesh of the horse and padded walls no space exists for a man.

Hencher puts the unlighted cigar between his teeth and steps onto the ramp. Silent and nearly broad as the horse he climbs up the ramp, gets his footing, squeezes himself against the white and silver flesh—the toe of one boot striking a hoof on edge, both hands attempting to hold off the weight of the horse—then glances down at Cowles, tries to speak, and slides suddenly into the dark of the van.

And Cowles shouts, doubles over then as powerless as Hencher in the van. The ramp bounces, shakes on its hinges, and though the brake holds and the wheels remain locked, the chassis, cab, and high black sides all sway forward once at the moment they absorb that first un-natural motion of horse lunging at trapped man. Shakes, rattles, and the first loud sound of the hoof striking its short solid blow to metal fades. But not the commotion, the blind forward swaying of the van. While Cowles is shouting for help and dodging, leaping away, he some-how keeps his eyes on the visible rear hoofs and sees that, long as it lasts—the noise, the directionless pitching of the van—those rear hoofs never cease their dancing. The horse strikes a moment longer, but there is no metallic ringing, no sharp sound, and only the ramp drags a little more and the long torch falls from the cab.

Then Cowles is vomiting into the tall grass—he is a fat man and a man as fat as himself lies inside the van—and the grass is sour, the longest blades tickle his lips. On his knees he sweats, continues to be sick, and with large distracted hands keeps trying to fold the grass down upon the whiteness collecting in the hollow of bare roots.

Hencher, with fat lifeless arms still raised to the head kicked in, hud-dles yet on the van's narrow floor, though the horse is turning round and round in the whitewashed stall. The jockey has left his chair and, cigarette between his lips, dwarfed legs apart, stands holding the long torch in both his hands and aiming it—like a rifle aimed from the hip —at Cowles. While Lovely the stableboy is singing now in a young pure Irish voice to the horse.

"Give me a hand with the body, Cowles, and we'll drag it into the stall," the jockey says. "Can't move it alone, cock, can't move it alone."

2

SIDNEY SLYTER SAYS

Fastest Track at Aldington Since War . . .

Thirteen Horses to Take the Field . . .

Rock Castle Remains Question in Reporter's Mind . . .

Oh Mrs. Laval, Oh Sybilline . . . Your Mr. Slyter has all the luck you'll say! Well, we drank each other's health again last night, and she confessed that she knew me right along, and I told her that everyone knows Mr. Sidney Slyter, your old professional. I never lose sight of love or money in my prognostications, do I now? But it's business first for me. . . . A puzzling late entry is Rock Castle, owned by one Mr. Michael Banks. And here's the dodge: if the entry is actually Rock Castle as the owner claims, then I know him to be a horse belonging to the stables of that old sporting dowager, Lady Harvey-Harrow, and how does he come to be entered under the colors (lime-green and black) of Mr. Banks? Something suspicious here, something for the authorities or I miss my guess. However, I shall speak with Mr. Banks; I shall look at the horse; I shall telephone the dowager. Meanwhile, Sidney Slyter says: wish you were here. . . .

It was Tuesday next and Margaret began to miss Michael in the afternoon. She tried to nap, but the pillow kept slipping through her fingers; she tried to mend the curtain, but her knees were in the way of the needle. Something was coming toward the window and it made her lonely. She went to the closet and from behind the duster and pail took down Banks' bottle of spirits and drank a very small glass of it. The missing of Michael came over her, the loneliness, the small grief, and she was drifting quickly down the day and time itself was wandering.

"Here puss, here puss. . . ."

Limping, bristling its hairs, the cat appeared near the pantry door. It ate quickly, choked on every mouthful, the head jerked up and down. The silver of the fish and speckles of the cat's eye caught the light. Now and then the dish scraped a little on the floor. Her back to the window, kneeling, Margaret watched the animal eat. And the cat, creature that claws tweed, sits high in the hallway, remains incorrigible upon the death of its mistress, beds itself in the linen or thrusts its enormous head into an alley, now sucked and gagged on the fish as if drawing a peculiar sweetness from the end of a thin bone.

But there was nothing sweet for her. She had dropped crumbs for the birds, she had leaned from the window, she had given the cat its dish. In the window—it looked out on the laundry court, was hard to raise—she had smelled the cool drifting air of spring and glanced at wireless antennas pulled taut across the sky. Annie must have heard the frame crash up, or must have caught the sound of her humming. Because Annie had come to the adjoining window, thrust out her blonde head, at twenty past two had jammed her sharp red elbows on the sill and talked for a while.

"Rotten day," Annie had said to her.

"Michael mentioned it would be clear."

"It's a rotten day. How's his horse?"

"Oh, he's a fine horse. A lovely horse. . . ."

"I don't know who Mike thinks he is, to go off and get himself a horse. But I've always wanted to kiss a jockey."

And Annie had taken up a little purse and counted her change in the window. Together they had heard a tram eating away its tracks, heard the hammer and hawking of the world on the other side of the building. It was spring in the sunlight and they leaned toward each other, and the smell of cooking mutton had come into the courtyard.

Now, between three and six, there was nothing sweet for her. Even her friend Annie had left the flat next door, and Michael was gone.

"I'm dead to the world," she said aloud.

Behind cataracts of pale eyes the cat looked across at her, cat with a black and yellow head which a good milliner, in years past, might have sewn to the front of a woman's high-crowned feathered hat. Margaret scratched on the floor, for a moment smiled. Her cat circled round the dish. It was so dark now that she could not see into the kitchen. From somewhere a draft began blowing the bottom of her skirt and she wondered what a fortune-teller—one of those old ladies with red hair and a birthmark—would make of her at this moment. There was the beef broth, water to be drawn and boiled, the sinister lamp to light, a torn photograph of children by the sea. Cold laurels in this empty room.

"He has only gone to look at the horse in Highland Green," she said. "It isn't far."

Once the madame of a frock shop had tried to dress her in pink. And even she, Margaret, had at the last minute before the gown was packed, denied the outrageous combination of herself and the color.

Once an Italian barber had tried to kiss her and she had escaped the kiss. Once Michael had given her an orchid preserved in a glass ball, and now she could not find it. How horrible she felt in pink; how horrible the touch of the barber's lips; how heavy was the glassed orchid on her breast.

Feeling lucky? Soon Michael would ask her that, after the sink was empty and her apron off. It was never luck she felt but she would smile.

In the darkness the cat swallowed the last flake of herring—Michael usually fed it, Michael understood how it wanted an old woman's milk to drink—then disappeared. It was gone and she thought it had left her in search of the whispering tongue of some old woman in a country cottage. So she stood, picked up the dish, made her way toward the smells of yellow soap and blackened stove. There was a bulb in the kitchen. But the bulb was bleak, it spoiled the brown wood, the sink, the cupboard doors which she had covered with blue curtains. She washed the cat's dish in the dark, lit the stove in the dark. For a moment, before the match flame caught at the sooted jets, she smelled the cold endless odor of greasy gas and her heart commenced suddenly to beat.

"Michael. Michael, is it you?"

But she turned, struck a second match, and the gas flames puffed up from the pipe in a circle like tiny blue teeth round the rim of a coronet and she herself was plain, only a girl who could cook, clean, sing a little. And then, in the light of the gas, she saw a stableboy's thin face and, outside, the mortuary bells were ringing.

. . . *The thin face of a pike and dirty hands—not black by earth, soot, or grease, but the soiled tan color of hands perpetually rubbing down a horse's skin—and wearing riding trousers of twill but no socks, and from the belt up, naked.*

"Now then, Mr. Hencher's with the horse, is that it?"

Together they walk in the direction of the stalls, passing a shovel in an iron wheelbarrow, a saddle pad covered with black flies, a whip leaning against a whited post. Over one stall, on a rusty nail, hangs a jockey's faded green-and-yellow cap.

They continue and from the rotted wood in the eaves overhead comes the sound, compact, malcontent, of a hive of bees stinging to death a sparrow. And the stableboy, treading hay wisps and manure between his shoes and the stones, points to the closed stalls and tells him of Princess Pat, Islam, Dead-at-Night, the few mares and stallions within.

And he hears them paw the dark, hears the slow scraping of four pointed hoofs.

"Smoke, Mr. Banks? I'll just have a drag or two before I go back in with him."

A growth of wild prickly briar climbs one side of the stall. There are no sounds within. Michael steps away, draws in his cuff, stares at the double doors—while the stableboy shoots back the bolt, slips inside. The horse stands head to the rear wall, and first he sees the streaks of the animal's buttocks, the high point that descends to the back. Then he sees the polished outline of the legs. Then the tail.

And at the same moment, under the tail's heavy and graying gall, and between the hind legs, he sees Hencher's outstretched body and, nearest himself, the inert shoes, toes down.

"How do you like him, Mr. Banks? Fine horse, eh?"

"Hencher," he whispers, "here's Hencher!"

Together they will bury Hencher with handfuls of straw, bolt the doors, wipe their hands, and for himself there will be no cod or beef at six, no kissing her at six, no going home—not with Hencher kicked to death by the horse. And forward in the dark the neck is lowered and he sees the head briefly as it swings sideways at the level of the front hoofs with ears drawn back and great honey-colored eyes floating out to him.

She heard the distant mortuary bells. Outside, over all this part of the city, returning fathers were using their weary keys. It was time to feed the cats, the dogs, the little broken dolls. It was never luck she felt, but Margaret waited, standing beside the coal grate in which they built no fire, waited for him to hang up his hat, untie her apron strings. When Banks had first kissed her, touching the arm that was only an arm, the cheek that was only a cheek, he had turned away to find a hair in his mouth.

Feeling lucky?

In how many minutes now she would nod, smile again, sit across from him and hold her pencil and the evening five-pound crostic, she wearing no rings except the wedding band and, in her otherwise straight brown hair, touching the single deep wave which she had saved from childhood.

Now and again from out the window would come the sound of lorries, the beat of the solitary policeman's step, the cry of a child. Later, after he had pulled the light string, she would dream of the crostics and,

in the dark, men with numbers wrapped round their fingers would feel
her legs, or she would lie with an obscure member of the government
on a leather couch, trying to remember and all the while begging for
his name. Later still the cat would come licking about for its old woman's milk.

The asparagus was boiling finally when the telephone rang. She
groped, found the instrument in the hallway, did not let the receiver
touch her ear. "Yes?" And even after the first words were spoken the
bell continued to ring, a mad thing ringing and ringing, trying to rouse
the darkened flat.

". . . the telephone's broken," she whispered into the cup, and her
hand was shaking. Then it went out of her head suddenly, and there
was only the dark terrible dustiness in the hall.

"Margaret?"

"Michael, is it you?"

"It is. Have you turned down the stove?"

"I think so, Michael."

"And the water off?"

"I think so."

"Good."

"Are you all right, Michael?"

"We're going up," and the voice was fainter now. "We're going up
for the Aldington. There's a hundred thousand in it. . . ."

"I want to come," she said.

There was a pause. And then: "I've thought of that. There's always
the train. You come by train. Tonight."

"Annie might join me if I asked her."

"Come alone. Just come alone."

"Yes, Michael."

After another pause: "You're the dear," he said softly in the dark
with traces of tenderness, and she heard the click and a child wailing
somewhere down the row.

"You're the dear," she repeated to herself in the kitchen. But she had
not turned off the stove and the asparagus was burned. She put a little
water in the pot and left it. An hour later she locked the flat, went down
the stoop, signaled a high-topped taxicab to carry her to the train at
Dreary Station. Hurrying she gave no thought to people on the streets.
She was a girl with a band on her finger and poor handwriting, and
there was no other world for her. No bitters in a bar, slick hair, smokes,
no checkered vests. She was Banks' wife by the law, she was Margaret,

and if the men ever did get hold of her and go at her with their trun-
cheons or knives or knuckles, she would still be merely Margaret with
a dress and a brown shoe, still be only a girl of twenty-five with a deep
wave in her hair.

A wife would always ride through the night if she were bidden. Would
ride through rainstorm, villages like Wimble, through woodland all
night long. All of it for Michael's sake: the station, the sign at the
end of the village, the cart with the single suitcase on it, the lantern
swinging beyond the unfamiliar spout, the great shadows of this
countryside. It was a lonely transport, there was a loose pin under
her clothes. And in this world of carriage seats, vibrations, windows
rattling, she stared at the other passenger, at the woman who had called
something out to her in Dreary Station and followed her aboard the
train.

A sudden roll of smoke passed the windows and she saw herself, and
her eyes ached and already she had been in her clothes too long. But
the crostics would be waiting when she returned. "What have you done
with the kiddies, Mrs. Banks?" asked the woman again.

Beyond the lights of crossings it was dark, the trees bent away from
the train, and Margaret felt the wobbling tracks running over the ties,
and each tie crushed under the wheels became a child. Children were
tied down the length of track: she saw the toads hopping off their bodies
at the first whisper of wheels, the faint rattling of oncoming rods and
chains, and she saw the sparks hitting the pale heads and feet. Then the
steam lay behind on the tracks and the toads returned.

"Done with them?" Margaret said. "I've done nothing with them.
There aren't any children."

The handle was rattling on her valise—she had not put it in the
rack—and her toes pressed against a sooty pipe. Her brown skirt was
drawn down completely, cloth over anonymous knees and heavy calves.
In her hand was the pink ticket. She sat backward with her shoulder
blades to the whistle engine, and looking out the window, she feared
this reversed and disappearing countryside.

"Oh," said the woman and flattened her paper, "I thought you'd
probably parked them with your mother."

"No. I didn't do anything like that."

"Weren't you ever parked when you were a child?"

"I don't remember. . . ."

"I was. I remember it," said the woman. "I was parked out more than I was home. For me there was nothing at the window, I used to eat my hands in the corner."

"I don't remember much of when I was a child," said Margaret. She noticed then a dead wasp suspended between the window's double sheets of glass. The train turned sharply and the overnight bag fell against her leg.

"Well," the woman spoke up above the noise. "Well," and coldly she reached a hand toward Margaret, "it used to be parking out for me." The woman paused, steadied herself, the train hissed round the turn. "But that's past. Now it's my sister leaves her kids with me of a weekend or summer. And I'm at the good end, now."

"All summer long?" asked Margaret.

"Some years, she does. I encourage it." And Margaret saw the wheels flattening the heads and feet.

A signal flashed. A yellow light then red, and levers, long prongs, pig-iron fingers worked in rust out there. The train swayed and stale water splashed in the decanters. The train smelled like the inside of an old man's hat—smelled of darkness, hair, tobacco—and the steam was up and she saw a car with its tiny lamps like match heads off in the blackness at a crossing. Were they merely waiting in the car? Or had the hand brake been set and were they kissing? Margaret felt the soot sifting into her bosom, she was breathing it down her nostrils. She wanted a wash.

"How old are they? Your sister's, I mean . . . her little children."

"Oh, young," said the woman, and Margaret looked at her. "But not so young they won't remember when they've grown. . . ." There were smells coming off the woman too, smells that lived on her despite the odor of coke and burning rails. Smells of shoe black and rotting lace, smells that were never killed by cleaning nor destroyed by the rain. The woman's strong body, her clothing, her hatpins and hair—all were greased with the smells of age.

"Monica's in the middle. Seven. She paints her nails."

"It's a nice name," said Margaret, and looking up, saw the woman's eyes like a female warden's eyes, black, almost beside each other, set into tiny spectacles with tweezers.

There were coffins in the baggage car and all through the night she smelled the cushions with their faint odor of skin tonic and old people's basketry and felt the woman watching her—wide-awake—and it was dark and stifling, a journey that made her muscles sore. The light began to swing on its cord.

The train had stopped. The door handle went down suddenly—after how long, she thought. Then the door opened and she saw the figure of a man who was standing on some country station ramp with the steam round his legs and a wet face. Margaret saw the night behind the man, heard the far-off ring of spanners or hammer heads against the locomotive's high black dripping wheels at the front of the train. The man was big, heavy as a horse cart of stone; there was not a wrinkle in his trenchcoat over the shoulders, his chest was that of a boxer. He blocked the door, held it, and his head came through. Hatless, dark hair, large straight nose. In one hand was a cigarette and he flicked the ash quickly into the skirts of his coat, as if he had no business smoking on the job. He swayed, leaned, his neck was red. He looked at the woman, and then at her; there was a movement in the dark eyes.

"All right now, Little Dora?" Nerve ends crossed in his gray cheek, it was a low conservative voice for kindness or bad weather.

"Right enough," said the woman without moving her hands. Her chin was squared. Then: "But I could do with a smoke," she added, and turned her spectacles toward Margaret.

"You don't mind if Little Dora takes one, do you, Miss?" He looked at Margaret, spoke to her from the empty ramp. His tie was loose and he was an impassive escort who, by chance, could touch a woman's breast in public easily, with propriety, offending no one. "You don't mind, Miss?" And there was nothing hushed in the voice, no laughter in the eyes, only the man's voice itself and his rainswept cheek and the cliff of his head with the old razor nicks, to startle her.

"It's all right, Larry, don't push it. I can wait," said the woman. "Seen this item, have you?" She tapped her newspaper, watched him. A short cough of the whistle swept back over them like smoke.

He leaned forward, holding the door, gripping the jamb, and the shoes were blackened, everything neat about the socks, the gray gloves were softly buttoned about the wrists and the hair was smooth. Only the hint of the tie was disreputable; it was red silk and loosened round the neck.

"I don't mind smoking," said Margaret quietly.

She followed them, and the man put up his collar against the wind and coldness of the night's storm. Down the wet planking, down the train's whole length of iron, walking and through her tears now looking at the heads asleep behind the train's dim and dripping windows. The rain had stopped, but there was a good wind. Despite it she thought she heard laughter and, farther on, the sounds of an infant crying and sucking too. In a brace on the wall of the station master's hut was a rusty ax; directly over the top of the engine she saw a few stars. But she was cold, so dreadfully cold.

"Bloody wild," the man said softly into her ear.

He was on one side of her, the woman on the other. The man took hold of her arm as if to escort her firmly, safely, through a crowd of men; the woman caught her by the hand. She breathed, was filled with the smell of the fog, saw the woman dart her cigarette into the night. At the platform's sudden edge, she saw a field sunk like iron under the stone fences, a shape that might have been a murdered horse or sheep, a brook run cold. The soot was acrid, it drove against her cheeks; the smell of oil was heavy in its packing and under it lay the faint odor of manure and wet hay and gorse.

"Feeling better?"

But she could not answer him. The wind had not disturbed his collar, he never blinked, eyelids insensitive to the rush of air.

"Larry," the woman plucked at his sleeve, shouted, "What have you on for tomorrow?" She clutched her spectacles, the lace was torn at her throat.

"Not much," putting his arm down upon her, round her, "sleep late . . . get Sparrow to do my boots . . . drive out to the Damps, perhaps. . . ."

"And come by the Roost?" she shouted.

"I'll look in on you, Dora. . . ."

Then his loose red tie was caught by the wind. It came out of the coat suddenly, and the red tip beat over the mist and thistles and wind off the end of the ramp. He waited a moment and carefully shut it away again.

"Had enough?" he asked.

They took her back down to the glass-and-iron door left open in the night, and she saw that it was the correct number on the door. With his hand still on her arm, and looking in as he had at first: "I expect you'll be wanting to see Mr. Banks tomorrow, Miss? Look sharp for him, Miss. That's my advice," and the woman laughed. When he stepped away, cupped his cigarette from view, once more the train began to move and the man stood waiting for his own door to be pulled abreast of him.

It was a good crowd. Margaret and the woman climbed down together. Men pushed close to the standing train and reached up, while steam boiled round their trouser legs, to tap the windows with their canes. The coffins went by on their separate trucks. Women with their stockings crooked, men with their coats wrinkled—sounds of leather, wood, laughter, and a bell still tolling. There were beef posters, hack drivers displaying their licenses, a fellow drinking from a brown pint bottle. Suddenly she felt the woman taking hold of her hand.

"Where will Michael be?" asked Margaret then, surrounded by the searching crowd. A stray dog passed after the coffins. For a moment she saw the man in the trenchcoat and his broad belt. He made a sign to the woman and, with three others dressed like himself, went under an arch to hire a car. On a wall was pasted an unillustrated poster: *You Can Win If You Want To.*

"Little Dora," a young woman was calling to them, "Dora!" She had red hair, dark near the crown. Her restless fingers touched the shoulder of a child whose hair was fastened with an elastic.

"You here too?"

"For the weekend only," the little girl's mother said, and fluffed her hair up on one side, kissed the woman's cheek. "But fancy you . . . such luck!"

"What's footing it, Sybilline?"

"It's the sunshine I want only," she said, holding the small girl's collar, "a rum, a toss, a look through a fellow's binoculars. . . . Will you take her, Dora?"

And after the child had changed hands: "This is Monica," she said to Margaret.

Margaret lost the far-off smell of grass when they went up the stairs. She had smelled it, wondered about it, sniffed it, the fresh clipped odor, the living exhalation of earth green and vast, a springtime of wet and color beyond the town's steam baths and shops and gaming rooms and the petrol pumps wedged between shuttered houses and hotels. Out there, over the steeple, over the wires, the wash, was the great green of the racecourse: the Damps. The grass itself; several ponds; the enormous stands with flags; the oval of roses in which men were murdered and where there fluttered torn-up stubs and a handkerchief—Margaret had tasted the green and then it was gone. Now the door closed and she smelled cheap marmalade and the rubber of pharmaceutical apparatus for home use. A small trunk stood by the door to the room. The woman, Dora, had a key in her hand.

"You seem to know the place, Little Dora."

"It's the first time for me."

"How then . . ."

"It's like all the rest."

The room was on the second floor. White, large, it had a closet with a sink in it. There were two brass beds covered with sheets, a picture of a girl in a lake. It was clean, but a pair of braces had been forgotten near the window.

3

SIDNEY SLYTER SAYS

Candy Stripe Looks Good . . .

Marlowe's Pippet Still Picked to Win . . .

Owner Refuses Comment on Rock Castle . . .

. . . extremely popular several seasons back. Well, Slyter excused himself from Mrs. Laval last night and talked by telephone to Lady Harvey-Harrow's groom. I couldn't reach the Manor House hence requested the stables, and Crawley the groom— he's as old as the dowager herself—Crawley said he had no recollection of the horse. That was his phrase exactly. (Heard stable rats nibbling corn in the background while Crawley tried to make it clear that his Lady, who might remember something helpful, had fallen off to sleep in the Manor House at sundown and could not be called.) Your Sidney Slyter will not take no. . . . Must drive to the estate. . . . Mrs. Laval just laughed—Oh Sybilline's lovely laugh—and said I should forget about Rock Castle. But what do women know of such mysteries? Slyter's got his public to consider. . . . This afternoon I confronted the en- igmatic Mr. Banks coming out of the Men's and offered him my hand, saying Slyter's the name. But he was white as my carnation and trembling; said he had no words for the Press; claimed he had an engagement with a lady, and I laughed at that. No apol- ogies. I told him my readers were betting on Marlowe's Pippet to win, and let him pass. . . . I want to know what's the matter with Mr. Banks. I want to know the truth about his horse. A case for the authorities without a doubt. And Sidney Slyter says: my prognostications are always right. . . .

THE CIGARETTE BURNED IN A SAUCER next to the brilliantine, and there was steam at the open lavatory door and sunlight at the raised window. Larry washed down to the muscles of his neck and arms, but the tips of his fingernails were black. He was whistling. Again he held the brushes in two hands, applied them simultaneously to the shine of his hair.

It was one o'clock, the racing crowd was at the Damps, and only the constable took a standing ale in the hotel's taproom while the wireless reported the condition of the horses. The foam was high on his tankard.

Larry whistled again, opened the bottom drawer, and from between layers of tissue lifted a vest of linked steel, shiny, weighing about five pounds. It fit over the undervest like silk. He turned sideways to adjust

the ties. Then he carried a moist towel to the bathroom, finished his
tea—it was bitter after the mouthwash and paste, and cleaner—and sat
in the horsehair rocker in the sun by the window. He raised his black
shoes to a footstool mauve and fringed with tassels, the sun began to
glow against the steel beneath his shirt. He had changed the water in
the flower vase first thing, so that was done; the pistol was loaded; he
smelled fish frying in the kitchen next to the Tap. A small biplane was
dragging a sign across the air in the direction of the spirited crowds:
Win with Wally. He glanced at the yellow petals, a corner of his pillow,
at Sparrow who was stretched on the bed. Then he nodded down at his
black shoes, thick and perfect as parade boots.

"Put a little spit on them, Sparrow," he said, and watched the other
climb off the bed, kneel, begin to polish.

Sparrow caught up with Larry near the Booter's. They walked by the
steam baths—it had a marble front and, waist-high, two protruding and
flaking iron pipes—walked by red petrol tanks, the beef posters, the
hedgerow upon which the birds were hopping, a novelty shop with a
rubber bride and groom in the window. On a low wooden door the
single word *Jazz* was chalked and beside the door stood a pot of drying
violets. Sparrow walked with the perspiration coming out on his chin;
the sun flashed from his mother's wedding band on his pinky. Larry
whistled and there was hardly a movement of the pale lips.

All about them was the stillness of the village: this watering place of
cocaine and scent, beer and feather mattresses and the transient rooms
of menservants, all deserted by sports and gypsies and platinum girls.
Deserted except for the constable, themselves, and the captive in the
white building. The small bets now—on a kiss, for show, for the cost
of lunch, the small and foolish bets for fun—were being placed elsewhere along with the serious wagers for a sick wife, burial of an aged
woman, relief from debt, a trip to the beach, and there were few risks
in the village now except those taken by the telephone operator who
made small business with anyone owning an instrument. The widow
who had held Michael Banks' face in her hands at breakfast was sleeping when Larry and Sparrow started their day; the constable's lips were
salty; the girl who had screamed was crying herself into dreams on the
floor. But Larry and Sparrow were walking through the odor of old
trees, through the village diaphanous and silent, walking now in search
of Thick and Little Dora.

On the stair, carpeted with rubber held firm by tacks, smelling of varnish and the rubber, a dark stair yet safe, the two men stopped to light up thin cigarettes; then Larry went first and Sparrow followed. From the end of the second-floor hall came the sound of a flushing toilet, the sudden swift plash of water in pipes, and a moment later the tinkling of a key. Nothing more. The hall, tinted green, was without decoration, without furniture except for a steamer trunk with lid half-raised on ancient petticoats and a bottle of silver-coated pills.

When he pulled open the door the little girl darted past, but Sparrow snatched at her arm—she smelled of Paradise Shore, had her hair full of pins—and twisted her round to the room again. He could feel the sweet pith of her arm, the ordinary thinness of flesh without ruffles. Under his fingers was a vaccination still bandaged and the spot was warm, a bit of radiance on the skin which, since her day in the clinic, she had attempted to hide under her short sleeve.

"Where's Sybilline?" asked the child, but Sparrow said nothing, letting his hand touch the hair that made him shiver just to feel it, to feel the pins which the girl had found and a few which Little Dora had stuck into it from a cardboard for her amusement. He put his hand in his pocket.

"Syb wouldn't want you running off," he murmured.

Everyone stared at Larry: Sparrow and the child now, and the two women, Little Dora with her shadow of mustache, steel spectacles, purple hat in place, and the captive Margaret whom they had dressed only in a white shapeless gown tied behind with cords. And two men, Thick with his ear close to a portable radio, listening to the sounds of sport —if not of horses then dogs or cars or motorcycles—and on the opposite side of the room from him, suit dusty and smelling of straw, the trainer Cowles, enormous and seated on an upended valise, shirt unfastened and his hair raised into a nasty crust. All of them stared, and there was no dirt on Larry's collar. Now Larry was in the room, and even when drunk he could comport himself. But he was not drunk, was at the other extreme from the full bottle, cognac preferred, which it took to make him laugh. Stood straight as he did when predicting, Larry who was an angel if any angel ever had eyes like his or flesh like his.

"My God," said Little Dora, "you've been bathing again." Her chin twitched.

"Afternoon, Cowles," said Larry over her head, "afternoon, Miss. Are you comfortable?" And he nodded to Thick, who turned off the radio. "Well," after a moment, "there's something sweet in the air. Wouldn't you say so, Sparrow?"

But he was looking at Margaret, at the bare feet, the whiteness of the charity gown, the shoulders sloping in the big armchair. "Well, Miss, you haven't answered my question." He waited, and she was deprived of everything, stripped as for some dangerous surgery.

"I'm comfortable," she said, and leaned forward in the chair.

"You're not wanting then."

"No. They tell me I can't see Michael. . . ."

"That's true, Miss. You can't see Mr. Banks. Right, Cowles?"

"He's engaged," said the trainer and laughed, face and neck still damp with a horse's drinking water.

Margaret's brown skirt, the shoes, the stockings had been burned and it was Thick who had returned with the playing cards and white gown. Little Dora had held it for her—"You won't be going into public in this rig, it's open behind!"—then fastened the ties. Once they had cut into her cousin's abdomen and she recognized the gown: whenever Thick had the chance, he whispered how he had attended his mother in Guy's Hospital in order to see the young women on the wards. Now she was herself attended and was ashamed to move. Thick had burned her things, identification card and all.

Suddenly she looked at Cowles: "Do what you want with me. But leave Michael alone. . . ."

"Don't listen to him," said the child Monica, and pushed the little table in front of Margaret, sat opposite and dealt the cards. "Just play with me," she said, turning up a golden queen, "we're friends." She was wearing a bright-green dress, too short, and she drummed on one of her pointed knees while staring at the figure on the card. Monica had the redness of her mother's hair at the back of her neck. "I bet I've got a jack under here."

Sparrow's own knees were aching. After being ground beneath the treads of an armored vehicle, the bones and ligaments of his legs had shrunk, in casts had become dry and grafted together. His knee caps were of silver and it was the metal itself, he claimed, that hurt. Now at either corner of his mouth the skin turned suddenly white and Larry took a step, held him up by the arm. Then under the shoulders, under the knees, Larry lifted him—Sparrow dropped the beret—and carried him to the bed where the small man lay whimpering.

"Take off his shoes, Cowles. Carefully, if you please."

Cowles did as he was told, the dark coat flapping down over his hands at the laces, while the others—the radio was on the floor, a chair scraped—moved all together toward the bed. Sparrow, at such mo-

ments, was in the habit of shutting his eyes, whether instantly crippled
in a picture palace, the Majesty, or in the Men's, whether caught in
Daphne's Row or in the room with tables and dirty silverware. He was
closing the lids now. They lowered, one or two lashes in each, slowly
obliterating the eyes, which were white and without tears. A single lick
of black hair lay on his forehead.

They were all at the bed, Thick and Larry on either side of the pillow
with Little Dora and Cowles—he was still holding the empty shoes—
and their expressions were unchanged even by Sparrow's moans. Margaret and the little girl came also, stood in the vicinity of Sparrow's
heart and lungs.

From his great height, drawing back his coat flaps and lapels so that
the gun and the gun's girdle—the holster, straps, strings—were visible,
slowly putting his hands in his pockets, Larry spoke the name, Larry
who had been the first to carry him the night he screamed, who had
sipped tea out of a tin cup while watching them give preliminary treat-
ment to the broken legs, and who had known immediately upon sight
of the buttocks tiny and gnarled that the injured man was a rider: "Sparrow." And Larry, who had greased his hair even in battle, was still
compassionate. "Sparrow," he said again and the moaning stopped, the
perspiration appeared, the slit eyes began suddenly to tighten and grow
shrewd.

"Dead and dying," came Sparrow's answering whisper at last, and
the wrists twisted in the enormous cuffs.

"Now then, Thick," said Larry, "roll up his sleeve."

Sparrow grimaced and all the while kept the round vague outline of
Margaret's face in his filmy sight. Larry took the tin packet from inside
his coat, from just beneath the armpit's holster, and opened it. He fitted
the needle to the syringe, broke the neck of the ampule, drew back the
plunger until the scale on the glass measured the centimeters correctly.
The tip of the needle dribbled a bit. He had tended to Sparrow in alleys,
bathhouses with crabs and starfish dead on the floors, in doorways, in
the Majesty, and the back of horsedrawn wagons on stormy nights. He
had jabbed Sparrow in the depths of a barroom and upright in the booth
of a phone; once on rough water with the rain beating down, once in
a railway coach with his ministrations hidden from the old ladies behind
a paper. Once too in the dark of a prison night, and many times, on
leave, with some strange fat girl wearing rolled stockings, or with a tall
girl carrying her underclothes in a respirator bag, standing idly by and
swinging the bag, pulling the rolled elastic, watching. As often as Spar-

row fainted, Larry revived him. Whenever Sparrow could stand on his feet no longer, whenever he went down in the crooked swoon, helpless as when he had first screamed from his bloody blankets—he had won a fiver from the kid of the battalion only that sundown—Larry the angel, the shoulder man, who later drowned the operator of the half-track in a shell hole filled with stagnant water and urine of the troops, took him up in his arms as carefully and coolly as a woman of long service. And with the needle and morphic fluid calmed him, standing then in suspect shadow, smoking, until Sparrow should rise, muttering, "Shivers and shakes," and proceed with his drugged and jittery step to a brief meal or to the job.

"This ought to do it," he said, and leaned forward, pinched as much of the flesh on Sparrow's arm as he could into a chilly blister. Then he punctured it, slid the needle beneath Sparrow's skin, gently pushed down the plunger. For a moment he could see the fluid lying like a pea just under the skin, then suddenly it dropped into a duct or into the mouth of a vein and was gone. He withdrew the needle and there was a tiny heart of blood on the tip of it. He watched, and in the middle of the tattoo—a headstone with "Flander's Field" in scroll beneath it—his pinch marks and the nick of the needle were still visible. He was casting a long shadow across Sparrow's torso, and the substance of his own head, the lines of his shoulders—constructed to catch a man's love for master tailoring—these lay lightly on the man in his agony. Then he looked across to Thick, who was stooping also and hiding his mouth behind a hand, keeping an eye on the bare needle. Thick's own forehead was trickling.

"He ain't going to need a transfusion . . . is he now, Larry?"

"Cover him with a sheet, for God's sake, and let's go," said Little Dora, and dug with mannish fingers into her stuffed side.

"Michael was sick once," whispered Margaret, and she was kneeling.

But this was not Sparrow's worst. Nor was it Daphne's Row or escaping in the manure wagon or trying to fix the needle behind the newspapers that time on the rocking train that had caused Larry himself to sweat and think of summoning the doctor who was bald and unlicensed and the best in the business for a man who had been stabbed or shot in the groin. None of these, but the time in the hock and antique shop—when the black cars passed up and down in front of the cluttered window and Sparrow had collapsed on a scabrous tiger skin, pulling a tea set with him and falling with his mouth jammed into the heel of a brass boot and he, Larry, had tried to squat beside and reach for him through a pile of bone and silken fans. His knee had crushed an old bellows and dust fell all about them, while paper weights rolled against the tiger's head. He had crouched there over Sparrow and had torn the tin packet. And a parrot in the back of the shop kept screaming, "Piss in his eye, piss in his eye!" from a great fortress-shaped wire cage. And while the cars hunted them up and down the street, while the parrot shrieked, he had freed Sparrow's arm from the cloth and had been too hasty, then, withdrawing the point, so that the needle broke, and the skin immediately turned blue. But even that day he had managed, watched Sparrow's cheekbones recede under a little color, helped him to crawl through the tunnel of Spanish shawls and so to escape, and had killed the parrot by stuffing his handkerchief into its shocked and gloomy face. Dragging Sparrow away he had heard the cage still swinging.

"That will do, I imagine," he said, and straightened. But no one else moved. First one, then by twos and threes the playing cards blew off the table and swished to the floor or landed on edge with tiny clacking noises, all face down except the queen. Thick wet his lips; Little Dora lifted back her veil; Cowles was biting his nails. Monica blinked her green and fearful eyes and Sparrow from the bed was sighing.

"Better now, Sparrow? Come along then. . . ."

"Wait!" said Little Dora. "You don't mean you're going without me, Larry! You wouldn't leave Little Dora behind! Not another day in the Roost. And I thought I'd be out today and have a throw and a lunch at the Pavilion. Ain't I going to get a finger in the Golden Bowl at least? Or at least a look at the Bumpy Girl? What the hell, I'm no matron. . . ."

But Larry opened the door a crack. "She wants watching, Dora." And, bracing Sparrow, raising his head slightly: "Use the ropes if you need to, Thick."

The door closed and Margaret remained kneeling at the empty bed. Little Dora tore off her gloves. Thick began to laugh.

There was a railing and Michael Banks took hold of it, then stared down into the darkness of five broad swinging doors. He was quite alone when he pushed through one of them. Underneath the grandstand and at the bottom of the steps he found ahead of him the empty reaches of the public lavatory—low ceiling, fifty feet wide and of concrete painted black and tiny brick cubes washed with a light-green color. There were a few bulbs in cages waist high between the urinals and toilet bowls. It was the rank darkness of the empty Tube; a man could hide even at the base of one of those toilets if he crouched low enough, made himself small.

He started to whistle softly and the sound coming from his own lips—he was not often a whistler, a smiler—made the words "barrels of fun" go round in his head. Slowly he unbuttoned his coat and listened. He was standing, he noticed, near a toilet that had no seat, one badly defaced in the row of urinals. Once he had seen a man die on a toilet—from fear—then had found a notice of the death in the papers. "Why are you always reading obituaries?" He remembered that ugly voice. "Who do you expect to find on the lists?" He couldn't say.

Now he peered ahead at a row of pipes with great brass valves—he had never been able to turn taps beneath a sink, could not bring himself to touch the copper ball, slime-covered, gently breathing, that lay in the bottom of a toilet tank—thinking that it wouldn't do at all to walk down there.

Then he heard the footsteps. They were none he knew, not those of Lovely, Cowles, or the jockey, who had a light and bitter tread. These were the sounds of a measured step, the left foot heavier than the right, the dragging of shoe nails against the stones. And Banks saw a movement, a mere breaking of shadow, at the end of the tunnel by which he himself had entered. He turned, starting toward the opposite end where the pipes loomed, but there too he saw the flickering of a white hand, fragments of darkness about to become the shape of a man. So he wheeled close against the nearest urinal and clutched at his clothing.

The man was beside him. A man smaller than Banks, humped over, with feet large as boxes and a slate strapped across his chest. The name of a horse was on the slate: *Rock Castle*.

Banks kept his eyes forward, said nothing. But down the tunnel's opposite length, climbing from behind the pipes themselves, the shape of the second man became complete. And at his side, in silent metamorphosis, appeared the third. The hanging slate of the first man banged against Banks' hip, and that of the second—all these carried the little boards, buckles and leather, wood frames splintered, pieces of slate chalk-dusted—caught him on the opposite side under the ribs. And the second man's nearest rubber, several sizes too large, smacked in the latrine water, moved again and lay beside his own wet shoe. Banks held tightly to his clothes, heard them shuffle, breathe, splash loudly. They

were just the three to stand beside him in the Men's—he knew it was
inevitable with the first echo of the footsteps—just the sort to gang up
on a lone man underground. But he also knew them for another kind:
in the glare above, all along the track's inner rail, great numbers of
these were posted, swiftly chalking, communicating with the crowd.
Dressed in rags, lean, fast as birds. These were the men who sat on the
rails with knees drawn up and scraps of paper fastened to their lapels,
soothsayers with craftiness and eyes that never stopped. Very method-
ical. For days he had seen them, the jaws unshaved, the looks of
intelligence, the slates slung like accordions from the wornout straps.
They were a system—"eunuchs," Cowles called them, "the mathe-
maticians"—but while clacking within arm's length of the hoof-cut turf,
each one sat in his astrological island, shabby, each figuring for himself
with twitching cheek muscles and numbers scratched on the slate. "The
bad-luck fellows," Cowles said of them.

Now Banks knew it to be so. The weight of the hands on the urinal,
the thickly rubbered foot, the hat in the band of which was a photograph of a nude woman, the slates—the name *Rock Castle* was scrawled
also on the other two—all this said as much.

And he was helpless now.

The first to come was whispering. Banks glanced quickly and saw a
scar hanging down from the eye like a hair, saw spectacles and a loose
soft collar partly torn at the seam. He tried to look away, but the man
went on with his whispering.

"I've got a word for you: *Sybilline's in the Pavilion.* Do you understand? *Sybilline's in the Pavilion. . . .*"

Down and back the length of the latrine it was a false and cheerful
sound. And behind the spectacles the man had watering eyes, eyes nearly
awash in the sockets, and he did not blink. On either side of his nose
—bookish—were grains of blood and scratches. When he whispered,
the saliva behind his lips, between his teeth, was tinted pink with blood
constantly trickling into the throat. The water round the eyes was clear.
And his limpid sight, the smile, his whispering, the signs of struggle, the
poverty of the cloth, his pink and golden gleam, the slate—these suggested unnatural occupation, the change in character: a man good for
certain kinds of hire.

"Don't move now, Mr. Banks, not a move if you please."

There was no smile, only the single flaw, the perversion, the staring
eyes and all round him the rank gloom, the chill, the burning of the
rusty lights.

"It's three to one now, Banks. Don't take it into your head to run off in a scare."

This whisperer was on his right; the second to come stood patiently on his left; Polka-dots—there was a neckerchief round his throat—had moved up close behind him. It was the triangle of his dreams, the situation he dreaded at the sound of sirens. He wanted composure when the whisperer touched his arm, saying, "You won't dart then. That's sensible. Why look here, Banks," smiling again, reaching into a pocket behind the slate, "What do you make of these?" And in his palm, suddenly, he held two small black balls, sovereign-sized in diameter and perfectly round. They appeared soft, made of tar perhaps, and left an oily dark stain on the skin as the man shifted them in his hand. "Ever seen one of these before? Pellet bombs. Quite a charge in them, Banks. Not enormous of course, but good enough to take a foot or a hand or eye without any question. Should you scare, Banks, and be so fancy as to skip on us, I'd throw one at you. And it would bring you to the flagging. But here," guiding him by the arm, "we don't need to risk a blasting. You won't be likely to run if you're sitting down. Now will you?"

They stopped at the broken toilet and Banks sat on it as best he could. They were standing close to his knees, making wet sounds with their boots and rubbers beside him, and it was worse than the crowds. Even the constable could help, he thought.

"Wait," he was squatting, staring up, could hardly see their faces, "what do you want?"

And the whisperer: "We could bash your brains," sucking sharply, feet trampling his own, huddling round him. "But," more easily, "that's not it for now. Later perhaps. Larry said to keep an eye on you all right. But Banks," catching him by the throat, pressing down upon him and smiling, "just take my word for it: *Sybilline's in the Pavilion.* She wants you to know, Mr. Banks, she thinks you'll understand. . . ."

And these three dropped back with their hands ready, arms hooked out defensively, and like boys flashing in an empty courtyard turned suddenly and—far apart, shoes scraping and slates caught close—raced off swiftly and with terrible clatter in the direction of the swinging doors.

He sat bent over in the quietness he had been looking for. It was a green world and he heard no echoes; they did not toss back any of their pellet bombs after all. He remained there on the piece of battered lavatory equipment for an endless time, and his eyes were half-shut.

4

SIDNEY SLYTER SAYS

Marlowe's Pippet Favored by Majority . . .

Retired Jockey to Ride Rock Castle in the Golden . . .

Owner Insists that Mystery Horse Will Run . . .

The wind's out of Slyter now; the hat's on the back of Slyter's head, all right all right. . . . Anyone got a drink? Anyone got a consoling word? Five pounds for the reader who sends me a bit of helpful information. . . . Because I took half a day to drive to the Manor House and return (if you know the uncharted moors on a summer day you know how desperately your Slyter drove). Arrived in time for tea—the little black cup you always suspect of being poisoned—and Lady Harvey-Harrow sent down to the empty stables for poor old Crawley. He came after a while, brushing through the cobwebs and removing his cap, and Lady Harvey-Harrow looked at him and said I was a gentleman from the Press. Still looking at him—mind you, not once my way—she asked him whether or not he agreed that the horse was dead, saying that it was her impression that the horse was dead but that if by chance the animal was still alive why those who had carried him off were welcome to such an old and useless horse. "What about it, now," I said, "dead or alive?" And the old man leaned over and stared hard as he could into Lady Harvey-Harrow's eyes and said—no more than a whisper—said that he had changed his mind and recollected having seen the horse not a fortnight ago in a shaded and gloomy place beneath the lone oak tree—the lightening tree he said—beside the river separating her Ladyship's heath from Lord Henry's land, and he remembered thinking how poorly the horse was looking at the time. I took up my hat and the old woman said she would not pursue the matter and suggested that I do the same. . . . How's that for a story to tell an established journalist? So Sidney Slyter's had it—for the moment—and Mrs. Laval is not in her accustomed room tonight. Unsatisfactory. But I'll get our men to check the files, that's what I'll do. . . .

How many are going to St. Ives?

Lines of people filed among the tables in the Pavilion, long lines wound between the little metal folding chairs all taken. They were coming down from the stands, from the stable area, from amusement tents, tramping across the beds of flowers left crushed or covered with spittle. White faces, a hat or two, a hearing aid, all packed together, stranger against stranger, and making their voices shrill over winnings or poor luck. The weight of them tipped a table up now and then, and spoons, forks with pastry on the tips, glassware, slid and fell from the edge. Those seated at the tables tried to drink, eat, talk, but everyone in the queues was laughing, stood staring down at the little round metal tops and puddles of lemonade and burned matches. There was a fat woman who carried her own sweets in a bag, and a cream puff had exploded against her cheek leaving bits of chocolate and egg white on her rosy skin. She was laughing from a deep stomach and dabbing with a fistful of handkerchief.

With the bottom of his trousers wet, brown hat on the back of his head, shirt crumpled and pinched lips smashed together, there was no happiness of the throng for Michael Banks, and he struck out at an elbow, at a shoulder blade, as hard as he dared. He saw the young woman immediately and gave a whistle. But it was drowned in the noise and upset of a waiter's tray.

She had a table to herself and had saved him a seat. She was drinking pink water and gin out of a tall glass and there was a second pink glass for him on the scratched metal table edge before his chair. A giant pair of binoculars lay between her glass and his and the long strap was bound safely round her wrist. Her red hair was like the orange of an African bird, and when she sipped, the jockey-pink rose water sent a delicate color up to a row of tiny pearls which she had sunk into the deepness of the hair.

"I'm Sybilline," she said.

He looked at the tip of her tongue and smelled the gin. Suddenly in the midst of weak eyes, puffy shirts, wallets stuffed with photographs of dead mothers and home, and on his person carrying still the clamminess, he found himself thinking he could bear the crowds for this, and felt his feet dragging, his fingers pressing white against the sticky metal of the chair. Yet he was brief.

"You wanted a word with me?"

"Oh, come off it now," she laughed. "Sit down and have a drink with Sybilline."

He did not remove his hat. He kept his back straight and with both hands seized the frosted glass, drank heavily. Everyone else wanted fish and chips or onions, but the gin and pink water was enough for him. There were fine soft flaming hairs on the woman's arms, freckles like little brown crystals out of the sea. The sun struck through the canvas and lighted her, here in the midst of a crowd which lifted his chair then allowed it again to settle. He hung on, swallowed, watched the way she breathed—there were holes cut in the tips of her brassière—and the way her fingers always curved round her windpipe when she brought her free hand to her throat. She was thin if anything and her skin was white as if it had taken all the skin's pigmentation, flesh color, to tint the hair.

"What did you want of me then?" he asked, and the chair was inching about beneath him, man and chair pressed into motion by the crowd on the Ouija board of the Pavilion's floor.

And quickly, brightening up: "I'm here for the weekend only and, fancy now, there's you! I've had a look through these," raising the strap of the binoculars, "and the fellow who owns them is gone. Aren't you glad? Things just come to pass, for a girl. For you, too, if you can only manage a little cheer in your face! Here, you carry them."

Slowly he put the strap over his shoulder. "But I haven't heard of you before," he said, and let the cold glass click against his teeth.

A small narrow man, appearing drunk and soldierly and wearing a red beret over an ear like a twist of leather, stumbled out of the queue and flung his arm round the woman's shoulder, shoved his cheek against the woman's cheek so that Banks saw the two heads together, the fair skin with its emulsion of cream and the scrap of the fellow's jaw, the green eyes meant for a mirror and the other eyes good only for sighting at a game of darts, the little red beret crushed into the softness of her orange hair. The man's breath stirred the pinkish curls and his short fingers were biting into the plain cloth above her breast. He was stooping, hugging her for balance, and Banks watched the two pairs of eyes, the twitching when movement came finally to the intruder's lips:

"Catch her while you can, Tosh," staring then, taking a breath too big for him, as if he himself had nobody in the world. "Stairways and stars, remember!" And Sybilline laughed, and with a hand on the man's thigh pushed him off so that he ducked quickly into the crowd.

Only her own eyes were left and Banks could not frown at them. "I'm a married man," he said. But there was a waltz coming out of the speaker, and she was laughing, twisting a curl the color of nail polish round her finger.

When they stood up, binoculars falling now against his hip, the fat woman and three others began fighting for the chairs, and his glass, still half-filled with gin, toppled and splashed on anonymous shoes and socks dropped carelessly below the ankles. But already Sybilline had him by the hand and Larry watched them going off through the crowd.

So Little Dora was left alone with Margaret. And Thick, driving the black van that had oil and sand smeared over the hand-painted name, was sent with Sparrow to the flat in the street at Dreary Station. Sparrow was agile now, climbed down from the cab and walked easily with the suitcase in his hand. Thick was grinning because he always liked a smashing. The sun lighted up the window boxes and the face of an old dog behind a fence; from far-off came the sounds of all the girls sewing in the factories.

"Gas johnnys," Sparrow told Mrs. Stickley and went with Thick to the flat and bolted the door from the inside. They took out the tools of the trade and in half an hour shredded the plant that the cat had soiled, broke the china quietly in a towel, stripped linen from the bed and all clothing out of the cupboards and drawers and closets, drank from the bottle found with the duster and pail. They cut the stuffing in bulky sawdust layers away from the frames of the furniture, gutted the mattress.

The high bells were ringing and Sparrow and Thick were done sawing the wood of the furniture into handy lengths, in sheeted bundles had carried out to the van the wood and the pieces of lingerie and puffy debris of their work. Bare walls, bare floors, four empty rooms containing no scrap of paper, no figured piece of jewelry or elastic garment, no handwriting specimen by which the identity of the former occupants could be known: it was a good job, a real smashing; and at dusk, on a heath just twenty miles from Aldington, they stopped and dumped the contents of the van into a quagmire round which the frogs were croaking. The two men smoked cigarettes in the gloom and then drove on.

Sybilline had let go of his hand and for a moment he did not lose her, stepping closely behind her figure, her red hair, quite certain she was lovely, even down to the open shoes and bare heels more red and wrinkled than he expected. But then the sound of a young woman's flat voice made him think of home, of Margaret; somebody knocked him in the side; and when he turned round again and discovered that Sybilline was gone he did not care. He was thinking of his wife Margaret and for the next hours fought alone through the crowd, thinking of her and sweating and becoming hungry.

And now, directly in front of the stands and just out of its shadow

—above him was the tower with the gilded face of the clock hung over with canvas and a scaffold's few swinging timbers—standing in one of the crowd's brief islands of space, he put a sandwich of hard salted bread and cheese to his teeth and chewed quickly. Others were sitting: a few women with their legs out straight on dirty towels or a folded sweater; a man wearing a tall gray coachman's hat with enormous red and green tickets sticking out of the band and now resting himself in an armchair, an overstuffed chair tonic-stained and running on make-shift wheels; a boy lying out on his back and asleep. But Banks, though breathing quickly and sweating, preferred to stand. He kept the cheese close to his mouth, bit into the bread. His long shadow was taking food.

"Buy a ticket," mumbled the man from his chair. In weariness and the heat he sought Banks' eyes but was too overcome to move. Banks turned a little and his shadow, like the arm of a sundial, pointed at someone else. He had found his air hole, a bit of room for his feet, and no one was at his elbow, nobody crowded. For once there was not a familiar face in sight, Margaret would wait. No longer did he care about the roses in the green behind him, but kept his eyes on the sandwich.

"He don't need a ticket. Can't you see?" One of the women, young, alone, with small carbon-black pock holes covering her face, sitting with her skirts out of place on the dirty incline of the clay spread before the stands, tore slowly into little pieces her own ticket, a dare that had failed, and glanced at the man in the chair. "He don't need your kind of luck, our kind of luck. Can't you see? God, what a thirst I've got!"

And ignoring her: "Buy a ticket," the man said again, and the wheels squeaked for a moment.

"God," the woman continued, and looked once at the sky, "they ought to shoot that Islam. Say," talking not to the prostrate man but to Banks, "you didn't bet on Islam, did you, mister? You'd know better, you would. He's broke my heart, that Islam. Say," he could feel a quickening of thought, a change in her eyes, "you wouldn't have a quid on you, mister?"

And quickly: "Watch out for her," the man said with an angry spinning of the wheels.

But Banks didn't care. He heard the voices of the man and girl—they were ringed round him and the bodies curtained out all except a far-off anonymous noise from the crowd—and he recognized the spent effort of the seller's voice and the appeal of the girl's. A little powder case was lying on its side next to her hip. But he had had enough of them and he was eating cheese.

"Here, I'll give you a quid," said a fat woman who was watching four or five chocolates melt in the palm of her hand.

The clay under his feet had grown hard with the spittle and rain, the sun, the endless weight of their bodies. It gave off an odor—of shoe leather, shredded tobacco, sweat. The sun was shining off their flesh. He moved his sundial's shadow again and peered at his teeth marks in the cheese; it made a dry bulb in his mouth and only the girl's remark about thirst had caught his attention. What if he showed her a pink lemonade and gin right now? She'd forget her Islam soon enough.

"Have one of my chocolates," said the woman.

He would watch out for all of them, he thought. Suppose he swallowed and looked at them, then said one word simply and clearly. What if he said "Larry"? The fellow in the chair would jump, most likely. But he buried the name, forgot it, thrust his face into the cheese which had no smell. He had never liked to stand while eating. Now he was grateful for the pause, the chance to stand apart though they were watching. Perhaps only the boy asleep was better off—no clock, no time, no witnesses for him. The face was bruised, bore the impression of knuckles beneath one eye. He would start, sit up, begin to cry if he heard the name of Larry, right enough.

Banks crumpled the sandwich paper and thrust it into his pocket.

"He's not so lucky," said the woman with chocolates, "he's only a kid." And she was looking at him squarely and he at her, and she had a man's thick lips, an arm she might throw about anyone's shoulder. "Tell us now," she said. "Are you the lucky boy? Have you been winning?"

He tried to look away. Then calmly, feeling the sun's pool hot in the top of his hat: "I've been picking them all correctly. But not for cash. . . ."

"You see," she shouted, "he hasn't got a quid!" And while laughing she licked the sweets, pulled a scrap of handkerchief from her skirt and began wiping the sticky palm. Her laughter awoke the boy and he groaned.

The girl laughed also, but less heartily, as if she might still hope to get what he did have.

"Shut up," said the man in the chair, "he's got more than that."

And over the heads of all those standing behind them, he saw the profile of Margaret's face. When he jumped, took the first long stride, he kicked something under his foot and in a moment knew it to be the young woman's powder case, without looking down, heard the tinkle and scrape of the contents scattering.

"Here, don't be rude . . . ," he heard the older woman say, and he was pushing, pushing away into the midst of them. And still there was the face and he gasped, slipped between two men in black, tried not to lose her, raised a hand. Here was surprise and familiarity, not out of fear, but fondness, and between them both perhaps three hundred others not moving, not caring what they lost in the sun.

"My God, what have they done to Margaret!" Because, for the moment only he saw the whole of her and she was wearing clothes he had never seen before—an enormous flower hat and a taffy-colored gown with black-beaded tassels sewn about the waist and sewn also just above the bottom that was dragging. A dress from another age, too large, too old, Margaret clothed in an old tan garden gown and lost. "She's not yet thirty," he thought, shoving, using his elbow, "where's their decency?" Then she was gone and he shouted.

"Watch who you're colliding with, young cock," said a voice in his ear.

He reached the spot where she had stood, but only a man, somebody's butler, with a small child on his shoulders, moved in her place now, and the man refused to talk. The child looked down at Banks.

So he turned, stumbled, and near the east corner of the stand saw the last of the taffy back rushing like the ghost of a doe, and they were hustling her—another woman and a man. "Wait!" he was only thinking it, "wait!" Here was the first taste from the cup of panic, seeing the girl, his wife, pulled suddenly away from him by an arm. When he reached the spot he found that Margaret had been caught at the top of the stairs leading down to the five swinging doors of the Men's, and he stopped, drew back, put his hand on the rail. A cigarette flung in anger, haste, was burning down there near one of the vaulted doors and he thought he could hear still the old public squeak of the hinge. He could not descend those stairs, and once more he was tasting lime. In the cool shadow he leaned, clutched the dusty iron, closed his eyes.

"Mr. Banks." It was Cowles, accompanied by Needles dressed in his silks. "Why, Mr. Banks, you'd better take care in the sun. Ain't that right, Jimmy?"

"I saw her . . . ," he managed to say.

"Who's that, Mr. Banks?"

"I saw my wife. . . ."

"Well, too bad for that, Mr. Banks, as the fellow says. Ain't that right, Jimmy?"

"They took her into the Men's."

"Unlikely, I should say. You'd better watch the sun, Mr. Banks. Come now," and he could hear the jockey shuffling his little boots, "come, you'd better join us at the Baths. They're bracing, Mr. Banks, very bracing. . . ."

"Fool," shaking the white gown in his face, "you fool!"

"But she pilfered the trunk, I tell you."

"I never let it happen . . . but you did. You fool!"

"And what's so smart about having a trunk full of clothes in the hall when you're trying to keep her naked?"

"Don't say smart to me, smart as a naked girl, you are! And I can't even take a slip to watch the Bumpy Girl without you letting her at a trunk full of clothes that would keep us all in style."

"You wasn't supposed to be taking a slip. You was supposed to stay."

"Don't throw it back at me, don't give us that! Just wait 'til Larry hears how it was you who was lax, you wait. . . ."

"Ah, Dora, I can't keep awake all day."

5

SIDNEY SLYTER SAYS

Mystery Horse's Odds Rise Suddenly . . .

Rock Castle's Trainer Suffers Gangman's Death . . .

Marlowe's Pippet: The Youngster Can Scoot . . .

. . . my great pleasure in announcing that I have sent five pounds, as promised, to one Mr. Harry Bailey, Poor Petitioners, Cock & Crown, East End. Mr. Bailey, carter by trade, suggests that, in his own words, "The horse will win. Ain't it the obvious fact which the old woman and her old groom are hidin'? My poor lame sister dreamt it now three nights in a row, that the horse will win. And all respects, Mr. Slyter, I'm of the opinion she's exactly right." There's a tip to make Sidney Slyter quake, there's one for your pals! Dead, alive, uncertain of age, uncertain of origin, suspected ownership—victory these things say to our reader in East End! Perhaps you've put your finger on it, Mr. Bailey—the simple conviction of your phrasing chills my heart, Mr. Bailey, with the suffering which our ancients knew—but we must not blaspheme the outcome of the Golden Bowl with such ideas of certainty. What have the rest of you to say? Anyhow, congratulations to Mr. Bailey, cheers to Mr. Bailey's sister. And five pounds to the next lucky person writing in. . . . But it's Sidney Slyter here, and my assistant Eddie has been put on the job of checking our files. Eddie will be checking them now and, any moment now, will be calling me direct from Russell Square. Eddie's just the boy for checking files. . . . And this is a new development: officials here have made it known that T. Cowles, of undesirable character and listed as trainer of Rock Castle, has been stabbed to death by members of a gang to which the victim Cowles himself belonged. And Sidney Slyter says queer company for Mr. Banks? Queer and dangerous? Fellow who operates the lift said Mrs. Laval was not available tonight; stepped out for dancing and bitters with a friend, he said. So Sidney can sit in the pub with the constable, or go throw dirty dice in the lane. But cheer up, cheer up, Eddie will be through to your Sidney Slyter soon. . . .

MICHAEL BANKS AND COWLES AND THE JOCKEY in his colors walked past the Booter's, past the barn and millinery shops until they reached the Baths, where they found the constable's two-wheeler leaning against the marble wall with water dripping from one of the iron pipes down to its greasy seat. A few bees were circling the klaxon and the water made a rusty summer's pool on the leather.

"Look out," said Cowles, "the old constable's after his cleanliness again."

"He's been drinking," the jockey said. "He wants to sweat away the beer. That's all."

The entrance to the Baths was on an alley. The building was of whitewashed stone and marble, and once, years before, the entire alley side had served as a sign. Now on the dirty white the paint was faded, but most of the letters in gold and brown could still be read: across the top of the wall and in a scroll "Steam Bathing" and under that the words "Good for Gentlemen," and then another slogan, "Steam Cleans and Cures." On either side of the door was painted the greater-than-life-size figure of a naked man, one view seen from the front, the other from the rear, both flexing their arms and both losing the deep red flesh of their paint to the sun and weather of harsh seasons.

Banks smiled once when he walked naked from the dressing room into the steam. He was immediately hot, wet in an instant, and felt his way through the whiteness that was solid and rolling and solid again all at once. Now and then four or five square feet would clear completely, and in one of these sudden evaporations he saw Cowles standing quite still and stretching, while the jockey was taking blind tentative steps, covering his face and mouth with the fingers and thumbs. But he heard the hissing, the sightlessness returned; they were groping in the same direction. Then: "Here, Mr. Banks," it was Cowles, obliterated but close to him in the steam, "lie here. There's room for three of us right here."

There were tables—three now pushed together—tables and shelves to lie upon, slippery and warm, and a collection of live red iron pipes upon which the Steam Baths operator and his two young boys threw buckets of icy water: and the steam smelled first of flame, cold mountain streams, and of the bare feet and ankles of the man and boys at work. And then it smelled of wood, stone floors, of white lime sprinkled between the slats on the stone; and of the bathers then, the molecules of hair oil and sweat from the skin. He breathed—and tasted, smelled the vapors filling the lung, the eye, the ear. So many clouds of it, so thick that the tin-sheeted walls were gone and only a lower world of turning and crawling and groaning men remained.

The shelving, wide enough for a man, was built about the room in tiers that reached nearly to the ceiling, all this space cut by braces, planks, verticals. Between the tiers were the tables with hands, feet, at the edges. It was a crowded ventless chamber and filled with noise, a confused and fearful roaring. But these men were prone and here activity was nothing more than a turning over or a writhing. Every few minutes the smallest of the two boys would fling a pail of ice water not on the pipes but across the flesh of a prostrate bather and the man would scream: no place here for undervests or socks, tie clasp or an address written out on paper.

". . . Lie next to me, Mr. Banks," and Cowles helped him up to the boards while the jockey climbed as best he could. Then the three of them were stretched out together and he felt that he himself was smiling. There was slime on the wood and steam was dripping down the braces, down the legs of soaking pine. By habit he started on his back and kept his hands at his sides, restraining his hands even when he felt the eyelids turning soft and his lips loosening, taking the seepage in. He heard the splashing of ice water but it was aisles away, and the steam was heaped up all about him, his lungs were hot. Then, later, he listened to Cowles succumbing, the flesh—a hand or foot—beating against the wood and growing still, the moans filled with resistance, helplessness, and finally relief as if confessing under the blows of a truncheon.

". . . Makes you feel . . . like . . . you'll never walk again . . . eh, Mr. Banks?" Now a whisper only and the head buried down under the fatty arms, one huge leg fallen over the edge, never to be retrieved.

Banks rolled over, making the effort to throw off the pinion and move despite the nervelessness of muscles, despite paralysis. "Excuse me, Needles," he said, but the jockey had his own discomfort and did not reply.

He always saved the stomach. It was best on the stomach and he waited until just that moment before he might not be able to roll at all, then tried it, and the exertion, the slickness of wood passing beneath his skin, the trembling of the propped arm—when these were gone there came the pleasure of shoulders sagging, of being face down in the Baths. Now he opened his eyes a little and his lips parted around the tongue. He thought of water to drink. Or lemonade. Or gin. He knew the torpor now, the thirst, with all the fluids of his body come to the surface and the hair sticking closely to his skull.

And then—not able to raise his head, drifting back from numbness and feeling the rivulets sliding down his flesh—he heard the sounds, the voices, that had no business in the Baths: not the steam's hissing nor the groans of bathers, but the swift hard sounds of voices just off the street.

". . . Gander at that far corner, if you please, Sparrow. And you, Thick, shadow the walls."

Moments later, back through the oppression: "Go down on your knees if you have to, Sparrow. . . ."

And the steam lay on the body of Jimmy Needles, and Cowles looked dead away. He thought he saw shadows through the puffs and billowing of the whiteness and he longed more than anything for a towel, a scrap of cloth to clutch to himself, to wipe against his eyes. In the anonymity of the Baths, amidst all those naked and asleep, he heard again the sounds and now he tried to rouse the trainer: "Cowles," whispering, "Come awake now, Cowles."

But then there was the ice blow of the water, and he heard the grunt of the child and pail's ring even before the sharp splash covered him from head to foot. He froze that moment and the skin of his shoulders, legs, back and buttocks pained with the weight of the cold more shocking than a flame. When he bolted upright, finished wiping the water from his eyes, he found that Cowles was gone and in a glance saw nothing of Needles except a small hand losing hold of the flat boards as the jockey shimmied down and away.

So he followed and several times called out: "Cowles, Cowles!" But he got no answer. He crouched and crept down the length of one wall, made his way in blindness and with the floor slats cutting into his feet. He moved toward the center and was guided by the edges of the tables.

And then there were three separate holes in the steam clouds and in one he saw the stooping figure of the man with the beret; in another he saw Thick scratching his chin; and in the last, the nearest, the broad tall body of Larry fully dressed, and his dark-blue suit was a mass of porous serge wrinkled and wet as a blotter. The cloth hung down with steam. The shirt, at collar, cuffs, and across the chest, was transparent as a woman's damp chemise and the chest was steel. He carried a useless handkerchief and the red was quickly fading from his tie, dripping down over the silken steel. Thick was wearing a little black hat that dripped from the brim, and Sparrow's battle trousers were heavy with the water of the Baths.

Banks squatted suddenly, then spoke: "What are you after now? Three beggars, isn't it?"

Without answering or looking down at him the men began to fade. Not gone suddenly behind the vapor's thick intrusion, but merely becoming pale, more pale as shred by shred the whiteness accumulated in the holes where they stood. A sleeve, a hand, the tall man's torso, a pair of wet shoes—these disappeared until nothing was left of the trio which, out of sight, continued then the business of hunting despite the steam.

"Go on," he heard himself saying, "go on, you bloody beggars. . . ."

Slowly he crawled under the braces of the table and after them. The steam was heavy and his eyes began to smart. He tore his calf on a splinter. Once more, and for the last time in the Baths, he came upon the toe of Larry's black boot, followed the trouser leg upwards to the lapel where a yellow flower was coming apart like tissue, saw the crumpled handkerchief thrust in his collar, the sheen of perspiration on the high cheeks, the drops of water collected around the eyes. But still there was the casual lean to the shoulders, one hand in one wet pocket as if he had nothing better to do than direct this stalking through a hundred and ten degrees and great dunes of steam. The boot moved, turned on the toe leather so that he saw the heel neatly strengthened by a bit of cobbler's brass, and the man was gone again, saying: ". . . Found him, Thick? Have a go under the steam pipes then."

And he himself was creeping off again, feeling his foot drag through a limpid pool, feeling the sediment on his skin. His hair was paste smeared across his scalp. He felt how naked he was, how helpless.

Then, still on all fours, he came to the corner. Under the wooden shelving, lying half-turned against a stretch of soapstone, bent nearly double at the angle of meeting walls, crowded into this position on the floor of the Baths was Cowles' body with the throat cut. Banks crept up to him and stared and the trainer was a heap of glistening fat and on one puffy shoulder was a little black mole, growing still, Banks realized, though the man was dead. And though this Cowles—he had had his own kill once, kept dirty rooms in a tower in the college's oldest quad, had done for the proctor with a fire iron and then, at 4 A.M., still wearing the gown darned like worn-out socks, had stolen the shallow punt half-filled with the river's waters and, crouched heavily in the stern with the black skirts collected in his lap, had poled off under the weeping willow trees and away, lonely, at rest, listening to the fiends sighing in nearby ponds and marshes—though this Cowles now lay dead himself his blood still ran, hot and swift and black. His throat was womanly white and fiercely slit and the blood poured out. It was coming down over the collar bone, and above the wound the face was drained and slick with its covering of steam. One hand clutched the belly as if they had attacked him there and not in the neck at all.

Just as Banks caught the lime rising at the odor of Cowles' blood he felt flesh striking against his flesh, felt a little rush of air, and Jimmy Needles lunged at him in passing and fled, hunting for the door. Before he himself could move he heard a sound from the wood above Cowles' corpse, glanced up, and peered for several moments in the congealed blue-tinted face of the constable: an old man's naked face reflecting cow and countryside, pint-froth and thatch in all the hard flat places of its shape.

"Here now, what's this deviltry. . . ."

But then Banks too was gone, no longer crawling but running, with the unhelmeted head of the constable and the sight of Cowles' freshly cut throat before him, reaching the door as he heard the hiss and exhalation of new blinding steam and the cry of the old nude member, only member, of the constabulary showered that moment from the small boy's icy pail.

His hand slipped on the knob but it shut finally against the pushing of the steam, and the jockey handed him a towel. He covered himself, leaned back, stared at the bench upon which, shoulder to shoulder, were seated the three of them—Sparrow and Thick and Larry—with pools at their feet. Banks held the towel with both hands under the chin, looked at the dark men on the bench and the row of clothes hooks curling from the wall behind them. There was water about his own feet now.

"What did you kill him for?" Watching Larry in the middle but seeing the silks fluttering over the hump at the peak of the jockey's spine: "Whatever for?" It was little more than a whisper above which he could hear the water falling from three pairs of hands, dropping from three sets of trouser cuffs. The flower had disappeared altogether from the blue lapel.

"Oh, come on," said Sparrow, getting up, wringing the beret, "let's have a dash to Spumoni's!"

In the dusk surrounding the Baths the bees swarmed straight off the klaxon and made a golden thread from the bicycle to a nearby shrouded tree.

It seemed hardly more than teatime but it was dusk, fast coming on to nightfall when there's a fluttering in steeples and the hedgerow turns lavender, when lamps are lit on ancient taxis and the men are parading slowly in the yards of jails. Castles, cottages and jails, a country preparing for night, and time to set out the shabbiness for the day to come, time for a drink.

Sparrow felt the mood: "Give us another liter of that Itie stuff," he said. The waiter filled their glasses and Larry heaped the plates with second servings of the spaghetti and tomato sauce. The waiter could see the blue butt and shoulder holster inside his coat. "Cheers," said Sparrow, while Jimmy Needles drank his health.

And between the tables: "You dance divine," said Sybilline, "just divine. . . ."

A quartet of scar-faced Negroes was playing something Banks had first heard out of gramophones in Violet Lane, something whistled by the factory girls on their way to work. No favorite now, no waltz carried on the tones of an old cornet, but music that set him trying to pump Syb's hand up and down in time with the piano player's tapping shoe. There was a trumpet, a marimba and bass and the piano on which a white girl was supposed to sit and sing. Beside his bench was a flabby fern in a bucket and the piano player kept a bottle there, under the dead green leaves. Banks could clearly hear the fellow's foot going above the syncopation of the racy song.

Banks had never learned to dance but he was dancing now. He pumped her hand and Syb wasn't afraid to move, wasn't afraid to laugh, and he found her spangled slippers everywhere he stepped and saw the drops of candlelight—on the tables there were candles fixed to the bottoms of inverted tumblers—swelling the tiny pearls pushed into the fiery hair. For a moment, admiring the decorative row of pearls, he thought of the faces children model out of bread dough and of the eyes they fashion by sinking raisins into the dough with their stubby thumbs. Then, with the hand on her waist, he felt a bit of Sybilline's blouse pulling out of her skirt and heard her voice, flitting everywhere fast as her feet, saying, "Let's have a drink-up, Mike, a rum and a toss. . . ."

The room was filled with people from the Damps—a racing crowd. In this room in the town surrounded by farm and vicarage and throaty nightingale there were people who did their banking in High Fleet Seven and others who did their figuring in the slums, all sporting now—it was the night before the running of the Golden—and ordering Spumoni's best. Like a theater crowd, a society in which the small person of Needles could go unnoticed, though wearing rainbow silks and cap and a numbered placard on his puffy sleeve. And Banks felt that he too went unnoticed, felt that he could drink and dance and breathe unobserved at last. There were enormous black-and-white paintings of horses about the walls along with the penciled handwritten names of endless guests.

There was the odor of whisky and Italian cooking, and the Negroes never ceased their melody of love and Lambeth Walk.

"Coo, Mike," she said just before they reached the table, "it's going to be a jolly evening." In Syb's voice he heard laughter, motor cars and lovely moonlit trees, beds and silk stockings in the middle of the floor.

Glasses in hand they did not sit, but stood beside the table, because she wanted to dance again and couldn't bear sitting down. They held hands while the small ex-soldier poured and Needles sucked in his cigarette and looked up at him.

"Mr. Banks," and it was Larry, lifting the fork, letting the candle shine across his face, "feeling a little better now?"

"Quite nicely, thanks," he answered.

"Bottom's up!" the girl said suddenly, and swallowed off the wine, balancing against his arm and tilting so that he saw the heart throb, the wine's passage down the throat from which she was capable of laughing, crying, whispering. So he drank also and it was the hard dry dusty taste of wine and he was warmed and pleasurably composed. He remembered not the Baths, the Damps, poor wretched Cowles, nor the rooms in Dreary Station, but a love note he had written at the age of twelve when the city was on fire. And remembering it he looked at Sybilline and saw in her eyes the eyes of an animal that has seen a lantern swinging on a blackened hill.

"Excuse us," he said, and put down the glass. "This is our melody."

In his arms she was like the women he had thought of coming out of comfort rooms. Or it was what they had done in the shelters or when the bands were marching—upright, holding each other close before the parting. One of his hands was on her body and the sequins kept falling off her blouse to the floor. They were dancing on sequins. He was able now, while holding her, to try and tuck in the blouse.

"It's shrunk," she murmured, "it'll never stay." But his fingers pushed in the cloth, and over the top of her auburn head he saw the piano player leaning to drink from the bottle pulled out of the bucket and saw the marimba player's black dusty hands—there was a big gold wedding band on one finger—shaking, trembling in mid-air. Everyone was talking horses, talking the Golden, but he was moving round the little floor with Syb.

"You know," pulling her head away from his brown lapels, but dancing, dancing, "that other chap was hopeless. Wouldn't even buy me an ice. But whatever did you do with his binoculars?"

He waited and then: "Gave them to a fellow selling tickets."

Later still, when she happened to see the jockey holding his head and Sparrow slipping something to the waiter—a Neapolitan with dirty shirt and mustaches—when the candles were softly dying and the wine was dregs—and still they were turning on the floor—then she laughed, spoke against his chest: "It'll be a jolly evening, Mike. I promise. We'll go to bed and you'll like my bed, Michael. . . ." And then in the middle of the floor with the others watching and Larry pulling sharply on his coat over the holster, sending Needles out for the hired car, then she gave him her own lips soft, venereal, sweet and tasting of sex.

But Sparrow stopped them kissing, tapped on his arm. "Come now, Banks, Larry says we're going to a proper place."

6

SIDNEY SLYTER SAYS

Marlowe's Pippet Smart in Practice Whirls . . .

Rock Castle Proves Ancient Champion . . .

Mystery Horse Possesses Danish Blood . . .

Harry Bailey of Poor Petitioners, Cock & Crown, East End, how
right you were! Fly up to Aldington, Mr. Bailey, fly to Aldington
with your poor lame sister, for Sidney Slyter says he needs you
now! Five pounds? Not half enough, I'd say! Sidney—God's silent servant—Sidney Slyter has his brimming glass, his fags,
lighter embossed with crop and stirrup, his hotel beds, and ladies
to converse with in the bars; has his hard sporting eyes red-
rimmed or not and under his titfor leaves of information about
the horses ever growing bone from bone and blood into blood.
And Sidney Slyter's got God's own careless multitude to shelter
in enjoyment and the luck of sport. But Mr. Bailey, my friend,
it took you puzzling over the problem while rubbing your dog's
worn ear and hearing the dreams of your ever-innocent lame
partner to perceive directly the horror at the end of our journey,
you to phrase the spoils of our fate! *The horse will win . . . the
horse will win. . . .* Amazing, Mr. Bailey, just amazing. . . .
Because Eddie Reeves came ringing through my wires at 4 A.M.
and what he read me was an accolade proper for the obituary
of the King of the Turf: *He's run the Golden before, Sidney.
Hear me Sidney? Entered in The Golden Bowl three times and
three times the winner. Hear me Sidney?* Then the dates; then
Eddie coughing through the dawn; then the minutes of each winning race. Then reading on: *Draftsman by Emperor's Hand out
of Shallow Draft by Amulet; Castle Churl by Draftsman out of
Likely Castle by Cold Masonry; Rock Castle by Castle Churl
out of Words on Rock by Plebeian—Bred by the Prince of Denmark, Sidney, bred by the Prince and commanded to win by the
Prince and ordained to win by the Prince and forebears of that
line, too. And by his order—just to get the royal stamp on him,
Sidney—the King's own surgeon transplanted a bone fragment
from the skull of Emperor's Hand into Rock Castle's skull. Then
presented by the Prince of Denmark to Lady Harvey-Harrow
on her sixteenth birthday. The horse will win, Sidney, the horse
will win. . . .* Rigid; fixed; a prison of heritage in the victorious
form; the gray shape that forever rages out round the ring of
painted horses with the band music piping and clacking; indomitable. And somebody knew all this already, and it wasn't Mr.
Banks. But who? Sidney Slyter wants to know: and Sidney Slyter
wants to know what's the matter with Mr. Michael Banks. . . .

IT WAS 4 A.M. IN THE DARKNESS that had begun with bees and warbling
and the fading of bells, and Thick had used the ropes. Now she was

bound, her wrists were tied together to the bedpost of brass, and Thick
was snoring. He had somehow got her back into the white gown but
had left the ties unfastened. It hardly covered her and despite the pain
she could feel the gauzy touch of the old hat against one bare leg. Despite the darkness of the night she could faintly see the shreds of
the long tasseled gown which he had ripped with his knife, muttering,
". . . Try to get big Thick in trouble, eh, try to make Thick look a
fool. . . ." and had strewed viciously about the room, across the floor.
A torn piece of the bodice was hanging over the closet door. And the
little steamer trunk—how desperately she had found it, rummaged
through the clothes of the long-dead woman. Cursing her, he had locked
the little steamer in the cellar. Locked all escape away, then beaten her.
And she had gone unconscious for an hour, for several hours, but there
was no sleep for her. A bed she could not know—upon it violence that
seemed not meant for her—this hour in which she could not sleep, arms
drawn back and flesh captured with Thick's rope, so tightly that her
hands were cold: she knew now the hunger of the abducted, knew how
the poor girls felt when they were seized.

Four A.M. and she was one of the abducted. She wanted to stand at
the window, hear a voice through the wall, find a flower pressed between the pages of a book, eat from a plate she recognized. But there
was only the darkness smelling so unfamiliar and the ropes that cut and
burned. She knew there was enormous penalty for what they had done
to her—but she could not conceive of that, did not require that: she
only wanted a little comfort, a bit of charity; with the awfulness, the
unknowable, removed. Once when a girl—and she had been a girl—
they had sent her away somewhere, and now the soreness, the sleeplessness, the sensation of invisible bruises reminded her of the hearth
with an uneasy fire on it and an old woman threading buttons, an endless number of buttons—blue and white and violet—on a string. She
was a child anything could be done to—and now, now a docile captive.
And when Monica, the little girl, awoke about this hour with her nightmares, Margaret took them to be her own bad dreams, as if in soothing
the child she could soothe herself.

But it wasn't soothing she wanted, it was a task or other to do. She
hadn't believed Thick's beating, really, though it put her out for an hour
or more. Later, lying strapped to the bed, she told herself it was what
she might have expected: it was something done to abducted girls, that's
all. She thought she had read a piece about a beating. And yet when it
came it surprised her. Though thinking now, listening, looking back

through the dark, she realized—this despite the article she had read—
it was something they couldn't even show in films.

Because his sweat smelled raw when he tied her. And because after
that, after he had grunted making the knots and cursed carrying the
trunk down, he had become silent and watched her for a while, his
precious radio telling them the time and starting a symphony, and then
he had told her he might have to tape her mouth and she hardly heard
it, listening to the low music and still feeling the hurt in her wrists and
to herself considering that never before had her hands been tied.

And he remarked: "You don't look half bad. Like that. . . ."

But he hadn't forgiven her, because it was then that he stepped nearly
out of sight across the room and she, hurting in the armpits as well as
wrists, decided to try just how much freedom she really had—with only
her arms drawn back to the post—and flexed a knee, the other knee,
moved one foot far on the mattress and rolled her hips as much as she
could. Until something told her she was being watched by Thick.

Then he came at her with the truncheon in his hand—it made her
think of a bean bag, an amusement for a child—and wearing only his
undervest and the trousers with the top two buttons open. He was in
his stockinged feet and cigarette smoke was still coming out of his nose.
She could see the dial of the little dry-cell radio in his glasses.

"I've beat girls before," whispering, holding the truncheon in the
dark, bracing himself with one fat hand against the wall, "and I don't
leave bruises. When it's done you won't be able to tell, you see. Plenty
of girls—maids, the nude down in Robin's Egg Blue, the tarts who run
the stitching machines, a kid named Sally. Used to operate in Violet
Lane, I did. Gaslight scenes is my attraction. And if I happened to be
without my weapon," raising a little the whiteness, the rubber, "the
next best thing is a newspaper rolled and soaking wet. But here, get the
feel of it, Miss." He reached down for her and she felt the truncheon
nudging against her thigh, gently, like a man's cane in a crowd.

"It ain't so bad," he whispered.

She was lying face up and hardly trembling, not offering to pull her
leg away. The position she was tied in made her think of exercises she
had heard were good for the figure. She smelled gun oil—the men who
visited the room had guns—and a sour odor inside the mattress. Perhaps
the little one called Sparrow had left it there. Or even Thick, now standing beside her in the dark, because Thick liked to sleep on it in the
afternoons. She remembered how earlier he had slept and how, after
she and the child returned to the table, Monica had found a jack, as

she thought she might, and won the game. And now, hearing the music, the symphony that old men were listening to in clubs, now she no longer would be able to play with Monica. She cared for nothing that Thick could do, but she would miss the games. There was a shadow on the wall like a rocking chair; her fingers were going to sleep; she thought that a wet newspaper would be unbearable.

Then something happened to his face. To the mouth, really. The sour sweat was there and the mouth went white, so rigid and distended that for a moment he couldn't speak: yet all at once she knew, knew well enough the kinds of things he was saying—to himself, to her—and in the darkness and hearing the faint symphonic program, she was suddenly surprised that he could say such things.

His arm went up quivering, over his head with the truncheon falling back, and came down hard and solid as a length of cold fat stripped from a pig, and the truncheon beat into her just above the knee; then into the flesh of her mid-thigh; then on her hips; and on the tops of her legs. And each blow quicker and harder than the last, until the strokes went wild and he was aiming randomly at abdomen and loins, the thin fat and the flesh that was deeper, each time letting the rubber lie where it landed then drawing the length of it across stomach or pit of stomach or hip before raising it to the air once more and swinging it down. It made a sound like a dead bird falling to empty field. Once he stopped to increase the volume of the radio, but returned to the bedside, shuffling, squinting down at her, his mouth a separate organ paralyzed in the lower part of his face, and paused deceptively and then made a rapid swing at her, a feint and then the loudest blow of all so swiftly that she could not gasp. When he finally stopped for good she was bleeding, but not from any wound she could see.

For how many minutes he had kept it up, she did not know. Nor how long ago it was when he started. Because when she first opened her eyes he was snoring and the radio had changed. Comics were talking and she could not understand a word of it. And because now she was like a convent girl accepting the mysteries—and still Thick snored—and no matter how much she accepted she knew it now: something they couldn't show in films. What a sight if they flashed this view of herself on the screen of the old Victoria Hall where she had seen a few pictures with Michael. What a view of shame. She had always dressed in more modest brown, bought the more modest cod, prayed for modesty, desired it. Now she was hurt—badly hurt, she expected. And she remembered a woman in the basement flat being run down by a bus and telling it: and she felt that way herself—still bleeding—felt the damage deep inside, aching in unanticipated places, paining within. There wasn't any Mrs. Stickley now, and that other woman—in the basement flat—had died.

She felt that she herself could die. In those early hours she had not thought to scream. But now she was prostrate in Little Dora's Roost and even Little Dora, who hated them playing cards, was gone. And without the presence of some other woman, any woman, she could die. Thick had been too rough with her, treated her too roughly, and some things didn't tolerate surviving, some parts of her couldn't stand a beating. She hadn't even her free hands with which to rub them.

So finally she sobbed several times in this hour before the dawn. The moon had failed, the last clothes off her back were torn to shreds, the ginger cake they had given her at noon sat half-eaten and bearing her teeth marks in a chipped saucer atop the wardrobe. The moonlight's wash reached the window and fell across the brass and Margaret on the bed: a body having shiny knees, white gown twisted to the waist, arms stretched horizontal to the end of the bed and crossed; gray mattress-ticking beneath the legs whose calves were swollen into curves, and the head itself turned flat in the same direction she had raised one hip, away from the farther wall against which Thick snored; and a wetness under the eye exposed to the wash of light and the sobs just bubbling on the lips. Margaret inert, immobile, young woman with insides ruptured and fingers curling at the moment of giving sound to her grievance.

The sobs were not sweet. They were short, moist, lower than contralto, louder than she intended; the moanings of a creature no one could love. But Monica must have heard them—Monica whom Little Dora had brought back to the Roost after Thick himself had gone to sleep—or perhaps those sobs merely coincided with sobs of the child's own. Because when Margaret sobbed aloud, Monica sat up screaming.

The girl was given to having nightmares. All day long she was clever, turning away her inoculated arm, hiding inside her fists the little sharp black lines of her fingernails, walking on heels to prevent the sole of her left sandal from flapping, winning every afternoon at cards, though she had no use for horses. At the sink in the closet she spent time daubing herself with drops of Paradise Shore from a vial—shaped like a slipper—which she carried in a small white purse with a handle. She was forever finding hairpins on the floor and putting them quickly to her head. And she drank tea with her legs crossed and her good arm—

the one without the scab—thrown over the back of the chair. Tall for her age, thin, not yet able to read, wearing socks that didn't reach to her ankles and a cameo ring tied from finger to wrist with a length of green ribbon, readily speaking of the pets—all suicides she said—which she had kept in their Farthing Maude flat, she was pale and bony and still smelling of dolls she had cared for, a girl expecting no favors in her bright-green dress, though sufficient enough in the daylight.

"She's being too friendly with the prisoner," Thick said whenever he could.

But at night there were horrors. At night she sweated her innocence and, bolting up in her shift, declared she'd been swimming in the petrol tank of a lorry, or watching three rubber dolls smartly burning, or sitting inside a great rubber tire and rolling down a steep cobbled hill in the darkness. And Margaret remembered these dreams.

Now Margaret's sobs and Monica's screams commenced together and continued together, variants of a single sound, screaming and weeping mingled. Margaret was lying with puffy red eyes closed but fully conscious of the mingling sounds. Monica was sitting upright on the brass bed next to her, not in the shift but merely in panties this night, and half the childish head of hair was down, the pins kept falling—a small body untouched, unidentified, except by arm bandage and the panties, and her eyes were shining open. Yet she was asleep, and between the two stripped beds and on the opposite wall the washed-back glow of the moon was lighting the cheap print in its glassless frame, print of a young woman who—in moonlight herself and with long hair drawn frontward across her chest, with two large butterflies sleeping upon her shoulders—was in the act of stepping into the silver pond to drink. So Margaret felt the two sounds coming from herself, starting from the same oppressive breast, as if the other half of sadness was quite naturally fear. And Margaret then opened her eyes and her face was toward Monica's bed and her arms were spasmodically flexing a little against rope and unyielding wrists and brass.

"Ducky," she whispered then, no longer sobbing, "Ducky. . . ."

Monica's head was lifted and the neck was stretched. There was a white thread hanging from the opened lips and it blew gently in the vibrations of the scream. The tooth-marked cake was on the wardrobe behind her.

"Ducky . . . wake up now, Ducky."

She was not awake yet, but she began to move: the graceless motions of the undressed dreaming child, fumbling off the bed, crouching and bending over as if the dream lay in the white innocent oval of her belly, stooped but holding the tiny hands out trembling to sense the night, and neither falling nor gliding across the distance between the beds yet coming on with a kind of limbless instinct, all disarrayed as an adult woman walking in the night. Until suddenly the little girl collapsed, fell forward, and buried the scream between Margaret's cheek and the ticking. And by touch of the child's skin, she knew that her own cheek was wet.

"Wake up, wake up," she whispered, and still Thick snored and she could not hold the girl.

But Monica's hands were clinging. She smelled the odors of soap and Paradise Shore and there was a hand upon her own shoulder making the flesh feel large, and the other small wedge-shaped hand was thrust between the mattress and her breast. Her lips were against the child's eyes and she could taste them. Somewhere she was losing blood, but there was no longer any sobbing or screaming. Only the melting dream, the feel of a dangling hairpin and at the foot of the empty bed next her own the dark-blue shade of one of Monica's sandals.

"Ducky," whispering against the eyes, "feeling a little better? There's a girl."

In the silence, glancing away from the face, she felt the child's fingers and touch of the cameo ring starting again at the round of her own shoulder; then traveling lightly away to the elbow and reaching the wrists, stopping. And followed by the other hand until both the child's arms were outstretched and come to a point atop her own, so that despite the cold and numbness she felt the grip, while somewhere below her waist she seemed to be sinking, caving in wall by tissue wall.

"Poor Margaret," said the little girl, "I could cry, I could. . . ."

"See can you do anything with the knots," she whispered then.

Monica knelt on the ticking near Margaret's head—a thin bent back, silver between the ribs, bowed as if for an old woman's drunken hand —and tried to work the rope ends.

"I can't," leaving off, soothing her fingers against the coolness of the brass. "What are we going to do?"

"Perhaps you could put a coat round me," she whispered at last. "If only Michael knew. . . ."

So the child fetched Little Dora's coat and spread it over Margaret and brought a glass of water and Banks' wife drank—some of it spilled and wet the mattress—and Monica dressed herself in the discarded green dress and sandals and socks. And on her own bare bed again: "Larry'll make him turn you loose. I promise."

"Yes. Go to sleep now, Monica." She watched the child lying firmly in the moonlight, watched two small hands carry the cake up and into the shadow of the mouth, listened to the rigid and fragile sounds of chewing. Later she heard Monica brush away the crumbs, lie still again.

Outside on a branch above the garbage receptacle, an oven tit was stirring: not singing but moving testily amidst the disorder of leaf, straw sprig, remnant of gorse, fluttering now and then or scratching, making no attempt to disguise the mood, the pallidness, which later it would affect to conceal in liveliness and muted song. A warbler. But a sleepless bird and irritable. Through drowsiness and barge-heavy pain she noticed the sounds of it and did not smile; saw rather a panorama of chimneys, fine rain, officers of the law and low yards empty of children; farther off there was a heap of tile and a young woman in rubber shoes, an apron and wide white cap, and there were bloodstains on the ticking.

She heard the door, and when it closed again it shook the picture of the woman bending at the pond. He was swaying in the room and stately drunk. Without feigning sleep and in innocence Margaret watched him, wondering what had changed him now, and smelled the dark rum which had stained the teeth, the lips, the tongue. The light was more than a wash—it seemed to come off the wardrobe's empty saucer, shine from the print of the pond, rise up from the worn flooring beneath his feet. Or the light was coming off the man himself.

Finally she understood this much: he was not fully dressed. The coat, the tie, the chemise-soft shirt, the undervest, were gone. And she was staring at naked arms, at white face and soot-black hair, at something silver that stretched and reflected the moon's pale tone from below his bare neck to the belted line of his trousers. And she thought that softly, ever so softly, he was humming as he swayed there, some sort of regimental march perhaps.

He moved then. Bringing the light, the glow, still closer—without any motion—he started down between the two brass beds, stopped—breathing near her shoulder—and fumbled in his pocket until he found and opened a little penknife that was only a sparkle before the curved sheet of steel. Despite the cold light of his chest she knew beforehand that his fingers would be hot, and his fingers were hot when, back turned to Monica, he stooped and reached—her own eyes were to the side and up and she saw the shining links like fish scales, and pressed to them the triangular black shape of the pistol—and began to cut. Once she saw his face, and it was the angel's whiteness except for a broken place at the corner of his mouth which set her trembling.

She waited and felt triumph while he cut. Then burning. For all his gestures were considerate, performed calmly and with care. There was sureness and the heated fingers. Yet there came his sound of breathing, and with exactitude he was yet slashing and the blade that went through Thick's ropes went into her wrists, her own wrists as well. They too began to bleed.

Even now, after how many hours, being able to move her arms, drag them back to her sides then cross them upon her stomach, chafe them, touch the welted wrists, even now there was little pleasure in it, feeling the scratches, cuts, stinging of the blood. "You've wounded me," she whispered, eyes to the ceiling and in darkness. "You cut me."

He said only: "I meant to cut you, Miss. . . ."

So sometime after 4 A.M. she tried to use her numb and sleeping arms, twice struck out at him, then found her hands, the bleeding wrists, the elbows, and at last her cheek going down beneath and against the solid sheen of his bullet-proof vest. At that moment sunlight roused the day's first warbling of the heavy oven tit, and Monica slipped away through the unguarded door.

Sparrow, having changed from wine to whisky and being drunk but not stately drunk, knelt in the middle of Larry's room and, surrounded by weapons of countless shape and caliber—black and oily, loaded, strewn across the floor and piled on the bed and on the horsehair rocker and the footstool, a collection of Webleys, Bren guns, automatics and revolvers to make the Violet Lane men whistle—and fumbling with string and paper, beret pushed all the way back and cupping the bald spot that protruded from the rear of his skull, fumbling and paying no attention to the woman crouched in the corner and sneering, tried to wrap something into a passable packet and failed until he cried, "Come over here, Little Dora, and give us a hand with this present for my boy Arthur."

7

SIDNEY SLYTER SAYS

Racing World Awaits Running of the Golden Bowl . . .

Classic Event Equivalent of Olympic Games . . .

Rock Castle's Owner: Pawn of Brutal Gang?

Somebody—angel of Heaven or Hell, surely—knew it all before.
Somebody, possessed of prescience and having time stuck safely
like a revolver in his pocket, knew all this already and went
about the business as sure of satisfaction as a fellow robbing
graves in a plague. Knowing Rock Castle's past, which was recorded; having only to know of that Danish blood which cir-
culated beneath the skin, only to know that the fact of this Rock
Castle—torn from his mare—predetermined the stallion's cyclic
emergence again and again, snorting, victorious, onto the salt-
white racing course of the Aegean shore; needing only this intelligence, that the horse existed and that the horse would win.
Then to make off with him, one night to take him from the
purple fields of the woman and groom too old, too feeble, and
too wise to care; then to choose and pose one ignorant and hungry man as owner and with threats and violence and the pleasures of life to hold him until the race was won. Simple. Easy.
Like taking sweets. . . . It might have been Sidney Slyter,
mightn't it? Or Harry Bailey of East End? It might have been
any one of us. . . . But it was Mr. Michael Banks. Because Mrs.
Laval's been holding out her hand and drawing near, enfolding
him. Because she told me so and has warned me off again,
warned me off. But what do women know of such mysteries?
They know too bloody much, I'd say. And Mrs. Laval, like all
the rest of them—the gang of them—Mrs. Laval knew it all
already. Every bit of it planned and determined in advance—the
kiss, the dance, the jealous deaths—all of them beforehand set
in motion like figures walking in the folds of the dirty shroud.
. . . What now of Sidney Slyter's view of the world? What now
of my prognostications? What of Marlowe's Pippet? And the
sport? But what power, force, justice, slender hand or sacrifice
can stop Rock Castle, halt Rock Castle's progress now? Sidney
Slyter doesn't know. . . . Nonetheless, Sidney Slyter will report
the running of the Golden Bowl for you. . . .

"Don't you know what eggs are good for, Michael?"

The hall bulb shone orange through the cracks round the door and
moonlight was coming through the cobwebbed window. Across the
floor boards the moon was one square and silver-tinted patch of light
within which, in a silken heap, lay a stocking that wanted fingering;

next to it a safety pin which, by moonlight and with point unclasped, looked charmed and filigreed, as personal as a young girl's fallen brooch. There was no sign of Cowles. There was nothing left of the jockey, not a boot or rubber jersey. Though out of the sounds of bottles smashing downstairs there came bursts of Jimmy Needles' laughter, loud and ribald and grievous.

It was 2 A.M. of the last night he spent alive—last darkness before the day and running of the Golden—and the covers were tossing. She had given a single promise and three times already made it good, so now he knew her habits, knew what to expect, the commotion she could cause in bed. And it was a way she had of rising and kicking off the covers with cart-wheel liveliness and speed each time she lost a pearl—and she had lost three pearls—and asking him to hunt for it through the twisting and knotting of the sheets. Now the covers were cartwheeling and falling about his shoulders all at once and there was the fourth to find. At the end of the bed-stead opposite the pillows she came to rest suddenly cross-legged and laughing, breathing so that he could see how far down she took the air.

"Don't ask me, Mike," hands above her head, hips wriggling a little at the apex of crossed legs, "I don't intend to help you. . . ." Then with a catch of sheet she idly daubed herself and laughed some more.

He came up crawling on hands and knees, still lagging after the tremor, the fanciful sex, and began to feel about in the tumult she had made of the sheets, himself not yet recovered from the breath of her own revival, the swiftness with which she turned from deep climactic love to play. As if she always saved one drop unquenched, the drop inside her body or on the tongue that turned her not back to passionate love but away from that and into attitudes of frolic. No moment of idleness or a yawn or slow recovery but each time surprising him by play and acrobatics, her fresh poses making his own dead self fire as if he had never touched her and making her body look tight and childish as if she had never been possessed by him.

"I can't find the bloody thing," he said.

"Go on," she said, and changed again, took one knee beneath her chin, "you find it." Then, while he searched beneath her pillow, felt down the center of the mattress and into the still warm hollows: "I've seduced you, haven't I, Mike," she said.

"You have," he answered. "Good as your word."

With Sybilline watching, he moved back and forth on the undulations of the springs, with moonlight striking across his spine, and his hands and knees softly sinking; and felt at last the opalescence, the hard tiny

tear of pearl on its needle shank, and held it up by the point for her
to see.

"You're a charmer, Mike," she said.

He reached out then to the skirt flung over the chair and stuck the
pearl in the row of three. There were no pearls left in her reddish pom-
padour, only the thick round of the hair and, as if it had been rumpled,
a coil coming down her neck and tickling. The bottles were still crashing
below them and someone was playing the widow's piano so quickly,
heavily, that Needles might have been running up and down the key-
board in his naked feet. But it was all bubbles and talk and musk and
closeness in the room and Banks cared nothing for the noise. As he
turned to face his Sybilline, began on hands and knees the several awkward motions it took to reach her, he knew remorse for the empty face
of himself once more: because her eyes were big and brown, steady and
temperate as those of a girl peering over a stile, while the rest of her
was still animated, quivering, with the fun. Thrice she had taken him
and he had thrice returned, riding into the bower that remains secretive
and replete after blouse and skirt and safety pin, silks and straps, have
all been discarded, flung about helter-skelter on the thorns. No more
now, he was fast returning to the old man. While she, his Sybilline, was
still tasting of that little shocking drop of incompletion that gave her a
maiden's blush, a shine between the breasts, as if she was always ready
for another go at it, another lovely toss.

After searching for all her pearls he was tangled in the covers now
himself. His skin was gray. His head was hanging but he smelled the
delicate stuff and blindly put his hand on her leg's underside, touched
the mild flesh for an instant, then let his fingers drag away. She wriggled
and was laughing.

"Be a sweet boy, Mike," she said, secluded with him from the party,
moving her bare shoulders in childish sailor fashion, "and fetch the
stocking."

So at two o'clock in the morning he labored off the bed—she gave
his arm a push—and took several steps until the moonlight caught him
round the skinny ankles. Standing there, with sheep passing outside
through darkened fields and the jockey screaming the first bars of an
enticing song, he could hear the girl behind him—and that was the fine
thing about Sybilline, the way she could kiss and play and let her spangles fall, keep track of all the chemistry and her good time, and yet be
sighing, sighing like a young girl in love.

He stooped, picked up the stocking, turned to hear her whistling through puckered lips.

Then: "I'll take that if you please, sweet Michael." She held the length of silk in her hands and he was scrambling over the tossed pillows, down the crumpled sheets, until the two of them were facing and once more cross-legged. The pharmacist's cure for women was on the edge of the sink, the smells were of the shores of paradise. Before his eyes and with the ends of her fingers, Sybilline drew the stocking out full length, held it swinging by the wide top and little toe, then in a quick gesture ran the whole porous line of it across her face and under her nose, just touching her nose, smelled it deeply and winked as she did so. And suddenly made a flimsy ball of it and with one hand lightly on his knee, reached forward and thrust the round of silk between his widespread legs and against the depths of his loin, rubbing, pushing, laughing. He flushed.

"You see," whispering, "you can win if you want to, Mike, my dear. But that's all for now." With lively arm she threw the balled stocking at the dusty moonlit glass and hopped off the bed.

He watched her dance round to the chair, dangle the blouse and skirt, replace the pearls and do a faint jazz step that kept her moving nowhere. Then she posed in the unbuttoned blouse and her fingers were sending off kisses and her legs, friendly and white and long, were the legs he had seen bare in the undergarment ads. Then she whispered through the oval of the skirt she was just dropping over her head: "Put on your trousers, Mike . . . we'll join the fun downstairs."

They stepped into the light of the orange bulb, held hands, walked along the widow's carpet to the start of the rail with grapes carved on the post. The hallway smelled of dust and nuptials; a rag was lying on the carpet. "We'll go down together," she said, and gave his arm a pinch. "We'll let them see we're untidy. But Michael," holding him midway on the stairs, "all the girls will love you, Michael. You're alluring! So don't forget, Mike, come back for me." And she kissed him, she whom he would never kiss in privacy again.

"I couldn't lose you, Syb."

She laughed for the two of them at the bottom of the stairs and her hair was redder than at any time that day. The lamplight shone upon it—lamps were lit all about the room, small bulbs and large, glass shades chiming and tinkling and strung with beads—and her eyes were brown and moist.

"There's that lovely girl!" shouted the widow, "and our funny boy. And look what she's done to him!"

Not only Jimmy Needles was playing the piano, but Larry as well, jockey and Larry having a duet together side by side and beating on the keys with nearly equal strength. On the bench before the upright, the little man in color and the large man in navy blue—hour by hour the wrinkles in the dampened suit were flattening—kept talking all the while they played and a bottle of rum stood on the seat between them. And Little Dora tried to listen. Sunk in a velvet armchair, wearing her lopsided matron's hat with a bit of feather now, her upper lip of pale hair wet with gin, eyes surly and black behind the glasses, stretched and recumbent on cushions as near as possible to the piano bench, she watched them, listened, in a torporous and deadly mood.

Sparrow was there. He was drinking whisky out of the widow's cup. The widow's daughter was in the crowd—a big girl in a child's dress pulled high who sat straight up and kept both hands on her knees, laughing and smiling out of a loose mouth and enormous eyes. And all the room was brown and filled with smoke and toy alligators and donkeys. Newspapers were strewn across the rug faded and worn with the footpaths of long-dead residents. A portrait of a Spanish nobleman hung above the mantel on which there burned a candelabra with smoky wicks and molten wax; and duplicates of Little Dora's chair, soft mauve contrivances on wheels, made humps along the walls. In volume nearly as loud as the piano the black wireless was turned up and an orchestra played out of the tufted speaker.

Kissing, noise, and singing: a late hour in the widow's parlor, and Banks saw Sparrow wave, watched Sybilline sit on the arm of Little Dora's chair and swing her foot, and noticed that the widow was keeping her eye on him. Plump, wearing the tasseled shawl, she suddenly leaned over Syb and the slouching woman, and after a moment Dora jerked round her head and stared at him. Then all three were laughing—even his own dear girl—and he started toward them, took a place at the jockey's side.

A barracks song was coming from the coffin box of the piano, old, fast-stepping. A golden mermaid stood holding a pitchfork on the ebony and she was bounded by wreaths, her fishtail curved over her head. Scars and finger-length burns marked the ebony, ivory was missing from the keys. Banks leaned against the trembling wood, and there was a pile of tattered sheet music ready to fall from the top and he had never heard such noise. Yet Larry went on talking—audibly enough, considering—and the jockey was nodding and beating upon the last key of the scale.

". . . And I told the Inspector he was making a horrible botch of it. I said it would never do. Who's pulling the strings I told him and he got huffy, huffy, mind you. I said the killing of the kids was no concern of mine but the hanging of Knifeblade was not acceptable, not in the least acceptable. You'd best not interfere, I said. There's power in this world you never dreamed of, I told him. Why, you don't stand a show-ing even with a little crowd at the seaside . . . and you'd better not bother with my business or my amusements. . . ."

"But didn't he try to stick you none the same," said the jockey.

"He did, but he failed. I knew him in Artillery, I knew his line. . . ."

Banks listened, looked at the white craven half of his face, the slicked black hair, the fingers hammering. He saw the man lift the bottle several times to his lips.

The jockey's sleeves were puffing out, the small black boots were hanging limp, one hand snatched down the goggles and through isin-glass he peered at the single key and at the two gray fingers he was striking it with—a rider who had a face shot full of holes and shoulders like the fragile forks of a wishbone on either side of the hump inside the silk. Banks put a sheet of the music on the rack and said, "Play us this piece, Needles. . . ." But the jockey did not reply.

There was a fire in the kitchen and it was Sybilline who told him to take the chair—"Don't you know what eggs are good for, Michael?" —and stood near him with her smile and the flush creeping up her cheek. They formed a regular crew: his Syb, the widow, the other one who looked as if she wanted to fight. Syb's throat was bare, the widow had plump hips and she was giggling. He could smell them: above the heat and moisture of the fire, the spice and flour odors of the laden shelves, the sweetness of old tarts and bread, he could smell the women strongest. And Sybilline kissed him immediately—leaning over, putting her face into his and her hand upon his neck—so that the other two could see. Still with mouths together, he found her breast for a moment and opened his eyes, saw the widow smiling—but it was a smile set and strained as if she could hardly keep from offering advice—and the other woman was smiling and Banks didn't care.

"Get out of here, Sparrow," the widow said all at once and looked down at him, became dimpled and rosy-cheeked again. Then Syb left him, stepped away with her compassionate mouth dissolving, becoming part of a pretty face again, and he could think of nothing except the stocking she had left upstairs—though they were roughing it in the parlor next to the kitchen and flinging about, dancing with the widow's girl, intent, all of them, on a smashing.

"Now, Mike, you'll have to eat," she murmured, and put a hand to her escaping loop of hair.

"But you been cheating, Sybilline," the widow said then, "you been going out of turn. The lady of the house has first prerogative and you been spoiling the order, Sybilline—if you please—you ain't been allowing me my prerogative." The little woman, youthfully plump except in the legs—she was standing on wiry, well-shaped legs—was preoccupied: it may have been she alone he smelled.

"Syb's always been a cat," said Little Dora, "first at the fellows, first in bed. She's a sister of mine but she's irresponsible, she is." And Banks could tell that this one, a fighter with her violet shadows and loosened boots, was interested: but probably she'd want to kill him first. There were no smiles behind those thick corrective spectacles.

"Well, Syb can do the cooking then," said the widow, and sat down beside him.

"I'll cook, I'd do anything for Michael!" There was the light step, the grace, the cheer, as she tossed her head and reached for the pan and the bowl of pure-white oval eggs. She got the butter on her fingertips and licked them, her blouse was untucked again and he could see the skin; the eggs were pearls and she was cracking the white shells with her painted nails. The widow was lighting a cigarette. Though he was watching Syb, he found that he was stroking the little widow's cheek and coming to like her in the kitchen with no one, except these three, to notice.

Beyond the half-opened door the parlor crowd sang "Roll Me Over in the Clover" and the name of Jimmy Needles was screamed out several times. But the women round him seemed not to hear; he hardly heard himself; the women were ganging up on him, doing a job on him. All three were noticing and he tried to pay no attention. They watched him eat. All three were smiling and taking his measure and he didn't mind. It was Sybilline who made him use the sauce.

"Here," reaching, tilting the thin brown bottle, "meat sauce is fine on fried eggs, Michael . . . didn't you know?"

The smell of the women—girlish, matronly—and the smell of the meat sauce were the same. As soon as it spread across his plate it went to his nostrils and they might not have bothered with their clothes, with procrastination. He kept his face in the plate and kept lifting the fork that had one prong bent, a prong that stuck his tongue with every mouthful. Brown and broken yellow, thick and ovarian, his mouth was running with the eggs and sauce while the whisky glasses of the women were leaving rings.

"Fetch him a slice of bread, Sybilline, he don't want to leave none of it on the china. . . ."

He shut his eyes and did not know whose hand it was, but the hand closed in a grip that made him slide forward on the chair and groan.

"You girls wait for me," said the widow in a voice he could hardly hear. Then: "You're a charmer, Mike!" and Sybilline was blowing him a kiss.

With his hands in his pockets, shirt collar open about the windpipe and the two muscles translucent at the back of his skinny neck, frowning and keeping his head down, he followed the swinging shawl into the din, the smoke, the noise of the piano that seemed to be playing on the strength of a grinding motor inside the box, though Larry and the jockey were still side by side on its bench. The widow stopped to fix her daughter's skirts and he bumped against the softest buttocks he had ever known, and apologized.

"I could love you right here," she whispered, "I really could. . . ."

He knew that. It was not the place for him exactly, but there was the sauce all over his lip and he thought that in another moment almost anywhere might do.

They reached the stairs in time. The corner turned, the hat tree with its multiple short arms thrust out in shadow, the carpeting, the widow's rail, the dust and orange bulb—suddenly the bedchambers were near and he was climbing. Up how many times, how many times back down. And it was merely a matter of getting up those stairs, and taking the precautions, and tumbling in, shagging with the widow as the night demanded. He saw her at the top for a moment; stumbled and paused and, clutching the rail, stared, while beneath the bulb she stood squeezing the tiny plump hands together.

Then she took hold of him, and behind the door at the end of the hall he dropped his trousers in the widow's sleeping chamber, heard her quick footsteps round the bed and in his hands caught the plumpness of the hips. Then under the wool those softest buttocks he had ever known. And he snapped off a stay of whalebone, flung it aside as he might a branch in a tangled wood; to his mouth drew her down and rubbed the sauce against her. She giggled and there was a dilating in the stomach.

"Go gently, Mr. Banks," fending, giggling, "go sweetly, please."

There was no cartwheeling now, no silk-stocking coil, no blushing or line of verse. Only the widow on the comforter and in his mouth the taste of eggs which had done the job for him. The moon had passed by the widow's room, but a transom was opened to the orange dimness of the hall. And under her three small rocking chairs with cushions, upon her bed—it was narrow and deep—and her rack of short broad night dresses and her stumpy bedside lamp, upon everything she owned or used there fell the rusty and sedentary light that, guiding no one, still burns late in the corridors of so many cheap hotels. The drawers were all half-open in her wardrobe; a pair of silver shears and a babyish fresh pile of curls lay on a table top before which she last had been trimming her dead ends of curls.

How long were the nights of love, how various the lovers. Holding his throat, standing in bare feet and with one hand wiping the hair back from his eyes, he stared down at the widow's cheeks again. It was her cheeks he had been attracted to and once more beside the bed he saw the tiny china-painted face with the eyelids closed, the ringlets damp across the top, the small greasy round cheeks he had wanted to cup in both his hands.

"Don't leave," whispering, not opening her eyes, "don't leave me yet, Mr. Banks."

In the hall he put on his trousers and shirt and took the stairs with caution. He was fierce now, dry but fierce. If there were prospects ahead of him he would take them up. There were shadows, tracks worn through the carpet by naked feet. More shadows, a depth of shadows, and not a vow to make or sentiment to express now on these old stairs—only the steepness and the wallside to guide his shoulder. Below, in the center of a love seat's cushion, he could see the outline of a hat and pair of clean white gloves.

"Mister . . ." He stopped, leaned his head against dusty wall plaster, and saw the big girl's figure at the start of the bannister below, made out her eyes and heard the moist and childish voice. She wore a sweater round her shoulders now. "Mister," the voice came fearfully, "there's someone wants to see you. A lady, Mister."

"I should imagine so!" He waited, then descended without noise, except for the brushing of his clothes against the wall, until he was only a step or two above the widow's girl. "I suppose you're not referring to yourself." He watched the loose lips, the eyes that brightened, watched the closing and opening of the sweater.

"She's a lady, Mister. She's at the other door. She give me half a crown to find you, and she told me not to get the whole house up, she did."

He nodded, leaned forward, gently kissed the girl.

She did not try to move, as if he had ordered her to remain exactly there by the darkened post with grapes. He paused at the love seat and noticed the red beret beside the hat and pair of gloves. The corridor smelled of water in the bottoms of purple vases and the piano was banging just beyond this emptiness. He kicked something—a cat's dish perhaps—and it slid down the passageway ahead of him. Then the wall was warm to his touch and he knew that behind it was the width of the kitchen chimney, briefly and in darkness saw the meat sauce bottle and Syb's painted nails.

He heard an engine running. He stepped into the pantry, one of several pantries, bare now without hanging goose or cutlery or stores of brandy, and faced the misty dew-drenched opening of the door. There was light coming in the windows—brass rods cut them, but they were curtainless—and he stood so that he was lighted by one of the windows just as she was visible against the sheet of fog. With a coat swinging, hair down to her shoulders, she was leaning in the doorway and her thin legs were crossed. When she heard him she turned her face, white at this hour, and dropped her burning cigarette—not outside, but into the shadows on the floor.

"Annie . . . good God, is it you?"

She laughed only. One long shank of the golden hair dragged across in front of her and buried the little wet coat lapel. The face then, the cheek, seemed set in gold. Arm hanging, body still tipped and ankles crossed, she made no movement other than a small twisting as if she were trying to scratch against the jamb.

"But you, Annie, I hadn't expected you!"

"Well," taking the hair in her fingers, holding it across her mouth, speaking through hair, "I shan't be bad or deceitful to an old friend. But I can tell a thing or two." And abruptly, as he smelled the dampness on her shoulders and reached for her, "You're sexed up, aren't you? The chap next door's been kissing and the girl next door has found him out!" She was twenty years old and timeless despite the motor car waiting off under the trees. At three o'clock in the morning she was a girl

he had seen through windows in several dreams unremembered, uncon-
fessed, the age of twenty that never passes but lingers in the silvering of
the trees and rising fogs. Younger than Syb, fingers bereft of rings, she
would come carelessly to any door, to any fellow's door.

"You'll have to lift me up," she cried, "I've got this far but I can't
take another step." Then laughed when he raised her, gold hanging
down and legs swinging at the knees, cheekbones making little slashes
beneath the skin, eyes big and black and body that had been tipping,
leaning, all collected now, wrapped in the coat and carried high against
his chest. They sat on the bare pantry floor in a corner and through the
adjacent windows came the misty streams like two searchlight shafts
touching and crossing just beyond their feet.

"Bottle's in the pocket. Have a drink if you want to." He did, though
first he put his palms on either side of the chilly jaw and leaned down
to Annie's mouth. With the hair spread out, eyes closed, her head was
pressed between his kiss and the hard empty floor. And the searchlights
moved steadily, the engine idled—it was smooth, low, indifferent—in
the blackness of the roadside and dripping chestnut tree.

"I'm sexed up, too," she said from the crook of his arm, and he
uncapped the bottle with his teeth. The crashing octaves, Needles singing solo, the screams and sounds of boots hardly reached them here,
though Annie remarked about the party and, after thinking, said she
did not want to go to it.

He opened her coat directly and ran his hand inside, up lisle and
tenderness until he found the seam, the tight rolled edge and drops of
warmth against his fingertips, and said, ". . . You want me to, you
really want me to?" She stood up then—he hadn't known that she could
stand—and with fingers steadying on his shoulders lifted first one tiny
knife-heeled slipper and the other, bending each leg sharply at the knee,
swinging alternate thin calves in an upward and silent dancing step,
removed the undergarment and the slippers, and came down slowly,
slowly, across his lap.

"I want you to."

Later, when they were dying down and moments before she slept:
"That Hencher," she said, "evict him, why don't you, Mike . . . throw
the bastard out." And the jaws, the cheeks, the eyelids all grew colder
and he left her there for the driver of the lacquered car.

Slowly, slowly, he went back up the hall with hands outstretched and
thinking of all the girls. He saw the hat tree's shadow, passed the love

seat and the staircase, empty now, and thought, she's gone off looking at her half a crown. Good thing.

He took a breath then and blinking through the smoke, rubbing his lips and blinking, holding Annie's gin bottle halfway to his lips and then forgetting it, found Larry towering in the parlor and Little Dora shouting up at him. Dora was wearing the jockey's striped racing cap and the long flat tongue of the visor protruded sideways from her trembling head.

"Take it off," she shouted, "let's see what you got!"

Sparrow, Jimmy Needles and the rest were crowded round them, laughing and showing their teeth through smoke and the white light of lamps with the shades ripped off now. But Larry towered, even while Dora caught him by the shirt, and there was the perfect nose, the black hair plastered into place, the brass knuckles shining on the enormous hand, and the eyes, the eyes devoid of irises. Tomorrow he would wear green glasses. For now he was drunk, drunk into a stupor of civility and strength, that state of brutal calm, and only a little trickle of sweat behind the ear betrayed his drunkenness.

"Come on, come on, you full-of-grace," pushing up against him, tearing the shirt, "let's see what you got!"

The pearl buttons came off the shirt and Banks stepped no closer, though Sybilline was there and laughing on one of Larry's arms. "Oh, do what Little Dora says," he heard her cry, "I want you to!" And there was a bruise, a fresh nasty bruise, beneath Syb's eye.

It was not a smile nor look of tolerance, but some wing-tip shadow —he was cock of this house—that passed across his face and Banks thought Larry had swayed. Yet he removed the wrinkled coat, allowed Sybilline to pull the holster strings, ungird him, allowed Little Dora to flap against him and rip off the shirt and, after Sparrow had undone the ties, once more waited while Dora took the undervest away in her claws. They cheered, slapping the oxen arms, slapping the flesh, and cheered when the metal vest was returned to him—steel and skin—and the holster was settled again but in an armpit naked now and smelling of scented freshener.

Larry turned slowly round so they could see, and there was the gun's blue butt, the dazzling links of steel, the hairless and swarthy torso of the man himself. In the process of revolving he looked at Sparrow, who went out then to the hired vehicle parked before the boarding house.

"For twenty years," shouted Dora again through smoke opaque as

ice, "for twenty years I've admired that! Does anybody blame me?"
Banks listened and amidst breaking glass, the tumbling of the mauve-
colored chairs, for a moment met the eyes of Sybilline, his Syb, eyes in
a lovely face pressed hard against the smoothest portion of Larry's arm
which—her face with auburn hair was just below his shoulder—could
take the punches. Banks looked away.

He left the gin bottle on a bolster and sprawled out shivering on the
love seat. They were finished with the final stanza of poor Needles' song.
He could very nearly taste the dawn, the face peering up out of a basin,
becoming old again, his full and wasting twenty-five. But he listened,
reached forward through the dark and then the shadow was in front of
him, Dora's bit of beard and a glimpse of the fibrous and speckled hams,
and he would have laughed except for the last jump inside of him.

"Got a cigarette," he asked her softly, and started trembling.

He was alone, finally, all alone and sore and the cartwheeling sheets
were piled in a white heap on the planking off the foot of the bed. The
last of them was gone; love's moonlight was no longer coming through
the glass; but there was light, the first gray negative light of dawn. The
mate of the oven tit had found a branch outside his window and he
heard its damp scratching and its talk. Even two oven tits may be snared
and separated in such a dawn. He listened, turned his head under the
shadows, and reflected that the little bird was fagged. And he could feel
the wet light rising round all the broken doors, the slatted crevices, rising
round the fens, the dripping petrol pump, up the calves and thighs of
the public and deserted visions of the naked man—the fire put out in
the steam-bath alley, the kitchen fire drowned, himself fagged and tasteless as the bird on the sick bough. But a sound reached him and for a
while he followed it: "Cowles . . . Mr. Cowles? Mr. Cowles?" The
widow's voice faded down in the direction of the barren pantry and
open door.

He let it go. He smelled the pillow touched by too many heads,
smelled the dry sweat of a night no more demanding—gone the pale
rectangle from which he had plucked the stocking, gone all the fun of
it. He thought of water against his lips but he could not move, stretched
upon his back and caught. But he must have moved his leg because
suddenly he felt it pricked, a sharp little pain in the skin, some bit of
foreign matter. He reached down slowly and took it in two fingers,
raised it high before his face: a single pearl on a pin that had been bent,
but a lovely rose color in the center where it held the light. Idly he

began to turn the pearl between his fingers. The hand hovered, fell, and he lost the pearl for good.

The shot went off just below his window. It was a noise in the very room with him, like a hand clapped upon his ear, and he thought of Jimmy Needles, the shoulder holster on the silver breast, thought of Sybilline and the widow. Then he was out of the bed, across the room and running.

He reached the street before the gunshot sound had died, ran into the dawn bareheaded and in time to see the warbler flying straight up from the thick brown tree with its song turned into a high and piping whistle. There were the frozen headlamps and black dripping tires of a double-decker parked across the street; a cottage with a hound clamoring inside; a poster showing bunched horses on a turn; an empty cart drawn back from the road. And at the corner of the boarding house, sprawled on the stones, the body of a child in a bright-green dress and, crouched over it, the puffing constable. A wet and sluggish sun was burning far-off beyond the wet foliage and crooked roofs.

He stopped—arms flung wide—then ran at the constable.

Because he recognized the child—she had always been coming over a bridge for him—and because now there was smoke still circling out of the belly, smoke and a little blood, and she lay with one knee raised, with palms turned up. And the old man crouching with drawn gun, touching the body to see where his shot had gone, old man with a star of burst veins in the hollow of either cheek, with his warts, the old lips that were ventricles in the enormous face, with brass and serge and a helmet like a pot on the head—there was nothing he could do but smash his fist against that puffing face. He did, and sent the helmet rolling.

The mists were drifting off, the leaves uncurling, the helmet was rattling about the street. And he kept driving the man, fighting the constable farther and farther away from the dead child, watching one of the mournful and unsuspecting eyes turn green and slowly close. Scuffling, panting himself, trying to take his punches with care, aiming at the blood that had started between the two front teeth. Then suddenly the constable—old, with a neck of cow's kidneys tied round by the high blue collar, and a nose that hooted in the struggle—gave it all back to him, blow for telling blow, finding his mark, punching in with the slobber and vehemence of his age. There was a straight look in his watering good eye, a quick and heavy hunching in the shoulders. His long hair, black and mixed with gray, went flying.

"Down you go, you little Cheapside gambler!"

The old man struck him full in the chest, once in the face, and once again on skin and cartilage of the aching chest. He fell, lay still—blindly reaching out for the little girl in green—and the constable drew back the boot furnished by the village constabulary and kicked him. After a moment of wheezing and blood-wiping, the old man strapped on the helmet, fixed his brass and replaced the warm revolver, took up his pipe from the mossy curb, and rubbing his arms and shins, disappeared to slowly climb the footbridge that was a hump of granite beneath the electric cables and ancient dripping trees.

It'll be a jolly evening, Mike, he dreamed, and the sun was shining on his lip when Jimmy Needles came out and dragged him to the safety of the house.

8

SIDNEY SLYTER SAYS

Freak Accident Halts Famous Race . . .

Thousands Witness Collision at End of Day . . .

Fatal Crash Brings Solemn Cry from Crowd . . .

. . . A beautiful afternoon, a lovely crowd, a taste of bitters and light returning to the faces of heroic stone—one day there will be amusements everywhere, good fun for our mortality. He has whistled; he has flicked his cigarette away; alone amidst women he has gone off to a fancy flutter at the races. And redeemed, he has been redeemed—for there is no pathetic fun or mournful frolic like our desire, the consummation of the sparrow's wings. . . .

IN THE PADDOCK and only minutes before the running of the Golden Bowl on a fast track and brilliant afternoon—high above them now the sun was burst all out of shape—Michael Banks and Needles listened to the dying of the call to saddle. A plaster held Banks' lips together at a corner of the mouth and impaired his speech; the jockey was sallow but Banks wore a large rose with leaves in his lapel; Lovely the stableboy kept whispering: "What a gorgeous crowd! Coo, what a gorgeous crowd!" They had tied down Rock Castle's tongue and now the horse's mouth was filled with a green scum. Round the paddock the crowd was twenty deep and silent, save for a rat-faced man at the spectator's rail who several times cocked his eyebrows, pointed at the silver horse, and said: "Rock Castle? Go on, I wouldn't take your money. Poor old nag."

Farther down, a mare set up a drumming with her hind hoofs, then was calmed. Men attending in the paddock spoke soothing words; a black horse was being led in tight circles, again the chestnut mare was dancing.

Banks took the camel's hair coat off the jockey's back, bared the resplendent little figure to sun and crowd. "Well, Needles," carefully hanging the coat on his arm, "Cowles always said he'd run like fire. Well, up you go, Needles."

Before he could take the jockey's leg in his hands, he heard the sounds of light and girlish hurrying, saw her stoop beneath the rail, saw the hair and the swinging coat similar to Needles'.

"Oh, good," cried Annie, "you've not started off! I thought I'd bring you luck."

"You can't come in the paddock," glancing about for the detectives, "you haven't any business here!"

"Oh, but I have, I have."

And Annie reached toward the jockey then, and even while Banks gripped the blown-out silken sleeve, she caught hold of Jimmy Needles' face in both her hands, leaned down and kissed the tiny wrinkles of his lips. Drawing away, golden hair uncombed and a printed card dangling from her buttonhole, breeze carrying off her laugh: "Oh, haven't I always wanted to? Haven't I just wanted to?"

Somebody whistled in the crowd.

"Tell you what," straightening the green glasses, cutting his profile across the sun, "I'll make it up to you. I'll make it up for the twenty years. A bit of marriage, eh? And then a ship, trees with limes on the branches, niggers to pull us round the streets, the Americas—a proper cruise, plenty of time at the bar, no gunplay or nags. Perhaps a child or two, who knows?"

Arm in arm, Larry and Little Dora, one tall and tough, the other squat and tough, strode along until they approached one hired car in a line of cars and, opening the rear doors, stooping, lifted Margaret from under a shabby quilt and off the floor, and, each gripping an arm and wrapping round her body the coat that belonged to Dora, started back still talking—now across Margaret's hanging head—about the streets and niggers and limes of the Americas.

"Coo, what a gorgeous crowd!"

But even the crowd was fixed. There were no more islands of space between the stands and the white threads of the rails upon which the lovely men were chalking, erasing, again chalking up their slates. Yet Thick had made a way for himself and could see all he needed to of the first turn; through long dark binoculars Sybilline watched the final turn; and in the center of the oval's roses, crouched down between two bushes, armed and grinning, Sparrow waited for signs of trouble, ready to shoot or turn as best he could to any threatened portion of the course. Sparrow always liked a race.

Banks saw nothing of the crowd but kept his eyes on Sybilline. Not once did she glance his way—though he was watched. He was being watched all right. Among the men on the rail he noticed the three who had accosted him, and wondered whether they would fling their bombs into a crowd just to bring one man down.

Then he heard the horses drifting slowly up from behind, the string of them unlimbering in the slow canter before the start. One of the jockeys was singing and Banks could not bear to raise his eyes, could not bear to see Rock Castle in that winding and nervous line, afraid to know that the horse had come this far. He kept his eyes down, began again his pushing and shoving, and there were only shoes to see: the open toes, pieces of nicked leather, buckles. Heel the color of a biscuit, slipper covered with diamond dust and glue, some child's boot tied with string. Shoes in motion or fixed at isolated angles amidst tickets, sweet wrappers, straws, and with the bit of stocking or colored sock or bare ankle protruding—shoes which end to end would have made a terrible marching column round the track the horses were soon to charge upon. He could not bear the faces, refused to look at them. On his own face the fresh plaster held the split corners of his mouth together and he was clean—it had not been easy to visit the Baths again but he had forced himself—and his narrow cheeks were shaved and his tie was straight. The only dirt was sleeplessness and he could not rid himself of that.

"Now, Sally, you'll see a little more from here," somebody said.

He kept pushing, trying to get beyond the crowd, trying for the north corner, where it was thinner at least. He saw the man with the gray tea-party topper and new supply of yellow, brown, green tickets stuck in the band, and he lowered his eyes again, thought of the night before and drinking-glasses with lipstick on the rims. He thought he should like to try it, try some of that, with Margaret. Once he stopped and lifted his head, but she was not in sight.

Then he was walking easily and into the glare of the hot sun, past the ranked petrol-smelling rows of empty cars, and there were little shattering bursts of light off the wipers and chrome and door handles, and only a few other people strolling here, laughing or pausing in the weeds by the rail. He leaned against a Daimler and tried to breathe. He noticed the pock-faced girl and it was clear she had found her quid: a big man with a sandy bush of mustache and gold links in his cuffs was holding her round the buttocks with one great hand. Another man and woman had their elbows side by side on the rail.

"Look," said the woman, and he heard no inflection, no rise or fall in her voice, "they're off."

Far away, back under clock and pennants, a terrible cheering went up. But it was the woman's clear statement that made him sick. He pulled his hand away from the radiator cap, set his foot down from the bumper, and tried to get close to her before the thirteen horses of the field should pass.

"Charlie, you're going to owe me a tonic," the woman said.

He heard the sound of hoofs and managed to stumble into the shadow of the pair by the rail. He nodded to the woman and she smiled, spoke again to her husband—"You might as well tear up your ticket!"—and he felt the coming breeze, watched a long hair on his sleeve. The mustached man had his back to the race. The girl was trying to see over his shoulder but he prevented her. And then the hair was saved between his fingers and he looked up, began to choke.

The blinders, the tongue tied down, the silver neck sawing in stride; the riders coming knee to knee with tangle of sticks and the noise; dust, the dangerous dust, rising high as a tall tree, and pebbles flying out like shots. He put an arm across his face, whispered *Margaret, Margaret,* and in the vacuum, the sudden silence, heard no hoofs, no roar, but only the thwacking of the crops and the clear voice of Jimmy Needles: "Make way for the Prince of Denmark . . . out of my path, St. James. . . ." He knew he must put a stop to it.

"You can't do that! Grab him, for God's sake, Charlie!"

But he was over the rail then and into the dust at last. It was a long way to go—directly across the track in the open sun—and he stumbled, tried to hold the hat. He heard his heart—far away a child seemed to be beating it down the center of a street in the End—heard the sound of air being sucked beneath the spot where the constable had landed two heavy blows, and his feet were falling upon the same loose earth so recently struck by iron.

He hadn't the strength to climb the second fence, instead went between the bars, going down, seeing his own dead shoe for a moment, feeling his hand slipping off the whitewash. Then he was on the green, splashed through an artificial pond, ran headlong into roses and hedges that came up to his shins. It was a park, a lovely picture of a park with a mad crowd down one edge and thirteen horses whirling round. His shoe came down on the blade of a shears some gardener had overlooked. He nearly fell. He would have to be fast, very fast, to stop them now.

He heard his shoes snapping off the thorns and trampling the grass, and yet he seemed only to be drifting, floating across the green. But it was a good run, an uphill run. The wind was catching his saliva when suddenly he veered round the man rising up between the rose bushes with a pistol. He saw the gun-hand, the silencer on the barrel like a medicine bottle, the quickness of Sparrow's waist-high aim, and then felt both shots approaching, overtaking him, going wild. And he reached the third and final fence, crawled through.

The green, the suspended time was gone. The child pounded on his heart with anonymous rhythm and he found that after all he had been fast enough. There were several seconds in which to take the center of the track, to position himself according to the white rails on his right and left, to find the approaching ball of dust ahead and start slowly ahead to encounter it. Someone fired at him from behind a tree and he began to trot, shoes landing softly, irregularly on the dirt. The tower above the stands was a little Swiss hut in the sky; a fence post was painted black; he heard a siren and saw a dove bursting with air on a bough. I could lean against the post, he thought, I might just take a breath. But the horses came round the turn then and once more his stumbling trot was giving way to a run. And he had the view that a photographer might have except that there was no camera, no truck's tailgate to stand upon. Only the virgin man-made stretch of track and at one end the horses bunching in fateful heat and at the other end himself—small, yet beyond elimination, whose single presence purported a toppling of the day, a violation of that scene at Aldington, wreckage to horses and little crouching men.

The crowd began to scream.

He was running in final stride, the greatest spread of legs, redness coming across the eyes, the pace so fast that it ceases to be motion, but at its peak becomes the long downhill deathless gliding of a dream until the arms are out, the head thrown back, and the runner is falling as he was falling and waving his arm at Rock Castle's onrushing silver shape, at Rock Castle who was about to run him down and fall.

". . . the blighter! Look at the little blighter go!"

Quietly, holding the girl's arm in the midst of the crowd: "Let me have the binoculars, Sybilline." Larry removed his green glasses, blinked once, and, still holding her arm so that the brass knuckles were brilliant and sunken into her flesh, looked through binoculars until the cloud went up.

"He's crossed us," whispered Sybilline, "he's crossed us, hasn't he?"

Out beyond the oval and past the broken threads of the rail the cloud stopped short and rose, spending itself dark as an explosion's smoke.

Then Larry was done and Sybilline took a look for herself: dust abruptly curling, settling down, horses lying flat with reins in the air, small riders limping among the animals or in circles or off toward the fence. And the silver horse was on its side with Banks and Jimmy Needles underneath. And three dirty-white Humber ambulances were racing up the track.

"Take me out to him . . . take me out to him, please."

But in the confusion—they passed the lined white faces of the man with tickets, the woman's husband Charlie, the older woman with chocolates smeared on her hands again—Larry and Syb and Little Dora hustled her behind the stands and out to the enormous car waiting in the line of cars, bundled her under the rags and quilting on the car floor. Thick was already sweating behind the wheel.

IT WAS A HEAVY RAIN, the sort of rain that falls in prison yards and beats a little firewood smoke back down garret chimneys, that leaks across floors, into forgotten prams, into the slaughterhouse and pots on the stove. It fell now on the roof of the stables in the Highland Green area and caused the trough beneath the pump to overflow, tore cobwebs off small panes of glass, filled wood and stone with the sound of forced rainwater. Timbers were already turning black, and the whistling of far-off factory hooters was lost in the rain.

Two chauffeur-driven automobiles approached with water spilling back from the wipers and cleaving down the hoods. They were black automobiles, though the rain gave them a deep-blue shine. They were high-bodied, carried special insignia, the radiator caps were nickel-plated. Grille to bumper they came into the cobbled yard and parked near the pump. The doors and windows remained shut, the engines continued to run; for half an hour the cars stood shedding the rain and no one alighted. Finally, when the rain failed to slacken, two men wearing waterproofs and bowlers got down—small men, Violet Lane detectives.

Wiping their faces with damp handkerchiefs, they went together down the wide walk between the rows of stalls, and the black cars followed at a little distance, low gears running smoothly as music boxes. The odor of rain-washed bridges drifted up to mix with dead smells of the stables: spread out from here were the gravel heaps, the leaking slate roofs and single rooms and roots and, farther on, the jewels, the places of execution, the familiar castle walls. All wet, all pitched in gloom. The two men knew this rain. It meant tea with lemon, housemaids out of mood, drops of water on spike fences and lickings for their boys. It meant women going it upright beneath the bridges and tall blue sergeants caped and miserable, helpless on all the corners. And it meant a dampness in the trousers that no coal fire could dry.

They stopped together at the stall door. They wiped their faces. They watched the water coming down the crevices in the wood, they inspected the hinges, the type of nail used, made note of a dead wasp caught on a green splinter. Then one pulled open the door and they stepped inside, looked up at the rafters, down at the straw, touched the wall planking with the very ends of their fingers, prodded the straw with their black shoes. And squatted and carefully took away the straw until Hencher's legs were uncovered to the knees. One fetched a black rubber ground sheet from his car; they rolled and sealed up the body. The straw would have to be sifted through a screen.

They posted one of the drivers to guard the stall until the laboratory boys could take the body and the straw. The driver stood at attention, a lonely man in an empty stable with his shoulders black with rain and his chin pulled into his collar. He smelled the burden on the other side of the wood. It was darker now and the rain heavier.

Between the two gently rocking cars—machines heavy with the sounds of their engines and streaming black—the Violet Lane detectives faced each other, stood close together and stared into each other's eyes. The mortuary bells were ringing and the water was coming off the brims of the bowlers.

"It's never nice to find these fellows in the rain."

"Well, I expect we'd best get on with it."

"We could trace him through the laundries."

"And there are always the tobacco shops, of course."

"Right. I've made out well before with the laundries."

"Go to it then. I'll try the shops. . . ."

And in gloom, with the bells stroking and the wipers establishing the uncomfortable rhythm of the hour, the two wet men withdrew to the cars and in slow procession quit the sooty stables in Highland Green, drove separately through vacant city streets to uncover the particulars of this crime.

SECOND SKIN

For Charlotte and Edwin Honig

NAMING NAMES

I WILL TELL YOU IN A FEW WORDS who I am: lover of the hummingbird
that darts to the flower beyond the rotted sill where my feet are propped;
lover of bright needlepoint and the bright stitching fingers of humorless
old ladies bent to their sweet and infamous designs; lover of parasols
made from the same puffy stuff as a young girl's underdrawers; still
lover of that small naval boat which somehow survived the distressing
years of my life between her decks or in her pilothouse; and also lover
of poor dear black Sonny, my mess boy, fellow victim and confidant,
and of my wife and child. But most of all, lover of my harmless and
sanguine self.

Yet surely I am more than a man of love. It will be clear, I think,
that I am a man of courage as well.

Had I been born my mother's daughter instead of son—and the
thought is not so improbable, after all, and causes me neither pain,
fear nor embarrassment when I give it my casual and interested
contemplation—I would not have matured into a muscular and self-
willed Clytemnestra but rather into a large and innocent Iphigenia betrayed on the beach. A large and slow-eyed and smiling Iphigenia, to
be sure, even more full to the knife than that real girl struck down once
on the actual shore. Yet I am convinced that in my case I should have
been spared. All but sacrificed I should have lived, somehow, in my
hapless way; to bleed but not to bleed to death would have been my
fate, forgiving them all while attempting to wipe the smoking knife on
the bottom of my thick yellow skirt. Or had my own daughter been
born my son I would have remained his ghostly guardian, true to his
hollow cheeks and skinny legs and hurts, for no more than this braving
his sneers, his nasty eye and the scorn of his fellow boys. For him too
I would have suffered violence with my chin lifted, my smile distracted,
my own large breast the swarming place of the hummingbirds terrified
and treacherous at once. Just as all these years I have suffered with a
certain dignity for father, wife, daughter, each of whom was his own
Antigone—the sand-scratchers, the impatient sufferers of self-inflicted
death, the curious adventurers for whom I remain alive. Perhaps my

father thought that by shooting off the top of his head he would force me to undergo some sort of transformation. But poor man, he forgot my capacity for love.

With Hamlet I should say that once, not long ago, I became my own granddaughter's father, giving her the warmth of my two arms and generous smile, substituting for each drop of the widow's poison the milk of my courageous heart. At night what a silhouette I must have made, kneeling, looming beside the child as she sat the always unfamiliar white statuary of the chamber pot. She must have known, I think, what happened to her mother, her mother's mother, her grandfather's father, and that she herself was the final accident in this long line of what I shall call our soft and well-intentioned bastardy. In the mirror our two heads—the bald one, the little silver one—would make faces together, reflecting for our innocent amusement the unhappy expressions worn once by those whom she and I—Pixie and I—had survived. So the all-but-abandoned Pixie, and my daughter, whose death I fought against the hardest, and my weightless wife, a flower already pressed between leaves of darkness before we met—these then are my dreams, the once-living or hardly living members of my adored and dreadful family, the cameo profiles of my beribboned brooch, the figures cut loose so terribly by that first explosion which occurred in my father's private lavatory. I know it was meant for me, his deliberate shot. But it went wild. It carried off instead dear Cassandra and hopeless, hysterical Gertrude. Went wild and left only myself alive.

Yes, my own feet at rest on the rotted window sill. But I am no mere sickened leaf on a dead tide, no mere dead weight burdening some gaudy hammock. In body, in mind, am I not rather the aggressive personification of serenity, the eternal forward drift or handsome locomotion of peace itself? As a walker, for instance, I am a tiger. I have always walked far in my white socks, my white shoes, and the extent and manner of my walking have always been remarked upon, with admiration or maliciousness, in the past. Since childhood I have walked into a room, or out, out into the shadowed greens or dangerous sand lots of the world, holding my chin lifted, my lips pleasantly curved and my eye round, measuring my steps so that they would never falter and keeping my hands in motion at my side, wishing never to appear intimidated by the death of my parents, wishing never to conceal the shame which I thought had left its clear and rancid mark on my breast. Even today I take these same slow-paced, deliberate, impervious footsteps, using the balls of my feet in proud and sensual fashion, driving a con-

stant rhythm and lightheartedness and a certain confidence into my
stride through the uninhibited and, I might say, powerful swinging of
my hips. Of course there are those who laugh. But others, like Sonny,
recognize my need, my purpose, my strength and grace. Always my
strength and grace.

In all likelihood my true subject may prove to be simply the wind—
its changing nature, its rough and whispering characteristics, the various
spices of the world which it brings together suddenly in hot or freezing
gusts to alter the flavor of our inmost recollections of pleasure or pain
—simply that wind to which my heart and also my skin have always
been especially sensitive. Or it may prove to be the stark elongated
brutal silhouette of a ship standing suddenly on the horizon of the mind
and, all at once, making me inexplicably afraid—perhaps because it is
so far off that not one detail reaches the eye, nothing of name, passengers, crew, not even smoke from the stack, so that only the ugly span
of pointed iron, which ought to be powerless but moves nonetheless and
is charged with all the mystery and inhuman distance of the compass,
exists to incite this terrible fear and longing in a man such as myself.
But for now the wind trails off my fingers, the ship fades. Because I
suppose that names must precede these solid worlds of my passionate
time and place and action.

There was Fernandez, then, my small son-in-law, who held up his
trousers with the feathery translucent skin of a rattlesnake, and who,
even in his white linen suit and with Cassandra's hand in his at the
altar, continued to look like the hapless Peruvian orphan that he was.
A breath smelling of hot peppers, dark and deeply socketed nostrils, flat
smoky brown skull that cried for lace and candlelight, in his jacket
pocket a Bible bound in white calfskin, and in his hand a bunch of
somber crimson flowers—this was Fernandez, who underwent a triumphant and rebellious change of character in the wedding car (it was
his own though he could not drive it, a sloping green-roofed sedan with
cracked glass, musty seats, bare oily floors rent and jagged so that the
road was clearly visible, the car Cassandra drove that day only with the
greatest effort and determination), this then was Fernandez, who caused
me, that day, to smile my most perspiring smile for the loss of my dear
blonde-headed Cassandra. But even then, of course, I could not have
imagined Fernandez on a bloody hotel room floor. And even now, after
the fact of these events—time has worked on them like water on old
knots—even now I cannot entirely castigate the memory of that Fernandez who was the groom. His favorite name for me was "good Papa

Cue Ball." For anyone else—except Cassandra, except me—that nick-
name would have been warning enough. But I would have welcomed
Fernandez then, Fernandez with his menacing green car, his piles of
tattered ration booklets, his heaps of soft smooth tires piled in the black
wooden structure where the chickens scratched, even had he threatened
me with the little hook-shaped razor blade he carried next to his Bible
in an Edgeworth tobacco tin. Welcomed him with opened arms, I am
sure.

But two more names will complete this preliminary roster of persons
whose love I have lost or whose poison I happily spent my life neutral-
izing with my unblemished flesh, my regal carriage, my impractical but
all the more devoted being. After Fernandez there was Miranda. I hear
that name—Miranda, Miranda!—and once again quicken to its false
suggestiveness, feel its rhapsody of sound, the several throbs of the vow-
els, the very music of charity, innocence, obedience, love. For a moment
I seem to see both magic island and imaginary girl. But Miranda was
the widow's name—out of what perversity, what improbable desire I
am at a loss to say—and no one could have given a more ugly denial
to that heartbreaking and softly fluted name than the tall and treacherous woman. Miranda. The widow. In the end I was Miranda's match;
I have had my small victory over Miranda; as father, grandfather,
former naval officer and man, I found myself equal to this last indignity;
to me her name means only ten months during which I attempted to
prolong Cassandra's life, ten subtle months of my final awakening.
Rawboned and handsome woman, unconventional and persistent
widow, old antagonist on a black Atlantic island, there she was—my
monster, my Miranda, final challenge of our sad society and worthy of
all the temperance and courage I could muster. Now I think of her as
my black butterfly. And now—obviously—the scars are sweet.

With the mention of my mother's prosaic name of Mildred I complete my roster, because there is no place here for Tremlow—my devil,
Tremlow—or for Mac, the Catholic chaplain who saved my life. No
place for them. Not yet. Of course the mere name of my mother has no
special connotation, no significance, but the woman herself was the
vague consoling spirit behind the terrible seasons of this life when unlikely accidents, tabloid adventures, shocking episodes, surrounded a
solitary and wistful heart. Like my father she died when I was young,
and I see her with most of her features indistinct. But she too was tall,
stoop-shouldered, forever smiling a soft questioning smile. I have no
recollection of her voice—some short time after my father's decision in

the lavatory she ceased to talk, became permanently mute—and my few visual memories of her are silent and show her only at a great distance off. Wearing her broad-brimmed white hat so immense and limpid it conceals her face and back in waves like tissue paper, she kneels in the garden strip next to the little chipped and tarnished electric sign which is the familiar urban monument of men in my father's profession and which, in my boyhood, identified our private house as the combined residence and working place of an active small-town mortician. I see my mother kneeling, hidden by the hat, inert and sweet and ghostly in the summer sun. She seems to me to be praying rather than gardening, and my imagination supplies the black trowel untouched by her white-gloved folded hands but stabbed upright, rather, into the earth at her knees. And then, in another fragment of memory, I see her seated in the middle of our lawn on one of my father's shellacked folding chairs and still dressed in white, still wearing the hat, while he, bareheaded and balding and in shirt sleeves, stands hosing down the long black limousine which was shabby, upholstered in red velvet except for the stiff black patent leather of the driver's seat, and often smelled of invisible flowers—that worn and comfortable old hearse—when it doubled on Sunday afternoons as our family car. The seated woman, the dripping machine, the man working his wrist in idle circles, this is the vision lying closest to the peaceful center of my childhood. And how much it contains: not only the still day of my youth but also the devotion and modest industry of my parents which gave my early life the proportions of a working fairy tale. For the president of the local bank, an unmarried teacher in the elementary school, two brothers dramatically drowned in a scummy pond at the edge of town, the thin mother of infant twins, three beautiful members of the high school graduating class decapitated in a scarlet coupé, a girl who had sold children's underwear in the five and dime, in our house all of them appeared, all were attended by my father and my mother as well, she in the parlor, smiling, he in the shop below, since she was always his perfect partner, the mortician's muse, the woman who more and more grew to resemble a gifted angel in a dreamer's cemetery as the years passed and the number of our nonreligious ceremonies increased. A few years only—yet all my youth—were marked by the folding and unfolding of the wooden chairs and sudden oil changes in the hearse, until that day my peace and excitement ended and my mother and I were only brief visitors in another undertaker's home.

At least I was witness to my father's death, in a sense was the child-accomplice of whatever dark phantom might have been materializing by his side that noon hour he finally locked himself in the hot lavatory—it was a Friday in midsummer—and rushed through the bare essentials of taking his life. Witness and accomplice because I was crouched with my ear to the door and because we talked together, curious but welcome conference between father and son, and because I played my cello to him and later fished from the trembling cupfuls of water in the bottom of the toilet bowl the little unused bullet which was companion to the one he fired. At least I knew it was for my sake, despite his confusion, his anger, his pathetic cries, and received the tangible actuality of his death with shocked happiness, grateful at least for the misguided trust implicit in the real staging of that uncensored scene.

How like my mother, on the other hand, to spare me: to disappear, to vanish, gone without the hard crude accessories of sweating water jug, pulmotor, stretcher, ambulance summoned from the City Hospital; gone without vigil or funeral, without good-bys. I missed her one morning and that was all. It makes little difference now that she died only twenty miles away and in the care of a half brother. It makes no difference to me. Because I missed her, I knew at once what had happened, I was alone, I could do nothing but alternate my days between the lavatory—endless brushing of teeth, plastering down of hair—and the back of the hearse where I instinctively stretched out to await my final vision of that experience denied me in space but not in time.

And in time it came, the moment when at last I sat up like a miniature fat corpse in the back of the solemn old limousine and found the cobwebs, the streaming motes, the worn velvet carpeting and various bits of silver and thin lengths of steel—the casket runners—all turned to dense geometric substances of light—orange, yellow, radiant pink—and in that blaze, and just as I clenched my hands and shut my eyes, knew that my father had begun my knowledge of death as a lurid truth but that my mother had extended it toward the promise of mystery—this at the instant I saw her, saw her, after all, in the vision which no catastrophe of my own has ever destroyed or dimmed.

She appears from a doorway in a large white house on a hill; clouds are banked heavily behind the house and hill and a deep morning sun appears to lie buried inside the enormous unmoving range of clouds; there is no one else in the great house with all its white chimneys and shuttered windows, silent, breeze-swept, filled with untouched tinkling crystal and dusty sleigh bells strung on long strips of dried and moldy leather, and my mother steps from under the portico, raises a gentle hand to the hat trembling with a motion all its own, and lifts her face, turns it left and right with the benevolent questioning glance of the royal lady prepared to greet either prince or executioner with her lovely smile which, from where I hide down the hill in a bush, is either innocent or blind. Then she is moving, skin and veils and featureless face—except for the smile—reflecting the peach and rose color of the filtered sun, descends one lichen-covered step and then another, sways and climbs up beside the driver of a small open yellow machine with wooden wheels, white solid tires and brass headlamps. The car is thumping up and down, but silently, and behind the single high seat is strapped a little white satin trunk, and the driver, I see, wears a white cap and driving coat, great eyeless goggles and a black muffler wrapped about his throat and hiding his mouth, nose, chin. With one gloved hand he grips a lever as tall and thin as a sword, and there is a sudden flashing when he contracts his arm; with his other hand he is squeezing the black bulb of the horn, though I hear nothing, and is sitting even straighter against the wind; and now he is gripping the steering wheel, holding it at arm's length; and now he turns his head and takes a single long look into my mother's face, and I see that she is admiring him—or pitying him—and I quiver; and then the tires are rolling, the trunk swaying, the muffler beating the air, and suddenly the white coat is brown with the dust of the road and the vehicle, severe and tangled like a complicated golden insect, is gaining speed, and I see that my mother is quite serene, somehow remains unblown, unshaken as the downward ride commences, and is merely touching her fingers to the crown of her familiar hat and raising a soft white arm as if to wave.

A waxen tableau, no doubt the product of a slight and romantic fancy. Yet I prefer this vision to my father's death. And by way of partial explanation, at least, I should make note of one concrete circumstance: that my mother, unable to bear the sound of the death-dealing shot— it must have lodged in her head like a shadow of the bullet that entered my father's—deafened herself one muggy night, desperately, painfully, by filling both lovely ears with the melted wax from one of our dining room candles.

But on now to the erratic flight of the hummingbird—on to the high lights of my naked history.

AGONY OF THE SAILOR

SHE WAS IN MY ARMS AND LIFELESS, nearly lifeless. Together we stood: the girl, young mother, war bride in her crumpled frock, and I in my cap and crumpled uniform of white duck—it was damp and beginning to soil after these nights awake, was bunched at the knees and down the front spotted with the rum and Coca-Cola from poor Sonny's upset glass—I hardly able to smile, perspiring, sporting on my breast the little colorful ribbon of my Good Conduct Medal and on my collar the tarnished insignia of my rank, and unshaven, tired, burned slightly red and lost, thoroughly lost in this midnight Chinatown at the end of my tour of duty and still wearing in my forgetfulness the dark blue armband of the Shore Patrol, and so protected, protecting, I holding the nearly lifeless hand and feeling her waist growing smaller and smaller in the wet curve of my arm, feeling even her cold hand diminishing, disappearing from mine and wondering how to restore this poor girl who would soon be gone. I looked around, trying to catch sight of Sonny where he sat in the booth with Pixie. And suddenly I was aware of the blind, meaningless, momentary presence of her little breast against my own and I, regretting my sensitivity but regretting more the waste, the impossibility of bringing her to life again—there in the small fleshed locket of her heart—I wished all at once to abandon rank, insignia, medal, bald head, good nature, everything, if only I might become for a moment an anonymous seaman second class, lanky and far from home and dancing with this girl, but felt instead the loose sailors pressing against us, all of them in their idiotic two-piece suits and laced up tight, each one filling me with despair because she and I were dancing together, embracing, and there wasn't even someone to give her a kiss. Here then was our celebration, the start of adventure and beginning of misery—or perhaps its end—and I kept thinking that she was barelegged, had packed her only pair of stockings—black market, a present from me—in the small tattered canvas bag guarded now between Sonny's feet.

There should have been love in our dark and nameless Chinatown café. But there was only an hour to spare, only the shotglasses flung like jewels among the sailors—each provided with his pocket comb,

French letters, gold watch and matching band—only the noise, the smoke, the poster of the old national goatfaced man over the bar, the sound of the record and torch singer, orchestra, a song called "Tanger-ine," only the young boys with their navy silk ties and Popeye hats, crowded elbows and bowls of boiled rice; only this night, the harbor plunging with battleships, the water front blacked-out, bloody with shore leave and sick with the bodies of young girls sticking to the walls of moist unlighted corridors; only our own café and its infestation of little waiters smiling their white-slave smiles and of sailors pulling down their middies, kicking their fresh white hornpipe legs; only ourselves—agitated eccentric naval officer, well-meaning man, and soft young woman, serious, downcast—only ourselves and in the middle of no romance.

So in the shame and longing of my paternal sentiment, flushed and bumbling, I felt her knee, her hip, once more her breasts—they were of a child in puberty though she was twenty-five—and touched the frock which I had found tossed over the back of the hotel sofa. I glanced down at her head, at the hair pinned up and her neck bare, at her face, the beautiful face which reminded me suddenly of a little death mask of Pascal. From one wrist she carried a dangling purse, and when it swung against my ribs—dull metronome of our constrained and hollow dance—I knew it was an empty purse. No stockings, no handkerchief, no lipstick or keys; no love, no mother, no Fernandez. There among all those sailors in the smoke, the noise, I pulled her to me, wincing and lunging both as I felt imprinted on my stomach the shape of hers, and felt all the little sinews in her stomach banding together, trembling. It was midnight—Pacific War Time—and I tried to collect myself, tried to put on a show of strength in my jaw.

"I've never been afraid of the seeds of death," I said, tightening my arm, staring over her head at the litter of crushed cherries and orange rind wet on the bar, "and if I were you I wouldn't blame Gertrude for what she did." We executed a fairly rakish turn, bumped from the rear, blocked by the tall airy figure of a bosun's mate—the uniform was stuffed against his partner in an aghast paralysis of love, bell-bottoms wrapped tight around the woman's ankles, the man's white face swaying in an effort to toss aside the black hair drenched in rum—and I looked down into my own partner's eyes which were lifted to mine at last and which were as clear as sea shells, the pupils gray and hard, the irises suddenly returning to sight like little cold musical instruments. I sighed—my sigh was a hot breath on her dry lips—I blushed, I got my wind again, and it was a mouthful of smoke, mouthful of rum, fragrance of salty black sauce and yellow plague.

"As you know," I said, "I grew up very familiar with the seeds of death; I had a special taste for them always. But when I heard about Gertrude something happened. It was as if I had struck a new variety. Her camel's-hair coat, her pink mules, her cuticle sticks scattered on the floor, her dark glasses left lying on the unmade bed in the U-Drive-Inn, I saw the whole thing, for that moment understood her poor strangled solitude, understood exactly what it is like to be one of the unwanted dead. Suddenly Gertrude and I were being washed together in the same warm tide. But in our grief we were casting up only a single shadow—you."

Quickly, artfully, I gave the bosun's mate a shove with my sea-going hip and, heavy as I was, stood hovering, sagging in front of Cassandra. I held her, with a moistened finger I touched her dry mouth, I raised her chin—unsmiling dimple, unblemished curve of her little proud motherhood—I watched her gray eyes and I waited, waited for the sound of the voice which was always a whisper and which I had never failed to hear. And now the eyes were tuned, the lips were unsealed—moving, opening wide enough to admit a straw—I was flooded with the sound of the whisper and sight of a tiny golden snake wriggling up the delicate cleft of her throat—still no smile, never a smile—and curling in a circle to pulse, to die, in the shallow white nest of her temple.

"I think you would like to know," she began, whispering, spacing the words, "you would like to know what I did with the guitar. Well, I burned it. Pixie and I burned it together." And in her whispered seriousness, the hush of her slow enunciation, I heard then the snapping of flames, the tortured singing of those red-hot strings. Even as I dropped her hand, let go of her waist, brought together my fat fingers where the Good Conduct Ribbon like a dazzling insect marked the spot of my heart in all that wrinkled and sullied field of white, even as I struggled with the tiny clasp—pinprick, drop of blood, another stain—and fastened the ribbon to the muslin of her square-collared rumpled frock, even while I admired my work and then took her into my arms again, hugging, kissing, protecting her always and always, and even while I gave her the Good Conduct Medal—she the one who deserved it; I, never—and shook long and happily in my relief: through all this hectic and fragile moment I distinctly heard the gray whisper continuing its small golden thread of intelligence exactly on the threshold of sound and as fine and formidable as the look in her eye.

"Pixie and I were alone, mother and daughter, and we did what we had to do. I think she disapproved at first, but once I got the kerosene out of the garage she began to enjoy the whole thing immensely. She even clapped her little hands. But you ought to have known," taking note of the ribbon, touching it with the tip of her pinky—no other sign than this—and all the while whispering, whispering those minimum formal cadences she had learned at school and gently moving, turning, arching her bare neck so I should see how she disciplined her sorrow, "you ought to have known the U-Drive-Inn was no place for a child. . . ."

I blushed again, I glanced down at the small bare feet in the strapless shoes—scuffed lemon shells—I welcomed even this briefest expression of her displeasure. "It was no place for you, no place for you, Cassandra," I said, and wished, as I had often wished, that she would submit to some small name of endearment, if only at such times as these when I loved her most and feared for her the most. A name of endearment would have helped. "You were too innocent for the U-Drive-Inn," I said. "I should have known how it would end. Your mother always told me she wanted to die surrounded by unmarried couples in a cheap motel, and I let her. But no more cheap motels for us, Cassandra. We won't even visit Gertrude in the cemetery."

She caught my spirit, she caught my gesturing hand: "Skipper?"—at least she allowed herself to whisper that name, mine, which Sonny had invented for me so long ago before we sailed—"Skipper? Will you do something nice for me? Something really nice?"

She was still unsmiling but was poised, half-turned, giving me a look of happiness, of life, in the pure agility of her body. And hadn't she, wearing only the frock, only a few pins in the small classical lift of her hair, hadn't she come straight from a sluggish bath tub in the U-Drive-Inn to the most violent encounter ever faced by her poor little determined soul? Now she held before me the promise of her serious duplicity, watching and gauging—me, the big soft flower of fatherhood—until I heard myself saying, "Anything, anything, the bus doesn't leave for another hour and a half, Cassandra, and no one will ever say I faltered even one cumbersome step in loving you." I gripped her small ringless hand and fled with her, though she was only walking, walking, this child with the poise and color and muscle-shape of a woman, followed her through the drunken sailors to the door.

In the dark, whipped by pieces of paper—the torn and painted remnants of an old street dragon—a sailor stood rolling and moaning against the wall, holding his white cupcake-wrapper hat in one hand and with the other reaching into the sunken whiteness of his chest, the upturned face, the clutching hand, the bent legs spread and kicking to the unheard Latin rhythm of some furious carnival. But on flowed Cassandra, small, grave, heartless, a silvery water front adventuress, and led me straight into the crawling traffic—it was unlighted, rasping, a slow and blackened parade of taxicabs filled with moon-faced marines wearing white braid and puffing cherry-tipped cigars, parade of ominous jeeps each with its petty officer standing up in the rear, arms folded, popping white helmets strapped in place—led me on through admiring whistles and the rubbery sibilance of military tires to a dark shop which was only a rat's hole between a cabaret—girl ventriloquist, dummy in black trunks—and the fuming concrete bazaar of the Greyhound Bus Terminal—point of our imminent departure—drew me on carefully, deftly, until side by side we stood in the urine-colored haze of a guilty light bulb and breathed the dust, the iodine, the medicinal alcohol of a most vulgar art.

"But, Cassandra," I said in a low voice, flinching, trying to summon the dignity of my suffering smile, all at once aware that beneath my uniform my skin was an even and lively red, unbroken, unmarked by disfiguring scars or blemishes, "look at his teeth, smell his breath! My God, Cassandra!"

"Skipper," she said, and again it was the ghostly whisper, the terrifying sadistic calm of the school-trained voice, "don't be a child. Please." Then she whispered efficiently, calmly, to the oaf at the table —comatose eyes of the artist, the frustrated procurer, drinking her in —and naturally he was unable to hear even one word of her little succinct command, unable to make out her slow toy train of lovely sounds. He wore a tee-shirt, was covered—arms, neck, shoulders—with the sweaty peacock colors of his self-inflicted art.

"There's no need to whisper, lady," he said. Up and down went his eyes, up and down from where he fell in a mountain on his disreputable table, watching her, not bothering to listen, flexing his nightmare pictures as best he could, shifting and showing us, the two of us, the hair bunched and bristling in his armpits, and even that hair was electrical.

She continued to whisper—ludicrous pantomime—without stopping, without changing the faint and formal statement of her desires, when suddenly and inexplicably the man and I, allied in helpless and incongruous competition, both heard her at the same time.

"My boy friend is bashful," she was saying, "do you understand? Let me have a piece of writing paper and a pencil, please."

"You mean he's afraid? But I got you, lady," and I saw him move, saw his blue tattooed hand swim like a trained seal in the slime of a drawer which he had yanked all at once into his belly.

"Father, Cassandra, father!" I exclaimed, though softly, "Pixie's grandfather, Cassandra!"

"No need to worry, Skipper," said the man—his grin, his fiendish familiarity—"I'm a friend of Uncle Sam's."

Yellow and silver-tinted, prim, Cassandra was already sitting on the tattooer's stool, had placed her purse on the table beside her, had forced the man to withdraw his fat scalloped arms, was writing with the black stub of pencil on the back of a greasy envelope which still contained— how little she knew—its old-fashioned familiar cargo of prints the size of postage stamps, each one revealing, beneath a magnifying glass, its aspect of faded pubic area or instant of embarrassed love. Alone and celebrating, we were war orphans together and already I had forgiven her, wanted to put my hand on the curls pinned richly and hastily on the top of her head. I could see that she was writing something in large block letters across the envelope.

She stood up—anything but lifeless now—and between his thumb and finger the man took the envelope and rubbed it as if he were testing the sensual quality of gold laminated cloth or trying to smear her tiny fingerprints onto his own, and then the man and I, the oaf and I, were watching her together, listening:

"My boy friend," she said, and I was measuring her pauses, smelling the bludwurst on the tattooer's breath, was quivering to each whispered word of my child courtesan, "my boy friend would like to have this name printed indelibly on his chest. Print it over his heart, please."

"What color, lady?" And grinning, motioning me to the stool, "You got the colors of the rainbow to choose from, lady." So even the oaf, the brute artist was a sentimentalist and I sat down stiffly, heavily, see-ing against my will his display of wet dripping rainbow, hating him for his infectious colors, and telling myself that I must not give him a single wince, not give him the pleasure of even one weak cry.

"Green," she said at once—had I heard her correctly?—and she took a step closer with one of her spun sugar shoes, "a nice bright green." Then she looked up at me and added, to my confusion, my mystifica-tion, "Like the guitar."

And the oaf, the marker of men, was grinning, shaking his head: "Green's a bad color"—more muscle-flexing now and the professional observation—"Green's going to hurt, lady. Hurt like hell."

But I had known it, somehow, deep in the tail of my spine, deep where I was tingling and trying to hide from myself, had known all along that now I was going to submit to an atrocious pain for Cassandra—only for Cassandra—had known it, that I who had once entertained the thought of a single permanent inscription in memory of my mother—gentle Mildred—but when it came to rolling up my sleeve had been unable to endure the shock of even a very small initial M, would now submit myself and expose the tender flesh of my breast letter by letter to the pain of that long exotic name my daughter had so carefully penciled out on that greasy envelope of endless lunchroom counters, endless lavatories in creaking burlesque theaters. So even before I heard the man's first order—voice full of German delicacies and broken teeth—I had forced my fingers to the first of my hard brass buttons, tarnished, unyielding—the tiny eagle was sharp to the touch—and even before he had taken the first sizzling stroke with his electric needle I was the wounded officer, collapsing, flinching, biting my lip in terror.

He worked with his tongue in his cheek while Cassandra stood by watching, waiting, true to her name. I hooked my scuffed regulation white shoes into the rungs of the stool; I allowed my white duck coat to swing open, loose, disheveled; I clung to the greasy edge of the table. My high stiff collar was unhooked, the cap was tilted to the back of my head, and sitting there on that wobbling stool I was a mass of pinched declivities, pockets of fat, strange white unexpected mounds, deep creases, ugly stains, secret little tunnels burrowing into all the quivering fortifications of the joints, and sweating, wrinkling, was either the wounded officer or the unhappy picture of some elderly third mate, sitting stock still in an Eastern den—alone except for the banana leaves, the evil hands—yet lunging, plunging into the center of his vicious fantasy. A few of us, a few good men with soft reproachful eyes, a few honor-bright men of imagination, a few poor devils, are destined to live out our fantasies, to live out even the sadistic fantasies of friends, children and possessive lovers.

But I heard him then and suddenly, and except for the fleeting thought that perhaps a smile would cause even this oaf, monster, skin-stitcher, to spare me a little, suddenly there was no escape, no time for reverie: "OK, Skipper, here we go."

Prolonged thorough casual rubbing with a dirty wet disintegrating cotton swab. Merely to remove some of the skin, inflame the area. Corresponding vibration in the victim's jowls and holding of breath. Dry ice effect of the alcohol. Prolonged inspection of disintegrating cardboard box of little scabrous dusty bottles, none full, some empty. Bottles of dye. Chicken blood, ground betel nut, baby-blue irises of child's eye—brief flashing of the cursed rainbow. Tossing one particular bottle up and down and grinning. Thick green. Then fondling the electric needle. Frayed cord, greasy case—like the envelope—point no more than a stiff hair but as hot as a dry frying pan white from the fire. Then he squints at the envelope. Then lights a butt, draws, settles it on the lip of a scummy brown-stained saucer. Then unstoppers the ancient clotted bottle of iodine. Skull and crossbones. Settles the butt between his teeth where it stays. Glances at Cassandra, starts the current, comes around and sits on the corner of the table, holding the needle away from his own face and flesh, pushing a fat leg against victim's. Scowls. Leans down. Tongue in position. Rainbow full of smoke and blood. Then the needle bites.

The scream—yes, I confess it, scream—that was clamped between my teeth was a strenuous black bat struggling, wrestling in my bloated mouth and with every puncture of the needle—fast as the stinging of artificial bees, this exquisite torture—I with my eyes squeezed tight, my lips squeezed tight, felt that at any moment it must thrust the slimy black tip of its archaic skeletal wing out into view of Cassandra and the working tattooer. But I was holding on. I longed to disgorge the bat, to sob, to be flung into the relief of freezing water like an old woman submerged and screaming in the wild balm of some dark baptismal rite in a roaring river. But I was holding on. While the punctures were marching across, burning their open pinprick way across my chest, I was bulging in every muscle, slick, strained, and the bat was peering into my mouth of pain, kicking, slick with my saliva, and in the stuffed interior of my brain I was resisting, jerking in outraged helplessness, blind and baffled, sick with the sudden recall of what Tremlow had done to me that night—helpless abomination—while Sonny lay sprawled on the bridge and the captain trembled on his cot behind the pilothouse. There were tiny fat glistening tears in the corners of my eyes. But they never fell. Never from the eyes of this heavy bald-headed once-handsome man. Victim. Courageous victim.

The buzzing stopped. I waited. But the fierce oaf was whistling and I heard the click, the clasp of Cassandra's purse—empty as I thought except for a worn ten dollar bill which she was drawing forth, handing across to him—and I found that the bat was dead, that I was able to see through the sad film over my eyes and that the pain was only a florid swelling already motionless, inactive, the mere receding welt of this operation. I could bear it. Marked and naked as I was, I smiled. I managed to stand.

Cassandra glanced at my chest—at what to me was still a mystery —glanced and nodded her small classical indomitable head. Then the tatooer took a square dirty mirror off the wall, held it in front of me:

"Have a look, Skipper," once more sitting on the edge of the table, eager, bulking, swinging a leg.

So I looked into the mirror, the dirty fairy tale glass he was about to snap in his two great hands, and saw myself. The pink was blistered, wet where he had scrubbed it again with the cooling and dizzying alcohol, but the raised letters of the name—upside down and backwards—were a thick bright green, a string of inflamed emeralds, a row of unnatural dots of jade. Slowly, trying to appear pleased, trying to smile, I read the large unhealed green name framed in the glass above the ashamed blind eye of my own nipple: *Fernandez*. And I could only try to steady my knees, control my breath, hide feebly this green lizard that lay exposed and crawling on my breast.

Finally I was able to speak to her, faintly, faintly: "Sonny and Pixie are waiting for us, Cassandra," as I saw with shame and alarm that her eyes were harder than ever and had turned a bright new triumphant color.

"Pixie and I been worried about you. You going to miss that bus if you two keep running off this way. But come on, Skipper, we got time for one more round of rum and Coke!"

With fondness, a new white preening of the neck, an altered line at the mouth, a clear light of reserved motherhood in the eye, Cassandra glanced at the little girl on Sonny's lap and then smoothed her frock— this the most magical, envied, deferential gesture of the back of the tiny white hand that never moved, never came to life except to excite the whole ladylike sense of modesty—and slid with the composure of the young swan into the dark blistered booth opposite the black-skinned petty officer and platinum child. I took my place beside her, squeezing, sighing, worrying, aware of my burning chest and the new color of her eyes and feeling her withdrawing slightly, making unnecessary room for me, curving away from me in all the triumph and gentleness of her disdain. I fished into a tight pocket, wiped my brow. Once more there was the smoke, the noise, the sick heaviness of our water front café, our jumping-off night in Chinatown, once more the smell of whisky and the sticky surface of tin trays painted with pagodas and golden monsters, and now the four of us together—soon to part, three to take their leave of poor black faithful Sonny—and now the terrible mammalian concussion of Kate Smith singing to all the sailors.

Duty gave still greater clarity, power, persistence to the whisper: "Has she been crying, Sonny?"

"Pixie? My baby love? You know Pixie never cries when I croon to her, Miss Cassandra. And I been crooning about an hour and a half. But Miss Cassandra," lulling us with his most intimate voice—it was the voice he adopted in times of trouble, always most melodious at the approach of danger—lulling us and tightening the long black hand— shiny knuckles, long black bones and tendons, little pink hearts for fingertips—that spraddled Pixie's chest limply, gently, "Miss Cassandra, you look like you been cashing in your Daddy's Victory bonds. And Skipper," sitting across from us with the child, glancing first at Cassandra and then myself, "you've got a terrible blue look about you, terrible tired and blue." Then: "No more cemetery business, Skipper? I trust there's no more of that cemetery stuff in the cards. That stuff's the devil!"

Cocked garrison cap and shiny visor; petty officer's navy blue coat, white shirt, black tie; two neat rows of rainbow ribbons on his breast; elongated bony skull and black velvet face—he called himself the skinny nigger—and sunglasses with enormous lenses coal-black and brightly polished; signet ring, little Windsor knot in the black tie, high plum-colored temples and white teeth of the happy cannibal; tall smart trembling figure of a man whose only arrogance was affection: he was sitting across from us—poor Sonny—and talking through the Chinese babble, the noise of the Arkansas sailors, the loud breasty volume of mother America's possessive wartime song. Poor Sonny.

"Skipper," once more the whisper of fashion, whisper of feminine cleanliness, cold love, "show Sonny, please."

"What's this? Games?" And casting quick razor looks from Cassandra to myself, shifting Pixie still further away from us and leaning forward, craning down: "What you two been up to anyway?"

I unhooked my stiff collar and worked loose the top brass button and then the next, gingerly, with chin to collar bone trying to see it again myself, through puckered lips trying to blow a cold breath on it, and leaned forward, held open the white duck in a V for Sonny, for

Sonny who respected me, who was all bone and blackness and was the best mess boy the U.S.S. *Starfish* ever had.

He looked. He gave a long low Negro whistle: "So that's the trouble. Well now. You two both grieving not for the dead but for that halfpint Peruvian fella who run out on us. I understand. Well now. Husbands all ducked out on us, wives all dead and buried. So we got to do something fancy with *his* name, we got to do something to hurt Skipper. Got to turn a man's breast into a tombstone full of ache and pain. You better just take your baby girl and your bag of chicken salad sandwiches—I made you a two-days' supply—and get on the bus. This family of ours is about busted up."

But: "Hush," I said, done with the buttons and still watching Cassandra—chin tilted, lips tight in a crescent, spine straight—and reaching out for the black angle of his hand, "You know how we feel about Fernandez. But Sonny, you'll find a brown parcel in the back of the jeep. My snapshots of the boys on the *Starfish*. For you."

"That so, Skipper? Well now. Maybe we ain't so busted up after all."

He puffed on his signet ring—the teeth, the wrinkled nose, the fluttering lips, the twisted wide-open mouth of the good-natured mule—and shined it on his trousers and flashed it into sight again—bloodstone, gold-plated setting—and took off his cocked and rakish hat, slowly, carefully, since from the Filipino boys he had learned how to pomade his rich black opalescent hair, and fanned himself and Pixie three or four times with the hat—the inside of the band was lined with bright paper medallions of the Roman Church—and then treated the patent leather visor as he had the ring, puffing, polishing, arm's length examination of his work, and with his long slow burlesquing fingers tapped the starched hat into place again, saying, "OK, folks, old Sonny's bright as a dime again, or maybe a half dollar—nigger money of course. But, Skipper," dropping a bright black kiss as big as a mushmelon in Pixie's platinum hair and grinning, waving toward Cassandra's glass and mine—Coca-Cola like dark blood, little drowning buttons of melted ice—then frowning, long-jawed and serious: "whatever did happen to that Fernandez fella?"

I shifted, hot, desperate, broad rump stuck fast and uncomfortable to the wooden seat, I looked at her, I touched my stinging breast, tried to make a funny grandfather's face for Pixie: "We don't know, Sonny. But he was a poor husband for Cassandra anyway." I used the handkerchief again, took hold of the glass. She was composed, unruffled, sat toying with a plastic swizzle stick—little queen—and one boudoir curl hung loose and I was afraid to touch it.

"Maybe he got hisself a job with a dance band. Maybe he run off with the USO—I never liked him, but he sure was a whizz with the guitar—or maybe," giving way to his black fancy, his affectionate concern, "maybe he got hisself kidnapped. Those South American fellas don't fool around, and maybe they decided it was time he did his hitch in the Peruvian Army. No, sir," taking a long self-satisfied optimistic drink, cupping the ice in his lip like a lump of sugar, "I bet he just couldn't help hisself!"

Then she was stirring the swizzle stick, raising it to the invisible tongue, touching the neckline of her wrinkled frock, once more whispering and informing us, tormenting us with the somber clarity of what she had to say: "Fernandez deserted his wife and child"—hairs leaping up on the backs of my hands, scalp tingling, heart struck with a hammer, fit of coughing—"deserted his wife and child for another person. Fernandez left his wife and child"—I clutched again the handkerchief, wishing I could extricate myself and climb out of the booth—"abandoned us, Pixie and me, for the love of another person. A man who was tall, dark-haired, sun-tanned and who wore civilian clothes. A gunner's mate named Harry. He had a scar. Also, he was tattooed," the whisper dying, dying, the mouth coming as close as it could to a smile, "like you, Skipper."

Then silence. Except for the shot glasses. Except for the tin trays. Except for the moaning sailor and the bay plunging and crashing somewhere in the night. Except for the torch song of our homeless millions. I slumped, Sonny shook his head, threw out suddenly a long fierce burnt-up hand and pure white dapper cuff: "Oh, that unfaithful stuff is the devil! Pure devil!"

The shaft goes to the breast, love shatters, whole troop trains of love are destroyed, the hero is the trumpet player twisted into a lone embrace with his sexless but mellow horn, the good-bys are near and I hear Cassandra whispering and I see the color in her eyes: "There aren't any husbands left in the world. Are there, Skipper?"

But Sonny answered, Sonny who took a shower in our cheap hotel, Sonny whose uniform was pressed dark blue and hard and crisp in a steaming mangle: "Dead or unfaithful, Miss Cassandra, that's a fact. Damn all them unfaithful lovers!"

Bereft. Cool. Grieved. Triumphant. The frozen bacchanal, the withered leaf. Taps in the desert. Taps at sea. Small woman, poor faithful friend, crying child—Pixie had begun to cry—and I the lawful guardian determined but still distressed and past fifty, nose packed with carbonated water, head fuming with rum, all of us wrecked together in a Chinatown café and waiting for the rising tide, another dark whim of the sea. But still I had my love of the future, my wounded pride.

"I think I told you, Sonny, that I'm taking Cassandra and Pixie to a gentle island. You won't need to worry about them."

"That's it, that's it, Skipper. These two little ladies are in good hands. Well now. Well, I understand. And I got a gentle island too if I can just find her. Wanders around some, true enough, but she sure is gentle and she sure just about accommodates an old black castaway like me. Oh, just let Sonny crawl up on that gentle shore!" He was nodding, smiling, with his long smoky five-gaited fingers was trying to turn Pixie on his lap, fondling, probing the fingers, gently feeling for the source of her tiny noise, and all the while kept the two great cold black lenses of his pink and white shell-rimmed sunglasses fixed in my direction. Nodding, at last beginning to croon through his nose—tight lips, menacing cheekbones—holding Pixie and shining all his black love into my heart.

But Pixie was crying. She was crying her loudest with tiny pug nose wrinkled, wet, tiny eyes bright and angry, tiny hands in fists, tiny arms swinging in spasms and doll's dress bunched around her middle, and her cry was only the faint turbulence of an insect trapped in a bottle. Amusing. Pitiful. A little bottle of grief like her mother.

"Pixie don't like this separation stuff," crooning, chucking her under the chin with the tip of his long black finger while Cassandra and I leaned forward to see, to hear: "Pixie don't approve of our family busting up this way." And she bent her rubbery knees, kicked, striking on the table the little dirty white calf-skin shoe that was untied, unkempt, forlorn, and then she was suddenly quiet, appeased, and smiled at Sonny and caught his finger as if to bite it to the bone with all the delight and savagery of the tiny child spoiled and underfed—rancid baby bottles, thin chocolate bars—through all her dreary abandoned days in wartime transit.

"That's the sign, folks! Pixie's ready! Time to go!"

I sat still, I flung my face into the smell of the empty glass, Cassandra took up her purse. And then we were in single file and pushing through the crowd of sailors. First Sonny—flight bag, paper bag stuffed with chicken salad sandwiches, Pixie riding high on his shoulders and thumping his cap—and then Cassandra—small, proud, prisoner of lost love, mother of child, barelegged and desirable, in her own way widowed and silvery and slender, walking now through anchors and booze and the anonymous cross-country passion of the Infantry March—and then in the rear myself—more tired than ever, bald, confused, two hundred pounds of old junior-grade naval officer and close to tears. This our dismal procession with Sonny leading the way. "Step aside there, fella, you don't want to tangle with the Chief!" Pixie was blowing kisses to the sailors; Cassandra was wearing her invisible chains, invisible flowers; and I refused to see, to acknowledge the scampering white-slavers, refused to say good-by to all those little Chinese waiters. Then out the door.

Long steel body like a submarine. Giant black recapped tires. Driver— another mean nigger, as Sonny would say—already stiff and silhouetted behind his sheet of glass and wearing his dark slant-eyed driving glasses and his little Air Force style cap crushed and peaked, ready and waiting to take her up, to start the mission. Concrete pillars, iron doors, dollies heaped high with duffel bags, no lights, crowds of sailors, odor of low-lying diesel smoke, little dry blisters of chewing gum under our feet, and noise. Noise of sailors banging on the sides of the bus and singing and vomiting and crying out to their dead buddies. The terminal. Our point of departure. And the tickets were flying and the SP's were ferocious ghosts, leaping in pairs on victim, lunging slyly, swinging hard with the little wet oaken clubs.

So at last we were packed together in rude and shameless embrace and at last we were shouting: "You go on now, Skipper," tall dancer, black cannon mouth, blow in the ribs, weighing me down with child, provisions, canvas bag, "you go on and get you a nice seat. Take your ladies on off to your island—I'm going to be on mine—no unfaithful lovers on my island, Skipper, just me, now you keeps your island the same. Good-by now, and you remember, Skipper, I'm going to lie me down on my island and just look at them pictures and think of you and Pixie and Miss Cassandra. So long!"

"Sonny!" Crying aloud, crying, bumping against him, bumping and trying to shift the wretched child out of our way, then falling against his tall black twisting form—glint of the buttons, bones of a lean steer, glimpse of a fading smile—then throwing myself and managing at last to kiss the two dark cheeks, warm, oddly soft and dry, affectionate long panther paws, kissing and calling out to him: "Good-by, Sonny. *Bon voyage!*" Then we were flowing on a rough stream toward the bus and he was gone. Poor Sonny.

SOLDIERS IN THE DARK

But Sonny was not gone at all. Not yet. The three of us were carried backwards and up into the great dark steel cylinder of our reckless ten-wheeled transport. We joined that monstrous riot for seats—one hundred and three men, a woman, a child, swallowed up for numerous sins and petty crimes into this terrible nonstop belly of ours and fighting hopelessly for breath, for privacy—and were lucky enough to snatch two seats together and to crouch down with flight bag and sandwiches between our legs and my hat askew and the skirt of Cassandra's frock crumpled above her knees. They were slim knees, bare, slender, glistening, disregarded. It was dark, the aisle was heaped high with white duffel bags. And did each of those sagging white canvas shapes represent the dead body of a bantamweight buddy saved from the sea and stowed away in canvas, at last to be lugged or flung aboard Interstate Carrier Number twenty-seven, bound nonstop for the great navy yard of the east? I looked for only a moment at Cassandra's knees and then quickly lifted my granddaughter to the pitch-dark window at my side. Pixie was crying again—insect going berserk in his glass, little fists socking the window—and the sailors were flashing their Zippo lighters and slowly, slowly, we were beginning to move. And then three figures struggled out of the flat gray planes and cumbersome shadows of the concrete, and dashed toward the front of the bus. The tall drunk bosun's mate was waving, Sonny was waving, and between them the moaning sailor was rolling his head, dragging his feet. The tubular door sprang halfway open and, "That's it," helpful, officious, out of breath, "get these fellas inside there . . . that's it!" And then Sonny was alone in the dark and we were backing slowly from the terminal in a wake of oil and compressed air. I pressed my face to the window, against the glass, too tired to make a farewell sign with my hand.

Off to one side, puffing, straightening his coat, Sonny continued to follow us. I saw his imperious arm, saw his slow imperious stride and the long fingers pointing instructions to the driver. Sonny held up his flat hand and we stopped; Sonny began to swing his arm and we started forward, turned, paced his tall backward-stepping shadow—anxious glance over his shoulder, summoning gesture of the long thin arm and flashing cuff—and then he stood aside and waved us on. I smiled, lost him, but even in the blast of the diesel heard what he must have communicated to his mean black brother in the cockpit: "You're OK. Now just keep this thing on the road. . . ."

Then I leaned back heavily and, pain or no pain, shifted Pixie so that she stretched herself flat on my chest and slept immediately. I lay there watching the stars and feeling my hunger grow. The paper bag was between Cassandra's feet, not mine, yet I could see the crushed bulk of it, the waxed paper and wilted lettuce, the stubby wet slices of white meat Sonny had prepared for us on a wobbling card table squeezed into the dirty porcelain lavatory of our cheap hotel. I could taste the white bread—no crusts—I could taste the black market mayonnaise. How many miles behind us now? Five? Ten? The bus was accelerating, was slowly filling with the smell of whisky—thick nectar of lonely travelers—and filled with the sounds of the ukelele, the tuneless instrument of the American fleet, and in her sleep Pixie was sucking her fingers and overhead the stars were awash in the empty black fields of the night. I thought of empty dry docks, empty doorways, empty hotels, empty military camps, thought of him fixing the sandwiches while we slept—pepper, salt, tin spoon and knife—saw him drinking a can of beer on the fantail of the *Starfish* on a humid and windless night. I saw him prostrate on his island of brown flesh, heard the first sounds of returning love.

"Cassandra? Hungry, Cassandra?"

He had diced celery into cubes, had cut olives into tiny green half-moons, had used pimento. Even red pimento. The moonlight came through the window in a steady thin slipstream and in it Cassandra's face was a small luminous profile on a silver coin, the coin unearthed happily from an old ruin and the face expressionless, fixed, the wasted impression of some little long-forgotten queen. I looked at her, as large as I was I wriggled, settled myself still deeper into the journey—oh, the luxury of going limp!—and allowed my broad white knees to fall apart, to droop in their infinite sag, allowed my right arm, the arm that was flung across sleeping Pixie, to grow numb. I was an old child of the moon and lay sprawled on the night, musing and half-exposed in the suspended and public posture of all those night travelers who are without beds, those who sleep on public benches or curl into the corners of out-of-date railway coaches, all those who dream their uncovered dreams and try to sleep on their hands. Suspended. Awake and prone in my seat next to the window, all my body fat, still, spread solid in the curvature of my Greyhound seat. And yet in my back, elbows, neck, calves, buttocks, I felt the very motion of our adventure, the tremors of our cross-country speed. And I felt my hunger, the stomach hunger of the traveling child.

"A little picnic for the two of us, Cassandra?"

She moved—my daughter, my museum piece—and hoisted the sack onto her lap and opened it, the brown paper stained with the mysterious dark oil stains of mayonnaise and tearing, disintegrating beneath her tiny white efficient fingers. Brisk fingers, mushy brown paper sack, food for the journey. She unwrapped a sandwich, for a moment posed with it—delicate woman, ghostly morsel of white bread and meat—then put it into my free hand which was outstretched and waiting. The bread was cold, moist, crushed thin with the imprint of dear Sonny's palm; the lettuce was a wrinkled leaf of soft green skin, the bits of pimento were little gouts of jellied blood, the chicken was smooth, white, curved to the missing bone. I tasted it, sandwich smeared with moonlight, nibbled one wet edge—sweet art of the mess boy—then shoved the whole thing into my dry and smiling mouth and lay there chewing up Sonny's lifetime, swallowing, licking my fingers.

My daughter was safe beside me, Pixie was sleeping on, dreaming the little pink dreams of her spoiled life, my mouth was full, the sailor was moaning. And now the distance threw out the first white skirts of a desert, a patch of poisoned water and a few black rails of abandoned track. I saw the salt mounds, the winding gulch, far off a town—mere sprinkling of dirty mica chips in the desert—and in the pleasure of this destitute world I was eager to see, eager to eat, and reached for another sandwich, stuffed it in. For Sonny.

But then I noticed her folded hands, her silent throat, the sack near empty on her lap, and I stopped in mid-mouthful, paused, swallowed it all down in a spasm: "Cassandra? No appetite, Cassandra?"

She did not answer. She did not even nod. And yet her face was turned my way, her knees tight, elbows tight, on one side not to be touched by thigh of sprawling father, on the other not to be touched by the stenciled name of the seaman whose duffel bag stood as tall as her shoulder and threatened her with reprehensible lumps and concealed designs, and in the thrust and balance of that expression, the minted little lips and nose, the bright nested eye, she made herself clear enough. No appetite. No sensation in a dry stomach. No desire. No orchids sweet enough to taste. Not the sort of woman to eat sandwiches on a bus. At least not the sort of woman who would eat in the dark. Not any more.

But I was alarmed and I persisted: "Join me, Cassandra. Please. Just a bite?"

She waited. Then I heard the firmness of the dreaming voice, the breath control of the determined heart: "My life has been a long blind date with sad unfortunate boys in uniform. With high school boys in uniform. With Fernandez. With you. A long blind date in Schrafft's. A blind date and chicken salad sandwiches in Schrafft's. With little black sweet pickles, Skipper. Horrible sweet pickles. Your sandwiches," the whisper dying out for emphasis, secret, explanatory, defensive, then rising again in the hush of her greatest declamatory effort, "your sandwiches make me think of Gertrude. And Gertrude's dark glasses. And strawberry ice cream sodas. And Gertrude's gin. I can't eat them, Skipper. I can't. You see," now leaning her head back and away, small and serpentine in the moonlight, and watching me with her wary and injured eyes, "nothing comes of a blind date, Skipper. Nothing at all. And," moving her naked fingers, crushing the wax paper into a soft luminous ball, "this is my last blind date. A last blind date for Pixie and me. I know you won't jilt us, Skipper. I know you'll be kind."

I wriggled. I blushed. I took the sandwich. I heard the catgut notes of the ukelele—vision of French letters floating downstream in the moonlight—I heard the black turbine roaring of our diesel engine, beyond this metal and glass heard the high wind filled with thistle and the flat shoe leather bodies of dead prairie rodents. And I was wedged into the night, wedged firmly in my cheerful embarrassment, and chewing, frowning, hoping to keep her feathery voice alive.

Our picnic, our predawn hours together on this speeding bus, our cramped but intricate positions together at the start of this our journey between two distant cemeteries, the nearly physical glow that begins to warm the darkest hour at the end of the night watch—when sleep is only a bright immensity put off as long as possible and a man is filled with a greedy slack desire to recall even his most painful memories—in all the seductive shabbiness of the moment I felt that I knew myself, heart and stomach, as peaceful father of my own beautiful and unpredictable child, and that the disheveled traveler was safe, that both of us were safe. We too would have our candy bars when the sun rose. Sonny had provided the sandwiches but I myself had thought of the candy bars, had slipped them secretly into the flight bag with Cassandra's stockings and Pixie's little fluffy pinafore. We too would have our ar-

rival and departure, our radio broadcast of victory and defeat. In the
darkness the driver sounded his horn—triple-toned trumpet, inane or-
chestrated warning to weak-kneed straying cows and sleeping towns—
and my lips rolled into the loose shape of a thoughtless murmur:
"Happy, Cassandra?"

"I'm sleepy, Skipper. I would like to go to sleep. Will you try?"

I chuckled. And she smoothed down her frock, brushed the empty
paper bag to the floor, pressed her hands together, palms and fingers
straight and touching as the child prays, and without glancing at me
lay her cheek on her clasped hands and shut her eyes. As if she had
toileted, donned her negligee, turned with her face averted and drawn
the shade. Modest Cassandra. While I chuckled again, grimaced, rolled
my head back to the window, grunted under the weight of Pixie—bad
dreams, little pig sounds—then sighed and swung away and dropped to
my army of desperate visions that leapt about in the darkness. But safe.
Sleeping. Outward bound.

But wasn't Cassandra still my teen-age bomb? Wasn't she? Even
though she was a war bride, a mother, a young responsible woman of
twenty-five? At least I thought so when at last I awoke to the desert
sunburst and a giant sea-green grandfather cactus stabbed to death by
its own needles and to the sight of Cassandra begging Pixie to drink
down a little more of the canned milk two days old now and pellucid.
And wasn't this precisely what I loved? That the young-old figure of
my Cassandra—sweet queenly head on an old coin, yet flesh and
blood—did in fact conceal the rounded high-stepping baby fat and
spangles and shoulder-length hair and dimples of the beautiful and
wised-up drum majorette, that little bomb who is all hot dogs and Egyptian beads? Wasn't this also my Cassandra? I thought so and for the
rest of the day the emotions and problems of this intensive fantasy saved
me from the oppressive desert with its raw and bleeding buttes and its
panorama of pastel colors as outrageous and myriad as the colors that
flashed in the suburban kitchen of some gold-star mother. Saved me too
from our acrobatic Pixie who at lunchtime added smears, little doll-
finger tracks and blunt smudges of Nestlé's chocolate to my white naval
breast already so crumpled and so badly stained. Smelling the chocolate,
glancing at the unshapely humps and amputated spines, thorns, of miles
of crippled cacti, I only smiled and told myself that the flesh of the
cheerleader was still embedded in the flesh of Pixie's mother and so
soothed myself with various new visions of this double anatomy, this
schizophrenic flesh. And toward sundown—more chocolate, more

smearing, end of a hot and untalkative and disagreeable day—when I was squinting between my fingers at the last purple upheaval of the pastel riot, I struggled a moment—it was a sudden cold sickening speculation—with the question of which was the greater threat to her life, the recklessness of the teen-age bomb or the demure determination of the green-eyed and diamond-brained young matron who was silvery, small, lovable with bare legs and coronet? It was too soon for me to know. But I would love them both, scrutinize them both, then at the right moment fling myself in the way of the ascendant and destructive image. I was still scowling and loving her, suspecting her, when the desert fireworks suddenly ended and the second night came sweeping up like a dark velvet wind in our faces.

"And we don't even have sandwiches tonight, Cassandra. Not one."

I felt the child's tiny knee in my groin—determined and unerring step—I felt her tiny hand return again and again to tantalize and wound itself against my unwashed cheek, absently I picked at the chocolate that had dried like blood on the old sailcloth or cotton or white drill of my uniform. And finding a plugged-up nipple secreted like a rubber talisman or ill omen in my pocket; watching Cassandra stuff a pair of Pixie's underpants into the flight bag; discovering that between my two white shoes there was another, the foot and naked ankle and scuffed black shoe of some long-legged sailor who had stretched himself out at last—in orgasm? in extreme discomfort?—and seeing Cassandra's face dead white and realizing that finally she had scraped the bottom of the cardboard face powder box which I had saved along with her stockings: all of it reminded me of the waxworks museum we had visited with Sonny, reminded me of a statue of Popeye the Sailor, naked except for his cap and pipe, which we had assumed to be molded of rubber until we read the caption and learned that it was made of eight pounds and five different brands of chewed-up chewing gum, and reminded me too that I could fail and that the teen-age bomb could kill the queen or the queen the bomb. The beginnings of a hot and hungry night.

But I must have lain there musing and grumbling for hours, for several hours at least, before the tire exploded.

"Oh!" came Cassandra's whispered shriek, her call for help, and I pinioned Pixie's rump, I sank down, my knees were heaved into flight, Cassandra was floating, reaching out helplessly for her child. In the next instant the rear half of the bus was off the road and sailing out, I could feel, in a seventy-eight-mile-an-hour dive into the thick of the night. Air brakes in full emergency operation. Accidental blow to the horn followed by ghastly and idiotic trill on the trumpet. Diving rear end of the bus beginning to describe an enormous arc—fluid blind path of greatest destruction—and forward portion lurching, hammering, banging driver's black head against invisible wall. Now, O Christopher . . . and then the crash.

Then: "Be calm, Cassandra," I said, and kept my hold on the agitated Pixie but uncovered my face.

And she, whispering, breathing deeply: "What is it, Skipper? What is it?"

"Blowout," I said, and opened my eyes. We were standing still. We were upright. Somehow we had failed to overturn though I saw her naked legs with the knees caught up to her chin and though everywhere I looked I saw the duffel bags lying like the bodies of white clowns prostrate after a spree of tumbling. And in this abrupt cessation of our sentimental journey, becoming aware of moonlight in the window and of the thin black line of the empty highway stretching away out there, and feeling a heavy deadness in my shoulder—twisted muscles? severed nerves?—I was able to glance at my free hand, to study it, to order flexing of my numerous and isolated fingers. I watched them. One by one they wiggled. Bones OK.

"Are you all right, Cassandra? Can you move your toes?"

"Yes, Skipper. But give Pixie to her mother, please."

So we disembarked. We joined the slow white procession of hatless sailors. In the dark and among the angular seventeen-year-olds with ties askew and tops askew, among all the boys red-eyed and damp from cat-napping and too baffled, too bruised to talk, we felt our way up the canted aisle until we reached the listing door, the puckered aluminum steps, the open night. I took her in my arms and swung her down, and out there we stood together, close together, frock and uniform both body-tight in the wind, ankles twisting and shoes filling with sand. The bus was a dark blue dusty shadow, deceptive wreck; our skid-marks were long black treacherous curves in the desert; the highway was a dead snake in the distance; the wind was strong. We stood there with the unfamiliar desert beneath our feet, stood with our heads thrown back to the open night sky which was filled with the tiny brief threads of performing meteors.

The wind. The hot wind. Out there it warmed the skin but chilled the flesh, left the body cold, and though we lifted our faces like startled sun-tanned travelers, we were shivering in that endless night and in the wind that set the long dry cactus needles scraping and made a rasping noise of all the debris of the desert: tiny cellular spines, dead beetles, the discarded translucent tissue of wandering snakes, the offal of embryonic lizards and fields of dead dry locusts. All this rasping and humming; all the night listening; and underfoot all the smooth pebbles knocking together in the hot-cold night. And she, Cassandra, stood there swaying and clasping Pixie awkwardly against her breast, swaying and trying to catch her breath behind Pixie's head; and the pale little fissure of Cassandra's mouth, the pale wind-chapped tissue of the tiny lips made me think of cold kisses and of goose flesh and of a thin dust of salt and of lipstick smeared helplessly on the white cheek. I took her elbow; I put a hand on her back and steadied her; I was surprised to feel the broad band of muscle trembling in her back; I thought of the two of us alone with a hundred and one sailors cut down and left for dead by a pack of roving and mindless Mexicans. Then in our roller-skating stance—hand to elbow, hand to waist—we began to move together, to stagger together in the moonlight, and over my shoulder and flung to either side of the harsh black visible track of our flight from the road I saw the prostrate silhouettes of a dozen fat giant cacti that had been struck head on by the bus and sent sailing. For a moment I saw them, these bloated shapes of scattered tackling dummies that marked the long wild curve of our reckless detour into the dark and milky night. Abandoned. As we were abandoned.

And then the lee of the bus. Clumps of squatting white shivering sailors. A pea jacket for Pixie. Another pea jacket for Cassandra. A taste of whisky for me. Little pharmacist mates clever in first aid and rushing to the sounds of chattering teeth or tidelands obscenity. While the black-faced driver hauls out his hydraulic jack and drags it toward the mutilated tire which has come to rest in a natural rock garden of crimson desert flowers and tiny bulbs and a tangle of prickly parasitic leaves. All crushed to a pulp. Mere pustules beneath that ruined tire.

It was the dead center of some nightmare accident but here at least, crouching and squatting together in the lee of the bus, there was no wind. Only the empty windows, shadows, scorched paint of the crippled monster. Only the flare burning where we had left the road and now the scent of a lone cigarette, the flick of a match, the flash of a slick comb through bay rum and black waves of hair, persistent disappointed sounds of the ukelele—devilish hinting for a community sing—only the cooling sand of the high embankment against which Cassandra and Pixie and I huddled while the sailors grew restless and the driver— puttees, goggles, snappy cap and movements of ex-fighter-pilot, fierce

nigger carefully trained by the Greyhound line—bustled about the enormous sulphuric round of the tire. Refusing assistance, removing peak-
shouldered military jacket, retaining cap, strutting in riding britches,
fingering the jack, clucking at long rubber ribbons of the burst tire:
"Why don't you fellows sing a little and pass the time?" But only more
performing meteors and this hell's nigger greasing both arms and whistling, tossing high into the air his bright wrenches. In the middle of the
desert only this American nigger changing a tire, winning the war.

I unlaced my dirty white buckskin shoes and emptied them. I glanced
at Cassandra. I glanced at Pixie who, even though cloaked in her pea
jacket, was beginning to play in the sand; I tried to smile but the driver
cavorting in the moonlight dispirited me and I wondered where we were
and what had become of poor dear Sonny. I hooked one foot onto the
opposite knee, gripped the ankle, brushed the sand from the sole of my
white sock, repeated the process. I glanced again at the night sky—
unmoved by celestial side show—and for some reason, scowling into
the salt and pepper stars, gritting my teeth at that silent chaos, the
myriad motes of the unconsciousness, I found myself thinking of Tremlow, once more saw him as he looked when he bore down upon me
during the height of the *Starfish* mutiny. Again I lived the moment of
my degradation. Then just as suddenly I was spared the sight of it all.

Because I had heard a sound. Cassandra's sleeping head lay in my
lap—high upturned navy blue collar of the pea jacket revealing only
the briefest profile of her worn and lovely little death-mask face—because I was awake and had heard a sound and recognized it. And
because suddenly that impossible sound established place, established
the hour, explained the tangled bright loops of barbed wire that apparently ran for miles atop the steep rise of our protective sand embankment. I listened, gently pressed the rough collar to her cheek, shivered
as I understood suddenly that the wire was not for Indians, not to im-
prison cows. Listened. And still the impossible sound came to me over
the wastes and distant reaches of the blue desert.

Bugle. This mournful barely audible precision of the instrument held
rigidly in only a single hand. An Army bugle. Taps. Across the desert
the faint and stately and ludicrous sound of taps. Insane song of the
forties. And slow, precise, each silvery dim note dragged all the way to
the next, the various notes weaving and wafting the sentimental mes-
sages into the night air. End of the day—who's listening? who?—and
of course lights out. But I listened to the far-away musical moon-
howling of that benediction into a dusty P.A. system built on the sands,

with a few stomach convulsions heard the final drawn-out bars of that impersonal cinematic burial song meant for me, for every bald-headed indoctrinated man my age. Taps for another bad dream. Brass bugle blown in the desert, a little spit shaken out on the bugler's sleeve.

So I knew that it was eleven o'clock of a hot-cold desert night and that we had come to stop not in the middle of nowhere but at the edge of some sort of military reservation—cavalry post of black horses that would explain the odor of dung on the wind? basic training camp with tequila in the PX and live ammunition on maneuvers? naval boot camp for special instruction in flying the blimp and dirigible?—and knew that whatever I had to guard Cassandra against it was not the Mexicans.

But now I was awake, alert, ready for anything. Hunching over my own daughter and my own granddaughter—outlandish bundles of pea jackets, flesh of my flesh—I became the solitary sentry with quick eyes for every shadow and a mass of moonlit veins scurrying across my naked scalp like worms. Fear and preparedness. Aching joints. Lap beginning to complain. But on the tail of the bugle and also miles away, several unmistakable bursts from a rapid-fire weapon. And I looked for a glow in the sky and tried to imagine the targets—cardboard silhouettes of men? gophers? antiquated armored vehicles?—and I listened and wondered when they would begin to shoot in our direction. Army camp, disabled bus, poor nomad strangers wandering through days and nights and hours that could be located on any cheap drugstore calendar: I took a deep breath, I stiffened my heavy jaw, I waited. In anger I heard a few more snorts of machine gun fire, in anger I nodded once more at the image of Tremlow the mutineer, in anger snapped myself awake.

"Cassandra," whispering, leaning close to her, lifting enormous collar away from her ear, touching the cold cheek, sweating and whispering, "wake up, Cassandra. We've got company. . . ."

Her open eyes, her rigid face and body, the quiver in the breasts and hips, and the outstretched rumpled figure was suddenly alert, half sitting up. And then she had thrust Pixie away, had hidden Pixie in a shadow on the sand. And then side by side Cassandra and I were kneeling together on our hands and knees, waiting with heads raised and red-rimmed eyes fixed on the barbed wire barricade directly above us.

"Men traveling on their bellies," I whispered. "Three of them. Crawling up the embankment to reconnoiter!" We heard the swishing sound of men pressed flat to the desert and, like children making angels in snow, swimming up the steep embankment through loose sand and

pebbles and low-lying dried and prickling vines. We heard their con-
centrated breathing and the tinkling sound of equipment. I recognized
the flat fall of carbine with each swing of invisible arm, recognized the
uneven sound of a bayonet drumming on empty canteen with each dragging motion of invisible haunch. Then a grunt. Then squeal and scurry
of little desert animal diving for cover. Then silence.

And then the heads. Three black silhouettes of helmeted heads suddenly there behind the wire where before there had been only the barbs,
the loops, the tight strands and the velvet space and salt and pepper
heavens of the whole night sky. But now the heads. All at once the three
of them in a row. Unmoving. Pop-ups in a shooting gallery.

And as Cassandra and I knelt side by side in the sand, stiff and
exposed and red-eyed in our animal positions, together and quiet but
vulnerable, the three heads began to move in unison, turned slowly,
imperceptibly, to the right and then to the left, in unison scanning the
horizon and measuring the potential of the scene before them. The tops
of the heavy helmets and the tips of the chin cups reflected the moon;
in the sharp little faces the eyes were white. Soldiers. Raiders. Pleased
with the scene. Their whispers were high, dry, choked with sand.

"Lucky, lucky, lucky! Ain't that a sweet sight?"

"Navy to the rescue!"

"Free ride on a Greyhound bus!"

The three of them looked straight ahead—intuitively I knew the
driver was still throwing his wrenches into the air, still trying to boss
the tire into place, and I groaned—and then in slow motion they began
to shift. The heads sank down until the men were only turtle shells and
hardly visible on the embankment; the muzzles of two carbines popped
into view; the man in the center raised his helmeted head and his white
hand and a pair of wire cutters, slipped and tugged and twisted while
the wire sang past his face and curled into tight thorny balls. Until they
could crawl through. Until they were free.

And then with heads down, shoulders down, rifles balanced horizon-
tally in their hanging hands, they swung in a silent dark green trio over
the embankment and down, down, like baseball players hitting the sand
and landing not on top of Cassandra and myself but in front of us and
to either side. Three sand geysers and Cassandra and I were trapped.

"Company C," panting, whispering, "Company C for Cain," panting
and aiming his gun and whispering, "Don't you make a peep, you hear?
Either one of you!"

Three small soldiers in full battle pack and sprawled in the sand, gasping, leaning on their elbows, cradling the carbines, staring us down with their white eyes. Web belts and straps, brass buckles, cactus-green fatigue uniforms—name tags ripped off the pockets—paratrooper boots dark brown with oil; they lay there like three deadly lizards waiting to strike, and all of their vicious, yet somehow timorous, white eyes began blinking at once. The middle soldier, the leader, wore a coal-black fingernail mustache and carried his bayonet fixed in place on the end of his carbine. All little tight tendons and daggers and hand grenades and flashing bright points and lizard eyes. Unscrupulous. Disguised in soot. Not to be trusted in a charge.

"Company C for Cain, like I said. But we been in that place for twenty-eight weeks and now we're AWOL. The three of us here are called the Kissin' Bandits and we're AWOL. Understand?"

And the smallest, young and innocent except for his big broken Brooklyn nose—my ghetto Pinocchio—and except for the foam which he kept licking from the corners of his mouth and swallowing, the smallest twitching there in the sand and prodding each word with his carbine and with his nose: "So on your feet, on your feet. No talking, and don't forget the kid."

Slowly, laboriously, indignantly I stood up, helped Cassandra, brushed the seat of my trousers, jerked the creases out of my uniform as best I could, indifferently picked off the cactus burrs, and took little Pixie into my arms.

They marched us to the cactus, in single file herded us thirty or forty feet into the shadow of that old fat prickly man of the desert and out of sight of the bus, the leader at the head of the column and swinging the carbine, slouching along lightly in the lazy walk of the infantryman saving himself, feeling his way with his feet, straggling all the distance of his night patrol—easy gait, eyes down watching for the enemy, back and shoulders loose and buttocks hard, fierce, inseparable, complementary, all his walking done with the buttocks alone—and in the middle Cassandra and myself and Pixie, and in the rear the tinkling dragging sounds of the boys with their cocked carbines and darting tongues and eyes. Raiders. Captives. Firing squad with the cactus for a blank wall.

"Now get rid of your eggs," said the one with the glistening mustache. "Dig your holes deep and bury them."

And there in the safety and shadow of the giant ruptured cactus, while Cassandra and I stood side by side and held hands under cover of her pea jacket, there and in unison the three of them unhooked their rows of dangling hand grenades, helped each other out of their packs and harnesses, freed each other of webbing and canteens and canvas pouches—watching us, watching us all the while—and then with unsheathed and flashing trench knives or bayonets held point down they squatted, dug their three black holes until at last they flung themselves back once more into sitting position and unfastened their boots, unbuttoned their green fatigues and then standing, facing us, watching us, suddenly stripped them off.

So the naked soldiers. White shoulder blades, white arms, white shanks, white strips of skin, white flesh, and in the loins and between the ribs and on the inside of the legs soft shadow. But white and thin and half-starved and glistening like watery sardines hacked from a tin. Naked. Still wearing their steel helmets, chin straps still dangling in unison, and still holding the carbines at ready arms. But otherwise naked. And now they were lined up in front of Cassandra, patiently and in close file, while I stood there trembling, smiling, sweating, squeezing her hand, squeezing Cassandra's hand for dear life and in all my protective reassurance and slack alarm.

"Leader's last," came the unhurried voice, "Baby Face goes first."

Lined up by height, by age and height, and each one nudging the next and shuffling, grinning, each one ready to have his turn, all set to go, and one of them hanging back.

"Drag ass, Bud . . . and make it count!"

His round young head was sweating inside the steel helmet, his freckled breast was heaving. I squeezed her hand—be brave, be brave—but Cassandra was only a silvery blue Madonna in the desert, only a woman dressed in the outlandish ill-fitting pea jacket of an anonymous sailor and in a worn frock belonging to tea tray, flowers and some forgotten summer house covered with vines. And in her hand there was no response, nothing. And yet her green eyes were searching him and waiting.

Then he leaned forward, eyes slowly sinking out of focus, tears bright on his cheeks, moon-face growing rounder and rounder under its rim of steel, and caught her behind the neck with a rough childish hand and drove his round and running and fluted mouth against the pale line of her lips. And sucked once, gulped once, gave her one chubby kiss, backed away step by step until suddenly Pinocchio made a wrenching clawlike gesture and threw him aside.

And Pinocchio's kiss: foam, foam, foam! On Cassandra's lips. Down the front of her frock. Snuffling action of the Brooklyn nose. But he couldn't fool Skipper, couldn't fool old Papa Cue Ball. So I squeezed again—brave? brave, Cassandra?—and felt what I thought was a tremor of irritation, small sign of impatience in her cold hand.

And then the third and last, the tallest, and the helmet tilting rakishly, the lips pulsing over the front teeth in silent appeal, the bare arm sliding inside the pea jacket and around her waist, and now the cumbersome jacket beginning to fall, to fall away, and now Cassandra's head beginning to yield, it seemed to me, as I felt her little hand leave mine and saw her returning his kiss—white shoe slightly raised behind her, pale mouth touching, asking some question of the slick black fingernail of hair on his upper lip—and saw my Cassandra raise a finger to his naked underdeveloped chest and heard her, distinctly heard her, whispering into all the shadowed cavities of that thin grisly chest: "Give me your gun, please," hanging her head, whispering, finger tracing meditative circles through the hair on his chest, "please show me how to work your gun. . . ."

But he was gone. All three were gone. They had whirled each to his hole, had flung in boots, carbines, helmets and fatigues, and had refilled the holes. Done with their separate burials they had fled from us in the direction of the unsuspecting sailors and the waiting bus, had run off with their stolen kisses and their crafty plans for travel. At the bus they used judo and guerrilla tactics on the bosun's mate, the moaning sailor and the noxious driver, and dressed like sailors they lost themselves in a busload of young sailors.

I turned and held out my free arm: "Cassandra, Cassandra!" I beckoned her with my fingers, with my whole curving arm, beckoned and wanted to tell her what a bad brush we had had with them, and that they were gone and we were safe at last. And she must have read my smile and my thoughts, I think, because she drew the pea jacket into place once more, thrust her hands carefully into the pockets, glanced soberly across the waste of the desert. And then she looked at me and slowly, calmly, whispered, "Nobody wants to kiss you, Skipper."

From that time forward our driver was dead white and licked a little patch of untweezered mustache all the while he drove. And so we recommenced our non-stop journey, rode with a fine strong tail wind until at last we reached our midnight (Eastern War Time) destination, found ourselves at last on the fourteenth floor of another cheap hotel. Here we stayed two days. Here I lived through my final shore patrol. And here I found Fernandez in this wartime capital of the world.

Be brave! Be brave!

THE ARTIFICIAL INSEMINATOR

AND NOW? And now?

And now the wind and the hammock which I so rarely use. For it is time now to recall that sad little prophetic passage from my schoolboy's copybook with its boyish valor and its antiquity, and to admit that the task of memory has only brightened these few brave words, and to confess that even before my father's suicide and my mother's death I always knew myself destined for this particular journey, always knew this speech to be the one I would deliver from an empty promontory or in an empty grove and to no audience, since of course history is a dream already dreamt and destroyed. But now the passage, the speech with its boyish cadences, flavor of morality, its soberness and trust. Here it is, the declaration of faith which I say aloud to myself when I pause and prop my feet on the window sill where the hummingbird is destroying his little body and heart and eye among the bright vines and sticky flowers and leaves: *I have soon to journey to a lonely island in a distant part of my kingdom. But I shall return before the winter storms begin. Prince Paris, I leave my wife, Helen, in your care. Guard her well. See that no harm befalls her.* My confession? My declaration of heart and faith? "I have soon to journey to a lonely island . . . guard her well. . . ." Monstrous small voice. Rhetorical gem. And yet it is the sum of my naked history, this statement by a man of fancy, this impassioned statement of a man of courage. I might have known from the copybook what I was destined for.

Because here, now, the wind is a bundle of invisible snakes and the hammock, when empty, is a tangled net-like affair of white hemp always filled with fresh-cut buds, only the buds, of moist and waxen flowers. Because it is time to say that it is Catalina Kate who keeps the hammock filled with flowers for me, who keeps it a swaying bright bed of petals just for me, and that Catalina Kate is fully aware that there must be no thorns among the flowers in the hammock.

But the wind, this bundle of invisible snakes, roars across our wandering island—it *is* a wandering island, of course, unlocated in space and quite out of time—and seems to heap the shoulders with an armlike weight, to coil about my naked legs and pulse and cool and caress the flesh with an unpredictable weight and consistency, tension, of its own. These snakes that fly in the wind are as large around as tree trunks; but pliant, as everlastingly pliant, as the serpents that crowd my dreams. So the wind nests itself and bundles itself across this island, buffets the body with wedges of invisible but still sensual configurations. It drives, drives, and even when it drops down, fades, dies, it continues its gentle rubbing against the skin. Here the wind is both hotter and colder than that wind Cassandra and I experienced on our ill-fated trip across the southwestern wartime desert of the United States, hotter and colder and more persistent, more soft or more strong and indecent, in its touch. Cassandra is gone but I am wrapped in wind, walk always—from the hips, from the hips—through the thick entangled currents of this serpentine wind.

Now I have Catalina Kate instead. And this—Sonny and I both agree—this is love. Here I have only to drop my trousers—no shirt, no undershirt, no shorts—to awaken paradise itself, awaken it with the sympathetic sound of Catalina Kate's soft laughter. And it makes no difference at all. Because I am seven years away from Miranda, seven years from that first island—black, wet, snow-swept in a deep relentless sea—and seven years from Cassandra's death and, thanks to the wind, the gold, the women and Sonny and my new profession, am more in love than ever. Until now the cemetery has been my battleground. But no more. Perhaps even my father, the dead mortician, would be proud of me.

No shirt, no undershirt, no shorts. And from my uniform only the cap remains, and it is crushed and frayed and the eagle is tarnished and the white cloth of the crown has faded away to yellow like the timeworn silk of a bridal gown. But it is still my naval cap, despite the cracks and mildew in the visor and the cockroaches that I find hiding in the sweatband. Still my cap. And I am still in possession of my tennis shoes, my old white sneakers with the rubber soles worn thin and without laces. Some days I walk very far in them. In the wind and on the business of my new profession.

And the work itself? Artificial insemination. Cows. In my flapping tennis shoes and naval cap and long puffy sun-bleached trousers, and accompanied by my assistant, Sonny, I am much esteemed as the man who inseminates the cows and causes these enormous soft animals to bring forth calves. Children and old people crowd around to see Sonny and me in action. And I am brown from walking to the cows in the sun, so brown that the green name tattooed on my breast has all but disappeared in a tangle of hair and in my darkening skin. An appealing sort of work, a happy life. The mere lowing of a herd, you see, has become my triumph.

Yes, my triumph now. And how different from my morbid father's. And haven't I redeemed his profession, his occupation, with my own? I think so. But here, now, this morning, with the broad white window sill full in my view—it is old, thickly painted, cool, something like the bleached bulwark of a ransacked sailing ship—and with the lime tree gleaming beyond the window frame and dangling under every leaf a small ripe lime, here with the hammock a swaying garden in the darkness behind me and the wind stirring my papers, stirring my old naval cap where it hangs from an upright of a nearby black mahogany chair, here I mention my triumph, here reveal myself and choose to step from behind the scenes of my naked history, resorting to this strategy from need but also with a certain obvious pride, self-satisfaction, since now I anticipate prolonged consideration of Miranda. I would be unable to think of her for very long unless I made it clear that my triumph is over Miranda most of all, and that I survive her into this very moment when I float timelessly in my baby-blue sea and lick the little yellow candied limes of my bright green tree. Seven years are none too many when it comes to Miranda, or comes, for that matter, to remembering the death of Cassandra or my final glimpse of Pixie when I left her with Gertrude's cousin in New Jersey. So now I gather around me the evidence, the proof, the exhilarating images of my present life. And now Miranda will never know how many slick frisky calves have been conceived in her name or, on her scum-washed black island in the Atlantic, will never know what a voracious and contented adversary I have become out on mine, on this my sun-dipped wandering island in a vast baby-blue and coral-colored sea. But Catalina Kate, I think, is my best evidence. And having summoned my evidence and stated my position, sensitive to the wind, to the green and golden contours of a country reflected in the trembling and in the fullness of my own hips, sensitive also to the time of cows, I can afford to recount even the smallest buried detail of my life with Miranda. Because I know and have stated here, that behind every frozen episode of that other island—and I am convinced that in its way it too was enchanted, no matter the rocks and salt and fixed position in the cold black waters of the Atlantic—there lies the golden wheel of my hot sun; behind every black rock a tropical rose and behind every cruel wind-driven snowstorm a filmy sheet, a transparency, of golden fleas. No matter how stark the scene, no matter how black the gale or sinister the violence of Miranda, still the light of my triumph must shine through. And behind the interminable dead clanking of some salt- and seaweed-encrusted three-ton bell buoy should be heard the soft outdoor lowing of this island's cows, our gigantic cows with moody harlequin faces and rumps like enormous upturned wooden packing crates.

But the evidence. Earlier this morning she appeared outside my window—Catalina Kate accompanied by little Sister Josie, who attends all our births and who remains faithful to some order that has long since departed our wandering island—appeared outside my window to tell me she was three months gone with child and to give us, Sonny and myself, a present with which to celebrate the happy news, a pound of American hot dogs wrapped up in a moldy and dog-eared sheet of soggy newspaper. Catalina Kate's own child! Her charcoal eyes, her hair plaited in a single braid as thick as my wrist and hanging over one lovely breast; her skin some subtle tincture of eggplant and pink rose, one hand already curved and resting on her belly where it will stay until labor commences, the other hand outstretched with her gift of hot dogs; here this girl, this mauve puff of powder who still retains her aboriginal sweaty armpits and lice eggs in the pores of her bare dusty feet, here this Catalina Kate and beside her the little black-faced nun who vicariously shares the joys of pregnancy and who smiles and who, despite her own youth and her little heavy robes of the order, reveals suddenly a splendid big mouthful of golden teeth. So the two of them stood there, flesh and innocence, until we had expressed our pleasure and Sonny had accepted the package of hot dogs—USA.—on behalf of both of us and I had completed their ritual, their girlish game, by reaching out the window where they stood in the deep sun and lime fragrance and with my fingertips gently touched her where she assured me the treasured life lay growing.

So in six months and on the Night of All Saints Catalina Kate will bear her child—our child—and I shall complete my history, my evocation through a golden glass, my hymn to the invisible changing serpents of the wind, complete this the confession of my triumph, this my diary of an artificial inseminator. At the very moment Catalina Kate comes due my crabbed handwriting shall explode into a concluding flourish, and I will be satisfied. I will be fifty-nine years old and father to innumerable bright living dreams and vanquished memories. It should be clear that I have triumphed over Cassandra too, since there are many people who wish nothing more than to kiss me when the midday heat occasionally sends me to the hammock or when the moon is full, stealing, gliding into the warmth and stillness of Plantation House, or in long silvery lines following me to the edge of a moonlit sea. For a kiss. For a shadowy kiss from me.

I receive the sweet ghostly touch of their lips, I kiss them in return. I stand glancing out over that endless ripple of ocean where we have wandered and will continue to wander, softly I call out a name—Sonny! Catalina Kate!—and watch the endless ribbon of our ocean road and smile. I hear the moving shadows and hear those long-lost words— "I have soon to journey to a lonely island in a distant part of my kingdom"—and I can only smile.

Poor Prince Paris.

THE GENTLE ISLAND

AND SO, fresh from the wartime capital of the world, we became her unwitting lodgers, Cassandra and I, Cassandra with her pretended mothering of Pixie, I with my recent and terrifying secret knowledge about Fernandez. Already the fall winds were gathering and every morning from my bedroom window I watched a single hungry bird hang itself on the wet rising wind and, battered and crescent-shaped and angry, submit itself endlessly to the first raw gloom of day in the hopes of spying from on high some flash of food in the dirty undulating trough of a wave. And every morning I stood blowing on my fingers and watching the torn and ragged bird until it flapped away on the ragged wings of its discouragement, blowing, shivering, smiling to think that here even the birds were mere prowlers in the mist and wind, mere vagrants in the empty back lots of that low sky.

Briefly then our new home. White clapboard house, peeling paint, abandoned wasp's nest under the eaves, loose shingles, fungus-like green sludge scattered across the roof. Widow's house, needy but respectable. In front a veranda—the old green settee filled with mice, heap of rotted canvas and rusted springs—and a naked chestnut tree with incurable disease and also two fat black Labrador retrievers chained to a little peeling kennel. Protection for the poor widow, culprits who heaped the bare front yard with the black fingers of their manure. And in the rear the widow's little untended victory garden—a few dead vines, a few small humps in the frost—and, barely upright and half-leaning against a weed-grown shed, the long-abandoned wreck of a hot rod—orange, blue, white, no tires, no glass in the windows, big number five on the crumpled hood—the kind of hopeless incongruity to be found behind the houses of young island widows. Our new home then, and with its cracked masonry, warped beams, sway-backed floors and tiny old fusty fireplaces packed with the rank odor of urine and white ash, it was just as I had dreamed it, was exactly as I had seen it and even smelled and tasted it during all my exotic hot nights at sea when I suffered each separate moment of my personal contribution to the obscene annals of naval history. This house then, and every bit the old freezing white skeleton I had been hoping for. So on my rickety pine bureau I propped my photograph of the U.S.S. *Starfish* and flung the flight bag in the bottom drawer and hung my uniform in the closet which contained three little seagoing chests made of bone and brass and dried-out cracked turkey skin. Propped up the picture, hung away the spotted uniform, admired the way I looked in a black and white checked shirt and dark blue thick woolen trousers. Ready for gales, ready for black rocks. Everything in order and as I had expected, even to the identical white bowls and pitchers and washstands in Cassandra's room and mine, even to the marble sink, lion claws on the tub and long metal flush chain in the john. Of course I could not have anticipated the black brassiere that dangled as large and stark as an albatross from the tin shower curtain pole. I stared at it a long moment—this first sign of the enemy—and then shut the old heavily varnished ill-fitting door. There was a tap leaking on the other side.

Of all those mornings, darkening, growing colder, dragging us down to winter, I remember most clearly our first in the widow's house, because that was the dawn of my first encounter with Miranda. Dead brown rotten world, heartless dawn. Innocence and distraction at half past five in the morning.

I awoke in my strange bed in my strange room in the old white worm-eaten house and heard Pixie crying her fierce little nearly inaudible cry and looked about me at the bare sprawling shadows of monastic antiquity and shuddered, smiled, felt my cold hands and my cold feet crawling between the camphor-ridden sheets. It was still dark, as black as the somber mood of some Lutheran hymn, the flat pillow was filled with horsehair and the blanket against my cheek was of the thin faded stuff with which they drape old ladies' shoulders in this cold country. And the wind, the black wind was rising off the iron flanks of the Atlantic and driving its burden of frozen spray through the abandoned fields of frost, across the green jetties, over the gray roofs of collapsing barns, driving its weight and hoary spray between the little stunted apple trees that bordered the widow's house and smashing the last of the dead apples against my side of the house. From somewhere nearby I could hear the tongue swinging about tonelessly in the bell hung up in the steeple of the Lutheran church, and the oval mirror was swaying on my wall, the gulls were groaning above me and Pixie was still awake and crying.

Stiff new black and white checked shirt of the lumberjack, dark blue woolen trousers—heavy, warm, woven of tiny silken hairs—my white navy shoes. I fumbled in the darkness and for a moment stood at my front bedroom window—silhouettes of bending and suffering larch trees, in the distance white caps of hectic needlepoint—for a moment stood at my rear window and watched the high weeds beating against the screaming shadow of the hot rod. And then I felt my way down to the cold kitchen and fixed a day's supply of baby bottles of milk for poor Pixie.

A lone fat shivering prowler in that whitewashed kitchen, I lit the wood in the stove and found the baby bottles standing in a row like little lighthouses where Cassandra had hastily stood them on the thick blond pine kitchen table the night before, found them standing between an antique coffee grinder—silver-plated handle, black beans in the drawer—and a photography magazine tossed open to a glossy full-page picture of a naked woman. It was five forty-five by Miranda's old tin clock and noiselessly, listening to the stove, the black wind, the clatter of the apples against the window, I took the bottles to the aluminum sink, primed the old farmhouse pump—yellow iron belly and slack iron idiot lip—discovered a pot in a cupboard along with a case, a full case, of Old Grand Dad whiskey, and filled the pot and set it on the stove. Then I plucked the nipples from the bottles and washed the bottles, washed the nipples—sweet scummy rubber and pinprick holes that shot fine thin streams of artesian well water into the sink under the pressure of my raw cold thumb—punched two slits in a tin can of evaporated milk—slip of the opener, blood running in the stream of the pump, fingers holding tight to the wrist and teeth catching and holding a corner of loose lip, grimacing and shaking away the blood—and as large as I was ran noiselessly back and forth between the sink and stove until the milk for Pixie's little curdling stomach was safely bottled and the bottles were lined up white and rattling in the widow's rectangular snowy refrigerator. I wiped the table, wiped out the sink, dried and put away the pot, returned the cursed opener to its place among bright knives and glass swizzle sticks, paused for a quick look at a photograph of a young white-faced soldier hung on the wall next to half a dozen old-fashioned hot plate holders. The photograph was signed "Don" and the thin face was so young and white that I knew even from the photograph itself that Don was dead. Squeezing my fingers I tiptoed back upstairs, leaned in the doorway and smiled at Cassandra's outstretched neatly blanketed body and at her clothes bundled on a spindly ladderback rocking chair that faintly moved in the wind. I leaned and smiled, sucked the finger. Pixie had fallen back to sleep, of course, in the hooded dark wooden cradle that sat on the cold floor at the foot of Cassandra's little four-poster bed.

And so I was awake, dressed, was free in this sleeping house and had forgotten the signs—the black brassiere, the naked woman, the full case of Old Grand Dad—and I could think of nothing but the wind and the shore and a set of black oilskins, cracked sou'wester and long black coat, which I had seen in an entryway off the kitchen. Back down I went to the kitchen and yanked open the door, dressed myself swiftly in the sardine captain's outfit and was shocked to find a lipstick in the pocket. Carefully I let myself out into the first white smears and streaks of that approaching day.

I tried to catch my breath, I socked my hands into the rising and flapping skirts of the coat, I smiled in a sudden flurry of little tears like diamonds, thinking of Cassandra safe through winter days and of a game of Mah Jongg through all the winter nights, and put down my head and made off for the distinct sound of crashing water. From the very first I walked with my light and swinging step and my chin high, walked away from the house ready to meet all my island world, walked actually with a bounce despite the wind, the crazy interference of the black rubber coat, the weight of my poor cold slobbering white navy shoes drenched in a crunchy puddle which I failed to see behind the kennel of the sleeping Labradors. The larch trees with their broken backs, the enormous black sky streaked with fistfuls of congealed fat, the abandoned Poor House that looked like a barn, the great brown dripping box of the Lutheran church bereft of sour souls, bereft of the hymn singers with poke bonnets and sunken and accusing horse faces and dreary choruses, a few weather-beaten cottages unlighted and tight to the dawn and filled, I could see at a glance, with the marvelous dry morality of calico and beans and lard, and then a privy, a blackened pile of tin cans, and even a rooster, a single live rooster strutting in a patch of weeds and losing his broken feathers, clutching his wattles, every moment or two trying to crow into the wind, trying to grub up the head of a worm with one of his snubbed-off claws, cankerous little bloodshot rooster pecking away at the dawn in the empty yard of some dead fisherman. . . . Oh, it was all spread before me and all mine, this strange island of bitter wind and blighted blueberries and empty nests.

I took deep breaths, battling the stupid coat, and I swung down a path of wet nettles, breathed it all in. Breathed in the salt, the scent of frozen weeds, the briny female odor of ripe periwinkles, the stench from the heads of blue-eyed decapitated fish. And the pine trees. The pine trees were bleeding, freely giving off that rich green fragrance which as a child I had but faintly smelled in the mortuary on Christmas mornings. Just ahead of me, just beyond the growths of crippled pine and still in darkness lay the shore, the erupted coast, and suddenly I the only-born, the happy stranger, the one man awake and walking this pitch-black seminal dawn—suddenly I wanted to fling out my arms and sweep together secret cove and Crooked Finger Rock and family burial mounds of poor fishermen, sweep it all together and give it life, my life. Pitching through brier patches, laughing and stumbling under the dripping pines, I hurried on.

And wet, rubbery, exuberant, I emerged into a clearing and stopped short, opened my eyes wide. I saw only a listing handmade jetty and a fisherman's hut with boarded-up windows, a staved-in dory and a tin chimney that gave off a thin stream of smoke. But beside the dory—gray ribs, rusted oarlock—there was a boy's bicycle propped upside down with its front wheel missing and a clot of black seaweed caught in the sprocket. And though there were days and days to pass before I met the boy—his name was Bub—and met also his fishing father and no-good brother—Captain Red and Jomo—still I felt that I knew the place and had seen that bicycle racing in my own dreams. I could only stop and stare at the useless bicycle and at two squat gasoline pumps pimpled with the droppings of departed gulls and wet with the cold mist, those two pumps once bearing the insignia of some mainland oil company but standing now before the hut and sagging jetty as ludicrous signs of the bold and careless enterprise of that outpost beside the sea. I knew intuitively that I had stumbled upon the crafty makeshift world of another widower. But how could I know that Captain Red's boat, the *Peter Poor*, lay invisible and waiting only fifty yards from shore in its dark anchorage? How could I know that we, Cassandra and I, would sail away for our sickening afternoon on that very boat, the *Peter Poor*, how know about the violence of that sea or about the old man's naked passion? But if I had known, if I had seen it all in my glimpse of Jomo's pumps and Bub's useless bicycle and the old man's smoke, would I have faltered, turned back, fled in some other direction? No. I think not. Surely I would have been too proud, too innocent, too trusting to turn back in another direction.

So I was careful to make no noise, careful not to disturb this first intact and impoverished and somehow illicit vision of the widower's overgrown outstation in the collapsing dawn, and staring at bleached slabs of porous wood and rusted nailheads I restrained my impulse to cup hands against the wind and cry out a cheery hello. And I merely waved to no one at all, expecting no wave in return, and gathered my rubber skirts and swept down the path to the beach.

Overhead the dawn was beginning to possess the sky, squadrons of gray geese lumbered through the blackness, and I was walking on pebbles, balancing and rolling forward on the ocean's cast-up marbles, or wet and cold was struggling across stray balustrades of shale. At my shoulder was the hump of the shore itself—tree roots, hollows of pubic moss, dead violets—underfoot the beach—tricky curvatures of stone, slush of ground shells, waterspouts, sudden clefts and crevices, pools that reflected bright eyes, big smile, foolish hat. Far in the distance I could see the cold white thumb of the condemned lighthouse.

But time, the white monster, had already gripped this edge of the island in two bright claws, had already begun to haul itself out of an ugly sea, and the undeniable day was upon me. I slipped, the coat blew wide, and for some reason I fell back and found myself staring up at a gray sky, gray scudding clouds, a thick palpable reality of air in which only the barometer and a few weak signals of distress could survive. An inhuman daytime sky. And directly overhead I saw the bird, the gray-brown hungry body and crescent wings. He was hovering and I could see the irritable way he fended off the wind and maintained his position and I knew that he would return again and again to this same spot. And against the chopping and spilling of the black water I saw the lighthouse. It was not safely in the distance as I had thought, but was upon me. Black missing tooth for a door, faint sea-discolorations rising the height of the white tower, broken glass in its empty head, a bit of white cloth caught up in the broken glass and waving, the whole condemned weight of it was there within shouting distance despite the wind and sea. I could even make out the tufts of high grass bent and beating against its base, and even through the black doorless entrance way I could feel the rank skin-prickling texture of the darkness packed inside that forbidden white tower, and must have known even then that I could not escape the lighthouse, could do nothing to prevent my having at last to enter that wind-whistling place and having to feel my way to the topmost iron rung of its abandoned stair.

Hovering bird, hollow head of the lighthouse, a sudden strip of white sand between myself and the mud-colored base rock of the lighthouse, little sharp black boulders spaced together closely and evenly in the sand, and then as white as a starfish and inert, naked, caught amongst the boulders, I saw a woman lying midway between myself and the high rock. Vision from the widow's photography magazine. Woman who might have leapt from the lighthouse or rolled up only moments before on the tide. She was there, out there, triangulated by the hard cold points of the day, and it was she, not I, who was drawing down the eye of the bird and even while the thought came to me—princess, poor princess and her tower—I looked up at the bird, still hovering, and then turned to the strip of beach and ran forward. But I stopped. Stopped, shuddered, shut my eyes. Because of the voice.

"So here you are!"

It was deep, low, husky, strong, the melodic tough voice of the woman who always sounds like a woman, yet talks like a man. It was close to me, deep and tempting and jocular, and I thought I could feel that enormous mouth pressed tight to my ear. It sounded like a big throat, shrewd powerful mind, heart as big as a barrel. And I was right, so terribly right. Except for the heart. Her black heart.

"My God. What are you doing down there?"

Somehow I opened my eyes, looked over my shoulder and raised my eyes from bright pink heart-shaped shell to bunches of weed to jutting hump of the shore to rising tall figure of the woman standing wind-blown on the edge above me. Looked and fought for breath.

Slacks. Canary yellow slacks. Soft thick canary yellow slacks tight at the ankles, cut off with a cleaver at the bare white ankles, and binding the long thighs, binding and so tight on the hips—yellow smooth complicated block of flesh and bone—that she could force only the tips of her long fingers into the slits of of the thin-lipped and slanted pockets. Slacks and square white jaw and great nest of black hair strapped in an emerald kerchief. Great white turtle-neck sweater and trussed white bosom, white breast begging for shields. Shoulders curving and muscular, unbowed. But yellow, yellow from the waist down, the tall easy stance of a woman proud of her stomach—lovely specimen of broad flat stomach bound and yellow and undulating down the front of the slacks—and staring at me with legs apart and elbows bent and eyes like great dark pits of recognition in the bony face. A strand of the black hair came loose and there was a long thick silver streak in it.

"Water's about twenty degrees," she said, and I heard the deep voice, saw the mountain of frosty breath, the toss of the hair. "You look like a damn seal. People shoot seals around here." And with one canary stride she was gone.

"Wait," I called, "wait a minute!" But she was gone. And of course when I looked again there was no bird in the sky and no poor white dead thing lying between myself and the blind tower on the rock. So I flung myself up the hump of the shore, knelt for a moment and carefully ran my fingers over the earth where she had stood—the footprints were real, real enough the shape of her large naked foot in the crushed frozen grass—and bewildered, cold, I sped off across those empty fields as best I could; cold and sweating, I found my way back to the sleeping house.

A once-white shutter was banging, the wind was whistling down the halyards of the clothesline, the nose of the hot rod peered at me through the tall grass, all was quiet around the kennel, and the house was sleeping, was only an old wooden structure with a tin mailbox on a post by the gate and crusts thrown out for the birds. Nothing more peaceful than the cord of cherry-wood—ash, spruce, hemlock, whatever it was —piled up for the dogs to foul. But I walked with the woman in my eye, entered the house with the vision of her handsome white face before me. Striking magic. Bold hostility. And I had begun now to suspect that sleeping house and I began to raise a first faint guard in my own defense, approaching the lopsided back storm door with care. But I was too late, of course. Too late.

I entered the darkness, drove the door closed with my shoulder and stood panting and dripping and leaning against the cold rough wall of the entrance way, stood glancing at broken flowerpots, hedge clippers hung from a nail, coil of anchor chain and pile of gunny bags, stared for a moment at a half-empty sack of charcoal briquettes. The place smelled of cold earth and congealed grease, was a wooden bin for the dead leaves and rubbish of the past. Apple cider turned to vinegar. Set of moldy and rusted golf clubs flung in a corner with rakes and a pair of rubber hip boots. But nothing that I could see to fear, and I tore off the sou'wester, pulled off the coat and hung them again where I had found them. Then I put my hand on the old-fashioned glass knob, gave it a gentle turn, and stepped into the kitchen. Cold, trembling, sighing, I was glad to be home. Then I stared at the cruel mess on the kitchen table.

Bottle of Old Grand Dad. Tall, burnished, freshly opened, bright familiar shape of every roadside bar—there was even a silver measuring device squeezed onto the neck instead of a cap or cork—that oddly professional and flagrant bottle of whiskey stood in the middle of the kitchen table, was a rude incongruous reality in the middle of the mess. And there was the mess itself: all of poor Pixie's baby bottles, all of them, bereft of nipples, emptied, lying flat and helter-skelter on the table

in little globs and pools of white baby's milk. I walked to the sink—
sides and bottom furiously splashed with the milk poured, shaken, from
the bottles—I walked to the table and picked up a bottle, turned it in
my hands, replaced it and picked up another, and I could make nothing
of this sad vehement litter, merely stood there with my face draining,
chin quivering, mouth working and twisting, trying to set itself into the
shape, the smile, of my self-sacrifice.

But the nipples. The horror of the nipples. I seized each of them one
by one, examined them closely and helplessly until I held five in the
palm of my hand, five nipples side by side and each one neatly cut off
about a quarter of an inch below the tip. Pair of steel shears spread
open near the Old Grand Dad. Bits of rubber glove made for a midget.
I looked and looked and then dropped them—considerable bouncing
like wounded jumping beans—and knelt on the floor, felt about under
the table for the sixth nipple which I never found.

I was still on my hands and knees and thinking about the pot, the
boiling water, the bottles to wash, the extra set of nipples to bring down
from my drawer upstairs, thinking of the bottles I had lined up in the
refrigerator—had I been watched even then?—when I heard the music.
Loud music at eight o'clock in the morning in that sleeping house. I
lifted my head, climbed to my feet, and slowly, more slowly than ever,
I hitched a little and straightened the front of my trousers, tucked in the
checkered shirt, stood listening with jaw jutting and tip of the ears
red hot.

Because of course it was not ordinary music. Not that morning, not
in that house. It was coming from beyond the dining room—sweet
tinkle of cut glass, spindle chairs, ghosts of little old seedless ladies
with chokers and gold wedding bands—was coming from the radio-
phonograph in the living room. With indignation I recognized the blasting exuberant strains of that brassy music. The *Horst Wessel lied* in full
swing, with percussion instruments and horns, trumpets and tubas, and
the heavy bass voices of all those humorless young marching men. The
Horst Wessel lied. I could hear the waves of praise, the smacking of the
drums, the maudlin fervor, the terrible toneless racketing of the military
snares, could see the muscles of the open mouths, the moody eyes locked
front, could feel the rise of their preposterous love and bravery, feel the
stamping feet, the floating sentiment—blue castles, beer, blood—the
catching treacherous rhythm of that marching song. And I was drawn
to it, drawn to it. With scowl and frown and hot wet palms, was nonetheless drawn to the impossible intensity of that barbaric unity, found

myself leaving the wreck of my efforts for Pixie in the kitchen and walking toward the sound, the incredible military mass of that captured phonograph record. I reached the door, stood in the open door, and those German soldiers were singing the song of death, the song of the enemy.

Canary yellow slacks, bare feet, a man's white shirt with open collar and sleeves rolled above the naked elbows. Oh yes, here was the second glimpse of her and she was on the floor in front of the fireplace, was kneeling and sitting back on her heels—wicked posturing, rank mystery of the triangle, bright and brazen cohesion between the rump and calves and canary yellow thighs—and her shoulders were thrown back and her powerful spine was a crescent and her broad hands were cupped on her knees. Her eyes were turned to the door and fixed on mine. No smile. Surrounded by leaves of an old newspaper. A tall glass of whiskey and a box of blue-tipped wooden matches waiting within reach on the brick apron of the fireplace. She waited and then jerked her head slightly toward the radio-phonograph, and I saw the picture of the dead soldier mounted upright in a silver frame on the cabinet.

"The *Horst Wessel*," she said above the din of the conquering music. "Don sent me the record." And then listening, abstracted in the pleasure of the loud marching song, slowly and with level eyes still on mine, she reached out one white hand, seized the full glass of whiskey, raised it in a salute in my direction: "Old Grand Dad. Bottle's in the kitchen. Help yourself."

She was waiting, watching me, and now I was bracing myself against the doorjamb, leaning against it, sagging against it, stood there with one wet shoe tapping time to the march. "Thanks. But I don't drink."

"Oh. You don't drink. Well then, you can light the fire." And she tossed the box of matches at my feet, put the glass to her mouth—thick glass, white teeth, burnished whiskey—began to pull at it like a man, and her neck was bare, bold, athletic, and her rump was a yellow rock in the saddle of her calves, and under the white shirt her breasts were crowned with golden crowns. I thought of poor Sonny and his rum and Coca-Cola, I thought of poor Gertrude stealing frantic sips of gin out of her cheap little cream cheese glasses, I thought of poor Pixie's milk curdling in the kitchen sink. But Don's widow was sitting on her heels and drinking, and all the young German men were singing for her, marching for her. I failed to see the spinning wheel and bumped it, that construction of brittle cobwebs five feet high, and thought it was going over. Then I stooped down quickly and stuffed a few leaves of newspaper between the logs and struck a flame.

Iron pot on a hook, iron spit for the impaling and roasting of some headless blue turkey, a little straw broom and dusty heart-shaped bellows, and on the andirons great solid brass balls fit for the gods. Suddenly the tall swallow-tailed flames and crackling puffs of orange and deep green light between the logs threw all these hand-forged or hand-made engines into relief, set them in motion, brought them to life, and I smelled the damp bursts of smoke and the widow was warming herself at the witches' fire. Beside the bellows was a coffin-shaped legless duck—faded decoy carved with a knife—that stared me down with two tiny bright sightless chips of glass. Fire in the antique shop. Dead duck. Smoke in my eyes.

"Take off your shoes, for God's sake," she said, and the mellow voice was loud above the chant of the SS men, the firelight landed in yellow lozenges on the slopes and in the hollows of her slacks, "you must be frozen. But go ahead, warm your toes while I tell you about Don."

And I could only nod, tug at the wet laces, free my heels, roll down the socks, wring them out—drops of steam on the hearth—could only make room for her and sit beside her on the cold wide naked planks of that floor with my hands propped behind me and my white feet and hers thrust into the heat. She dropped down on an elbow, crossed her long straight legs at the ankles, held out the whiskey glass—but it was not for me, that whiskey, at least not then—and breathing deeply, straining at the nostrils, shirt binding and slackening across her breasts, she began to wheeze. To wheeze! The big white knuckles of the fingers holding the glass, her crowned breasts, the mighty head of black hair, the stomach girding her in front like the flexible shape of a shield, the fluted weight of neck and arms and legs, all the impressive anatomy of this Cleopatra who could row her own barge, this woman who could outrun horses on the beach or knock down pillars of salt, everything about her revealed perfect health, denied this sudden swirling of mud or rattling of little pits in her chest. But even above the raucous melody of the eager Germans and their impossible military band I heard it: the sound of obstructed breathing, tight low crippling whine in the chest. Yet her eyes on mine were direct and heavy and dark, were large and black and fierce and cracked by spears of silver light. She wheezed on, mocked by the competitive fire, waiting for the steel needle to descend once more into the grooves of plodding Reichstag hysteria, and then whacked herself once on the uppermost yellow thigh and began to talk.

"That's him in the picture," she said without moving, without pointing, merely assuming that I had seen it when I entered the room. I nodded. "That's Don. Young, good-looking boy. He stepped on a land mine, God damn him. In Germany. He took a wrong step and then no more Don. Poof. I met him in South Carolina. There he was, toward sundown standing at a country bus stop in South Carolina. The end of nowhere and burning up at the edges. Nothing but the road, a tree smothered with dust, the little three-sided shed where they were supposed to wait for the bus, a field full of scarecrows. And in front of the shed and surrounded by perhaps twenty cotton pickers, there was Don. I saw him. Short, limber, smile all over his face, head of tight blond curls, overseas cap like a little tan tent on the side of his head. Bunch of tattered damn black cotton pickers out for blood and this wonderful bright little guy with his smile and curly hair. Don. A little angle in South Carolina. So I gave him a lift. Sense of humor? My God, he had a sense of humor." And suddenly she was choking on a snort of laughter, choking, gasping, giving my now toasty bare foot a friendly push with hers. And now her wheezing had found another depth, and each word came out shrouded in its cocoon of gravelly sound, its spasm of spent breath, and there were streaks of moisture at the hairline and on her upper lip. She took another slow drink of whiskey and the silver strand of hair hung down, the voice was deep.

She set down the glass and filled her lungs and said: "Good God, I married him for his humor. Because he was light on his feet and light in his heart. And because he was quick and talented and because he was just a boy, that's why I married him. Why I gave him a lift and followed him to Galveston, Texas, and married him. Don. Three dozen roses, a brand new hot plate, a rented room outside Galveston, and one day Don telling me he had been elected company mascot—what a sense of humor, what a winsome smile—and that night our celebration with a spaghetti dinner and bottle of dago red. I should have known then that it couldn't last. My God. . . ."

The golden foot was struggling against mine, the perspiration was as thick as rain on her lip, her shirt was wet and through it I could see the sloping shoulder, the handsome network of blue veins, the companion to the black brassiere that was still hanging in the john upstairs. Stretched full-length at my side she was wheezing and staring into the light of the fire, and now there were dimples, puckers, unsuspected two wild hands. But it was everywhere. And now her voice was coming through the smoke and for a moment I could only listen, breathe in the terrible odor, keep watching her despite my tears.

"I don't really believe in this stuff," drinking in enormous whiffs of greasy smoke, "but sometimes it helps a little. Don told me about it, found an ad in the Galveston paper," filling her lungs with punk and dung and sparks, "he was such a sweet airy little clown. Five months of marriage to Don," swirling, sinking, drifting now on the fumes of the witches' pot, "and then a land mine in Wiesbaden or some damn place and no more Don and me a widow. . . ."

"I'm a widower myself," I said, and I stood up carefully, avoided the large white hand that was reaching for my trouser leg, stared once at the little unmoving face of the dead soldier, and started out of the room.

But just as I approached the door: "Well," I heard her say, "we'll make a great pair."

And when I reached the upstairs hallway Pixie was screaming in her cradle and Cassandra was wrapped in a musty quilt and stood trying to coil up her hair before the oval mirror. I heard the gasping breaths below turn to laughter and for a long while hesitated to enter my icy room. Because of the dressmaker's dummy. Because she had placed the dummy—further sign of industry in the island home, rusted iron-wire skirt and loops of rusted iron-wire for the bold and faceless head, no arms, torso like an hourglass, broad hips and sweeping behind and nar-row waist and bang-up bosom all made of padded beige felt, historical essence of womanhood, life-size female anatomy and a hundred years of pins—she had placed this dummy at the head of my bed and dressed it in my naval uniform so that the artificial bosom swelled my white tunic and the artificial pregnancy of the padded belly puffed out the broad front of my official white duck pants which she had pinned to the dummy with a pair of giant safety pins rammed through the felt. Cuffs of the empty sleeves thrust in the pockets, white hat cocked out-rageously on the wire head—desperate slant of the black visor, scream-ing angle of the golden bird—oh, it was a jaunty sight she had prepared for me. But of course I ignored it as best I could, tried to overlook the fresh dark gouts of ketchup she had flung down the front of that defiled figure, and merely shut my door, at least spared my poor daughter from having to grapple with that hapless effigy of my disfigured self.

And moments later, scooping Pixie out of the cradle, tossing her into the air, jouncing her in the crook of my arm, smiling: "Have a good sleep, Cassandra? Time to start the new day." In the mirror her little curves in the canary yellow slacks, and now her chest was maniacal, was as trenchant and guttural and insistent as the upturned German record itself. So I looked at her then, forced myself to return the stare of those vast dark eyes, and she tried to shrug, tried to toss back the thick length of silver hair, but only glowered at me out of her stricken heaviness and abruptly tapped herself on the chest.

"Asthma." Tapping the finger, squaring the jaw, watching me. "I get it from too much thinking about Don. But it's nothing. Nothing at all. . . ."

I nodded. And yet the fire had fallen in and the pot and spit were glowing and her knee was lifting. Her lips were moist, pulled back, drawn open fiercely in the perfect silent square of the tragic muse, and I leaned closer to smell the alcohol and Parisian scent, closer to inspect the agony of the muscles which, no thicker than hairs, flexed and flickered in those unhappy lips, closer to hear whatever moaning she might have made above the racket of her strangulation.

"What can I do? Isn't there something I can do?"

"The secretary," she said. "Bring me the box in the middle drawer. Saucer too. From the kitchen."

So I embarked on this brief rump-swinging bare-and-warm-footed expedition, and with the woolen pants steaming nicely around my ankles and the checkered shirt pressing against my skin its blanket of warm fuzzy hairs, I glided heavily to the little chair, the papers, the oil lamp —God Bless Our Home etched on the shade—and calmly, backs of the hands covered with new warmth, licking my lips and feeling that I might like to whistle—perhaps only a bar or two, a few notes in defiance of the *Horst Wessel*—I returned to the cold kitchen with hardly a glance, hardly a thought for the remnants of poor Pixie's breakfast and lunch and dinner. Solicitous. Professional search for a saucer. Long-faced scrutiny of the cupboards. The hell with the nipples.

And then I was kneeling at her side, leaning down to her again with the box in one hand and the dish in the other, and though she was heaving worse than ever with her eyes still shut, nonetheless she knew I was there and tried to rouse herself. "What next?" I asked, and was startled by the quickness of her reply, shocked by the impatience and urgency of her rich low voice.

"Put some powder in the dish and burn it. For God's sake."

Sputtering match, sputtering powder, glowing pinpricks and smoke enough to form a genie. I tried to fight the smoke, the stench, with my cold sleepy face was puffy and pitted, was black and white with shadow, and the faded quilt was drawn over her shoulders and her hair was still down.

"What's burning?" she said. "What's that awful smell?" But in the mirror I put a finger to my lips, shook my head, though I knew then that the noxious odor of grief, death and widowhood would fill this house.

CLEOPATRA'S CAR

SHANKS OF ICE HANGING FROM THE EAVES, the wind sucking with increasing fury at the wormholes, Miranda standing in the open front doorway and laughing into the wind or bellowing through the fog at her two fat black Labradors and throwing them chunks of meat from a galvanized iron basin slung under her arm, the ragged bird returning each dawn to hover beyond the shore line outside my window, empty Old Grand Dad bottles collecting in the kitchen cupboards, under the stove, even beside the spinning wheel in the parlor—so these first weeks froze and fled from us, and Cassandra grew reluctant to explore the cow paths with me, and my nights, my lonely nights, were sleepless. I began to find the smudged saucers everywhere—stink of the asthma powders, stink of secret designs and death—and I began to notice that Cassandra was Miranda's shadow, sweet silent shadow of the big widow in slacks. When Miranda poured herself a drink—tumbler filled to the brim with whiskey—Cassandra put a few drops in the small end of an egg cup and accompanied her. And when Miranda sat in front of the fire to knit, Cassandra was always with her, always kneeling at her feet and holding the yarn. Black yarn. Heavy soft coil of rich black yarn dangling from Cassandra's wrists. Halter on the white wrists. Our slave chains. Between the two of them always the black umbilicus, the endless and maddening absorption in the problems of yarn. It lived in the cave of Miranda's sewing bag—not a black sweater for some lucky devil overseas, nor even a cap for Pixie, but only this black entanglement, their shapeless squid. And I? I would sit in the shadows and wait, maintain my guard, sit there and now and then give the spinning wheel an idle turn or polish all the little ivory pieces of the Mah Jongg set.

And marked by Sunday dinners. The passing of those darkening weeks, the flow of those idle days—quickening, growing colder, until they rushed and jammed together in the little jagged ice shelf of our frozen time—was marked by midday dinners on the Sabbath when Captain Red did the carving—wind-whipped, tall and raw and bald like me, his big knuckles sunk in the gravy and his bulging eyes on the widow—and when Bub waited on table and ate alone with Pixie in the kitchen, and Jomo—back straight, sideburns reaching to the thin white jaws, black hair plastered down with pine sap—sat working his artificial hand beside Cassandra. On Sundays Jomo worked his artificial hand for Cassandra, but I was the one who watched, I who watched him change the angle of his hook, lock the silver fork in place and go after peas, watched him fiddle with a lever near the wrist and drop the fork and calmly and neatly snare the full water glass in the mechanical round of that wonderful steel half-bracelet that was his hand.

Those were long Sunday meals when the Captain spoke only to say grace and ask for the rolls; and Bub stood waiting at my elbow and smelled of brine and uncut boy's hair; and Jomo sat across from me, solitary—except for Cassandra at his side—and busy with his new hand; and Miranda drank her whiskey and cursed the weather and grinned down the length of the table at the quiet lechery that boiled in old Red's eyes; and Cassandra, poor Cassandra, merely picked at her plate, yet Sunday after dreary Sunday grew heavier, more ripe to the silent fare of that cruel board. Dreary and dull and dangerous. So at the end of the meal I always asked Jomo how he had liked Salerno. Because of course he had lost his hand in the fighting around Salerno. A city, as he said, near the foot of the boot. What would I have done without Jomo's hand?

Family and friends, then, gathering week after dreary week for the Sabbath, meeting together on the dangerous day of the Lord, pursuing our black entanglement, waiting around for something—the first snow? first love? the first outbreak of violence?—and saying grace, watching the slow winter death of the oak tree, feeling wave after wave of the cold Atlantic breaching our trackless black inhospitable shores. And then another Sunday rolling around and the sexton rushing to the Lutheran church to ring the bells—always excited, always in a hurry, can't wait to get his hands on the rope—and once again the frenzied sexton nearly hanging himself from the bellpull and another Sunday ringing and pealing and chiming on the frosty air.

So the gray days died away and the hours of my lonely and sleepless nights increased, each hour deeper and darker and colder than the one before and with only the dummy—mockery of myself—to keep me company, to follow me through the cold night watch. Luckily I found an old brass bed warmer in the closet behind the trunks and every night I filled it with the last coals of the fire and carried it first to Cassandra's room, devoted fifteen minutes to warming Cassandra's bed, and then carried it across the hall—hot libation, hot offering to myself—and

shoved it between the covers where it spent the night. And I would lie
there in the darkness and everywhere, except in my feet, suffer the bruis-
ing effects of the flat frozen pillow and the cold mattress, and clutching
my hands together and waiting, knowing that even the coals would cool,
would remember one of Jomo's phrases spoken when he thought I
couldn't·hear—blue tit—and in the darkness would begin to say the
phrase aloud—blue tit—aware that in some mysterious way it referred
to the cold, referred to the way I felt, seemed to give actual substance,
body, to the dark color and falling temperature of all my lonely and
sleepless nights. Then I would dream with Jomo's incantation still on
my lips. And I would dream of Tremlow leading the mutiny, of Gertrude's grave, of Fernandez mutilated in the flophouse, and I would
awaken to the sound of the wind and the sight of my white spoiled
uniform flapping and moaning on the dressmaker's dummy. Blue tit.
And at dawn a hard tissue-thin sheet of ice in the bottom of the basin,
big block of ice in the pitcher, frozen splinters like carpet tacks when I
stumbled to the bathroom to empty the bed warmer down the john.
Standing in that bathroom, shivering, blinking, bed warmer hanging
cold and heavy from my hand, I would always lean close to the bathroom mirror and read the message printed in ornate green type on a
little square of wrinkled and yellowed paper which was pasted to the
glass. Always read it and, no matter how cold I was, how tired, I would
begin to smile.

> *Wake with a Loving Thought.*
> *Work with a Happy Thought.*
> *Sleep with a Gentle Thought.*

I would begin to smile, begin to whistle. Because it tickled my fancy,
that prayer, that message for the new day, and because it was a talisman
against the horrors of blue tit and saved me, at least for a while, from
the thought of the black brassiere.

So the changes of those cold days. Until the local children became
glum Christmas sprites and the first snow fell at last—sudden soaring
of asthma powder stench, dirty little volcanoes smoldering in every
room—and the night of the local high school dance loomed out of the
fresh wet snow and I, I too, was swept along into the glaring bathos of
that high school dance. Kissing in the coatroom. Big business out back

in the car. Little bright noses in the snow. Jomo's hook in action. Beginning of our festive end.

"Ready, Skip? Ready yet, Candy? They'll be here any sec. . . ."

Even in the cold and echoing bathroom—lead pipe, cracked linoleum, slabs of yellow marble—and even with the cold water running in the tap and the snow piling against the window and the old brown varnished door closed as far as it would go, still I could hear her calling to us from the parlor, hear the sound of her tread in the parlor. But though her voice rose up to us crisp and clear and bold—a snappy voice, a hailing voice, deeply resonant, pathetically excited—and though I resented being rushed and would never forgive her for daring to invent and use those perky names, especially for shouting up that cheap term of endearment for Cassandra when I, her father, had always yearned hopelessly for just this privilege, nonetheless it was Saturday night and the first snow was falling and I too was getting ready, after all, for the high school dance. So I could not really begrudge Miranda her excitement or her impatience. I too felt a curious need to hurry after all. And perhaps down there in the parlor—kicking the log, sloshing unsteady portions of whiskey into her glass, then striding to the window and trying to see out through the darkness and heavy snow—perhaps in some perverse way she was thinking of Don, though her chest was clear and though from time to time I could hear her laughing to herself down there.

Laughing while I was making irritable impatient faces in the bathroom mirror. Giving myself a close shave for the high school dance. Trying to preserve my own exhilaration against hers. And it was pleasurable. After a particularly good stroke I would set aside the razor and fling the water about as wildly as I could and snort, grind my eyes on the ends of the towel. Then step to the window for a long look at the black night and the falling snow.

Wet hands on the flaking white sill. Sudden shock in nose, chin, cheeks, sensation of the cold glass against the whole of my inquisitive face. Kerosene stove breathing into the seat of my woolen pants, eyes all at once accustomed to the dark, when suddenly it coalesced—soap, toothpaste, warm behind, the cold wet night—and I smiled and told myself I had nothing to fear from Red and saw myself poised hand in hand with Cassandra on the edge of the floor and smiling at the awkward postures and passions of the high school young. I stared out the window, tasting the soap on my lips, watching the snow collect in the black crotch of a tree—slick runnels in the bark, puckered wounds of lopped branches crowned with snow—that grew close to the window and glistened in the beam of the bathroom light, and I felt as if I were being tickled with the point of a sharp knife. Thank God for the sound of the tap and of Cassandra's little thin shoe spanking across the puddles of the bathroom floor. I waited, face trembling with the coldness of the night.

"Skipper. Zip me up. Please."

"Well, Cassandra," I said, and turned to her, held out both hands wide to her, "How sad that Gertrude can't see you now. But your dress, Cassandra, surely it's not a mail-order dress?"

"Miranda made it for me," tugging lightly at a flounce, twisting the waist, "she made it as a surprise for me to wear tonight. It has a pretty bow. You'll see. It's not too youthful, Skipper?"

"For you?" And I laughed, dropped my arms—antipathy toward my embrace? fear for the dress?—and wiped my hands on the towel, frowned at the thought of Miranda's midnight sewing machine, stood while with straight arm and straight fingers she followed the healing needlework on my skin, traced out the letters of her lost husband's name—did she, could she know what she was doing? know the shame I felt for the secret I still kept from her?—then by the shoulders I turned her so I could reach the dress where it hung open down her back. "Of course it's not too young for you, Cassandra. Hardly."

"And we're not making a mistake tonight? We shouldn't just stay home and let Miranda go to the dance alone with Red and Bub and," pausing—moment of deference—whispering the name into the little clear cup of her collar bone, "and with Jomo?"

"Of course not," I said, and reached for the zipper, probed for it, quickly tried to work the zipper. "It's only a high school dance, Cassandra. Harmless. Amusing. We needn't be out late," pulling, fumbling, trying to work the zipper free, "and think of it, Cassandra. The first snow. . . ."

She nodded and plucked at the bodice, fluffed the skirt, put one foot in front of the other, and with each gesture there was a corresponding ripple in the prim naked shape of her back and a corresponding ripple in the dress itself. That dress. That green taffeta. Flounces and ruffles and little bright green fields and cascading skirt. Taffeta. Smooth for the palm and nipped-in little deep green persuasive folds for the fingers. Swirling. Shining. Cake frosting with candles. For a fifteen-year-old. For a cute kitten. For trouble. Green taffeta. And when we went down the stairs together, Cassandra holding up the knee-length skirt, I following, steadying myself against the flimsy bannister, I saw the green bow, the two full yards of fluted taffeta with a green knot larger than my fist and streamers that reached her calves. Bow that bound her buttocks. Outrageous bow!

So I zipped the zipper and in the mirror full of contortion, mirror crowded suddenly with hands, elbows, floating face, I tied my tie and spread a thin even coating of Vaseline on my smooth red scalp—protection for the bald head, no chafing in wind or snow, trick I learned in the Navy—and grinned at myself in the glass and buffed my fingernails and struggled into my jacket and rapped on Cassandra's door—exposure of black market stocking, gathered green taffeta hem of skirt, hairpin in the pretty mouth—and waited and waited and then escorted her down the dark stairs.

"Candy! My God, Candy! She looks like a dream, doesn't she, Skip?"

Before I could reply or smile or make some condescending gesture they hugged each other, hooked arms and crossed the parlor to the fire, in front of the fire held hands, admired each other, babbled, swung their four clasped hands in unison. Girlish. Hearts full of joy. The big night. Miranda was dressed in black, of course—her totem was still hanging in the bathroom—and around her throat she wore a black velvet band. Her bosom was an unleashed animal.

"My God, Candy, we're just kids. Two kids. Two baby sitters waiting for dates! And they'll be here any sec!"

"And me, Miranda?" Squirming, shrugging, raising my chin toward the cracks in the ceiling, "What about me, Miranda?"

"You?" She laughed, showed her big white knees, pretended to waltz with Cassandra in front of the fire. "You're the Mah Jongg champion. Boy, what a Mah Jongg champion you are!" And suddenly locking Cassandra's face between her bare white hands, and swaying, smiling at Cassandra's little downcast eyes: "My God, I wish Don were here," she said. "I wish Don could see you tonight, Candy."

"Watch out for the asthma," I murmured, but too softly and too late because the dates were stamping on the veranda, banging on the door, and she was gone, was already rushing down the hall and kissing them, throwing herself on the sniffling figures standing there in the cold.

And under my breath, quickly: "First dance, Cassandra? Please?"

"I can't promise, Skipper. I can't make promises any more."

Then the fire shot high again and the black beauty was herding them all into the parlor—Jomo, Bub, Grandma who looked like a little corncob tied up with rags—and they were all blowing on their fingers, kicking the snow off their boots, sniffling. Red ears. Mean eyes. Smears of Miranda's lipstick on each of the faces.

"Have a drink, Jomo?" she said, and hugged his narrow black iron shoulders with her long white arm, ran her other hand through Bub's wet hair. "Just one for the road?"

"Can't. Red's out in the car. Waiting."

The long-billed baseball cap, the steady eyes, the flat black sideburns sculpted frontier-style with a straight razor, pug nose and skin the color of axle grease and little black snap-on bow tie and lips drawn as if he were going to whistle through his teeth—this was Jomo and Jomo was looking at Cassandra, staring at her, with one oblivious snuff of his pug nose expressed all the contempt and desire of his ruthless race. It was the green taffeta bow, of course, and before he could finish his contemplation of that green party favor, green riddle as big as a balloon, I stepped in front of him, and hoping, as I always hoped, that one day he would forget and give me his cold hook of steel, I thrust out my hand.

"Evening, Jomo," I said. "How's the cod? Running?"

He waited. No artificial hand. No real hand. Only the soft light of fury sliding off his face, only one more baffling question to ask his old man about and to hold against me. So he turned to Miranda, jerked his head toward the door.

"Anyways, Red's got a pint in his pocket. Let's go."

But the little old woman, mother of the Captain and grandmother of his noxious sons, was pushing on Bub's sleeve and pointing in my direction and trying to talk.

"She wants to say something," Bub said. "Tell Bub," he said, and stuck his ear down to the little happy bobbing clot of the old woman's face. Crushed once with a clam digger. Dug out of a hole at low tide. Little old woman with love and a sense of humor.

"All right," I said, "what is it? And how is Mrs. Poor tonight?" I smiled and glanced at Cassandra—shining and silent cameo by the hearth—and smiled again, squared my shoulders, leaned my head slightly to one side for Mrs. Poor who was clinging to Bub's arm and pumping with excitement in all the little black muscular valves of her mouth and eyes. Every Saturday Red went down to feed her doughnuts, and on Sundays after grace he would sometimes tell us about her health and happiness. "Well," I said, knowing that she was shrewd, not to be trusted, that the little rag-bound head was stuffed with Jomo's jokes and snatches of the prayer book which she knew by heart, "well, tell us what Grandma wants to say tonight."

Bub looked at me, wiped his nose. "She says all the girls are sweet on you. You're apple pie for the girls, she says. All the girls go after a rosy man like you. Real apple pie, she says." And Bub was scowling and the old woman was nodding up and down, grinning, pointing, and Miranda was kneeling and fixing Cassandra's bow.

"What a nice thing to say," said Cassandra. "Don't you think so, Skipper?"

Jomo leaned over and smacked his thigh. "God damn," he said, "that's good."

And going down the hall toward the open door where I could see the snow driving and sifting—Miranda first, then Cassandra and Jomo and Bub and last, as usual, myself—I noticed Bub's quick ferret gesture, quick fingers nudging his brother's arm, and clearly heard his young boy's voice cupped under a sly hand, in the darkness saw his boy's feet dance a few lewd steps to the fun of his question:

"What's that thing she's wearing on her ass?"

And Jomo, in a dead-pan voice and puppet jerk of the silhouetted head: "Never you mind, Bub. And watch your language. You got a mouth full of rot."

"Maybe. But I'd like to kill it with a stick."

Old joke. Snickering shadow of island boy. Jackknife shadow of older brother. But then the snow, the darkness, the packed and crunching veranda, the dying oak and the picket fence heaped high with snow, and beyond the fence, low and throbbing like a diesel truck, the waiting car. It was a hot rod. Cut down. Black. Thirteen coats of black paint and wax. Thick aluminum tubes coiling out of the engine. And in the front an aerial—perfect even to the whip of steel, I thought—and tied to the tip of the aerial a little fat fuzzy squirrel tail, little flag freshly killed and plump, soft, twisting and revolving slowly in the snow, dark fur long and wet and glistening under the crystals of falling snow. The lights from the house were shining on the windshield—narrow flat rectangle of blind glass already half-buried like the silver hub caps in the heavy snow—and I glanced back toward the house and waved and, blinking away the snow, licking it, thinking of another departure, "*Au revoir,* Grandma," I called softly, "take good care of Pixie." Then I stumbled to the car with wet cheeks and with a smile on my wet lips.

I took hold of the handle. Turned, pulled, shook the handle. "Come on, Bub," I said, leaning down, rapping on the glass, shading my eyes

and attempting to peer into the car, "open the door, you're not funny."
I squinted, brushed at the snow with a cold hand. I saw the two heads
of hair and the knife-billed baseball cap between them in the back, saw
Bub laughing, poking at Captain Red who sat behind the wheel holding
the pint bottle up to his lip. I saw the pint bottle making the rounds.

"All right," I said, when the door came open at last, "now get out
for a moment, Bub. You can sit on my lap."

"Now wait a minute. Just you wait. I got this seat first. Didn't I? If
there's any lap-sitting to be done, it's you who's going to do it. Now
you want to ride to the dance with us you better just climb into the car
and have a seat. Right here." Pointing. Laughter. Bottle sailing out the
window. Captain Red—tall man dressed in his Sunday duds, shaved, fit
to kill—blowing the horn three times. Three shrill trumpet blasts
through the falling snow.

"But, Bub," leaning closer, trying to whisper into his ear, "I'm bigger
than you are. I'll be too heavy."

And the shout: "Never you mind about that. I'll do the worrying,
you just do what I say. And I say you can sit on my lap or you can
walk!"

Then there was the meshing of metal, the hard shower of snow,
sparks under the snow, and if I hadn't leapt—puffing, pumping, displaying blind humiliating courage since it's always the fat man who has
to run to catch the train—surely I would have been left behind, left
standing there with my hopeless breath freezing on the dark night air.
An evening at home. Evening with Grandma. Up and down to the lavatory. Smiles. But I did leap, sucked all possible breath into my lungs
and desperate, expecting and even willing to be maimed, for five or ten
steps plowed along beside the moving car and then jumped, ducked my
head, got a grip on the dashboard and back of the seat, hunched my
neck and shoulders—presence of mind to save fingers, feet, loose ends
of cloth and flesh from the slamming door—and perched there, balanced there absurdly on Bub's tough wiry little lap. Steaming upholstery, six steaming people. Smells of gasoline, spilled whiskey, fading
perfume, antifreeze. And Bub. With my head knocking against the roof
of the car I knew him for what he was: a boy without underwear, holes
in his socks, holes in his pockets, rancid navel, hair bunched and fur-
rowed on the scrawny nape of his neck, and the mouth forever breathing
off the telltale smell of sleep and half-eaten candy bars. This country
boy, this island boy. Filled with fun. With hate. With smelly self-
satisfaction.

"Jingle Bells, everybody," cried Miranda, "sing along with me!" But we were swerving, skidding, sliding through the snow and all at once the lights of the high school were flickering above the tombstones in the cemetery on the hill.

And into the tiny exposed orifice of Cassandra's ear: "I got dibs on the first dance," said Jomo, and I understood the meaning of her down-cast eyes and through the snow I heard that the bass drum was out of time with the rest of Jack Spratt's Merry Hep Cats.

But how long, oh my God, how long did I endure that drummer—pimples, frightened eyes, chewing gum under his chair, some kind of permanent paralysis in his legs—how long endure the cornet—begging for alms—or the little girl with the accordion—black and white monster on her bare knees—or the poor stick of a schoolteacher at the upright piano or the paper cups of pop, the wedges of chocolate cake—chocolate on the lips, cheeks, melting all over the hands—how long endure the concrete walls, steam pipes, varnished and forbidding floor, the red, white and blue bunting hung from the nets, how long endure the moth-ers or the fat old men waiting around for the belly-bumping contest? How long? How long endure all this as well as the sight of Jomo going after Cassandra with his damnable hook? Long enough to be tempted into love once more, long enough to perspire in that cold gymnasium, to win the belly-bumping contest—treachery of my long night—long enough to have my fill of pop and chocolate cake. Too long, oh God, much too long for a man who merely wanted to dance a few slow numbers and amuse his daughter.

"If the power fails," and I startled at the sound of Red's deep voice, glanced at the uncertain yellow glow of the caged lights, glanced at the windows filled with wind and snow, "if it fails there's no telling what all these kids will do. Might have quite a time in the dark. With all these kids." And the two of them, widow in black, Captain Red in black double-breasted suit, swung out to the middle of the floor, towered above that handful of undernourished high school girls and retarded boys. Two tall black figures locked length to length, two faces convulsed in passion, one as long and white and bony as a white mare's face, the other crimson, leathery, serrated like the bald head to which it belonged, and the young boys and girls making way for them, scattering in the path of their slow motion smoke, staring up at them in envy, fear, shocked surprise. From the side lines and licking my fingers, swallowing the cake, I too watched them in shocked surprise, stuffed a crumpled paper napkin into my hip pocket. Because they were both so big, so black, so oblivious. But if this was the father, what of the ruthless son? What of Cassandra? What dance could they possibly be dancing?

I was her guardian, her only defense, and I tossed off my Coke—fifth free Coca-Cola, thoughts of Sonny—crushed the cup, and in my heavy dogtrot ran the whole length of that cold basketball court and in the darkest corner saw a flash of steel, the sheen of bright green taffeta. And paused. Bumped a proud mother. But started out onto the floor anyway. Alone. Breathless. Trying to avoid the dancers.

"Say there," behind me the woman's voice, sound of Sunday supper in the Lutheran church, "that fellow's got a nerve."

"Don't he though? And all these young boys in uniform and men like that going around scot free? Lord God. Ain't it a crime?"

The boys were wearing their white shirts—frayed collars, patches in the sleeves—and their wrinkled ties, the young girls were wearing their jerseys, homemade skirts, glass earrings—hand-me-downs—their cotton socks and saddle shoes. And I was among them and I looked into their frightened eyes, looked through the jerseys, and despite my desperation I was able to keep my wits about me—interesting little blonde, sweet raven head—and was not ashamed to look. Sixteen, seventeen, even nineteen years old and undernourished and undeveloped as well. Daughters of poor fishermen. Daughters of the sea. Anemic. Disposed to scabies. Fed on credit, fed on canned stock or stunted berries picked from a field gone back to brier, prickly thorns, wild sumac. Precious brass safety pins holding up their panties, and then I saw the pins, all at once saw the panties, the square gray-white faded undergarments of poor island girls washed in well water morning and night and, indistinguishable from kitchen washrag or scrap of kitchen towel, hung on a string between two young poplars and flapping, blowing in the hard island wind until once more dry enough and clean enough to return to the plain tender skin, and of course the elastics had been worn out or busted long ago and now there were only the little bent safety pins for holding up their panties and a few hairpins for the hair and a single lipstick which they passed from girl to girl at country crossroads or in the high school lavatory on the day of the dance. Plain Janes, island sirens, with long skinny white legs—never to know the touch of silk—and eyes big enough and gray enough to weep buckets, though they would never cry, and little buttocks already corrupted, nonetheless, by the rhythm of pop melodies and boys on leave. I steadied myself on a thin warm shoulder. "Don't be afraid," I murmured, "it's only Papa Cue Ball," and smelled the soap in her straight shining hair and saw that her skirt had once belonged to Mamma—poor skillful pleats—and that her face revealed the several faint nearly identical faces of a little Dionysian incest on a winter's night.

"You leave Chloris alone," her partner hissed, and I yanked my hand from her shoulder, blushed at the realization that I had been squeezing her little thin rounded shoulder.

"No harm meant," I said under my breath. "Just lost my footing. She's all yours," and I smiled at the relentless black walnut eyes, wheeled and cut in on Jomo, took Cassandra right out of his arms.

"OK, Jomo," I said, "I'm cutting in."

It was the far dark corner of the gym and there was a young marine sitting on top of a pile of wrestlers' mats, and I noticed his mouthful of bright cigar, his crooked smile in the dark, the glint of the bottle he didn't even pretend to hide. Three or four younger boys were hanging around the marine and sharing his bottle, waiting for word from Jomo and talking in lewd tones about Cassandra and me. By the way they turned their heads and covered their mouths and jerked their thumbs at us I knew perfectly well that they were talking in lewd tones about us. Country haircuts—except for the shaved marine—and the country ears and country Adam's apples. Inheritors of the black Atlantic. Boys who talked a lot but never danced. And of course the marine, the pride of the school, the pride of the woman at the piano. Sophomore in uniform. Leather head. Twenty-seven wounds in the rib cage. Telling them how he raped the little Japanese children. Cocking his knee in the darkness, passing the bottle. Promising to show them all twenty-seven scars in the john.

And glancing to the left, to the right, leaning down as close as I could to Cassandra, and fighting all the while against the current and trying to draw away from Jomo's friends in the corner—but there was no escaping the shadows, the arrogant glow of the cigar—and trying to subdue the electrical field of green taffeta and worrying, apologizing for my graceless steps, "It's a tough crowd, Cassandra," I said, "I don't like the looks of it."

She was stiff, her back was stiff, her arm was suddenly unsupple, she was making it hard for me. And I wanted to see her face—how could she, why did she turn away from me?—and wanted to feel the taffeta yielding, wanted some sign of her happiness. "You aren't having fun, Cassandra?" I said, and squeezed her hand, wondered whether I might not be able to imitate the sons of the sea and whirl her around by that little tapering white hand for our amusement, hers and mine, and whirl her so that her skirts would rise. But there was only the varnished floor, only the stiff shadows of ropes and acrobatic rings looping down from the darkness overhead, only the steam pipes along the walls with their enormous plaster casts like broken legs, and it was discouraging and I wanted to take her to the cloakroom and take her home. "Refreshments, Cassandra? How about some chocolate cake?" And seeing a movement in the vicinity of the indolent marine and talking closer to her ear, more quickly, "Or Coke, Cassandra? Join me in a little toast to Sonny?"

But one of his admirers had taken the marine's peaked cap, had hung it on the side of his head and was sauntering in our direction, swaggering. The cap was flopping against his neck, the pubic hair was curling around his ears, he was whistling—despite the clarion cornet and choking accordion—and he was advancing toward us casually, deliberately, shuffling our way from the darkness of giggling drinkers and lolling marine. Then a punch on my arm, jab in my ribs, and a boy's brogan landed in a short swift kick just above my ankle and Bub was saying, "Come on, Sister, let's dance," and threw his arms around her and hopped from side to side, snorting and snuffling happily into the green. Proud of his rhythm. Proud of the hat. Bub acting on orders. Bub determined to work his hands under the green bow. And Cassandra? Cassandra's eyes were closed and she was resting her palms lightly on the heavy wooden humps of his boyish shoulders. As I started away I saw them converging on her—Jomo, Red—saw the menacing horizontal thrust of the baseball cap, the bright arc of the swinging hook, the enormous black figure of Captain Red with his tie pulled loose. They began cutting in on each other, spitting on their hands or giving her up without a word, standing by and serving as outriders for each other, and at once I understood that they were taking turns with her and that this then was their plan, their dark design.

"Me?" I said. "Someone wants me? Outside?"

She grinned, a tiny girl, messenger with bobbed hair, and said she would show me the way. Mystery. Trap set by the marine? Cruel joke? But I decided that Miranda must be having asthma out in the snow and that my little girl guide—spit curls, washed and fed, eyes like a little mother cat, and plump, liberal with her own lipstick, well-mannered and ready for the juice of life—must surely be the daughter of the frenzied sexton who was so dead set on hanging himself from the bell ropes of the Lutheran church. So I followed her.

"Like the dance?"

"Why, yes," I said, startled, trying to keep up with her, to keep in close behind her, "yes, I do. It gives me an idea of what my own high school reunion might be like," and I was using the back of my hand, then my handkerchief, trying to catch the scent of her.

"I bet you were popular," she said. She was not giggling, spoke with no discernible mockery in her voice, this child of chewing gum kisses and plump young body sweetly dusted with baby talc, "I bet you'd have fun with the kids in your school or with your classmates even after thirty or forty years or whatever it is. You don't look like a kill-joy to me." And leading me into a cold dark corridor, concrete, bare lead, whistling with the cold wind of my own distant past: "You know what?" speaking clearly, matter-of-factly, while I joined her hastily at the dead weight of a metal fire door and the snow began driving suddenly through a narrow crack and into our faces, "I bet all the girls go for you. Am I right? Aren't you the type all the girls go after?"

"Well, Bubbles," I said, and like Carmen's her black hair was curled into little flat black points, "you're the second person to mention this idea tonight. So perhaps there's something in what you say."

"I knew it," she said, and we were pushing together, forcing the wrinkling door to yield, small plump girl and tall fat man straining together, beating back the snow, smelling the cold black night of the silent parking lot and breathing together, testing the snow together, "I knew you were the shy unscrupulous type. The type of man who might get a girl in trouble. A real lover."

"No, no, Bubbles, not in trouble. . . ." But I was shivering, smiling, setting straight the core of my boundless heart. A real lover. I believed her, and I lifted my broad white face into the wet tingling island snow. We had been able to open the door about a foot and so stood together hand in hand just outside the building. Together, the two of us. Blood under the skin and alone with Bubbles, scot free again.

A pale lemon-colored light from the gymnasium windows lay in three wavering rectangles on the snow. Pale institutional light coming down from the high school wall. And beyond the cold wall, beyond the tenuous light stretched the parking lot with its furry white humps of buried automobiles and, at the far edge, the black trees tangled like barbed wire. Behind the trees was the cemetery, and I could just make out the crumbling white shapes of the tombstones, the markers of dead children, the little white obelisks in the island snow. It was the place of rendezvous for the senior class, of passion amongst the fungus and the marble vines, of fingernail polish on the lips of the cherubim. So I felt that

Bubbles and I were alone in some cheap version of limbo, and I chuck-led, warmed the fingers of my free hand, and loved the trees, the perfect star-flashes of the snow, the nearness of the little cold cemetery, the buried cars, and at my side the small wet girl. But where, I wondered, was the heavy wolfish shadow of Miranda? Where the shadow of the woman who should have been clutching her chest and wheezing out there in the middle of that field of enchanted snow?

"I don't see anyone," I said. "Are you sure you've got the right person?"

"You're supposed to meet her in the cemetery. Lucky you."

I nodded. "But it looks so far."

"Don't be silly," smiling up at me, shining her curls and eyes and earrings up at me through the snow, "it isn't far. So good-by for now."

"All right then," I said. I dropped her hand, licked my chapped lips, tried and failed to imitate the bright promise of her young voice. "Good-by for now."

Then I put down my head and started across the lot—six feet and two hundred pounds of expectant and fearless snowshoe rabbit—and wondered how many couples there were in the cars and whether or not I would dare to ask Bubbles for a kiss. I wondered too what Miranda could possibly be doing in the cemetery. And at that moment I had a vision of Miranda leaning against a lichen-covered monument in her old moth-eaten fur coat and signaling me with Jomo's flashlight, and I hur-ried, took large determined strides through the trackless snow.

But I stopped. Listened. Because the air seemed to be filled with low-flying invisible birds. Large or small I could not tell, but fast, fast and out of their senses, skimming past me from every direction on terrified steel wings and silent except for the unaccountable sharp noise of the flight itself. One dove into the snow at my feet—nothing but a sudden hole in the snow—and I stepped back from it, raised my hands against the unpredictable approach, the irregular sound of motion, the blind but somehow deliberate line of attack. Escaped homing pigeons? A covey of tiny ducks driven berserk in the cold? Eaglets? I found myself beating the air, attempting to shield my eyes and ears, thought I saw a little drop of blood on the snow. And I was relieved with the first hit. It caught me just behind the ear—crunching shock at the base of the head—and still it might have been the ice-encrusted body of a small bird, except that despite the pain, the vigorous crack of the thing and my loss of breath, and even while I reached behind my ear and discov-ered my fingers covered with ice and blood, I was turning around, stooping, trying and of course failing to find the body. With the second hit—quite furious, close on the first, snowball full in the face—my relief was complete and I knew that this time at least I had nothing to fear from any unnatural vengefulness of wild birds.

Tremlow, I thought, when the hard-packed snowball of the second hit burst in my face, Tremlow, thinking that only Tremlow's malice—it was black and putty-thick, a curd incomprehensibly coughed up just for me—could account for the singular intensity of this treachery intended to befall me in the parking lot, could account for the raging meanness behind this ambush. I stood my ground, spitting snow, shaking the snow out of my eyes, dragging the snow away with my two hands and feeling the sudden purple abrasions on my cheeks, trying to dodge. Not a shadow, not a curved arm, not a single one of them in sight. But the barrage was slowing, though losing none of its power, none of its accuracy, and I could see the snowballs now and they were winging at me from all angles, every direction. I swung at them, growled at them, helpless and wet and bleeding, and still they came. The third hit—blow in the side, sound of a thump, no breath—sailed up at me slowly, slowly, loomed like a white cabbage and struck me exactly as I tried to step out of its path. Tracer bullet confusion of snowballs. Malevolent missiles. From every corner of the lot they came, and from the vicinity of the all-but-hidden cars—lovers? could this be the activity of island lovers? nothing better to do?—and even, I thought, from as far as the cemetery.

I fought back. Oh, I fought back, scooping the snow wildly, snarling, beating and compressing that snow into white iron balls and flinging them, heaving them off into the flurry, the thick of the night, but I could find no enemy and it was a hopeless sweat. "Tremlow!" I shouted, raising my head though I felt in tingling scalp and quivering chin the unprotected condition of that bald head as target, "Tremlow! Come out and fight!" A hoarse shout. Unmistakable cry of rage addressed to the phantom bully, the ringleader of my distant past. Perhaps from somewhere, from some dark corner of the world, he heard.

Because it ceased. I saw no one, heard no human sound, no laughter, and the last of the discharged snowballs fell about me in a heavy but harmless patter like the last great duds of a spent avalanche. Final lobbing to earth of useless snowballs. Irregular thudding in the snow. Then safe. Then silence. Only the gentle puffing fall of the now tiny flakes, only the far-off wind, only the muffled sound of Jack Spratt's Merry Hep Cats commencing once again in my ears. Only the yellow light on the snow. And of course the blood and snot on the back of my hand.

I waited. And slowly I controlled my temper and my pain, controlled my breathing, brushed the palm of my hand over my scalp and regained my usual composure. I was wet and chilled, but I smiled when I saw what an enormous ring I had trampled all about me in the snow. The great stag that had been at bay was no longer at bay. Tremlow, if he had ever been there, was gone. As I walked slowly back along the deep path I had cut from the fire door to the center of the parking lot I forgot about the demon of my past and began to muse about that enemy of the present who was, I knew, only too real. How was it possible, I wondered, for a man to throw snowballs with an artificial hand?

But it was my night of trials and when I returned to the gymnasium, blinking, wiping face and hands with my handkerchief, trying to reset the sparkle in my watering eyes, I saw the two of them at once—Jomo, Cassandra—saw that the hook was buried deep in the bow, that the two of them were dipping together to the strains of a waltz—Jomo leading off with a long leg thrust between her legs—and that Jomo was panting and that his trousers were sopping wet up to the knees. Poor Cassandra like a green leaf was turning, floating, waltzing away out of my life, a green leaf on the back of the spider. My teen-age bomb and her boy friend. And I might have charged him then and there, might have struck him down when two little white roly-poly women cut me short, caught my arms, hung a numbered placard around my neck, pushed me forward like little tugs—dirt in the girdles, dough in the dimples, mother's milk to spare—and the music stopped, girls giggled, someone stood on a Coca-Cola crate and shouted: "Take your places, belly-bumpers! Gather about now, folks, for the contest!"

And another voice: "Make them take off their belts, hey, Doc! Buckles ain't fair!"

And the first: "Ladies, pick your bumpers . . . bumpers in place . . . come on now, fellows, we got to start!"

Laughter. Calls of encouragement. Eight pairs of bumpers—including me—to fight it out pair by pair. Then a circle in the crowd, silence, boy with the bass drum and boy with the cornet standing there to beat and blow for each winner. And I who had always considered myself quite trim, heavy but rather handsome of form, holding up my trousers, perspiring now, I was called upon to make sport of myself, to join in the fleshly malice of this island game. Perverse. The death of modesty. But I could not refuse, could not explain that there was some mistake —rising to the catcalls in that human ring—could do nothing but accept the challenge and bump with the best of them and give them the full brunt of belly, if belly they wanted. I noticed that the old-timers were drinking down last minute pitchers of water so that they would rumble. But I was not intimidated. I would show them a thing or two with my stomach which all at once felt like a warhead. *Allons*. . . .

The fat began to fly. It was an obscene tournament. And if I had lost the night even before my abortive journey to the parking lot, or if I had begun to suffer the hour that would never pass when I first set foot in Jomo's car, or if I had tasted the thick endlessness of the night with my first hurried mouthful of chocolate cake, knowing that I was sealed more and more tightly into some sort of desperate honeycomb of dead time with every drink the bare-headed marine took from his bottle—drinking to my frustration, drinking me dry—and if I had already begun my endless sweat at the mere sight of dancers dancing, what then was my dismay among the belly-bumpers? What then my injury—pain of bouncing bags, cramp of belligerence low in the gut—what then my confusion and drugged determination as I stood there facing the glazed eye of time? Dimly I heard Doc's voice, "Hey there, no hands!" And slowly, slowly, I forced myself to learn the stance with body sagging to the front, back bowed, shoulders drawn tightly to the rear, elbows pulled close to the ribs and sharply bent, hands limp, fingers limp, barely holding up the trousers, forced myself to balance on the balls of my feet, to balance, pull in the chin, thrust, sail forward and bump, shudder, recover. Without moving my feet. Dead time. Spirited dismay.

Sweat in the eyes, breathless. Partners face to face, hands set and loose and dangling like little fins, bellies an inch apart, two mean idiotic smiles. Ready. And then the signal, crowd pressing in to see, and then the swaying start, the first bump, the grunt, the rhythm of collision, and in and out, up and down, forward and backward with shirt tails working loose in front and the bottom of the belly popping out and visible and pink and sore, bump and shudder and recover—tempo steady but blows rising in strength—until the look of surprise, the tottering step, the blush of defeat, and Skipper wins again. Another blast on the cornet, more blows on the drum. Some clapping, my weak smile. Then off again, off on another round.

I vanquished the local butcher, came up against Red's cousin, fought on until I nearly met my match in Uncle Billy. Because he was last year's champion and wanted to win. Because bare as the day he was born he weighed four hundred and eight pounds on the fish factory scales. Because he was sixty-three years old and prime. Because he wore no un-

derwear on bumping days and bumped with his shirt unbuttoned,
bumped with his blackened gray cotton workshirt pulled out of his
pants and hanging loose and flowing wide from neck to somewhere
below the navel. Because he also wore rubber-soled shoes and, tied in
little fingerlike knots at the four corners, a red bandanna on his big bald
head—nigger neckerchief to frighten opponents and keep the sweat out
of his eyes—and from a heavy chain locked around his throat a big
gold bouncing crucifix. And because he whispered in constant violation
of the rules, and because he rumbled. Uncle Billy who knew all the
tricks. King of the fat.

Old volcano belly. Worse than a horse, louder than a horse. Rum-
bling, sloshing, bearing down, steering his terrible tumescence with the
mere sides of his wrists and for a moment I saw their faces in the
crowd—Miranda, Jomo, Red, Bub, Cassandra, all in a row, all smiling—and I thought I saw Cassandra wave, and then I was laboring to
keep my balance, to hold my stride, while with every painful encounter
I could feel that Uncle Billy hadn't even begun to exert himself and was
only biding his time, waiting me out.

And the catcalls: "Come on, Uncle Billy, bust him open!"

And close to me and through his little hard teeth the constant whispering: ". . . never been on a woman. Never had a woman on me. No
sir. . . . Always saved myself. For supper, that's my big meal, and for
bumping. . . . I eat a full loaf of bread whenever I sit down to table.
And I make a habit of drinking one full gallon can of sweetened corn
syrup every day. . . . So you know what you're up against. The picture
of health," nodding the nigger neckerchief, tossing his cross, patches of
short white whisker beginning to shine on his fat cheeks, "because the
Good Lord gave me so much flesh that little things like piles or stones
or a cardiac condition don't mean a thing. . . . Never know they're
there. . . . Now wait a minute," going up on his toes, eyes bright,
shadow of a jawline appearing above his jowls, "don't you try to trick
me, now. . . . You look out for Uncle Billy because I measure eighty-
nine inches around the middle and I'm just letting you get winded before
I bust you right open as the fella wants me to. . . ."

Then: "Your mother," I whispered as we hit, "you bumped bellies
with your mother, did you?"

Socko. Straight to the heart. *Touché.* And in that lapsed moment,
single faltering moment when he tried to determine the exact nature of
the insult—smile swallowed up in a gulp, jaw unhinged, blinding light,
pain in the muck of his morality—I shifted my weight and gave him

everything I had and hooked him, hit him hard and at a fine unsettling angle, managed to work a little hipbone into the blow, man to man, final and fiercest of the thwacking sounds, and his flesh was surrendering against mine even before he sagged, gasped, staggered back from me in defeat, even before I heard the asinine cacophony of drum, cornet, and crowd. I shut my eyes and felt as if at last I had struck the high gong of the carnival.

"No hard feelings," I said, and wiped my face on my sleeve.

"You win, Mister. But here," fumbling with the chain, holding out his hand, "do me a favor and take this as a gift from me. I got it when I beat the Reverend Peafowl at belly-bumping. But now you deserve it more than me."

So with the chain and crucifix in my pocket and a five-pound chocolate cake in a box under my arm I set off calling through the crowd for Cassandra. And of course she was gone. All of them were gone. I was alone, abandoned, left behind. Outside I stood for a long while looking down into the violent ragged hole the fleeing hot rod had torn in the snow, stood watching all their scuffed and hurried footprints now filling slowly, gently, with the first snowfall which was still coming down. The gymnasium lights went off and the trees, the building, the sky behind the snow were all a deep dark blue. There was nothing to do but walk, so I shrugged, put my hands in my pockets, put my head down and started my journey home. Alone.

Trying to hurry, trying to keep out of the deepest drifts, trying to hurry along for Cassandra's sake. There were little black shining twigs encased in icicles, and fence posts and sudden gates opening through the snow. And my wintry road was littered with the bodies of dead birds—I could see their little black glistening feet sticking up like hairs through the crusty tops of the snow banks—and far off where the snow was falling thickest I could hear the sloshing and breaking of the black wintry sea. No lights. No cars. Not even the howl of a dog. It was a late winter night on the black island and I was alone and cold and plowing my slow way home. Digging my way home with my wet feet. Gloomy, anxious, hearing the ice castles shattering in the branches overhead and falling in tiny bright splinters around my ears.

Then the house, the kennel, the sword points of the picket fence, the chestnut tree under full white sail. At last. And thinking of the foot warmer with its brass pan of bright hot coals and seeing the hot rod black and squat and once more covered with new snow, seeing that car and so knowing I was in time after all, I began to clap the snow from my arms and to run the last few steps to the creaking cold veranda where wrapped in a quilt on the frozen glider and smoking a cigarette Miranda sat huddled and waiting for me in the dark. Miranda. Woman in the dark. Wet eyelashes.

"You," I said with my hand already on the old brass knob, "what do you want?"

"Skip," throwing off the quilt, stretching her legs, pitching the cigarette over the broken rail, "don't go in, Skip. They're young. Let's leave them alone."

"Where were you?" I said, and paused, pulled the door shut again softly, faced her. "Do you know what happened to me in that parking lot? Do you? As for running off without me at the end, a pretty cruel trick, Miranda."

"Never mind, for God's sake. They're only kids. But let's go out to the car, Skip, and leave them alone."

"Car? You mean Jomo's car? I wouldn't set foot in his car, Miranda. And besides, I want to go to bed."

"My car, for God's sake. Out back," and her breathing was clear and full and I could see the single gray streak thick and livid in her hair and already she was going down the steps and wading knee-deep in the untrampled snow and I was following her. Against my will. Against my better judgment. Shivering. Watching her closely. Because she had changed her clothes and was wearing the canary yellow slacks that had turned the color of moonlight in the snow and a turtle-neck sweater and a baby-blue cashmere scarf that hung below her knees and dragged in the snow. And the little wet flakes twinkled all over her.

"No snowballs," I said. "I'm warning you."

She muttered something without turning her head and I missed it, let it go by. The snow was falling in fine little stars but I was too cold and wet to enjoy it. Once I glanced back over my shoulder at the house and though there was not a single light in a window I thought I saw the dark head and torso of someone watching me in a downstairs window—Grandma? Jomo? Bub?—but I could not be sure. Apparently the night was full of snares and sentries and I hesitated, wiping the fresh snow out of my eyes, and then I heard Miranda rattling at the wrecked car and I hurried on.

Tall weeds matted deep in the snow. Crystals as big as saucers tucked in the eaves of the rotting shed. Outline of an old wheelbarrow. And canted up slightly on one side next to the shed the smashed and abandoned body of the wrecked hot rod—orange, white, blue in the soft cold light of the snow—and in that dark and gutted and somehow echoing interior Miranda with one white naked hand on the wheel. Dense shadow of woman. Queen of the Nile.

"Hop in," she said, and I heard her patting the mildewed seat, heard her ramming the clutch pedal in and out impatiently.

I tugged, stopped, stuck my head in, looked around—pockets of rust, flakes of rust, pockets of snow, broken glass on the floor—and slid onto the seat beside her. And the glass crackled sharply, the springs were steel traps in the seat, the gearshift lever—little white plastic skull for a knob—rose up like a whip from its socket, the dashboard was a nest of dead wires and smashed or dislocated dials. There was a cold rank acrid odor in that wrecked car as if the cut-down body had been burned out one night with a blowtorch, acrid pungent odor that only heightened the other smells of the night: rotting shed, faint sour smell of wood smoke, salt from the nearby sea, perfume—*Evening in Paris*—which Miranda had splashed on her wrists, her throat, her thick dark head of hair. A powdery snow was blowing against us—no glass in the windows, no windshield—and scratching on the roof of that dreadful little car, and I felt sick at last and wanted only to put my head between my knees, to cover my bare head with my arms and sleep. But I pushed the gearshift lever with the toe of my shoe instead, glanced at Miranda.

"Like it? Bub's going to fix it up for me in the spring. It only needs a couple of new tires."

"Your lipstick's crooked," I said, and sniffed, stared at her, ran my fingers along the clammy seat.

"Yours would be crooked too, for God's sake. But you can thank Red for that." She smiled, close to me, and the lines in her broad white face were drawn with a little sable brush and India ink and the mouth was a big black broken flower still smeared, still swollen, I knew, from the Captain's teeth. "Need I say more?" she said, and snapped out the clutch, picked up the fuzzy end of the baby-blue cashmere scarf and rubbed it against her cheek.

"That's all right, Miranda. I don't care anything about your private life. Shouldn't we be going back to the house?"

"We just got here, for God's sake. Relax. You're just like Don, never sit still a minute. But of course Don was love."

Silence. Hand pulling up and down aimlessly on the steering wheel. Snow falling. Snow singing on the roof. Then a movement in her corner,

sudden rolling agitation in the springs, and her tight yellow statuesque
leg was closer to mine and she was reaching out, pressing the cashmere
scarf against my cheek.

And quickly: "What about Cassandra?" I said. "She won't do anything foolish?"

Another drag of the rump, leg another few inches closer, and she
leaned over then—slowly, slowly—and with long moody deliberation
removed the tip of the scarf from my cheek and wrapped it twice around
my throat and fastened it in a single knot with one tight sudden jerk.
Too vehement I thought. But tied together neck to neck. Hitched. And
feeling the cashmere choking me, and seeing the head thrown back
against the mildewed seat and the long leg bent at the knee and the
angora sweater white and curdled all the way through—solid, not a
bone to interrupt that mass, no garment to destroy the rise of the
greater-than-life-size breasts—at last I felt like a sculptor in the presence
of his nubile clay—to hold the twin mounts, Oh God, to cast the
thighs—and quickly I flung my right hand out of the wrecked car window, heard something rip.

"Cassandra? Cassandra?" she said, showing me the deep black formless mouth, the hair on the back of the seat: "Like mother, like daughter,
isn't that about it? You and your poor little Candy Cane," she said, and
she was laughing—low mellow mannish laugh, scorn and intimacy and
self-confidence—and with one foot resting on the dashboard and the
other hooked to the edge of the seat she rolled up the bottom of the
sweater and took the heavy canary yellow cloth in both bony hands
and, tensing all her muscles, pulled down the slacks and swung herself
up and away on one cold and massive hip. Away from me. Face and
hands and eyes away from me. Laughing.

Icebergs. Cold white monumental buttocks. Baffling cold exposure.
Classical post card from an old museum. Treachery on the Nile. Desire
and disaster. Pitiless. A soft breath of snow swirling in that white saddle,
settling in the dark curves and planes and along the broad rings of
the spine. And laughing, shaking the car, muffling her deep low voice
in her empty arms she said: "Red's sleeping it off right now. So how
about you?"

Drunk? Out of her mind with passion? Or spiteful? Who could tell?
But in the rusty disreputable interior of that frozen junk heap she had
mocked me with the beauty of her naked stern, had challenged, aroused,
offended me with the blank wall of nudity, and I perceived a cruel
motive somewhere. So I clawed at the scarf, tore loose the scarf, and

supporting myself palm-down on her icy haunch for one insufferably glorious instant I gathered my weight, rammed my shoulder against the loud tinny metal of the rusted door—no handle, door stuck shut—and kicked myself free of her, kicked my way out of the car and fled. Burning. Blinded. But applauding myself for the escape.

When I reached the front of the house I realized that the snow had stopped and that the slick black hot rod under the chestnut tree was gone. When I reached Cassandra's room, puffing through the darkness, feeling my way, I knew immediately that she was not asleep, and without pausing I dropped to my knees beside her and took her cold hand —no rings—and confessed to her at long last that Fernandez was dead. That I had found him dead at the end of my final shore patrol on Second Avenue. That I thought she should know. Pixie stirred from time to time but did not wake. Then at the doorway I stopped and glanced back at the rumpled chunky four-poster bed, the black shadow of the cradle on the warped floor, the windowpane covered with snow.

And softly: "We were wrong about him, weren't we? Just a little? I think so, Cassandra."

In my own room I discovered Uncle Billy's crucifix in my pocket and pulled it out, held it in the palm of my hand and stared at it, then hung it around the neck of my white tunic on the dressmaker's dummy. Gold was my color. Another medal for Papa Cue Ball. Someone—Miranda? Red? Jomo? Bub? even Grandma was not above suspicion—had filled the foot warmer with water, and it was frozen solid. I frowned, set it carefully outside my door—blue tit—and inched myself into the cold comfort of that poor iron bed with bars.

Sleep with a gentle thought, I remembered, and did my best.

VILE, IN THE
SUNSHINE CRAWLING

Yes, I have always believed in gentle thoughts. Despite everything, including the long-past calumnious efforts of a few cranks in the Navy Department, I have always remained my mother's son. And how satisfying it is that virtue—tender guardian, sweet victor, white phantom of the boxing ring, which makes me think of the days before the mutiny when Tremlow vainly attempted to give me boxing lessons every late afternoon in a space cleared among the young bronze cheering sailors on the fantail—how satisfying that virtue always wins. I have only to consider Sonny and Catalina Kate and Sister Josie and myself to know that virtue is everywhere and that we, at least, are four particles of its golden dust.

Yes, everywhere. In getting down to business with one of the cows, in blowing the conch that calls the cows across the field to me, in noticing from time to time the remarkably rapid growth of the child, another fleck of golden dust inside Catalina Kate, in splitting a pawpaw with Sonny or spending an hour or two over the year-old newspaper Catalina Kate had wrapped the hot dogs in, or calling out "No beat the puppy!" to the small black bowlegged boy who wallops the little pink squealing bitch every afternoon between the overgrown water wheel and our collapsing barn, in all this, then, the virtue of life itself.

In the very act of living I see myself, picture myself, as if memory had already done its work and flowered, subjected even myself to the golden glass. Broad white window frame, white shutter with all but a few slanting lattices knocked out, long mahogany table, cane chairs, rusted hurricane lamp suspended by a chain from the ceiling that rises to a peak, pagoda style, and houses the bats; gray clay-colored wooden floor, hemp hammock filled with red petals, odor of slaves and curry and wine and hibiscus soft and luxurious on the dark air. Cup of the warm south. Beaded bubbles. And myself: drawn up to the table, studious, smiling at the thought of the little dark faces pressed into the enormous green and yellow leaves curling in at the window, frowning and smiling both with my upper body leaning on the table and my feet bare and my toes playing in the rich dust under the table, eyes and mouth burning slightly with the fever of our constant and deceptive temperature. Myself. Lunged quietly against my long table—bottle of French wine, bottle of local rum, handful of long thin unbanded black cigars stuck like pencils in a jam jar, swarms of little living fleas in the grooves of my note-taking paper—lunged at the table and seeing myself and smiling at the thought of yesterday, yesterday when I sat in the swamp with Sister Josie and Catalina Kate, and ruminating over the latest development of Kate's precious pregnancy—Kate has only about three more months to go, it occurs to me—and teasing the fleas.

And so I have already stepped once more from behind the scenes of my naked history and having come this far I expect that I will never really be able to conceal myself completely in all those scenes which are even now on the tip of my tongue and crowding my eye. The fact of the matter is that Miranda will have to wait while I turn to a still more distant past, turn back to a few of my long days at sea and to several other highlights of my more distant past. Mere victory over Miranda is nothing, while virtue is everything. So now for my past, for the virtue of my far-distant past.

But first my afternoon in the swamp.

God knows what time it was, but we had finished eating our noon meal of the sea creatures Big Bertha somehow digs out of the conchs, and Sonny was sleeping out in the barn and I was sitting at my table and toying with—yes, even after seven years I still wear it around my neck on its thin chain—toying with Uncle Billy's crucifix and thinking about certain problems of my profession. I was noticing that the insides of my hands were the color of golden straw, and was listening to the doves when suddenly a face appeared among the flat green and yellow leaves and spotted shadows outside my window, a tiny face as smooth as a wet kidney and the color of the black keys on a piano. Tiny little face without a line, with eyes like great timid pearls and a little nut-brown mouth and masses of artificial gold teeth—young as she was she had had all her teeth extracted and nice gold teeth installed for beauty's sake—and around the little black head the truly gigantic mauve headpiece of her official habit and the white thing that looked like a priest's collar shoved vertically over her tiny face. Serene, serious, silent.

"Sister Josie," I said, "is it really you? How nice. But Sister Josie, what do you want?"

Somber child. Dark wonderfully cowled little head in the corner of the window. Little black cheekbones. Pearls beginning to dissolve and more luminous and gentle than ever. Ready to open her mouth, this child, this black girl, thin devoted example of missionary madness. Sweating. Hot as the devil. Long time to answer. And then she smiled and in a murmur she asked me to come with her because Catalina Kate was asking for me and had sent her, Sister Josie, up to Plantation House to persuade me, if she could, to join her in a little walk down to the swamp.

"Well, of course, Josie," I said, and reached for my old yellowing cap and cocked it on my head, "I was wondering about Kate since you usually dog her tracks, don't you, Josie?"

Vigorous nodding in the corner of the window. Trembling of the little dark features. Master coming. Gift of God. Ecstasy. As usual I was pleased with her happiness and smiled and told her to wait for me by the water wheel. I extended my hand slowly, gently, and let it come to rest on the broad white sill so that it was directly in the path of a little black newborn lizard which I had noticed while listening to Sister Josie's soft interminable plea. And for a moment we watched the baby lizard together. It was black, fuzzy, about an inch and a half in length. It was covered with frills and tendrils, wore leggings, had absurdly large feet for its size and an absurdly large blind head. Ugly. And while we watched—did Josie make the sign of the cross?—the baby lizard crawled onto the back of my hand and stopped, little tail twitching at a wonderful rate, and stood still as I lifted him slowly into the warm sweet air that hovered between Sister Josie and myself. Lifted him up to my nose.

"Do you see, Josie? He hasn't any eyes. And look at that tail, will you? Excruciating!"

We laughed. Then I took a deep breath, puckered my lips and blew so that he sailed off in an orgy of somersaults and plopped onto a bright golden spot next to Josie's cheeks.

"I'll have to improve my aim, Josie," I said, and, laughing, shooed her off to the water wheel. No doubt the little lizard would turn into a dandy big fellow when he grew older. But I have always favored the birds, especially the hummingbirds, over the lizards and butterflies. Give me the mystery of birds or the strength and sweetness of honest-to-God animals like cows any time. What better than the little honeysuckers or the leather hides and masticated grass and purple eyes of my favorite cows? As for a blackbird sitting on a cow's rump, there surely is the perfect union, the meeting of the fabulous herald and the life source. And there are always the ground doves to give voice to my vision, soul to my love.

Since I was up and about I looked in on Big Bertha—mass of black fat, calico rags, old brazen face and dusty hands and fat breasts decorated with the fingerprints of the babies she had nursed, all of her crouched over the mortar and pestle and fast asleep—and I grinned at her, raised my finger to the visor of my cap in salute to her. I strolled around to feed a few fistfuls of green grass to the ducks, squatting, pulling up the grass, enjoying the greed of the ducks and the way they wagged their white tails. Then to my feet again and on through the shadows of the lime trees—perfect little pale yellow globules dangling amidst the riffling green leaves and shadows and nearly invisible thorns—until I came out into the sun and approached the barn.

I stood in the doorway, crossed my legs, leaned against the hot porous upright—remarkable labor of the wood ants—thrust my hands into my pockets and stared up at the star-shaped hole in the roof. Interesting star-shaped hole with a shaft of sunlight driven through it like a stake. Dry and sagging timbers, roof that would soon collapse and be no more. Sonny—my ingenious Sonny—wanted to remove some of the planks from the walls to repair the roof. But I preferred the barn as it was, or as it would be. We would just have to get along, I told Sonny, with a roofless barn, and I was pleased when he slapped his thigh and said, "Oh, you means a roofless barn. I understands you, Skipper. That's good!" I knew I could always count on Sonny.

I walked into the barn then and stood at the foot of Sonny's hammock and smiled down on him. Poor Sonny. Sleeping in the heat of the afternoon. Hands clasped behind his head, light streaming in the little rivers between his ribs, hammock swaying, one long black shrunken leg dangling out of the hammock, hanging down. He was naked except for a pair of combat boots—no laces, leather turned to white fungus—and a pair of my castoff white jockey shorts and a sailor hat with the brim reversed and airslits, diamonds, cut around the crown. And he had changed in seven years—thinner, a few white kinks in the hair, some of the rich oily luster gone from his black skin, incurable case of boils on one of his thighs—but was Sonny, still Sonny with every black bone showing and a smile sleeping on those living lips which looked as if they had been split open in a fight. The nearby shaft of sunlight cast a glow on the patched hemp of the hammock and sent little shadows dancing and shivering up and down this black length of Sonny in his stretched and swaying bed. I left him in peace, walked softly to the other end of the barn where Oscar the bull was watching us.

"What's the matter, Oscar," I said, "jealous of my attentions?"

Confusion and hatred in the crossed bloodshot eyes. Dust swirling out of the shaggy white head of hair when I rumpled it. Flies in the ears. Mean old bull begrudging every invisible drop of his scattered seed. Flies, lice, mud. But marvelous shaggy machinery for my purposes.

"Don't be jealous, Oscar," I said softly, "your time will come." And I laughed and gave the brass ring in his nose a little tug and turned my back on him, walked out to the hot radiance beyond the doorway. I paused for a moment, squinted, fanned myself briefly with my cap, then made for the water wheel.

She was nearly invisible against the water wheel, my little blessed chameleon with bowed head and folded hands. But she was there and waiting. Patient and perspiring in the shade of the wheel. Each time I saw the water wheel, and I saw it a good many times each day, I stopped, always perplexed and startled to see its life-giving gloom. Because it was about twenty feet tall, this fusion of iron wheel and fragment of stone wall, and useless, absolutely useless, and inexplicable, statuary of unknown historic significance now drenched with green growth, robbed of its power. The wheel that could never turn, the wall that had ceased its crumbling. No water. And yet in every cracked iron cup, in every dark green furry ribbon of the climbing plants, in every black hanging leaf and every swaddling vine—there was even a little crooked gray tree growing out of the side of it—it appeared to be spongy and dense and saturated, seemed to drip with all the waters of the past and all the bright cold waters that would never flow. Monolith of forgotten industry, what on earth had it crushed? What sweetness extracted? The birds were singing and chirping among the red berries and in secret crevices in the moss. I listened until I could disregard no longer the little nun standing there meekly under the towering wheel.

"Well, Josie," I said, and stepped forward briskly, "Let's go and see what this is all about. OK, Josie?"

She told me that she was ready to go, though her little silk voice was so soft I could hardly hear it above the sound of the birds, and she told me that Miss Catalina Kate was hoping I would go to her. I smiled.

"Lead on, Sister Josie," I said, and sauntered along behind her as she picked her way down the hot path trying to avoid the thorns in the high grass. The wind was rolling about in that high grass—stretching out to sleep? getting ready to spring?—and there were trees growing out of trees, smooth gray trunks and bushy heads of hair, flowers like painted fingernails and occasionally underfoot a sudden webbing of little roots tied in knots. But Sister Josie had nimble feet and knew where she was going.

"Do I smell guavas, Josie?"

Vigorous nodding.

"Why don't you pick a load on our way back, Josie? I'm very fond of guavas."

More nodding, long soft statement of acquiescence.

When we passed the pile of dried conchs and stepped out onto the beach the bush was on our right and the sea on our left and the bush was impenetrable and the beach was a quarter-mile strip of snowy pink sand and the tide was sliding in, frothing, jumping up in little round waves. So there was much wetting of shoes and trouser bottoms and swaying skirts during that last quarter mile of our walk. Above us through the dead coconut leaves the sun was an old bloody bone low in the sky. I whistled, hummed, blinked, licked salt. Paused to help Sister Josie climb over the windfalls or crawl through the sea grape trees.

"Lovely spot, Josie," I said. "Good for the soul."

"Oh yes, sir." Furnace of gold teeth, habit soaked to the knees. "That why she here, sir."

"But surely she doesn't mean to have the child out here, Josie? Does she?"

"Oh, yes, sir. She want the baby in the swamp, sir."

"Well, there's courage for you, Josie."

"Yes, sir."

And then the bush fell away on our right and the beach swept wide into the sea on our left and rose, straight ahead, into a long white sandy shelf, and Sister Josie and I were in the open and pulling each other to the top of the broad sandy shelf. A fisherman's hut, a white stump, the green transparent tint of the endless sea on one side and on the other, where the shelf dipped down into a little rank stagnant crescent, the swamp. The beginning of the swamp. Dark green tepid sludge of silent waters drifting inland among the ferns and roots and fuzzy pockets and pools of the infested swamp. Harem of veiled orchids, cells of death.

"You see, Josie," smiling, raising my hand, gesturing, feeling the ocean breeze on my neck and smelling the lively activity of the fields of

sunken offal in the swamp, breathing deeply and seeing how the pale
blue-green light of the ocean met the dark greens and heavy yellows of
the swamp, "you see, Josie, a true freak of nature. Wonderful, isn't it?
And that fisherman's hut, who knows what's been going on in that
fisherman's hut, eh, Josie? How about it now, a few small sacrifices to
the gods?"

And head lowered, eyes lowered, voice soft and serious: "Sometimes
she sleep there, sir."

The ants were racing through the holes in my tennis shoes and the
tide was a rhythmic darkening of the sand and something was beating
great frightened wings in the swamp. There were bright yellow turds
hanging from a soft gray bough over the hut, and I began to scratch.
But then I looked down and saw what I had somehow failed to see in
my first sweeping glance at the warmer side of the sand shelf and beginning of the swamp. And I took slow incredulous footsteps down that
sandy incline, leaned forward, held out my hands.

"Kate. Are you all right, Kate?"

She was lying there and watching me. Must have been watching me
all the time. Lying there on her stomach. Chin in her hands. Naked.
Legs immersed halfway up the calves in the warm yellowish pea soup
of that disgusting water. And stuck to her back, spread eagle on her
broad soft naked back, an iguana with his claws dug in.

"Kate, what is it, Kate. . . ."

But she only smiled. I stopped, hand thrust out, and kneeled on one
knee in front of Catalina Kate who had the terrible reptile clinging to
her back. His head reached her shoulders, his tail dropped over her
buttocks, and he might have been twenty or thirty pounds of sprawling
bright green putty. Boneless. Eyes like shots in the dark. Gorgeous bright
green feathery ruff running down the whole length of him. Thick and
limp and weak, except for the oversized claws which were grips of steel.
Kate was looking at me and smiling and the iguana was looking at me,
and I heard the noise of locust or cricket or giant swamp fly strangling
behind a nearby bush.

"Hold on, Kate," I whispered, "don't move. Just leave him to me."

So then I rose carefully from my position on one knee and tried to
think of what to do, of how to go about it. There at my feet was Kate,
and she was stretched out flat on the sand, had dug a nice deep oval
hole for her belly, and her naked skin was soft and broad, mauve and
tan, and the shadows all over her arms and calves and flanks were like

innumerable little bright pointed leaves. At one end of her the scum from the swamp water lay in fluffy white piles against her calves; at the other her black hair was heaped up in a crown, shaped in oil, and the long thick braid hung down over one shoulder into the sand. A child with real pink sea shells for ears, child with a disappointing nose but with lips as thin as my own and bowed, moist, faintly violet and smiling. A dark mole—beauty mole—on one cheek. Body as big as Big Bertha's. A garden, but shaped by her youth. There at my feet. Kate.

And on her back the monster.

So I straddled her—colossus over the reptile, colossus above the shores of woman—and hearing the lap and shifting of the sea, and wiping my palms on my thighs and leaning forward, I prepared to grapple with the monster. My eyes were already shut and my hands already feeling downwards, groping, when Josie, little Sister Josie, took courage—for her it must have been courage—and called out to me.

"Oh, no, sir. No, sir. Don't touch iguana, sir. Him stuck for so!"

She had risen from her seat on the stump in front of the fisherman's hut, wringing her hands, squeezing her ankles together beneath her skirts, doll in the sunshine, straight and small, but sat down again quickly as soon as I glanced at her. Little black face, pained eyes, ankles and knees and hands all rigid and pinched together, unbearable hot weight of cowl and little buttoned shoes and God knows how many skirts. I was in no mood to take advice from Sister Josie and told her so.

"That's all right, Josie," I said. "I'll handle this."

From inside the rich brown layers of drapery or from one of her sleeves she produced a tiny Bible and licked a finger, began to read. She looked like a little black beetle hunched up and reading the Bible in the sunlight. The forked tongues were crying out in the swamp. I shook my head. And lunged down for the iguana.

I got him with the first grab. Held him. Waited. And with my feet buried deep in the sand, my legs spread wide and locked, my rump in the air, tattered shirt stuck to my skin like a plaster, nostrils stoppered up with the scum of the swamp, heart thumping, I made myself hold on to him—in either hand I gripped one of the forelegs—and fought to subdue the repellent touch of him, fought not to tear away my hands and run. Cool rubber ready to sting. Feeling of being glued to the iguana, of skin growing fast to reptilian skin.

"Now," I said through clenched teeth, and opened my eyes, "now we'll see if you're any match for Papa Cue Ball." And slowly I pulled up on him, gently began to wrestle with him. He yielded his putty, stretched himself, displayed a terrible elasticity, and everything rose up to my grasp except the claws.

"It's just like being in the dentist's chair, Kate," I muttered, and grinned through my own agony, "it'll be over soon." But Catalina Kate gave no sign of pain, though now her head was resting on her folded arms and her eyes were closed. So I kept pulling up on the iguana, tugged at him with irritation now. With every tug I seemed to dig the claws in deeper, to drag them down deeper into the flesh of poor Kate's back in some terrible inverse proportion to all the upward force I exerted on the flaccid wrinkled substance of the jointless legs or whatever it was I hung on to so desperately. And he wouldn't budge. Because of those claws I was unable to pull him loose, unable to move him an inch, was only standing there bent double and sweating, pulling, muttering to myself, drawing blood.

"Well, Kate," I said, and let go, stood up, wiped my brow, "it looks as if he's there for good. Got us licked, hasn't he, Kate? Licked from the start. He means to stay right where he is until he changes his mind and crawls off under his own power. So the round goes to the dragon, Kate. I'm sorry."

I climbed off, dipped my hands in the scummy water—even scummy water was preferable to the iguana—rubbed them, wiped them on my trousers, mounted the slope, flung myself down in the sand beside Sister Josie. And grimacing, pulling the visor down fiercely over my eyes, "There's nothing to do but wait," I said. "We'll have to be patient."

"She plenty patient already, sir. She already waiting."

"That's right, Josie," I said, "you young ladies better stick together."

Sister Josie read her Bible, I twirled Uncle Billy's crucifix on its gold chain until the sun came down. And we waited. Coconuts knocking together, sun drenching the sand, dry bones scraping in the middle of the swamp, peacock tails of ugly plants fanning and blazing around the edge of the swamp, a little pall of late afternoon heat settling over us. Like Sonny and Big Bertha and the rest of them I must have dozed. Because suddenly I was leaning forward to the stillness of the warm south and trembling, giving the nun a signal on her little knee.

"Do you see, Josie? Do you see? The iguana moved!"

It was true. He had unhooked his claws and slid down onto Kate's right hand and deep rosy shoulder and upper arm, and now his ruff was humming, his tongue flexing in swordplay, swishing in all the tiny hues of the rainbow, and the eyes were dashing together like little sparks.

"He's hungry! Do you see that, Josie? He's hungry now, he's going off to hunt flies! Thank God for Kate. . . ."

So he plopped from her shoulder and waddled down to the scum, this bright aged thing livid in the last thick rays of the sun, and inch by steady inch pushed himself under the lip of a broad low-hanging yellow leaf and into the scum, and lashing his tail, kicking suddenly with his stubby rear legs, he disappeared. Succubus. I would have gone after him with a stone had it not been for the failing light and for Catalina Kate who had raised herself up on her arms and was smiling and beckoning and opening to me like some downy swamp orchid.

I ran to her and sank down next to her, panting, brushing the sand from her breasts.

"Well done, Kate!" I whispered, "well done, my brown Joan of Arc. You know about Joan of Arc, don't you, Kate? The lady burned up in the fire?"

Smiling. But a gentle smile and only faintly visible. A color in the face. Touch of serenity about the eyes and at the corners of the mouth. Nothing but the radiance of the fifteen or sixteen years of her life on this our distant shore, our wandering island.

I took her hand. I covered her back with the remnants of my own dissolving shirt and I reached down into the enormous egg-shaped hole in the sand and helped Kate to feel with her soft young fingers what I could feel with mine: the warmth of the recent flesh and the little humped hieroglyphic in the warm sand.

"Feel the baby, Kate? Unborn baby down there in the sand, eh, Kate? But no more iguanas, you must promise me that. We don't want to let the iguana get the baby, you know."

She nodded. Kate understood. And that's all there was to it. I helped her to her feet and arm in arm we climbed the little velvet slope of sand together and walked up to Sister Josie—another sign of the cross, big gold flash of teeth—who rose, held out her arms and embraced my own nude Catalina Kate. That's all there was to it. Except walking back alone to Plantation House in our moment of darkness, brushing aside the leaves and thorns and stumbling knee-deep in the salty foam, I saw the few lights and long black silhouette of a ship at sea and smiled to myself since apparently our wandering island has become quite invisible. Only a mirage of shimmering water to all the ships at sea, only the thick black spice of night and the irregular whispering of an invisible shore.

So now I sit staring at the long black cigars and at the bottle of French wine. Perhaps I will open the French wine when the child is born, drink off the French wine when the child is born on the Night of All Saints. And now I goad myself with the distant past.

So hold your horses, Miranda! Father and Gertrude and Fernandez, sleep! Now take warning, Tremlow!

WAX IN THE LILIES

"WE CAN SELL THE TIRES ALONG THE WAY if we have to, Papa Cue Ball," said Fernandez, as in pairs we rolled them—white walls, retreads, dusty black tires as smooth as balloons—from his little improvised garage to his old disreputable forest green sedan. "Besides, I couldn't leave them behind. They might be stolen. Nobody's honest these days, Papa Cue Ball. The war makes everybody steal."

"You know best, Fernandez," I said. "But there isn't room for all these tires. And what will your bride think of setting off on her honeymoon in a car loaded up to the hilt with black market tires? Not very *sympathique*, Fernandez?"

"Look, Papa Cue Ball, look here," letting two fat ones roll to a stop against a fender, and then leaping into the car, leaping back into the dust again, "I throw out the seat—so—I throw out all this ugly stuff from the trunk compartment—what would anyone be doing with all these rags—and we have plenty of room for the tires. As to your second objection," stooping to the nearest tire, glaring up at me darkly—I hastened to give him a hand—and speaking slowly and in the most severe of his Peruvian accents, "it will be a very short honeymoon, Papa Cue Ball, I assure you. A very short honeymoon."

I smiled. In the long summer twilight of the trailer camp—soft magenta light through temporary telephone poles and brittle trees, distant sound of schoolboys counting off like soldiers, sound of tropical birds caged up behind a neighbor's salmon-colored mobile home—and with his little shoulders square and hard under the white shirt, and his trousers, little tight pleated trousers, hitched as high as the second or third rib, and wearing the white linen shirt and crimson braces and the rattlesnake belt and tiny black pointed boots, surely Fernandez looked like a miniature Rudolph Valentino—eyes of the lonely lover, moistened lips—and I could only admire him and smile.

"Short but passionate, Fernandez?" I said then, and laughed.

"Don't try to be indelicate with me, Papa Cue Ball. Please."

"You misunderstand me, Fernandez," I said, and paused, frowned, extended my hand. "Since you have married my daughter I thought I could speak to you—well—frankly, and also joyously."

"OK, OK, good Papa Cue Ball. Let's forget it."

"Just as you say, Fernandez," I said, and reached out, took his small cool hand in mine, shook hands with him. "I share your happiness, Fernandez, I want you to know that," I said, and for a moment I leaned against the old waiting automobile and my head was light and my mouth was dry and tart and bubbling with the lingering dry aroma and lingering taste of the warm champagne. Because I had considered champagne indispensable. And I had supplied the champagne, carried it to the City Hall in a paper bag, and after the service and in the dim institutional corridor between the City Clerk's office and a Navy recruiting office we three had sipped our warm champagne straight from the bottle. I had counted on paper cups, but as luck would have it, the water cooler was dry and filled with dust and there was not one paper cup to be found in the holder. Toward the end of the bottle, when there were only a few drops of our celebrative wine remaining, I kissed the bride, there in the dark corridor of the City Hall. And now I remembered the kiss, the champagne, the City Clerk with dirty fingernails, and I wanted only to please Fernandez, to please Cassandra, to make the day end well.

So I did my share of the work and together we rolled the last of the unruly bouncing tires out to the waiting Packard and stowed them aboard. The chickens, little red bantams, and little white frightened hens, were cackling in the makeshift garage and squawking in sudden alarm, and I was tempted to toss them my remaining left-hand pocketful of confetti—yes, I had thrown my fiery flakes of confetti at Cassandra on the hot sidewalk in front of the red brick City Hall—but Fernandez had told me that the chickens were good layers and I thought better of it, left the confetti in the pocket where it was. Instead I stooped and clucked at the chickens, tried to nuzzle a little white stately hen under my arm. But it was a suspicious bedraggled bird and much too quick for me.

"The car needs some water, good Papa Cue Ball," Fernandez called from the steps of his stubby one-man aluminum trailer—it sat on blocks like a little bright bullet in the fading sunlight—so while Fernandez gathered together his guitar and cardboard suitcase and extra pair of shoes and drew down the shades and locked the trailer, I managed to attach the hose to the outdoor spigot, pried open the enormous and battered hood, braced myself against the smashed-in grille and filled up the great black leaking radiator. Then I flung down the hose—nozzle lashing about in a perverse and frenzied circle, lashing and taking aim and soaking the lower half of my fresh white uniform—and dropped the hood and wiped my hands on an oily rag, straightened my cap, smoothed down the pure white breast of my tunic and gently shooed away the chickens and patted the old battered-up green hood of the car. The sun was going down, the champagne was tingling and Cassandra, I knew, was waiting where I had left her with Gertrude at the U-Drive-Inn.

"Ready, Fernandez?" I called. "Bride's waiting, Fernandez."

Then Fernandez must have felt the champagne also because suddenly the three broken car doors were tied shut with twine and I was behind the wheel and the sun was turning to gold the tall white plastic Madonna screwed to the dashboard and Fernandez was sitting up straight beside me with a bunch of crimson flowers in one hand and a large unlabeled bottle of clear liquor in the other. I waved to a fat red bantam hen, and the two of us, Fernandez and I, called good-by forever to his life in the splendors of Tenochtitlan Trailer Village. As we drove out between the rows of mobile homes—wingless airplanes, land yachts, or little metal hovels with flat tires and sagging aerials—suddenly I had the impulse to pat Fernandez on the knee, and did so and smiled at him through the sunlight which was full in my face.

"Courage, Fernandez," I said softly. "She's a charming girl."

"Don't worry about me, Papa Cue Ball," cradling the bottle, clutching the flowers in his tiny bright mahogany fist, "Fernandez is no innocent."

Sand flats, mountains of gravel, abandoned road-working machines, conveyer belts, fields of marsh and silver oil tanks, hitchhiking soldier, a pony ring, and the aged dark green Packard swaying and knocking and overheating on that black highway south.

"Faster, Papa Cue Ball, the hour is very late."

Nonetheless I thought we had better eat—hamburgers in toasted golden buns at the side of the road, butter and pickle juice running through our fingers, two cold bottles of Orange Crush for the dark-faced groom and perspiring good-natured naval officer who gave the bride away—and my better sense told me that someone must attend to the Packard—unpardonable delay in lonely service station, gallons of gasoline, buckets of water, long minutes in the rest room where we, Fernandez and I, took our first drink of the colorless liquor which burned away the Orange Crush and killed the champagne—so that the

sky was dark and the moon was a lemon curd by the time we reached
the little suburban oasis called El Chico Rio and honked the horn in a
prearranged enthusiastic signal—so many longs, so many shorts, so
many trills—and parked in front of Gertrude's accommodations in the
U-Drive-Inn.

"Where are the flowers, Fernandez?" I whispered, and set the hand
brake. "Quickly, hold the flowers up where she can see them."

"The flowers were foolish, Papa Cue Ball." Glum. Somber. Squaring
his shoulders at the Madonna. "I dropped them in the big wire basket
in the toilet back there at the Texaco station. A good place for them."

But I pushed him out of the car then, straightened his linen jacket,
squeezed his hand, and turned, smiled, removed my stiff white cap—
civilian habit I was never able to overcome—because Gertrude's door
had opened and there was a light on the path and Cassandra was walking toward us carefully in high heels, and Cassandra was composed,
calm, silvery and womanly and serene as she came walking toward Fernandez and myself and the old hot smashed-up Packard in these her
first moonlit moments of matrimony. I caught my breath, held out my
arms to her. And glancing down, I whispered, "Kiss her, for God's
sake, Fernandez. Look how she's dressed up for us. You must do
something!"

And it was true. Her hair was down, yet drawn back slightly so that
we could see the little diamond pendants she had clipped to the lobes
of her tiny ears; her waist was small and tight and her little silver breasts
were round; she was cool, her dress was crocheted and white; and in
honor of Fernandez, in honor of his Peruvian background, she wore
draped across her narrow shoulders a long white Indian shawl with a
fringe made of soft white hair that hung down below her knees. She
carried a black patent leather purse, new, and also new a small black
patent leather traveling bag monogrammed, I discovered once she got
into the car, with a large golden initial C. We could smell the perfume
and breath of talcum powder and sharp odor of nail polish—pink as
the color of a peach near the stem, still wet—even before she reached
the car, and I felt myself choking and gave Fernandez a shove, and
dropped my cap and reached out and caught up the purse, caught up
the traveling bag. Pride. Embarrassment. My daughter's porter.

But he did not kiss her. He merely secured the bottle of liquor under
one arm and put his little heels together and bowed, bent low over
Cassandra's soft white hand. The fingers of her other hand—two silver
bracelets, a silver fertility charm—were curled at the edge of the high

tight collar and her eyes were bright. Then I saw her breasts heaving again and knew that everything was up to me.

"Well, Cassandra," I said, "my little bride at last!"

"My bride, Papa Cue Ball," ruffled, holding the bottle by the neck, "you misunderstand, Papa Cue Ball."

"Naturally, Fernandez," I said, and smiled and felt Cassandra touch my arm and wished that I hadn't already kissed the bride in the City Hall. "But are we ready to go? And shall I drive, Fernandez? I'd be happy to drive. If only you two could sit in back. . . ."

"The three of us will sit in the front seat, Papa Cue Ball. Naturally. And remember, please, this is my honeymoon, the honeymoon of Fernandez. I am the new husband and on my honeymoon my wife will do the driving. So that's settled. The wife drives on the honeymoon. And you will sit in the middle if you please, Papa Cue Ball. So let's go."

I helped Cassandra into the car and managed to jam her traveling bag among the tires and slid in beside her, sighed, settled down with Cassandra's purse in my lap and her smooth white ceremonial shawl just touching my knee. It was the first time Fernandez had cracked the whip, so to speak, and she took it well, Cassandra took it well. I glanced at her—mere doll behind the wheel, line of firmness in her jaw, little soft hands tight and delicate on the wheel—and her eyes were glistening with a new light of pride, joy, humility. Obedient but still untamed. Shocked. Secretly pleased. Mere helpless woman but summoning her determination, pushing back her hair, suddenly and with little precise white fingers turning the key in the ignition and, with the other hand, taking hold of the gearshift lever which in Cassandra's tiny soft hand was like a switchman's tall black iron lever beside an abandoned track.

"Got your license with you, Cassandra?" I asked. "But of course you do," I murmured in answer to my own question and smiled, caressed the little black patent leather purse in my lap, then balanced the purse on my two raised knees, played a little game of catch with it. How carefully, slowly, Fernandez climbed back into the old Packard which he himself was unable to drive, and then took hold of the broken door handle and pulled, pulled with all his might so that the door slammed shut and the car shook under the crashing of that loose heavy steel. Another side of Fernandez? A new mood? I thought so and suddenly realized that the enormous outdated Packard with all its terrible capacity for noise and metallic disintegration was somehow a desperate equivalent of my little old-world Catholic son-in-law in his hand-decorated necktie and crumpled white linen suit.

"OK, Chicken," he said, another vagary of temper, another cut of the lash, and without a word to me he thrust the bottle in my direction, "we want to head for the hideaway. And please step on the gas."

"I'm with you," I wanted to say to Cassandra as I took the bottle, held the purse in one hand and the tall clear bottle in the other, "don't be afraid." But instead, "Away we go!" I cried, and rolled my head, glanced at Cassandra, put the clear round mouth of the bottle into my own aching mouth and shut my eyes and burned again as I had first burned when I leaned against the tin partition in the Texaco filling station and sampled the rare white liquor of the Andes.

"My wife drives well. Don't you think so, Papa Cue Ball?"

"Like Thor in his chariot," I said. "But a toast, Fernandez, to love, to love and fidelity, eh, Cassandra?"

Moonlight, cold dizzying smell of raw gasoline, dry smell of worn upholstery, sensation of devilish coiled springs and lumps of cotton in the old grease-stained front seat of the Packard, wind singing through Cassandra's door and the hot knocking sound of the engine and a con-stellation of little curious lights winking behind the dashboard, and I was snug between Cassandra and my son-in-law of several hours now, and the Madonna was standing over me and holding out her moon-struck plastic arms in benediction. She was the Blessed Virgin Mary, I knew, and I smiled back happily at her in the moonlight.

"Skipper?" Cassandra was staring ahead, whispering, driving with her bright new wedding ring high on the wheel, "Light me a cigarette. Please." So I opened the purse—how long now had I been waiting for an excuse to open that purse? for a chance to get a peek inside that purse even in the smelly darkness of the speeding car?—and found the cigarettes and a little glossy unused booklet of paper matches and put one of her cigarettes between my lips and struck one of the matches— puff of orange light, sweet taste of sulphur—and smelled the blue smoke, and placed the white cigarette between the fingers which she held out to me in the V-for-victory sign. And during all the long miles we chalked up that night—tunnels of love through the trees, black Pa-cific deep and hungry and defiant down there below the highway, which was always honeymoon highway to me when that night had passed— and until we reached the hotel far up in the mountains, that was all Cassandra said to me, but it was enough. She had changed. There is a difference between a young bride with crimson flowers and a young woman driving a dirty old forest green Packard with her white pointed toe just reaching the accelerator and a cigarette burning in her pretty mouth. What bride wants to keep her eyes on the road? So she had changed. She would never lose the invisible encyclopedia balanced on the crown of her head and would always be identified for me with the BVM. But behind her anticipation—why else the new purse? why else the patent leather traveling bag? or why the monogram?—and behind whatever vision she may have had of matrimony, there was a change. Still hopeful, still feeling joy, but smoking an unaccustomed cigarette and tasting fate. In the darkness I noticed that one of her pendant earrings had disappeared, and I was sorry and irritated at the same time, wanted to tell her to remove its mate or to let me take it off myself. But I held my peace.

And Fernandez? Fernandez, I knew, was drunk. At least he was a jealous custodian of the bottle, or inconsiderate groom, a testy son-in-law. And forty or fifty miles beyond El Chico Rio the black sprawling ominous interior of the Packard was filled suddenly with the elated piercing sounds of a wolfish whistle, and I saw that Fernandez was sitting on the edge of the seat with the bottle gripped between his knees and two fingers stuck between his teeth, grinning, staring at Cassandra, whistling those two loud terrible notes of his crude appreciation, and I knew that Fernandez was drunk or at least that he had given way, at last, to the psychic tensions of his mysterious past.

"Control yourself, Fernandez," I said, trying at any cost to preserve the humor of our journey, "we have a long night ahead of us."

"The heart cries out," he said, dully, morosely, "the heart demands satisfaction, nothing less. But my wife will know what I mean," nodding, wiping his brow. "Know what I mean, Chicken?"

The mere expression on her white face appeased him, though not for long because all at once we could see the moon shattering on the black chaos of the Pacific far below us and the first cigarette package was empty and Fernandez was hunched in the furthest dark corner of the car.

"Fernandez?" Softly, cheerfully, touching him lightly on the shoulder: "Are you all right? Shall we stop for a minute?"

"Drive on, good Papa Cue Ball, drive on," he said, and I saw that he had removed his shoes, removed his green socks, rolled the white linen trousers up to his knees. What next? His legs were perfect white shapely bowling pins, and he was arching one foot, wriggling the toes, flexing one calf.

"Hey, Chicken! You like cheesecake? You like cheesecake, Chicken?"

The Packard swerved once—headlights chopping through the trees
—but Cassandra applied the brakes, steadied her hands on the wheel,
and we recovered again, accelerated, sped around a curve with the moon
going great guns again and Fernandez quickly repeating the marriage
service to himself in Spanish. And then my heart was floating in a dark
sea, in my stomach the waves were commencing their dark action. And
yet for two more hours I was aware of everything, the climbing Packard,
sudden feeling of elevation, hairpin turns in the road, small rocks in the
road, Cassandra's white skirt riding above her knee, moon flitting behind stark silhouetted peaks, the white plastic Madonna fixed and comforting on the dashboard, clearly aware of Fernandez sitting upright and
all at once talking happily at my side.

"It's silver mining country, Chicken. You see? Mountains of the great
silver deposits. Think of the lost cities, the riches, thousands of little
sure-footed burros laden with silver. Do you understand my feeling,
Chicken? Silver is the precious metal of the church, the metal of devotion, ceremony, candlelight. The treasure of the heart, the blessed metal
of my ancestors and of my somber boyhood. Out of these mountains
they dug silver for old coins, Chicken, silver for the heavy girdles of
young brides. Think of it. . . ."

And slumped between them I listened, held my peace, drifted higher
and higher into those black gutted mountains. There were ravines and
cliffs and falling boulders all waiting to finish off the Packard, and we
left our tire tracks in patches of fresh snow. Yet I merely grinned to
myself, tried to imagine what our exact altitude might be.

. . . stumbling forward with the monogrammed traveling case in my
hand, in the beam of the headlights stumbling, trying to breathe, feeling
exhilarated despite the dizziness and pain in my eyes. "Is this it, Fernandez?" I called over my shoulder, hatless and suddenly hot and cold
at the same time. "Pretty high up, Fernandez!"

"This is it, Papa Cue Ball," he called back to me. "Honeymoon Hide-
Away, which is the best place in all Southern Cal for the young men
and women who have just taken the vows of marriage!"

Narrow rock-strewn deserted place, beginning of a steep gorge ringed
with peaks, and I stumbled, paused, struggled for breath, looked up at
the cold diminishing stars and birdless peaks. We were trapped, I knew.
And yet I was unaccountably pleased to see that at the end of the headlights' dull beam there was a shattered stone wall of a demolished building and leaning against it, fat and sullen and holding a little hairless dog

in her arms, a Mexican woman who remained alone now with her little dog in all this rubble. I wondered how long she had been leaning there waiting to meet us.

"Señorita," I called, *"buenas noches!"* And I waved—she was a match for me, the fat brown unsmiling mother of that wrecked mining town—and hurried after her with the blood draining from my eyes and my heart pounding. Around the corner I found only a single sharply inclined street of the abandoned mining town, only a barred window, a row of doorless openings, a chimney fallen intact across the street like the skeleton of some enormous snake, a few streaks of moonlit mortar and a few jagged heaps of dislocated stone still lodged there in the bottom of the sheer gorge. Ruin. Slow collapse. The rank odor of dead enterprise.

But there was light in the hotel and the heavy long empty bar was ornamented with the plump naked bodies of young Victorian women carved in bas-relief and lying prone on their rounded sides down all the length of that dark dusty wood. A light in the Hide-Away, and I rushed inside, dropped Cassandra's traveling case beside the bar.

"Three beers, *Señorita*," I said—she was standing in the shadows next to an old nickel-plated cash register that looked like a cranky medieval machine of death—"and the rooms are ready? You've got the rooms ready for us, I hope?"

She waited. Her small eyes were bright and glittering in the shadow, she could have been afraid or sullen but there was beauty still in the dark reticence of her enormous size. Then she moved, stood the little silver hairless dog on the bar—obedient, trembling, scared to death— and turned her back on me, groaned and stooped out of sight. It was a slow intimate process, the procuring of that first beer, headless, tepid, drawn in a small Coca-Cola glass and from what spigot or rancid keg I was unable to see, but at last she set the glass in front of me and braced herself against the bar, moved the dog out of my arm's reach. Then she turned again and in the same way produced the second glass, and the third, until the three glasses stood in a bitter row and the dog tipped its sharp trembling ears at me from the far side of the cash register. I thought the woman's eyes were warmer when she slid the last beer in line, at least her breath—rich, flaring, full of provocative hot seasoning and rotten teeth—was closer to my face and stronger.

"Now the rooms," I said. "You've got the two rooms? OK?"

She nodded.

"Excellent," I said, "excellent. You're a real old queen of the Pampas." She watched me, resting her breasts on the bar, and there was still beauty in the lines of her greasy face, still a strange promise of strength and gentleness in her short blackened fingers. I smiled, picked up the glasses, and was just arranging them on a dusty table when I noticed the soldier, a lone soldier near the jukebox with his dark head on his arms and khaki shirt wet and clinging to his thin ribs, and heard Fernandez calling out in the darkness beyond the fallen wall.

"In here, Fernandez! In here, Cassandra! Can you see the light?"

I waited, paced up and down. There was the odor of mildewed cardboard, odor of pack rats under the sagging floor, the Mexican woman had tacked an out-of-date girlie calendar above the jukebox. Then they appeared—I knew at once that they had been holding hands—and I embraced Fernandez, embraced Cassandra, seated them at our private table and sighed, smiled at both of them, winking at Fernandez, winking happily at Cassandra, and took a quick sip of my flat tepid beer.

"So, good Papa Cue Ball, you have seen to everything and all is in order?"

"All in order, Fernandez. Except for our unfortunate friend over there," and I nodded in the direction of the soldier, tried to catch Cassandra's eye over the rim of my glass. Fernandez turned, glanced at the sleeping figure, shrugged.

"It's nothing, Papa Cue Ball. Merely a drunk GI. The GI's are all over the place these days. Don't give it a thought. But look, a woman of my own color! A very good omen, Papa Cue Ball, a very good omen."

"I thought you'd be pleased, Fernandez."

"Fernandez is very pleased. And Chicken," looking now at Cassandra, putting his little brown hand on her wrist, "do you see that she's a woman who has borne many children? Do you see from her size that she's a woman of many glowing and painless births? Take heart from her, Chicken. Put a little flesh on the bones. . . ."

And interrupting him quickly: "Well, what do you think of having the wedding supper now, Fernandez? Pretty good idea?"

"Magnificent, good Papa Cue Ball. You think of everything!"

Tortillas. Soft brick-colored beans. Bitter nuts, half-moons of garlic, fish sweated into a paste with hard silver slices of raw onion. Ground meal, green peppers the shape of a finger and the texture of warm mucilage and filled with tiny black explosive seeds, and chicken, oh the tortured chicken skewered and brown and lacerated, running with pink blood and some kind of thick peppered sauce, chicken that fell away from the bone and in the mouth yielded first the delicate flavor of tender

white meat and then the unexpected pain of its unleashed fire, chicken
and murky soup and bits of preserved vegetable poisoned in such a way
as to bring a sudden film to the eyes and pinched dry shriveling sensations to the nose and throat. So Fernandez kept calling out in Spanish
to the Mexican woman, and the Mexican woman—now there was a
new glazed color in her cheeks, a new odor of hot charcoal amongst
the other smells of her enormous and unrevealed self—kept coming to
us with still another clay pot steaming in one brown hand and always
the little dog shaking helplessly in the other. And Fernandez ate, cocking
his head, holding the food appreciatively on his tongue, then nodding,
chewing, demanding more, and of course I ate right along with him,
cooling myself, saving myself with innumerable glasses of the beer which
was suddenly sparkling and as cold as ice.

"You know about the *cojones*, Papa Cue Ball? This is a feast for the
cojones, let me tell you. . . ."

So that's what our old mother of the mesquite was up to, and I
blushed then, glanced at Cassandra—poor Cassandra, soft and unsmiling in the light of the half-candle which the fat woman had brought
with the first brusque Spanish command—and bit down as hard as I
could on a little tough root that was filled with devils. I was always
afraid that Cassandra would marry a marine like so many of the girls
she knew at school, but what would those marine wives think if they
could see her now, waiting out this wedding night in the dark dining
room of an empty hotel which was once the call house of our little
abandoned and evil-smelling and still collapsing silver town? For that
matter, what was I to think? No doubt I was too full, too excited, but
eager, strangely eager nonetheless, to think.

In the end there was candy—what secret cache expended loyally for
the sake of Fernandez? what dirty old shoe box or earthen pot lovingly
exhumed and made to yield up this cracked plate of thick dark sticky
chunks of sugared fruit?—and two twisted black Mexican cigars and a
tiny glass filled to the brim—rare cordial? primitive aphrodisiac?—for
Cassandra. I ate, I smoked, I looked the other way when I saw her
slender white fingers reach for the glass.

"Well, Fernandez," I said, and pushed back my chair, stood up, blew
the ash off my black cigar—sickening cigar, heavy pungent odor of bad
dreams—and for a moment held myself where the food lay, "how about
a little music, Fernandez? Shall we try a song?" The sallow wizened face
looked up at me and he was unable to smile, unable to speak, unable
even to nod, but the eyes told me that he wanted me to try a song.

Cassandra was still holding the full glass, Cassandra still untouched by these disreputable ghosts or the chorus of the pack rats below the floor. The candlelight was flowing in her hair and on her ring finger there was a little bright chip of fire. I wanted to suggest that I call out the titles of the numbers and that she, my poor Cassandra, select our song. But clutching the back of the chair I looked down at her and the phrasing of this well-intentioned thought never came to my lips.

I left them together, left the two of them sitting together in the midst of the debris of the feast of the *cojones,* as my son-in-law had said, and somehow turning abruptly toward the dusty colors of the obsolete jukebox, I knew that once I walked away from the table, away from the wreckage of the indelicate wedding supper, I would be walking away from them forever. It was a difficult moment, an awkward pause. But I stepped out, telling myself I always enjoyed the mystery of push buttons and the flamboyance of bright undulating colors.

Unsteady steps across the rotten floor. A good look at the white neck of the sleeping soldier. And then the old machine, the colored water moving through the tubes, the rows of bright square buttons and, inside the dusty glass, the rows of printed song titles each one of which was a further notch in my knowledge of romance. I leaned down, hands on knees, never looking back at the table, and very carefully and slowly read each one of those little romantic titles twice. Then I made my choice, fumbled around in my pocket for a coin, pushed the bright button down. A click, a scratching sound, then music, and I started to wag my head to the rhythm of that awful tune.

Listening, swaying, smiling, hands still on knees, I did my best to dream up a little reverie of my own, a little romance of my own, and I did my very best, stood it as long as I could, then simply had to turn around and did so, humming along with the record, snapping my fingers, putting another nickel in the slot, turning slowly—oh I wasn't going to miss a trick that night—until I stood facing them once more, but in shadow and with the colored lights revolving and dissolving across my poor wrinkled uniform. They had gotten up from the table —Fernandez, Cassandra—and I was just about to call good night to them, thinking that they wouldn't leave the room until I called good night to them, when I saw the Mexican woman taking charge of them, watched with a curious shrinking sensation on my lips, my smile, as she took Cassandra's submissive white face between her greasy hands and kissed her in the middle of that mere ghost of a white brow and then let go of Cassandra and quickly gave Fernandez a couple of coaxing pats on his white linen rump, and then pushed them out the door.

"Good night, you two," I called anyway, and was alone with my music, the drunk GI, the woman who began clearing away the debris. Alone with the miniature silver dog. But not for long. Because before I could sit down with the drunk GI Fernandez retuned, breathless, guarded, already smelling of Cassandra's scent, and held out to me the Edgeworth tobacco tin in which he kept his spiv, that terrible little weapon made of a broken razor blade.

"For you, Papa Cue Ball," he said. "Take it. In case that one there," jerking his elbow at the soldier, "in case that one tries to cause you any trouble when he wakes up. It's better to be ready for him, just in case. . . ."

"Thanks, Fernandez. But wait," trying to detain him, watching him slip off not toward the shrouded staircase but toward the littered street outside, "where are you going?"

"For the guitar, Papa Cue Ball. There would be no romance without my green guitar."

But I was alone. Alone in this mining town of rusted iron pipe and settling rock and corrugated paper turned to mold. Alone with my heavy stomach, my heartburn, the dizziness I still suffered from the altitude. I paced up and down the dark room, I tried unsuccessfully to make friends with the wretched little silver dog. Apparently the woman expected me to climb to my own room upstairs and sleep, but I told her that I had spent so many months at sea that I found it difficult to sleep in a bed ashore. Why didn't she bring me a beer, I asked her, and also one for the soldier and, if she liked, a beer for herself as well? She nodded, and then she put her fat brown hand on my arm and gave it a squeeze.

I told her I would sit down and keep the soldier company. So I pulled out a chair and took a seat. The head of black curly hair was buried in the crossed arms, the khaki shirt was disheveled, the cuffs were unbuttoned and drawn back from the thin gray wrists, and I noticed the outline of a shoulder patch which had been removed and no doubt destroyed.

"Hey, Joe," I said. "Wake up, Joe. How about joining me for a beer?" No answer. No sound of breathing, not even the faint exhalation of a low moan. I leaned close to the hidden head to listen but there was nothing. I touched his elbow, I shook him by the arm. "Joe," I said, "two lone servicemen ought to join forces, don't you think?" But there was nothing. Only the rats, a little wind through the timbers, the first wailing chords struck on the guitar upstairs.

Then, on a tray this time, she brought out three beers and also a tin basin of warm water and a scrap of rag. And slowly she put down the glasses, arranged the rag and basin next to the GI and sat close beside him. We drank to each other—dark eye on mine, little silver dog huddled between her breasts—and still holding her glass and without taking her eyes from mine she reached out her free hand, took a chubby fistful of black curly hair and pulled the GI upright, let his head loll over the back of the chair.

"Is he OK?" I whispered, "is he alive?"

She nodded, drank another sip of beer. Then she showed me the back of her small shapeless hand, held her hand up like a club.

"You did it?" I whispered and pushed aside my beer, leaned away from the two of them. "You mean you did that to him yourself?"

More nodding, more sipping, a soft shadow of pride passing over the greasy brown contours of her round face, more searching looks at me. And then suddenly she finished off her beer and, softly talking all the while to the dog and now and then glancing at me, she cradled the GI's head and dipped the rag and went to work on him. With age-old tenderness she ran the rag over the lips, under the eyes, around the nose, again and again dipping the rag, squeezing, returning with heavy breath to the gentleness of her occupation. The white face began to emerge and already the water, I could see, was a soft rich color, deep and dark.

When the dog tipped its tiny nose over the edge of the basin I stood up. And quickly, without commotion, I left them there, the preoccupied fat woman bent over her task and the soldier moaning in the crook of her arm—he had begun to moan at last—and I groped my way outside and knelt at the nearest pile of rubble and upchucked into the rubble to my heart's content, let go with the tortillas, the hot tamales, the champagne, nameless liquor and beer, knelt and clung to a chunk of mortar and gooseneck of rusted pipe and threw open the bilge, had a good deep rumble for myself.

Anyone who has gotten down on his knees to vomit has discovered, if only by accident, the position of prayer. So that terrible noise I was making must have been the noise of prayer, and the effect, as the spasms faded and the stomach went dry, was no doubt similar to the peace that follows prayer. In my own way I was contrite enough, certainly, had worked hard enough there in the rubble to deserve well the few moments when a little peace hung over me in the wake of the storm that had passed.

I breathed, I smeared my face in my handkerchief, I climbed to my feet. It was a job done, and now the night, I knew, was going to fly away fast. Too bad for them, I thought, too bad for me. It hadn't ended well but it had ended.

And now I was wandering and the opera house was like a decapitated turret or the remains of a tiny and monstrous replica of a Rhine castle. A few curtain wires flapping loose in the wind, a couple of sandbags and a little gilt chair upside down in the entrance hall, a pile of handbills. Another house of pleasure for the men in the drifts. And how many performances did my Mexican love attend? How many with some other little hairless rat-shaped dog tucked under her arm? How many with a mouthful of *pepitas* and a heavy hand on her rolling thigh and bright candles lit all the way across the little stage? I would never know. But there was life yet in that miniature lopsided castle of bygone scratching orchestras and flouncing chorus girls and brawling applause. So I began to feel my way up the narrow stairs. I climbed as high as the first balcony, climbed up into the fading night and could go no further, for the second balcony, the roof, the stage, all of it was gone and there was only a scattering of broken glass, the wind in my face, the feeling of blackness and a good view of the pitiless gorge and hapless town. I could make out the squat deeper shadow of the far-off Packard, I could hear the guitar. The dawn was rising up to my nostrils.

And then I saw those two enormous soft rolls of faded tickets which—by what devilish prank? what trick of time?—had been printed up for a movie that had starred Rita Hayworth, I remembered, as the unfaithful mistress of a jealous killer who escaped from prison midway through the first reel of the film. Shotguns, touring cars, acid in the face, long hair soaking wet in the rain—it was a real find, that memory, those rolls of tickets, and I scooped them up and tore them into ten-foot lengths and tied them to the broken railing, to upright twists of iron, to the arms of ravaged chairs, and watched all those paper strips snapped out onto the wind and listened to the distant sounds of my little son-in-law shouting at my poor daughter and beating on the neck of the guitar, and emptied my pockets, threw my remaining handfuls of confetti out onto the wind. It was a fete of mildewed paper and wild sentiment, a fete for three.

And in that flapping dawn—sky filled with rose, silver, royal blue— I opened the Edgeworth tobacco tin, for a long while stared at the razor blade inside. Then slowly, can and all, I tossed it over the edge of the first balcony. And seven and a half months after that flapping dawn in the mountains Pixie poked her little nose into the world—premature, an incubator baby—and sixteen months after that same rose and silver and royal blue dawn they were putting Gertrude's poor body into the ground. Thank God for the old PBY's and for a captain who did not interfere when I left the ship to be on hand back home as needed in City Hall or maternity ward or cemetery. Thank God for the boys who flew those old PBY's straight to the mark.

"That's all you are, Papa Cue Ball. The father of a woman who produces a premature child. The husband of a woman who kills herself. I renounce it, Papa Cue Ball. I renounce this family, I renounce this kind of a man. Can you explain? Can you defend? Can you speak to me with honor of your own Papa? No. So I renounce, Papa Cue Ball, I will escape one of these days. You may take my word. . . ."

"If you don't wish to come, Fernandez, then you may stay behind."

"That's what I wish. I do wish it, Papa Cue Ball, now that you put the words in my mouth! And believe me, I will follow my heart. . . ."

In front of the mirror in the little room stacked knee-high with the cardboard cartons which I had half-filled with poor Gertrude's clothing, I was having trouble with the sword. Our limousine was waiting, scheduled to depart from the U-Drive-Inn, while the hearse was scheduled to depart, of course, from the mortuary. Or rather our limousine was scheduled to rendezvous with the hearse at the mortuary, the two black vehicles to proceed on from there together. And we were late and I was having trouble with my sword. Poor Gertrude. In the mirror I saw the smart dark blue uniform—it was Christmas, after all, the Christmas of '44 and time for blues—saw the polished brass buttons, the white shirt still open at the neck since the baby was playing with my black tie, saw my bald head, freshly shaven cheeks, furrows over the bridge of my nose, and the unhooked and unwieldy sword. It was not my sword, it was the old man's sword, and I had borrowed it late on that last night on the *Starfish*. I had thought a sword necessary for Gertrude's funeral and now a couple of hooks were giving me trouble and the black scabbard was growing heavy in my hands.

"Cassandra," I said into the mirror, "I wish you'd cry. And Sonny," leaning forward, looking around for him in the mirror, "can't you give me a little help with the captain's sword?" Sonny was beginning to mourn, grief was beginning to overtake him in this ransacked room in the U-Drive-Inn, and he was scowling at Fernandez and holding Pixie on his lap. It was Sonny who had given the baby my black tie.

"All's you got to do is speak up, Skipper. You knows that. I've helped the old man with his sword, and I can help you with it. You knows that."

Sleeve of her camel's-hair coat dangling from one of the boxes. Odor of gin. A scattering of small change, cuticle sticks, keys, all gleaming in the far corner of the room where I had been going over them, sorting things out. And on a fluffy beribboned hanger hooked to the top slat of the Venetian blinds her negligee, her pink negligee—I had rinsed it in the bathroom sink the night before, hung it to dry—now doing its long empty undulating dance in the cool currents of the air freshener that was humming low on the west wall. Poor Gertrude. I could never hold a grudge against Gertrude. No matter the motorcycle orgies with members of my own crew, half a season on a nearby burlesque stage, the strange disappearances, insinuating notes to Washington, and bills, bruises, infidelity here at the U-Drive-Inn, and even a play for faithful Sonny, no matter how she had tried to injure me or shame Cassandra, still I could never despise the early wrinkles, the lost look in the eyes, the terror I so often saw on the thin wide mouth, the drunken floundering. She was a helpless unpretty woman with dyed hair. She got a rash from eating sea food. She gave a terrible ammunition to those young members of my crew with whom she managed to have her little whirlwind affairs. And her early V-letters were always the same: "I hope they sink you, Edward. I really do." She said she was going to drink up my insurance money when I was gone. Poor Gertrude. "You are going to hate me, Edward," she wrote, "at least you won't deny me hate, will you?" But she was wrong. Because the further she went downhill the more I cared. And Gertrude was no match for my increasing tolerance.

"Now give me my tie, Sonny," I said, and there was the empty camel's-hair sleeve, the sword at my side, my own uneasy look of consternation in the mirror. "The baby will have to play with something else. On the double, Sonny, we're late already."

"What about the child, Papa Cue Ball? You don't intend to leave the child with me?"

"Yes, Fernandez. That's the plan. Exactly."

Then Sonny helped me with the knot and gave me his arm and Cassandra found my hat in the bathroom. Gertrude's fingerprints were everywhere, her smell was everywhere—sweet lemon and a light haze of alcohol—and in the wastebasket a crumpled tissue still bore the lipstick impression of her poor thin lips stretched wide in the unhappiness of her last night alive.

And Sonny: "Look at that baby there, Skipper. She sure misses her Grandma!"

I nodded.

So I leaned on Sonny and Cassandra preceded us—bright sun, black limousine, bright shadows in the empty driveway—and so at last, and only twenty-five minutes late, we pulled away from the U-Drive-Inn and headed east in fairly heavy traffic to keep our rendezvous with Gertrude's hearse. I could tell they had vacuum-cleaned the inside of our limousine. The upholstery was like gray skin and the sun was hard, brilliant, silent through the clear glass.

"Them swords are the devil to sit down with, Skipper. Ain't they?"

I agreed with him. And then: "If we used the jump-up seats we could be carrying six instead of three. Did you notice that, Sonny? Wonderful room in these limousines. But I wonder why there aren't any flowers?"

The traffic was heavy and all the other cars were filled with children. I could see them through the sealed glass, the smooth bright silence of our slow ride. Faint brand-new automobile smell, hard light, subtle sensation of new black tires humming gently through the perfect seat—gray skin, foam rubber, a bed of springs—and rising like a thin intimate voice into the receptive spine. And of course the driver. Something familiar about the driver—charcoal chauffeur's jacket, white collar, charcoal chauffeur's cap, dark glasses—a curiously muffled and familiar look about the driver. But I couldn't place him and went back to stroking the warm handstrap and staring at the tints that were beginning to appear in the curves and along the edges of our shatterproof glass.

"Ask him if he has his lights on, Sonny. Funeral cars always have their lights on, don't they, Sonny? We'd make better time with lights, I'm sure."

We were only forty-eight minutes late, exactly, when we drifted to a marvelous stop beneath the bright green caterpillar awning and waited while the driver climbed the smooth white marble steps to report inside. The place looked empty. No sign of the hearse. No attendants in black swallowtails. Nothing. Then Sonny went in after the driver—grief riding his shoulders, dreading the interior of this establishment which was like home to me—and in close conversation, stooping, black shoes making startled noises on the marble, they returned together. Sonny opened the car door, stuck his head in, and Cassandra and I—Cassandra in her trim black dress, hair drawn tightly under the little hat—leaned forward as one. The black face was wet and the long black cheeks were more hollowed out than ever. His panther hand was trembling.

"Been some mistake, Skipper," shaking his head, fanning himself with his black chief's cap, "hearse gone on ahead without us. The man inside couldn't tell us a thing. Anyways, we got to get a move on now."

"Well, hop in, Sonny," I said. "Let's go." Then leaning forward, touching the stiff driver's charcoal arm and wishing I could see his face, "Listen," I said, "it's a matter of life and death. Do you understand?"

"Got his lights on now, Skipper," nudging me, peering down into my face, staring at me with those hard-boiled eggs of his, "and them lights ought to help for sure."

"That's good, Sonny," I said. "I'm glad."

Then suddenly the highway was wide open, clear, a long rising six-lane concrete boomerang with its tip driven into the horizon and all for us. Soft gray seats and chrome and the sunlight standing still on the ebony dashboard, and only the highway itself took my attention away from the chrome, the felt padding under our feet, so that for a moment I saw the lemon trees, the olive groves, the brown sculpted contours of the low hills.

There was a shadow in the front seat next to the driver, a dark amorphous shadow that swelled and tried to change its position and vague shape according to the curves in the road, black shadow that seemed to be held in its seat by the now terrible speed of the Caddy. The driver had both hands on the wheel and now the speed was whispering inside my spine. I noticed that the tints of the window and windshield glass had slid, suddenly, onto Cassandra's black dress, were shining there in the black planes of her body, and that she was looking at me. The black shadow was snuggling up to the driver.

"Hurry up," I said as loud as I could, leaning forward and fighting against the sword at my side, "hurry up, will you? We haven't got all day."

And then the turn-off, the gentle incline over gravel, a long sweeping glimpse of the lemon sky, the archway flanked by two potted palms—there was an angel floating between the palms—the still sunlit aspect of the cemetery at the end of the day. And a little sign which I saw immediately—*Speed six miles per hour*—and far off, at the top of a dun-colored hill, a little activity which I tried not to see. Sonny was suffering now, moaning to himself, and doing a poor job of controlling his fear of graveyards.

"Look, Sonny," I said, "isn't that the hearse?"

"Appears to be the hearse, Skipper. Sure enough."

We crawled toward the hill and toward the green speck—it proved to be a tent for mourners—and toward the other elongated speck, black and radiant, which was the hearse. The sky was a pure lemon color, quite serene.

"But, Sonny," clutching his arm, reaching up quickly for a fierce grip on the handstrap, "it's moving, isn't it? It wasn't moving before, but it's moving now."

"Appears like you're right, Skipper. That hearse just don't want our company, I guess."

And then the stillness of the limousine, the grease and steel sound of the door opening—we left the car door open behind us, large and empty and catching the sun—and Sonny holding one of my arms and Cassandra the other, and we were walking across the carpet of thick green imitation turf in the gentle light on top of the dun-colored hill, and no one was there.

"All right," I said, "they can begin. Let's get it over with."

But I knew better. There was no one there, the place was empty. The remains of flowers were scattered around underfoot, red roses, white carnations, the debris of real activity, I could see that. But I rushed to the tent, for a long while stood looking into the darkness of that warm tent. There was a shovel lying on the ground and the smell of earth. Nothing else.

The flowers were heaviest where the digging had been going on. Piled up, kicked out of the way, crushed. And there were a few strips of the thick green turf lying more or less around the edges of what had been the hole, and the three of us, standing there together, gently touched the green turf with the toes of our shoes. They must have thought they were burying a piano, and judging by the width and depth of the new earth the hole must have gone down a hundred feet. There was the deep print of a workman's boot right in the center and I squatted, kneeled, brushed it away.

And kneeling, weighing a handful of the new earth in my cold hand: "So they went ahead without us," I said. "They put poor Gertrude into the ground without us. You know," looking up at the two black figures rising into the soft lemon sky, "I told them I wanted Gertrude to have a white casket. A white casket with just a touch of silver. But they might have put her into mahogany and gold for all we'll ever know. How can we tell?"

I stood up, raised my palm, straightened out my fingers: "Pretty sandy stuff, isn't it, Sonny?" I said, and tossed it away, wiped my hand on the back of my pants. I turned to go.

And then the whisper, the quick soft whisper full of love and fear: "Ain't you got something for the grave, Skipper? Got to leave something for the grave, Skipper. Bad luck if you don't."

I nodded, thought a moment, pointed. He understood. Sonny understood and unhooked the hooks and raked out a little trough about three inches deep in the loose skin-colored soil. He buried the sword about three inches deep in the loose soil, tamped it down. Perhaps he was right. Perhaps we would have had worse luck had we not left it there. At least it was no great loss.

The driver took us the long way around the cemetery on our way out, drove us at six miles per hour along the gentle road that was like a bridle path through a hovering bad dream. At the far end of the cemetery there was a line of eucalyptus trees, and leaning forward, staring out of the tinted glass and between the trees, I saw a mountain of naked earth heaped high with flowers—dead flowers, fresh flowers, an acre-long dump of bright tears for the dead—and I knew that poor Gertrude's flowers would soon land on the pile.

"When we get home, Cassandra," I said, and leaned back against the perfect cushion and shut my eyes, "I want you to try on that camel's-hair coat. I think her camel's-hair coat might fit you, Cassandra."

THE BRUTAL ACT

WHITE LIFEBOAT. I heard something, steel, ratchet, a noise I must have known was descending cable, and there was an eclipse of the porthole, a perfect circle of blackness flush against the side of the ship at the spot where the great ring of brass and glass was hooked up with a little chain. The porthole was always open as it was now because I liked to catch the first pink edges of the tropical dawn, first breath of day, first patter of bare feet on the deck above. But it had never gone black before, that porthole of mine, and for a moment—squall? tidal wave? another ship between ourselves and the sun?—I felt what it was like to be faintly smothered in some new problem of seamanship. Slowly I put on my cap, set aside my torn gray copy of the serviceman's abridged edition of the New Testament. Then carefully I thrust my head through the porthole and attempted to twist myself about and look topside. No luck at all. So I looked down. Suspended a long way below me, yet out of reach of the waves, motionless, a white lifeboat was empty and absolutely still down there. For some reason I lowered the port, spent precious minutes screwing tight the brass lugs, even though I was swept immediately by my usual swift fear of ocean nausea. Then I looked at my wrist, 0500 hours, and then I locked the cabin door, climbed topside. For three days, in a sudden effort to keep abreast of Mac the Catholic chaplain, I had been reading the New Testament each dawn. The lifeboat destroyed all that.

I came out with a light in my eyes and the brisk wind catching my cap by the visor, and dead ahead was an enormous field of shoal water emerald green in the dawn. East, I thought and smiled, blotted a little fine spray with the back of my hand. I had to shade my eyes. But the lifeboat was there all right, though swung up as she should have been on giant fishhooks of steel and not suspended above the waves where I had first seen her, and she was motionless up there, hauled now a good distance above my head, and she was as large as someone's private cruiser and, in her own shade, a solemn white. I wondered whether or not it was the same boat. But the fishhooks were canted slightly, the blocks were pulled from under her, the giant tarpaulin lay heaped on the deck, and after a moment I knew that it must be the same boat. I stood there, shaded my raised eyes, waited.

Because someone was standing on her bow. He was nearly a silhouette to me, and yet I took him all in, the long spread legs, the fist on the cable, the faded denim jeans, the flapping sky-blue shirt, the long black hair whipped in the wind, the white hat rolled up and stuck halfway down the front of the jeans. I watched him in the shelter of the white lifeboat and in the bright warmth of the sun. But he was a man of the wind, a tall bony man of this sudden topside wind, and he was bracing himself on the enormous soft white prow of the lifeboat and grinning down at me.

I cupped a hand, tried to see into the sun, called up to him: "Tremlow? Started painting the shack yet, Tremlow? How about knocking off early for a little boxing?"

It was the windward side of the ship, the eastern side, and even in the shelter of the boat the air was loud so that I could hear nothing but whistling overhead and far forward a heavy singing in the anchor chains. But I could see him and he had moved one foot so that it rested now against his rigid knee, and he was shaking his head at me, still grinning.

"By the way, Tremlow," squinting, cupping my hand again, "who told you to take the tarp off the lifeboat? The tarp's supposed to be on the lifeboat at all times. See to it, will you?"

I gave him a half-salute then—mere boy only a third my age and six feet five inches tall and a perfect Triton—and turned on my heel. The lifeboat remained a white impression in my mind, a floating thick-sided craft with a wide beam, deep draft, brass propeller, an enormous white sea rover with something amiss. But at least I had been too quick for Tremlow, once again had managed to avoid his deliberate signs of insubordination.

I took my bearings and made my way aft in time to help Mac into his vestments. We were in the sick-bay which was the most suitable spot on the ship for holding Mass, as I had insisted to the old man, and a few of the men leaned up on their elbows to watch.

"How goes it, Mac?" I said.

"Late as usual," he said.

"No rush, Mac," I said, "no rush," and slipped the purple stole around his damp shoulders. "Did you notice the coral shoals off our starboard side around 0600 hours, Mac? Like a field of underwater corn or something. Or perhaps it was a couple of acres of broken bottle-green glass, eh, Mac?"

But I could see that he wasn't listening, so I opened the white locker where he kept the cross and took it out, unwrapped it, gave it a few licks with the chamois.

"OK, Mac," I said, "all yours."

I was in the middle of my four-year stint on the U.S.S. *Starfish* and it was a bright pink and green dawn in early June and I was helping Mac, seeing how I could give him a hand. Helping Mac serve Mass though in the background, just hovering in the background, just doing what I could to help Mac start his day. I wanted to tell him about the lifeboat but kept quiet, busied myself with the various odd chores of Mac's silent hour. But the bell was tinkling and I was trying to make myself look small. From far forward near the anchor chains the mushy rapid-fire sounds of a machine gun died away. I nodded, glanced significantly at Mac, because they knew better than to have machine gun practice when Mac was holding services in the afterpart of the ship. I walked over to a porthole—sea the color of honey now, sky full of light—then turned at a nearly inaudible little SOS from Mac and put a towel on my arm, stationed myself in the background. But not before I had seen that one of the black pelicans was flying high off our starboard quarter with his broken neck thrust forward and homely wings wide to the wind. The bird was good medicine for the lingering vision of the white lifeboat though not good enough as I discovered. Even the hours I had devoted to helping the chaplain failed to save me.

The sick and wounded were first and we made quick work of them, Mac and I, passing from bed to bed with the speed of a well-oiled team, giving to each man his short ration of mysterious life, freely moving among the congregation, so to speak, and stooping, pausing, wiping the lips—it was my job to wipe the lips—then disengaging the hands that clasped our wrists and hurrying on. I leaned over, felt the impression of parted lips through the linen, shut my eyes and smiled down at the unshaven face. "Feeling a little better today?" I whispered softly because Mac was already murmuring to the man ahead, and I daubed once more at the lips with the linen towel. "We'll get you off to a good start anyway." And I carefully found a clean spot on the towel.

And then the medicos were kneeling and it was 0730—time was passing, that much I knew—and Mac was straightening up and signaling to me to throw open the infirmary doors. So I threw them open, nodded to a couple of familiar faces, hurried back to Mac. Blond hair faded almost to white, wet blue eyes, enormous unhappy face like the tortured white root of a dead tree, tall brawny heavyweight wearing vestments and purple stole and khaki shirt and pants, poor Mac, and I watched the watering eyes, the dimples that were really little twitching scars in his great pale cheeks, watched Mac and everything he did as if I knew already what I owed him and as if all those days were upon me when Mac would be gone.

"Cheer up, Mac," I whispered, "there's a pelican following us. That's a good sign, isn't it?"

But still he was not listening, so I looked around, asked one of the medicos to bring me a fresh towel. Mac was standing in front of the cross with his chest caved in and his clasped hands trembling and his walleyes large and yellow and fixed on the silent faces of the men. I stood beside him, nudged him, and in a louder whisper tried again.

"The men are pretty devout, Mac, at least they aren't taking any chances. They're waiting for you. Let's go."

More tinkling of the bell. Infirmary jammed with men. Faces looking in at every porthole. Silent faces watching until they could have their turns inside. And inside all the heads were bare—gray pebbly helmets carried by chin straps or stuffed under perspiring arms—and tan or black or blond or red almost all of them were shaved, packed together like so many living bones, and in the silence and looking over Mac's white shoulder I thought that all those young vulnerable skulls must have been cast from the same mold. The men were breathing—I could see the movement of their chests—they were waiting to return to battle stations, to return to work. Somebody coughed.

And then Mac shuddered and began. They pressed forward at 0800 hours, pressed toward the cross, all of them, with the blank vaguely apprehensive faces of young sailors who never know what's coming—ocean, destruction, living dream—on their way toward the unknown. Blue denim, white canvas, wind-burned skin, here and there a thin-lipped smile, a jaw hanging down. I saw Sonny in the crowd, saw him trying to elbow his way to the makeshift altar and sneaking a couple of extra steps whenever he could. I smiled.

"Let me get up there," I heard him whisper, "me next," and then he too was in the front row and on his knees and when we passed, Mac and I, passed with cup, plate and towel, I felt the tug on my sleeve and knew suddenly that Sonny's reverence was not all for God. "Got to speak to you, Skipper," he whispered as I touched the corner of the towel to the shapeless swelling of those trembling lips, "got to have a word with you right away. . . ."

I nodded.

So at 0940 hours the last stragglers crossed themselves and we were done. Mac went below for a shower while I wrapped the cross in the chamois, stowed it again in the white cabinet. The sea was still a honey-colored syrup streaked with green, the blue of the sky had faded nearly to white, I thought I could smell the spices of a distant land on the smooth clear moving air. If only I could have heard a few birds; I always missed the song of the birds when we were at sea. At least the pelican, sweet deformed lonely creature, was still high off the barrels of our sternmost guns.

I stooped under number three turret then and began to whistle, forgetting as usual that it was bad luck to whistle on a ship. Sonny slid out from behind a funnel, we fell in step.

"Well," he said, "we got troubles. Oh my, we surely got troubles now. Ain't you noticed anything peculiar yet today? You ain't seen a thing to make you suspicion the ship ain't exactly right? Well, let me tell you. Somebody is fiddling with the boats. How's that? Sure as I know you is you I know somebody is fooling around with them lifeboats. That's bad. But that ain't all. Somebody else has broke into the small arms locker. Yes sir, somebody has busted into that locker and swiped every last small arms on the ship. Ain't that just the devil? But you want to know what I think? Here's what: I think they means to kill all the officers and dump the bodies in the lifeboats! Some kind of devilish thing like that, you wait and see. . . ."

I returned to my cabin and unlocked it, opened the porthole, hung my head out of the porthole where there was nothing to see except the golden water, the paste of foam, the passing schools of bright fish, the shadow of the ship sliding down to the deep. And all the while overhead there was a stealthy clamor around the white lifeboat—I remembered that 33 *persons* was stenciled on the bow—and I nodded to myself, closed up the port again, because poor faithful Sonny was never wrong. But at least the ocean was calm and I wasn't sick.

So I spent the day in my damp bunk reading, still trying to catch up with Mac, spent the day in hard meditation and drinking warm clear water from the regulation black Bakelite pitcher which I filled at the tap. Around 1600 hours I went topside briefly to assure myself that Tremlow had not abandoned his interest in the lifeboat. He had not. I saw him stow a wooden box—sea biscuits? ammunition? medical supplies?—under the tarp and then with heavy grace and fierce agility drop down beneath the tarp himself and begin to laugh with someone already secreted in that hot white arc. Standing flat against steel, beautifully hidden, I looked skyward then—the poor pelican was gone—and then I skimmed down below again and poured myself another glass of water.

When I felt the sunset imminent I simply spread open the New Testament over my eyes and fell asleep. . . .

I woke even before Sonny kicked with his old black blucher on my cabin door, woke in time to hear him muttering, grunting under the weight of an axe, flapping and sweating down the companionway toward my cabin door. But the cabin was filled with moonlight and there was no hurry. I ran my fingers over the books in the little shadowy bookcase screwed to the steel plate at the head of my bunk until I found the slot for the New Testament and shoved it home. Then I emptied the remains of the water pitcher into my right hand and rinsed my face, snorted, wiped my face on the rumpled sheet. The moon filled the cabin with its pale nighttime color; my palms and the backs of my hands, I saw, were green. I was covered with green perspiration. But I knew I wasn't going to be sick this time, had nothing to fear from my ocean nausea now.

And opening the door: "Topside, Sonny," I said, "the first thing to secure is the pilothouse."

"Now I want to tell you," panting, chugging along with the bright fire axe, leading me through the darkness and into the sudden green pools, "now you want to watch yourself. They's got a ringleader."

"Ah, yes," I said, "a ringleader."

"A ringleader, just like I says. And they been having a party. That's right! They been having a party on the fantail ever since the dark come down. And they're full of beans! Hear? You hear it?"

A shot, a tinkle, a scream from somewhere aft, the far-off massed clatter of running men. Hand on iron, foot on a rung, I paused and gave the ship my craning and hasty inspection: a black ship in a bright lunar field, and high above us little steel cups were whirling on the mast and there was smoke in the smokestack. The bow dipped, then recovered itself.

"Now about this party," pulling me around, pointing upward with the luminous head of the axe, for a moment thrusting his enraged face close to mine, "that devil been the whole show, that's the devil got them stirred up this way."

"Tremlow?"

"You got the name on your lips. You ought to know. That's him. Now this devil thought up a party and worked the whole thing out hisself and I was down there on the fantail too—old nigger spy, that's Sonny—and I want to tell you I never seen a party like that before. It sure stirred them up. You know how? Hula-hula, that's how. I tell you, when he done the hula-hula, he had them men in the palm of his hand."

"Tremlow?" I said, "Tremlow doing some kind of Hawaiian dance?"

"That's right," but whispering, drawing me back into the protection of a funnel and pointing firmly, contemptuously, out to a white stretch of the deck where half a dozen of them suddenly raced by dragging burden, victim, spoils of some sort through the green glow of that southern night. "Yes, hula-hula. That's what I mean and with all the trimmings. He danced that dance hisself. And you know what? He got them full of intoxication, that's it, downright intoxication, with all that hula-hula stuff, got them cheering and bumping around and dancing themselves, the way he beat around there in the middle of that moonlit fantail with two fellows playing those little tinny stringed instruments and two more beating on galvanized iron pots for drums. He even had a real grass skirt that swooped all the way down to his ankles and a shirt fixed over his head so you couldn't tell whether he was a chief or one of them hula-hula girls. It did the trick, so I guess it didn't matter which he was. That devil. . . ."

Another shot, another brief turbulent huddle, the arc and soar of something pushed, tossed, heaved and then sailing overboard. And the deep green velvet night was in my face, the whole ship glistened under its coating of salty moisture, and now there was the moon itself adrift in its own mirrored ocean and the ship was in the sway of the moon, and Tremlow, so Sonny said, had done his dance.

"It must have been amusing, Sonny," I said, and I was hanging on tightly to the moonlit ship though she was still, flat in the water like a melting iceberg. "But I hope they don't bother Mac. He's discouraged enough already, eh, Sonny?"

"That chaplain? That chaplain's on the skids. We coming to each man for hisself now, you wait and see. . . ."

"Yes. But wait a minute," I stopped short, caught hold of his sleeve, leaned out over the rail, "there, do you feel it, Sonny? Quick, what's happening?"

Rigid. Black wet nose in the air. Long black paw held up for silence. And then: "Turning." And moving his head then until his white hallelujah eyes were again fixed on mine, and looking at me and sighing with the hopelessness of all nigger warnings and prognostications, he repeated the word: "Turning."

"Changing course, Sonny? Are we? Out with it, is she changing course to starboard?"

"Turning," he repeated, "turning to port. Now you're the one wants to secure the pilothouse, now here's your chance."

"On the double," I said, and the axehead lunged, the ship was straining, moving into the tension of a giant curve, leading us into some forbidden circle. And then the PA was coughing, whistling, piping the madness of its call to Battle Stations and suddenly and dead ahead of us, the green moonlight and black shadows assumed a more solid and dangerous shape: lifeboat, bridge wing, pilothouse, it was all there, each piece in its proper place and rising in tiers and frosted together like the sections of some giant wedding cake. Then hand over hand and up the last green frosted rungs and feeling the whole of that starboard bridge wing heeling down slightly under the centrifugal force, strain, of that tight turn, and bringing each other to a standstill at the open door of the pilothouse where he, Tremlow, was clutching the spokes and even yet trying to get another degree out of the locked wheel.

Moonlight. Green brass binnacle. Green brass barometer. Madness on the decks below, clatter of falling helmets, bodies stumbling, falling, diving into gun mounts, and up here in the wheelhouse our near-naked wireless operator, Tremlow, at the helm of the ship. Sonny began to swing high the axe, but I stayed his arm, for a long moment could only stand there waiting, holding my breath, surveying that ludicrous scene of Tremlow's plan. Because there was Tremlow in the moonlit pilothouse, alone on the bridge, and he was wearing only the long grass skirt and the sweat of the dance was still bright and slick and heavy on his arms, his shoulders, his long muscle-banded back.

"Let go, Skipper," whispering, shuffling, "let me chop him down!"

And then there was the flash of the head, the toss of the long black hair, and Tremlow leapt from the wheel and assumed a crouch. The grass skirt was matted into a smooth bulky fibrous round over the terrible bones of his hips, fell long and sharp and undulating to his bare ankles. Even when he crouched it swished. The wheel was abandoned and the brass speaking tube was calling us, fiercely, shrilly, and moonlight was all about Tremlow and suddenly was also falling flat on a long dark flank that had come out of the grass like a tiger.

"No, no, Sonny," I whispered, holding the arm, turning away the axe, keeping my eyes on the muscles bunching up to spring, "when I hit him, you take the wheel. We must think of the ship. . . ."

So the bright axe fell under our feet. And Sonny sprang out of the way and I threw up my guard. The moon, I noticed, made luminous scar-shaped blotches on the slick brown of that violent breast and flashed and swam and was scattered in all the sharp folds and blended spaces of that now hissing and roaring grass skirt which was coming at me and barely covered him, swinging, swaying in his headlong strides. He was still grinning.

"Tremlow," I tried to say when he socked me. He knocked down my guard with a tap of his bright fist, and vaguely I thought that it wasn't fair, that he was supposed to respect my age, respect my rank, that he was supposed to be down in the shack communicating with the rest of the fleet. Knocked down my guard and socked me in the mouth, and I should have ducked at least because the line of that blow was as clear as hate in the steady eyes, though I still missed the idea, the plan, which was surely riding far forward by then in Tremlow's eye.

"Wait," I said, and my mouth was bleeding, "wait a minute . . . you don't know what you're doing . . . you'll be sorry, Tremlow."

But he hit me in the mouth again. Same fist, same mouth, more bloody mud, more pain. Why not the nose, I thought, or the naked eye, or the stomach, why this furious interest in my loose and soft-spoken mouth?

"Tremlow," I said, tried to say, "you're on duty . . . and Battle Stations . . . the shack . . . please."

We went over the rail, off that wing of the bridge and down, down, with his fist wedged among my bloody teeth and the grass skirt flying, and together, locked together in his hate we burst through something—canvas, I thought, the tarp!—and landed together in a black embrace. Faint odor of dried-out bilge. Faint odor of new hemp. And of cork and lead and paint. And feeling another kind of pain, suddenly I knew that we had fallen together into the bottom of the white lifeboat—33 persons—and that we were not alone. For a moment, hearing laughter, listening to Tremlow swear, for a moment my eyes in darkness found the star-shaped hole in the tarpaulin overhead, and for that single moment I watched the gentle moon pulsing to all the limits of the great canted star cut in the canvas. I must have moaned.

Because the star fled and suddenly the fight went on and the tangle

f the tunic with deep awkward pleats. And the dark bright blue
rd on my arm—white letters SP a mile high—and then the gaiters.
canvas things with laces and hooks and eyes and canvas straps to
der the instep, little canvas sleeves to bind the ends of the white
ers to the fat ankles, and it must have been two o'clock in the
ing, Eastern War Time, when I sat on the floor in our shabby room
e cheap hotel trying to fasten on the gaiters, puffing, struggling,
ng my lips in silence because Cassandra and Pixie too were both
ng in the single bed. And finally the cap, my old white garrison
-eagle going to seed on the front, golden threads of the eagle turn-
ack—the old cap pulled square on my head to simulate, if possible,
oliceman's style, the policeman's look of authority. My rig, my
rig. Thank God she never saw me in that rig.

was raining. Once more we were across the street from a Grey-
d terminal, though it was an eastern rather than a Pacific terminal
hough we were in a hotel instead of a Chinese restaurant, and it
raining. A vaguely familiar terminal, the return to a hardly altered
ness, the city-wide relentless song of the rain, and in a wet envelope
y pocket, my orders. A final shore patrol for Skipper. More shore
ol, more drunks in a dream, more faces inside the cage. Didn't they
w I had had enough, that I was done with the sea? At least I with-
this information from Cassandra, kept her from knowing that she
ld be alone that night while I, her father, was off exposing himself
od knows what harm. So we crossed the street in the rain at half-
one in the morning—no more 0130 hours for me, no more—and
for the nearest doorway and in the red-eyed pain of interrupted
sy slumber we shook ourselves like dogs in front of the desk clerk
piled into the dingy, self-service elevator.

ven from across the street and through the rain I spotted that hotel
what it was: a place for suicide.

"Where are we, Skipper?" she asked once, but I shook my head. I
ded time, I needed silence, I had to think. The elevator had a tic in
atchets and one of the push buttons had fallen out, it banged from
e to side in its dismal shaft and smelled like the flooded lavatory of
bus we had just escaped from. There was a crumpled six-inch black
dline in the corner. We groaned and banged our way up the shaft.
A place for suicide obviously, and my orders were in my pocket and
nny was three or four thousand miles away that moment in Southern
. Surely I couldn't seek help from the clerk who had sent us up with

of arms, legs, hands, began to twist again in the sloping darkness inside
the boat which all the while I never forgot was white, and my whole
poor self told me that the others, whoever they were, were piling on.
There seemed to be a purpose in that struggle, but still it escaped me.
And then hands, the crook of a naked arm, everyone pulling in a different direction in the darkness until all at once they seemed to work
together, those hands, that vicious elbow, and I heard the ripping of
cloth and felt myself floundering, flopping helplessly, because they had
gotten a little rough water cask under my stomach and were rolling me
in some odd fashion on that little rough barrel. And in the darkness.
Forever in the darkness and crippled, bleeding away my good blood in
my poor battered mouth. There was no laughter now.

"What the hell!" I said, or at least thought deep in my heart, and
over the barrel then I began to fight like a fish. Oh, I grunted at them,
gagging on blood, grinding the top of my bald head into the invisible
deck, and I flexed every possible muscle and bucked, did my best to
buck, thrashed around good and plenty in the darkness with someone
breathing his hot breath into my ear and the cloth ripping away from
my flesh as if they were running the tip of a hot wire down the length
of my thigh.

And then: "Dear God," I said, but this too was merely a quick sensation deep in the heart because the grass skirt—wet rough matting of
cruel grass—was rammed against me and there was only darkness and
a low steady fatigued scuffling sound in the bottom of the white lifeboat
along with my last spent cry of pain.

But they must have had an accomplice stationed on the deck because
the darkness bolted then, myself and water keg and kneeling men all
knocked together, smashed, set whirling in the very darkness that had
been tipped, freed, cut loose, was now falling. Surely there was an accomplice who pushed her out and cut the cables, because one moment
I was tumbling in the darkness and the next I was standing straight out
of the star-shaped hole with my hands raised up and my eyes thrust up
into the moonlight. The lifeboat was falling but I was standing inside
the star with my head in the air and my eyes fixed on one tiny figure
far above who was leaning out over the deck, throwing down a rope.
It was Mac. Mac with his vestments flying and his tiny face white with
fear, Mac who flung down the rope and, hand over burning hand—I
was free on the end of that rope when the lifeboat struck—pulled me
back aboard.

Struck, yes, and the splash reached up and soaked my legs even while I clung to the rope and twirled slowly around and around on the end of it.

"Pull her up, Mac," I whispered, "for God's sake. . . ."

There were three lifeboats, as it turned out—Tremlow was in the lead—and on the cold deck I lay half-naked and propped on my side and watched the three of them turn away from us in the moonlight and sail away. Three white sitting ducks in the moonlight. And perhaps I should have unlimbered one of the three-inch guns and ordered them picked off. It would have been easy. And they deserved it. But I lay on the deck half-naked and wet and shivering and thought I saw Tremlow small and dark and confident at the tiller of that first white gently rolling boat. So I let them go. Merely watched and wondered what the sun would do to Tremlow in that grass skirt, wondered what he would say when he was picked up. Claim to be a survivor of a torpedoed ship? God knows. Or perhaps, I thought, perhaps they would never be picked up.

"Let him go on dancing," I said to Mac and tried to smile.

They disappeared like three drops of milk dissolving in a creamy soup, those three boats. And wiping my nose, rubbing myself gently, lying at Mac's feet on our wet and unyielding deck I watched them, watched those three little white boats until they were gone. Follow the leader, I thought. And later, much later, I reported the group of them to be missing in action and told the old man we lost the boats in a storm.

The floating paradise, the brutal act, a few memories on a distant shore. . . .

. . . *dropped to my knees beside her and took her cold hand—no rings—and confessed to her at long last that Fernandez was dead. That I had found him dead at the end of my final shore patrol on Second Avenue. That I thought she should know.*

Yes, I thought she should know. And yes, I told her the truth, made my confession, got it off my chest that night the snow fell into the trembling arms of the larch trees on our black and ragged island rooted fast in the cold and choppy waters of the Atlantic. Yes, I told her, my own daughter. For her own good. For her own good and mine, for our mutual relief. And yes, yes, I thought she might spare herself if she knew the truth, might spare her own life somehow. But I was wrong, of course.

The truth. Yet wasn't I deceiving her even then? certain details, withholding others, failing somehow tonality of the thing? Well, I should hope to God! I or anyone else convey the true tonality of Second I was by Cassandra's little lumpy four-poster—little for years under that embroidered pillow—in the col prim rotting house with fresh white snow on the sagg dark trenches—Puritan graves—awake and listening Second Avenue could not survive that moment in a v why did I wait, why bother to talk to her at all? Bec acted then and there, should have done something speak, in the middle of the flickering darkness of Se I should have left the body, bodies to be true to fa found them in the flickering chaos of the cheap roo Avenue hotel, flophouse, whatever it was, and po driven the gray Navy pickup truck back to that othe self, and waked her and bundled her into a blanket a half-asleep, back down those twenty or so wet block up the broken tiles of those stairs and into the roon she could have taken a good look at him with her own what I should have done. I know it now. But I waite

Yes, I waited those two or three months, and they ference, they tipped the scale, shadings of the true to and certain details were kept to myself. Cassandra ne stance, that I took care that she should not be alone matter, yet it might have helped. And I never told her felt as if it were going to boil over like a car radiator. other small points omitted, gone. And I shall never fo loss. A hair's breadth might have kept Cassandra from merely a hair's breadth. Now I shall never really forgive

But if I missed those many years ago I won't miss ag everything, for what I told her as well as what I didn' upstairs bedroom of the cold island house, everything now to restore a little of the tonality, to set to rights small recognition, a brief scene of blood, some light of fections.

There was the regulation .45 caliber Navy automatic stuck like a four-pound T-bone steak point down on n web belt—too small, they were always too small for around the girth of my white tunic and squeezing me,

skirt
brassa
Little
go un
trous
morn
in the
movi
sleep
cap—
ing b
the p
poor

It
houn
and
was
dark
in m
patr
kno
held
wou
to C
past
ran
une
and

for

nee
its
side
the
hea

Sor
Ca

malice, oh, with what obvious malice to the fourteenth floor which was really the thirteenth floor, I knew. Never have I been taken in by the number fourteen in a cheap water front hotel but have always known beforehand that other number it concealed. The light went out when we reached the fourteenth—thirteenth—floor and, knowing I could not trust Cassandra alone, I gasped, fumbled for the door lever in the darkness, caught my fingers in a joint that was packed with grease.

So we disembarked quickly into the bare corridor, and as I was turning the key in the lock I saw the figure down on its knees with scrubbing brush and pail at the far end of the corridor and I knew that for the moment at least Cassandra was safe. A lucky break on our unlucky floor.

The single bed, the broken radio, the cigarette burns on the chiffonier, the stains on the toilet seat, the broken window shade which came down in my arms. A room in the wartime metropolis of the world for Cassandra, a cut above a flophouse for Cassandra, just the place for her, with its hairs on the pillows and old disreputable impressions on the gray sheets. How little I knew.

"Are you trying to look like Mussolini, Skipper? You look like Mussolini, Skipper, you really do when you hold your chin out that way."

I smiled. "You're tired, Cassandra," I said, "you better hop right on in. Big day coming up, Cassandra."

So it was 2 A.M. and mother and infant were sleeping together in the narrow bed with the loose springs which on many another night gave quick unconcealed clamor to the hidden desires of young servicemen, and I was lacing my gaiters in the middle of the floor and staring at the rain-refracted puddle of neon light that my feet were in. It always rained hardest between midnight and early dawn, I thought.

And then hat, gun, gaiters and envelope of orders and I was ready, paused for a last look at the two of them in the lonely bed. "Grandpa's going on shore patrol," I whispered, "be a good girl." I carried a straight-backed chair with me and left the door ajar when I stepped into the hall.

I set down the chair, cleared my throat, beckoned slowly with my finger. From far down the hall she peered at me, dropped the brush into the pail. She swept away the wings of hair with her wet hands and gasped, rolled her eyes at me, climbed to her feet and bundled up the rags of her skirt and came to me as if I were pulling her in steadily on a golden string. She was plucking herself into a vague new shape, her

eyes were white and fixed on mine, to those young eyes I must have
looked like General Douglas MacArthur in the bare corridor of that
disreputable hotel.

Sixteen years old and haggard, dismayed by the faint lingering sensation of her missing youth, confused by her age, already a sallow and
lonely legend of the late-night elevated trains. Scrub woman and still a
child. And staring at the phantom officer high in that vulgar building
while the rain fell.

"Late for you, Sissy," I said. "Pretty late for you, isn't it?"

Something crossed her face then and she wiped her nose and tried to
conceal what must have been a pain in her side. I drew her close to
me—fragile jaw, transparent flesh, a certain color in the hair, human
being despite the rags, the tin pail, endless vigil on the fourteenth floor.
I glanced at the crack in the door, the chair, and back to the girl with
her eyes, bright nose, lame spirit, carfare rolled up in the top of her
stocking.

"Now, Sissy," I said, "can you sit in the chair? Do you think you
can do that?"

She looked inward for some obscure source of moral vision, then
measured the distance to the chair, then looked long and hard at me,
then, "That's it, that's it," I said, and then she sat down.

"Now, Sissy, listen to me. I must go down in the elevator now, and
I will be gone until the light comes through the window over your
bucket and brush. You see it, Sissy? Now you must stay in the chair
until I return. Don't let anyone go into the room, don't let the lady
come out. And if you hear the lady moving about in the room, you go
to her and stay with her. Do you understand me, Sissy? You must keep
awake and take care of the lady. Take good care of the lady."

And stinking elevator, empty desk, rain in the street. And at the curb
and occupied, I knew, there was the small gray windowless pickup truck
with its official number and spotlight on the driver's side. It had the
unmistakable look of all penal vans, the rain was a thin film over its
dents and bruises. Each dent, each chip in the official gray paint meant
a thrown brick or a struggle in the street, a punchy body smashed
against the side of the gray truck and beaten up, carried away. I sighed,
craned up for a final sight of the fourteenth floor and straightened the
big blue brassard on my arm and climbed into the truck. The engine
kicked over and we pulled out into the deserted thoroughfare of glistening worn trolley track and black girders of the elevated overhead,
began to cruise, to weave rhythmically between the girders.

Twenty blocks of girders, fruit carts shrouded for the night, occasional strip-tease theaters—light bulbs, ticket booth, bright naked posters in the rain—while armed merchant ships waited on both the rivers and GI's drank their late glasses of beer or Nedick's orange juice. Cruising down Second Avenue through the rain, killing a last official night toward the end of the war, fat and uncomfortable and fatigued—gaiters too tight, poor circulation—until, as luck would have it, we saw the crowd and the chief who was driving popped on the light, the little spotlight, and speared the crowd.

"Got your hackles up, Chief?" I asked, "the boys ought to be able to do a little bloodsucking right here, don't you think?"

So we hit the curb, drove over the curb, cut a swath through the rain, and just in time I braced myself against the battered tin dashboard and saved my head.

"Why, look," I said, "they're mostly women," and all the gray tin doors flew open at once and we were accosting the women on Second Avenue and looking for trouble.

"Blew your buttons already, Chief?" I said, but he didn't hear me.

And from deep in the crowd and choking herself with the bathrobe collar and shaking the bright rain in her long blonde hair and pulling the robe tight in the middle: "Hey, girls, the Navy's here!" she said. But the bare throats were still—no laughter—and the robes and negligees were wet, the lips were wet, the eyes were full of something they had seen upstairs. No love. Mere sheep huddling away from death. Though the blonde pushed forward then and gave a tug on her bathrobe cord.

"What about you, Happiness?" she said. "What about you, Honey?" But her eyes were full of another face, not mine, and something, I could tell, was wrong.

"All right," I said. "Now tell me. Any sailors in trouble around here?"

And watching me, letting the rain run down her cheeks: "Upstairs," she said.

"Thought so," I said. "Well, Chief, lead the way."

The entrance hall was dark and crooked and full of rotten vegetables, stray cats, one of the dark doorways off lower Second Avenue and lean, improvident, brushed here and there with scum. And there were five flights of stairs. Five long flights. Already the chief and the other gray members of our shore patrol—three more pairs of gaiters, three hickory sticks—and even the women had passed me on the second landing when I stopped for breath. Already the chief and armed sailors and women sounded like dark dray horses in an abandoned warehouse overhead, and I was puffing up the stairs with my hand ready on the T-bone steak and my full heart beating slow time to the climb.

The top. Rain on a little window, rain among broken aerials, another dark corridor in one more house of crumbling skin and I waited—a foot on the last step, foot on the landing, forearm across the upraised thigh—and took a few slow breaths to quiet everything.

"What is it, Chief?" I called, and tried to loosen my tight gaiters.

Then I walked down the corridor, pushed through the women, and looked for myself. I pushed through, blood or no blood, and fell to my knees beside his body while my face began to tingle and my stomach started to boil up like the radiator of an overheated car. I looked at the body and I swayed, glanced once about the room. And at least Fernandez had found his hideaway, his true hideaway, at last. Peruvian face mask, a pair of black castanets, long white tasseled shawl like the one he had once given to his bride, these he had hung at interesting artistic angles on that sagging wall of skeletal white lath and flaking plaster. Another rain-refracted neon light flicked on and off through the window, lit up a portion of the wall and fell across me where I was kneeling close enough to touch him and to memorize forever each shattered line of that little corpse. There was a woven straw chair with an enormous high rounded back and gently curving arms and a solid basket bottom, and the assailants, murderers, whoever they were, had knocked it over, hacked away at it with some kind of sacrificial hatchet. And they had found his collection of old silver coins, had flung the old bright coins all about the room where they glowed like blood money, old silver coins of honor, in the flickering cheap neon light. But no matter how destroyed, it was still his hideaway, I could see that: here on the top floor of the building of condemned lives, here he had gathered together his bric-a-brac—earthen jugs, horsehair switch, dried poppies in a little Chinese vase—here feathered the poor wrecked nest which I had found, stumbled into, invaded with my gaping shore patrol.

He was naked. Covered with blood. Yes, Fernandez lay on his back on the floor and his neck was fastened to the iron leg of the day bed with one of the strings of the smashed guitar. The murderers had jumped on the belly of his new guitar and smashed it. There was a white mountain-goat rug flung across the day bed but they had killed Fernandez on the hard bare floor. Stabbed, beaten, poked and prodded, but he was finally choked to death with the guitar string.

And the fingers. Yes, all five fingers of the left hand. All five. The

clasp knife, the wine-dark pool, the fingers themselves, it was clear, too
clear, what they had done and that the severed fingers were responsible
for the spidery red lines scattered over everything. The wild tracings,
the scene of blood—I touched him on the shoulder once and then I
managed to reach the corridor and, while the blonde held me under the
arm and cupped her wet hand on my forehead, I doubled over and let
everything in my hot stomach boil up and out.

When I returned to the room I pried open the window and let the
rain beat in. I remained standing on my feet and staring at the second
body until the job was done. The other belonged to a sailor and was
fully clothed in white bell-bottomed pants, crumpled white middy
blouse. A big man face down. Hands buried beneath the face. Legs
kicked far apart. Killed by the single driving blow of another clasp knife
which they had left in his back.

"His name's Harry," the blonde said.

"Harry," I said. "Poor Harry."

And then all of her weight was on my arm, her voice suddenly tremulous, she was crying. She said she knew what had happened and
wanted to tell me. So I righted the hatcheted straw chair and made her
sit down, held her cold hard hand and looked at Harry while the hand
squeezed and the elbow shook and the voice talked on. She said that
she had heard the noise upstairs and that there was nothing unusual
about the noise, but that when the man came down and banged on her
door, another sailor, she said, and as big as Harry, very much like Harry
in fact, she told him she didn't want to with anyone who had just been
fighting, that she wasn't going to give herself to anybody with a swelling
eye and the blood still on his knuckles and running out of his nose. But
she couldn't help herself, she said, and it wasn't bad, all things considered. So he waited until it was over and then while she was trying to
do something with her hair and he, the sailor, was still breathing hard
on her bed, why then he caught her eye and kept looking at her and
told her all about it. He and a couple of others had killed a little fairy
spic upstairs, that it was a game they had to let some fairy pick them
up and then, when they were in the flophouse room, to pull out the
knives. . . .

"He waited, you see? Waited until he was done to tell me. So now
for ten bucks the blood's on my hands too, and all over I'm dying, I
can feel it. That guy there, that Harry," pointing down, drawing the
robe tight between her knees, "he came in too soon, you see, and tried
to save his buddy, so they killed him. . . . I wish it was me."

I let go of her hand, I helped to turn up the bathrobe collar, I wrapped the white mountain-goat rug around her lap. Her head was down. I touched the thin blonde hair on the back of that small ageless skull and spoke to the chief, made it clear to him that I didn't want to see the sailor's face.

And then the chief gave orders: "Get the basket stretcher out of the truck. You two, wrap him in the sheet. But leave the little one alone, he's not ours. . . ."

Was Tremlow's first name Harry? Was it Tremlow lying now at the bare feet of the streetwalker sitting in the shiny partially chopped-up straw chair? Tremlow killed at last while defending my little lost son-in-law? Or was it Tremlow who had swung the sacrificial hatchet, destroyed the hideaway, lopped off the fingers? This, I thought, was more like Tremlow, but I could not be sure and was careful that I would never know.

I looked again and saw the little white calfskin book lying near the left hand of Fernandez. It was a book from the past, a soft white unread book just out of reach where I left it.

"Don't worry," I called softly to the bowed figure on the straw chair, "there's no blood on your hands."

And web belt, meaty automatic and gaiters, these I dropped into the back of the pickup truck with Harry's body, stared at the sheeted form bound into the mesh of the basket, and stepped away, flagged down a taxi, returned as quickly as I could to the predawn silhouette of my own cheap hotel.

She was sitting in the straight-backed chair, poor Sissy, and wide awake, clear providential eyes fixed on the elevator. I held the door so it wouldn't bang and took off my cap and smiled. Then wrinkled and bloodstained and more haggard than Sissy herself, I approached her slowly and helped her out of the chair and took her into my arms and kissed her. Her mouth tasted like old wax paper but it was the kiss of my life.

And we were wrong about him, Cassandra, weren't we? Just a little wrong, Cassandra?

"Papa," I cried, "no, Papa. Please. . . ."

"I shall do it, Edward, I tell you. See if I don't. . . ."

"But please, please, what about Mamma, Papa? What about me?"

"Some things, Edward, can't be helped. . . ."

And crouching at the keyhole of the lavatory door, soft little hands

cupped on soft fat knees and hot, desperate, hopeful, suddenly inspired:
"Wait, Papa, wait, I will play for you, poor Papa."

"No, no, Edward, never mind . . . it will do no good. . . ."

But I raised one of my hands then, clapped it over my lips, waited.
And when I failed to answer him there was only silence behind the
lavatory door. Was he caught off guard? Uncertain? Or stricken even
more deeply with despair, sitting on the old brown wooden toilet seat
with vacant eyes and pure white boneless mortician's hands clasped
vacantly between his knees? I knew by the peculiar intensity of that
prolonged silence that I was safe for awhile, that he could do nothing
at least until I had played him my Brahms. It was the dripping faucet
that gave the silence its peculiar tight suspended ring, the dripping faucet
that convinced me: it would hold his attention until I could play my
Brahms.

"Are you there, Edward?"

But as small and fat and ungainly as I was, and as much as I wanted
to talk with him, plead with him, I had just been inspired and knew
enough, suddenly, not to answer. One sound, I understood, and he
might well blow his head off then and there.

"Edward?"

But his voice was weaker while the monstrous dripping was louder,
more dominant, more demanding. And my cheeks were fatter than ever
with my held breath, my ears throbbed, my eyes throbbed, I stole away
into the bright noon sun of that hapless Friday in midsummer. I flew
to my room, as much as any inspired and terrified fat boy can fly, and
for those few moments—mere sunlit suspended moments saved by a
rotten washer in the right-hand faucet in the lavatory sink—for those
extra moments of life he was none the wiser.

I ran to my room though I was not a quick child, ran with my short
plump bare arms flung out in front of me and not a sob in my throat,
not a snuffle in my little pink naked rosebud of a nose, so bent was I
on staying his hand with my cello. And the sunlight, bright sunlight
coming through every window in planes as broad as each sill and filled
with motes and little stationary rainbows that warmed leg, knee, pudgy
arm, home full of light and silence and suspended warmth. And only
the two of us to share my Brahms.

The cello was under my bed and without thinking I flopped to my
hands and knees and hauled it out, and then tumbled it onto my bed,
turned back the corners of the old worn-out patchwork quilt in which
my mother always wrapped that precious instrument. Cello in the sun-

light, tiny shadows beneath the strings, wood that was only a shell, a thin wooden skin, but dark and brown and burnished. The sunlight brought out the sheen of my cello—tiny concentric circles of crimson moons—brought out the glow of the thick cat strings. I stood there, put my palm on its thin hard belly, and already it was warm and rich and filled with my slow awkward song.

So I tightened the strings, tightened the bow and hugged the now upright cello and held my breath, trotted back silently—bulging sway-backed child, bouncing cello—to my lonely sunlit post by the locked door. And then—no noise, no noise—the terror of touching the cello's middle leg to the floor and of resting the waxen neck in my shoulder and pressing down a string and raising the bow, flinging up the bow and staring at the keyhole and waiting, watching the keyhole, smiling, in silence holding everything ready for the song.

"Now, Papa," I said suddenly, and there was a startled jumping sound behind the door, "now I am going to play!" And my arm fell and the bow dragged, sawed, swayed to and fro—hair on gut, fat fingertips on gut—and the cello and I rolled from side to side together. I kept my eyes on the little black hole in the door, with every ecstatic rhythmic roll crossed and recrossed my legs.

So I played for him, played Brahms while my father must have been loading the pistol, played while he swept an impatient and frightened hand through the gray thinning hair and made fierce eyes to himself behind the door. I played with no thought of him, really, but he must have gagged a little to himself in there, choked like a man coughing up blood for the first time as he tried to decide how best to use the nickel-plated weapon, forced his fingers inside the trigger guard. I suppose the first sounds of the cello must have destroyed the spell of the faucet. So I played on, phantom accomplice to his brutal act, and all the while hoping, I think, for success and pleased with the song.

And then: "Edward!"

Bow in mid-air. Silence, catch in my throat, legs locked. Because his voice was loud. He had gotten down on his knees and had put his mouth to the keyhole: "Edward," he said firmly, "stop it!"

And then cello, legs, bow, myself, heart, Brahms, all locked together for a moment of immobile frenzy because I heard the lock turn in the lavatory door and thought he was coming out to me.

"Edward! I have opened the door. There is no point in making someone break down the door to get me. . . ."

So the bow swung free and again I was squatting, leaning close to the door: "But, Papa, may I come in then?"

The shot. The tiny acid stink at the keyhole. And the door opened slightly of its own accord, hung ajar so that I saw one twisted foot, trouser cuff jerked above the ankle, and my own release, my cry, my grief, the long shocked moment when I clung to the cello and heard the terrible noise and wondered when it would ever end. He may have spoken to me one last time—"Good-by, Edward"—but I couldn't be sure. The shot, after all, killed everything.

Everything, that is, except my love. But if my own poor father was Death himself, as I think he was, then certainly I was right to tell Cassandra how familiar I was with the seeds of death. Wasn't I myself, as a matter of fact, simply that? Simply one of those little black seeds of death? And what else can I say to Father, Mother, Gertrude, Fernandez, Cassandra, except sleep, sleep, sleep?

LAND OF SPICES

HIGHLIGHTS OF HELPLESSNESS? Mere trivial record of collapse? Say, rather, that it is the chronicle of recovery, the history of courage, the dead reckoning of my romance, the act of memory, the dance of shadows. And all the earmarks of pageantry, if you will, the glow of Skipper's serpentine tale.

Cinnamon, I discovered when I was tossed up spent and half-naked on the invisible shore of our wandering island—old Ariel in sneakers, sprite surviving in bald-headed man of fair complexion—cinnamon, I found, comes to the hand like little thin brown pancakes or the small crisp leaves of a midget tobacco plant. And like Big Bertha who calls to me out of the black forest of her great ugly face I too am partial to cinnamon, am always crumpling a few of the brittle dusty leaves in my pockets, rubbing it gently onto the noses of my favorite cows. And what better than cinnamon for my simmering dreams?

Yesterday, if I can trust such calculations in my time of no time, yesterday marked the end of Catalina Kate's eighth month. Four weeks to go and right on time, and Kate has stretched and swelled and grown magnificently. My Kate with a breadbasket as big as a house, tight as a drum, and the color of old brick and shiny, smooth and shiny, under the gaudy calico of that tattered dress. And wasn't Sister Josie pleased? "Baby coming in four weeks, Josie," I told her. And weren't we all? But yesterday was also the day I knocked up Sweet Phyllis in the shade of the calabash tree. A big day, as I told Sonny, a big day all around.

"Cow's calling, Skipper. Just hear if she ain't!"

Dawn. The first moment of windy dawn, and the bright limes were dancing, the naked flesh hung down from the little cocoa trees, and already the ants were swarming. Red-eyed Sonny stood there—metamorphosed, waiting forever—among the broad leaves and shadows framed in my large white rotting casement. Sonny was waiting, yawning, rubbing his eyes in my view of the world.

"Cow's calling for sure. And ain't that Sweet Phyllis, Skipper? Sounds like Phyllis to me!"

"All right, Sonny," leaning forward, scratching myself, smearing the ants, watching the shifting torso in my window, listening, "it's all right, Sonny. She'll wait." I could hear the faint far-off appeal, the dumb strained trumpeting of Sweet Phyllis in heat. She sounded ecstatic, was making a brassy sustained noise of grief. Sonny had a good ear.

"Tell Big Bertha to fix us a lunch, Sonny. We might as well make a day of it. And tell Bertha that she and Kate and Josie may come along if they'd like to. Fair enough?"

"Oh, they'll want to come along, Skipper," grinning, shifting softly and erratically in the window with his arms pressed tight to the long thin torso and somehow active, up to something, though in no way suggesting his intention to be off, to be gone about my business, "them girls wouldn't miss a hot fete for Phyllis if you allows them the privilege and lets them get off from work, Skipper, you knows that!"

The old smashed petty officer's cap this time, the indecent angle of the cap, the long shrunken torso like a paste of hickory ash and soot, the fixed grin, the unshaved black jaw working. "Well, Sonny," I said, "how about it? Are you going to tell Big Bertha what I told you?" And then, listening, watching, returning his grin: "Sonny," I said softly, "Sonny, are you relieving yourself against Plantation House? Under my very window, Sonny? You have no scruples. You have no scruples at all."

And shaking his head in pretended pain, showing me that long wry black face and contorting his brows, blinking: "That's right, Skipper," he said, "I don't have none of that scruples stuff. No, sir!"

So that's how yesterday began, with the live sounds of the calling cow and Sonny's water. It ended after dark with a bath, one of the prolonged infrequent sandy sea-splashing baths for Sonny and myself. And in between, only our little idyl down with the cow. Only the five of us in the shade of the calabash tree with Phyllis. And the girls, as Sonny called them, added their charms to the cows' and enjoyed our little slow pastoral down in the overgrown field with Phyllis and Alma and Edward and Freddy and Beatrice and Gloria. More water, of course, and a little song and so many soothing hands and a nap on a pile of green calabashes and the taste of guava jam, it couldn't have been a better time for Phyllis, a better time for us.

"All right," I said, "everyone here? Now let's not have a lot of noise. I don't want you making a lot of noise and frightening that cow. You hear? I don't want to get kicked." And then I started off, leading the way. And Sonny in the old chief's cap and ragged white undershorts followed, and then Big Bertha with our lunch on her head in an iron

pot, and then beautiful sway-backed Kate and Sister Josie, who in her
mauve hood and cowl, long mauve skirts hiding her little black shoes,
loved all the wild cows and mockingbirds and indecent flowers. In a
long single file and in that colorful order they followed me through the
bush, and I was the Artificial Inseminator of course, and in one hand I
carried the little black tattered satchel and in the other hand swung
Uncle Billy's crucifix. A slow languid single-file progress through the
bush with the women jabbering and the orchids hanging down from the
naked Indian trees and Sonny slapping flies and the sun, the high sun,
piercing my old white Navy cap with its invisible rays. And I swayed,
I swung myself from side to side, opened up our way along that all-but-
obliterated cow path on the saw-toothed ridge among the soft hibiscus
and poisoned thorns and, yes, the hummingbirds, the little quick jewels
of my destiny. From the frozen and crunchy cow paths of the Atlantic
island—my mythic rock in a cold sea—to this soft pageant through leaf,
tendril, sun, wind, how far I had come.

"Got to go a little faster now," I said, and raised the dripping satchel
so they could see it, "must hurry it up a little, Sonny and young ladies,
or the ice will melt."

And from the other side of the ridge and on the floating air she was
calling us, Sweet Phyllis, was holding her quarters rigid and sticking her
nose through the calabash leaves and blaring at us, blaring forth the
message of her poor baffled fertility. It was a signal of distress, a low-
register fire horn, and I recognized more than Sweet Phyllis's voice drifting over the ridge.

"You hear it, Big Bertha?" I said, "hear it, Kate? And you, Sister
Josie, do you hear it too? They're all calling now. Alma and Beatrice
and Gloria and Edward and Freddy—hear them calling? They've gotten
the idea from Phyllis, eh? All of them think it is time for a hot fete,
even the steers. Isn't that so, Josie?"

Little black Josie, old Bertha with the pot on her head, my dusty
rouge-colored pregnant Kate with her club of dark hair hanging down
to her breast and her belly slung down and forward near the end of her
time—they giggled, each one of them, and pointed at the wet shirt clinging to my enormous back, pointed at the dripping satchel. I smelled
them—little nun, old cook, mother-to-be—and knew that they were in
a processional, after all, and that each one of them was capable of love
in her own way.

"The way things is going, Skipper, old Sonny's about to start a little
calling of his own any minute now. I just feels a big call catching right

here in this skinny throat of mine. Got to bellow it out any minute, Skipper, damn if I don't."

"You want to call too, Sonny," I said. "Why not? A little calling wouldn't hurt you. It's the hammock that's bad for you, Sonny. Too much time in the hammock is bad."

And I laughed, glanced over my shoulder—Sonny flopping along in his unbuckled combat boots, Sonny pulling up his drawers—and the three dark women were watching us and listening. Love at last, I thought, and I thrashed out onto a small golden promontory above the field. Blue sky, bright pale blue of a baby's eye, our golden vantage point, the field below; and in the center of the field the dark low sprawling shape of our deep green tree, and under the tree the cows—two steers, four heifers, six young beauties in all—and in the branches of the tree, which were tied together, knotted together like tangled ribbons in a careless head of hair, the birds, a screeching and wandering tribe of birds that were drawn to Phyllis's song like ourselves and now swarmed in the tree. Love at last. I smiled over my shoulder and we started down.

To the last we held our single file. To the last we maintained our evenly spaced formation, our gentle steps, delicate order, significant line. Tennis shoes filled with burrs, white trousers torn, old rakish and rotting white cap, shreds of once-white shirt plastered to my mahogany breast and back, and except for these I was naked. Sniffing the sweet air and keeping my chin lifted, and swaying, riding slowly forward at a heavy contented angle I, Skipper, led the way. I knew the way, was the man in charge—the AI—and there was no mistaking me for anything but the leader now, and they were faithful followers, my entourage. Down we went, and the tennis shoes and combat boots and little black pointed shoes from the missionary's museum and two other lovely pairs of naked feet hardly touched the earth, hardly made a sound, surely left no prints in the soft wild surface of the empty field. It was a long slow day with the cows, a picnic under the calabash tree, a gentle moment, a pastoral in my time of no time.

We maintained our places in line up to the very tree itself, and then one by one and without breaking file we stopped and folded aside the tender branches, one by one entered the shade, joined the loud animals in the din of the birds. The spot I chose for entering was not an arm's length from Sweet Phyllis's dripping nose which was thrust through the leaves and sniffing us, giving the sound of desire to our approach. But she was not frightened. And as soon as I entered that grove of shade I rested my hand on her shoulder, thrust my own nose through the leaves, was just in time to watch Kate take the last twenty or thirty steps of our amorous way.

She was like a child, like a young girl, because despite her weight and swayed back, despite sore muscles and the rank sweat on her exotic brow, she was taking those last steps with her hands held behind her back—backs of her hands nesting in the small of her back—and with her elbows held out like wings, and she was waggling her elbows, tossing her head, taking light happy strides on her naked toes. It was a sinuous slow-motion seductive cantering, the heavy oblivious dance of my young Kate. Despite the water under her skin. Despite the big precious baby inside the sac.

"Come along, Catalina Kate," I cried, "I'm watching you!"

And then we were all together and the bellowing stopped, the birds simmered down, Bertha wedged the iron pot into the above-ground roots of the tree, and I—humming, musing, stripping off the rags of my shirt—I squatted and opened my official black satchel and removed the little sad chunk of ice, deposited the little smooth half-melted piece of ice in the lip of the spring that was a black puddle among the lesser roots at the far edge of the tree. And carefully—down on my knees, smiling—I took the little glass bottle from the satchel and weighed it in my hand—a mere nothing in the hand, but life, the seeds of life—and stood it carefully on the chunk of ice. Safe now. No worry now. I could take my time.

"See there, Kate? That's Oscar. Oscar in the little bottle, Kate! For Sweet Phyllis, do you understand?"

And smiling, glancing at the bottle, glancing at me, fixing the shiny black club of plaited hair between her young breasts and indifferent to the sweat that trickled down her bare throat and down her arms, down the sides of her young face and even into the corners of her dark eyes, she said softly: "Oh, yes, sir, Kate know what you mean."

"Good girl," I said, "I'm glad." And then: "Well, what about it, Bertha, time to eat? Poor Sonny looks pretty hungry to me!"

So while the spring kept Oscar cool, the five of us sprawled close together and held out our hands to the fat black arm that disappeared inside the pot and came up dripping. Calypso herself couldn't have done better. Sweet guavas and fat meat that slid into the fingers, made the fingers breathe, and crushed leaves of cinnamon on the tongue and sweet shreds of coconut. We ate together under the dark speckled covering of the tree, sprawled together, composed, with no need for wine, and the cows stood about and nosed us and a blackbird flew down and sat on Sonny's cap. We ate together among the smooth green oval calabashes that were as large as footballs, and lay among the calabashes and licked our fingers. I told Josie to take off her shoes—"Take them off, Josie," I said, "you have my permission." And while she was trying to unfasten the little knotted strings Edward took it into his head to jump up on Sweet Phyllis and the bird hopped wildly about on Sonny's cap. And my namesake—reluctantly I say that name, reluctantly admit that name—left bright thick gouts of mud on each of Sweet Phyllis's soft yellow flanks.

And Sister Josie spoke. Holding the tiny broken-heeled shoes in her lap and poking a little naked foot from under the madness of the mauve skirts, at last she felt the need to speak, to speak to me: "Edward trying to walk down the road on Phyllis, sir?"

"Of course he is, Josie," I said softly, "of course he is."

"Walk down the road for babies?"

"Yes, Josie. That's what he wants."

So we ate out of Bertha's pot, watched Edward jumping up, watched Freddy using his nose for life—"See how he goes at it, Kate," I said, "no holding him back"—Freddy ramming his head straight out and nuzzling, drawing back his lips, that famished steer, and snuffling and waving marvelous long streamers from his glazed bubbling nose. And in our lazy heap we noticed idly that Alma and Beatrice and Gloria were playing tricks with their tails or trying to mount each other or one of the steers.

"Poor Alma," I said. "She looks like Pagliacci, don't you think so, Sonny? But look there, Sonny, when Beatrice tops Gloria and then Gloria tops Beatrice you really have something, don't you, Sonny? Divine confidence, isn't that it? Blessed purpose anyway, eh? And who's to say nothing will come of it?"

They planted their hoofs among our legs—sticky hoofs, outstretched legs—and they lowered their brown eyes on us, and Gloria licked my cheek and Beatrice even lay down next to little Josie, cow's head next to cowled head, breaths mingling.

"Now, what about this poor little Sweet Phyllis, Skipper? You going to make her wait all day?"

"In good time, Sonny," I murmured. "She'll wait, she'll keep, don't worry."

The blackbird danced, the cows switched flies or picked off torn little leaves with their big teeth or tried to get everything started up again, the black spring continued to steep the roots of the tree and keep Oscar cool. We dozed. And Sonny sighed for Bertha, put his long skinny panther paw on Kate. "Hugging is all right, Kate," I thought to say, "but nothing more, Kate, do you understand? You mustn't hurt the baby." Then I pulled little Sister Josie's swaddled head down to rest on my broad steaming mahogany chest, gave her Uncle Billy's crucifix to hold.

"No lady of the cloth ever had it this good, Josie," I whispered—shoe-button eyes unmoving, mouth big with gold—and in my half-sleep I heard the animals and through a warm speckled film saw Kate kneeling and rinsing out Sonny's drawers in the spring, then standing in shadow and turning, reaching, as I seemed to see the very shape of the earthbound child, and hanging Sonny's white drawers on a dead limb to dry. Shades beneath the calabash tree, soft sounds, leaf-eating dreams, grove of perpetuation. Silence. The tree was suddenly still, perfectly still, down to a bird. Love at last.

But we awoke together, and like Josie, Catalina Kate must have felt the need to speak, must have thought that it was her turn to speak to me, because she was leaning over Sonny and looking down at me, and I could see the shoulder, arm, small face, naked hair, and I heard what she was saying: "God snapping him fingers," she said, and that sudden moment of waking was just what she said, "God snapping him fingers," though it was probably Edward breaking a twig or one of the birds bouncing a bright seed off the smooth green back of a resounding calabash.

And on my elbow, suddenly, and wide-awake in my old time out of time: "Yes, Kate," I said. "Snapping for you!" She giggled. And had the hours passed? Days, years? I put down the thought because I was wide-awake and the sharp harmony was like a spear in the ribs.

"Now, Sonny," I said, and already I was crouching at the lip of the spring, "let's take care of Phyllis. What do you say?"

Black spring, black ferns, last remnant of ice the size of a dime, bright little glass bottle upright, gleaming, cool. The genie had wreaked havoc on Oscar, I thought, and I picked up the bottle—the bull in the bottle —and weighed its fragile cool weight in my palm.

"Come, now, Sonny," I said briskly, "let's be done with her. Where's the tube?"

He whipped it out of the satchel then, that resilient tube, long amorous pipette, and I snapped the neck of the bottle, stuck an end in the bottle and caught the other end between my teeth and quickly sucked the few pure drops of Oscar into the pipette and dropped the empty bottle down the spring and popped my finger over the end of the tube to keep Oscar where I wanted him.

"Battle stations, everyone," I said softly, but they were already moving, dancing, and the somehow suspicious cows were already composing themselves into a single group-attitude of affection, and the arms were raised, curved, quick and languid at the same time. Apparently some brief intelligence was stirred in Alma, Freddy, Edward, Beatrice, Gloria, because suddenly they had sense enough to keep out of our way, and drew back and hung their heads and watched us with big round glowing sylvan eyes.

Late afternoon under the calabash tree. Closing in on Phyllis. Speckled shadows. Trembling, smiling, soothing. A cow and her sisters. And it was a simple job for me, and nothing for her, merely a long hair rolled up lengthwise and lost in a hot muscular blanket of questing tenderness, but nonetheless we smiled, closed in carefully and in our own sweet timeless time, expectant, bemused, considerate, with fingers and arms and in soft dalliance transplanting the bull and stopping the tide of the heifer.

Late afternoon and only faint sounds of breathing, brief shifting activity in the shadows, and Sonny was embracing the smooth alerted head while Catalina Kate and Josie were posted on her starboard side, were rubbing and soothing and curving against her starboard side and Bertha, Big Bertha, was tending the port. And I was opposite from Sonny and knew just what to do, just how to do it—reaching gently into the blind looking glass with my eye on the blackbird on Sonny's cap—and at the very moment that the loaded pipette might have disappeared inside, might have slipped from sight forever, I leaned forward quickly and gave a little puff into the tube—it broke the spell, in a breath lodged Oscar firmly in the center of the windless unsuspecting cave that would grow to his presence like a new world and void him, one day, onto the underground waters of the mysterious grove—and pulled back quickly, slapped her rump, tossed the flexible spent pipette in the direction of the satchel and grinned as the whole tree burst into the melodious racket of the dense tribe of blackbirds cheering for our accomplished cow.

And wasn't she an accomplished cow? And wasn't it, this moment of conception, this instant of the long voyage, a time for bird song and smiling and applause? So she gave a sprightly kick then—one pretty kick from Sweet Phyllis but too late, much too late, because I had seen that pretty kick coming even before I took Oscar's little bottle off the

ice and was standing back well out of her way and smiling when she
let fly so prettily in the face of her fate—and then, and only two years
old, she gathered herself in sulky modesty and pushed through the
screen of leaves and without much hurry but with clear purpose trotted
off alone across the empty field. I waved, I watched her diminishing and
rising and falling brown body until it turned into the heavy bush and
was gone.

"Well, too bad, Phyllis," I said to myself, "you won't quite catch up
with Kate," and I smiled and shook my head.

And then Sonny was pulling on his sun-bleached underdrawers and
Bertha was hoisting up her pot and Josie was putting on her shoes and
Kate was plaiting her long dark hair again and trying to arouse my
heart, I thought, with sight of the child. Any time now, I knew, and the
sun would die.

"Good-by to the dark-eyed cow," I said. "And now Big Bertha and
Catalina Kate and Sister Josie, I want the three of you to return to
Plantation House together while Sonny and I go down to the south
beach and have our bath. You lead the way, Bertha; be careful, Kate;
remember what you do at sundown, Sister Josie."

So I retrieved Uncle Billy's crucifix from Sister Josie, and they
started off.

And in darkness and in silence Sonny and I made our way to the
south beach and naked except for our official caps sat together in the
sand on the south beach, ground ourselves back and forth, back and
forth in the abrasive white sand and scrubbed our calves, thighs, even
fleshy Malay archipelagos with handfuls of the fine sand that set up a
quick burning sensation in tender skin. By the time we waded out to
our shoulders the moon was on the water and the little silver fish were
sailing in to nibble at the archipelagos. My arms floated out straight on
the warm dark tide, I rinsed my mouth with sea water and spit it back
to the sea, I tasted the smooth taste of salt. When we rose up out of
the slow-motion surf the conchs were glistening at us in the moonlight.

"I tell you what, Sonny," I said, and dried the crucifix, pulled up my
tattered white pants, "why don't you look in on Josie or see what Bertha's fixing us for chow? I just want to stop off a moment at the water
wheel. OK?"

So I left him at the corner of the barn and whistled my way to the
water wheel and found her waiting. I stood beside her, mere heavy
shadow leaning back against dark broken stone and moonlit flowers,
and I smelled the leaves of cinnamon. I put my arm around her and

touched her then, and part of the dress—sweat-rotted dissolving fragment of faded calico—came off in my hand. But it was no matter and I simply squeezed the cloth into a powder and dropped it and put out my hand again.

Her eyes were soft, luxurious, steady, in the darkness she reached out and tore off a flower—leaf, flower, taste of green vine—and looking at me put it between her teeth, began to chew.

"Saucy young Catalina Kate," I whispered, "eight months pregnant and still saucy, Kate? Iguana going to get you again if you keep this up."

She giggled. I felt the shadow then, the firm shadow of tiny head and neck, little upswept protecting arms. Felt, explored, caressed, and by the position of the moon and direction of the scent of spices I knew that the island was wandering again, floating on.

"Now tell me, Kate," mouth close to her ear, hand holding her tight, "what's it going to be? Little nigger boy, Kate, or little nigger girl?"

And spitting out the leaf and smiling, putting her hand on mine: "Whatever you say, sir," she said, "please God. . . ."

Yesterday our pastoral, tomorrow the spawn. A mere four weeks and I will hold the child in my own two hands and break out the French wine, and after our visit to the cemetery, will come to my flourishing end at last. Four weeks for final memories, for a chance to return, so to speak, to the cold fading Atlantic island which is Cassandra's resting place. And then no more, nothing, free, only a closed heart in this time of no time.

So on to the dead reckoning of my romance. . . .

DRAG RACE ON THE BEACH

RED SUN IN THE MORNING, sailor's warning. I knew that much. And hadn't I sworn off the sea? After my one thousand days and nights on the *Starfish* hadn't I sworn off the sea forever? There was my mistrust of the nautical life, the suspicion of my tendency toward seasickness, the uneasiness I had come to feel in the presence of small boats whether in or out of the water. My sympathy for all the young sun-tanned and shrapnel-shredded sailors in deep southern seas would never die, but I was done with the water, the uncomfortable drift of a destructive ocean, done trying to make myself acceptable to the Old Man of the Sea. So what drew me to the *Peter Poor*? How to explain that dawn in March which was an eastern blood bath, in the first place, and full of wind? Why did I interrupt our Mah Jongg games or my friendly fights with the black Labradors? Having recovered from the indignities of that crippling December dance, and having spent three frozen months in the calm inside the gale—trying a little of the Old Grand Dad myself now, not much, but just a little, and building the fires, drying the dishes, dragging Pixie down the cow paths on a miniature creaky sled with turned-up wooden runners—why, having watched the snow at the window and having kept my mouth shut during all those Sunday dinners and having learned to sleep at last on those hard cold nights, why, suddenly, did I trot right down to the dock with Cassandra and submit myself to the *Peter Poor* which was a fishing boat and didn't even have a head?

"Go on, Skip, don't spoil the fun. It's a good way to see the island. And Skip," clicking the needles, giving the log in the fireplace a shove with her bare toes, "it's just what Candy needs. My God, Skip, how could you refuse?"

And toying with the East Wind, watching her: "What about you, Miranda?" I said, "it's not like you to miss a good time?"

And throwing back her head and twinkling the light in her glass and laughing, "No, no, I've already been out sailing with the boys. Besides, every girl deserves to be the only woman on the *Peter Poor* just once in her life."

254

But Cassandra only looked at me and took my hand.

So it was on a red dawn in the month of March that I succumbed to the idea of Crooked Finger Rock and sunken ships and a nice rough ghostly cruise around the black island, succumbed and gave Cassandra the one chance in her life to be the only woman on the *Peter Poor*. And it was in the month of May that I raced down the beach for my life in Miranda's hot rod, in May, the month of my daughter's death. And in June that we got out of there, Pixie and I, June when I packed our flight bag and hurried out of that old white clapboard house and carried poor Pixie off to Gertrude's cousin in New Jersey. Four months. Four short months. A brimming spring. And of course I know now that there was a chance for Cassandra up to the very moment she swung her foot gaily over the rail of the *Peter Poor* and stood with her hair blowing and her skirt blowing on the cluttered deck of that water-logged tub of Red's. But there was no chance really for Cassandra after that. No chance at all. The second of the four seasons sucked her under, the sea was cruel. March, then May, then June, and the last fragments, the last highlights, last thoughts, the time of my life.

Red sun in morning, sailor's warning. That's it. And the dawn was lying out there on its side and bleeding to death while I fidgeted outside Cassandra's door—accomplice, father, friend, traveling companion, yes, old chaperon, but lover and destroyer too—and while Miranda waltzed around the dark kitchen in her kimono and tried to fix an early break-fast for Pixie. Dawn bleeding from half a dozen wounds in its side and the wind blowing and my old bird fighting its slow way across the sky.

"Hurry, up, Cassandra," I called through the closed door, blowing on cold fingers, stuffing a fat brown paper sack—lunch for two—under my arm and watching the bird, "you'll have to hurry a little, Cassandra, if the Captain is going to make the dawn tide." Even upstairs in the cold dark house I could feel the tide rising, feel the flood tide reaching its time and turning, brimming, waiting to sweep everything away. But there was no need to hurry. I should have known. I should have known that Red had been waiting seven months already for this tide, this dawn, this day at sea, and that he would have waited forever as long as he had any hopes at all of hearing her heels clicking on the deck of the *Peter Poor*, that he would have let the *Peter Poor* list forever in the green mud for the mere sight of Cassandra coming down his weedy path at six o'clock in the morning, would have sailed the *Peter Poor* onto rocks, shoals, reefs, ledges, anywhere at all and under any condi-tions if he could once persuade Cassandra to climb aboard. No hurry.

And yet perhaps I was aware of his baldheaded, wind-burned, down-East, inarticulate seagoing licentious patience after all, and fidgeted, marked the stages of the dawn out of the intuitive resources of my destructive sympathy. God knows. But she appeared to me then, un-smiling—unsmiling since the blustery high school dance when I had done my best to tell her everything, make her understand—and wearing a little pale blue silk kerchief tied under her chin.

"I thought you were going to wear slacks, Cassandra," I said. "Slacks are more appropriate to a boat, you know. Much more appropriate than a full skirt, Cassandra. But of course it's too late now anyway."

We went downstairs together—shadows and little playful drafts on the stairs, and if it wasn't a big prize bow for a high school dance then it was a big billowing rust-colored skirt for a windy day—and in the kitchen she hugged Miranda and kissed Pixie's forehead. Then hot coffee, standing up, and then another hug, another kiss, and then good-by.

"While we're gone, Miranda," I said, "don't fool around with the nipples or do anything harmful to the child. OK, Miranda?"

"My God, Skip, you've got a sore memory, haven't you? But every-thing's forgiven, Skip. Don't worry."

The wind, the red sun, and I tried to take her arm under the chestnut tree, but she walked on ahead of me with the kerchief tilted back and her two small white hands pressed down flat against the tiny round abdomen of the orange skirt which lunged and kicked and whirled in woolen fury. The hard thin mature white legs were bare, I could see that, and I tried to come abreast of her again on the empty road.

"That skirt's going to give you trouble, Cassandra," I said, just as all at once she turned off the road and began to run lightly down the weedy path with the skirt whipping and fumbling about her legs and the tight kerchief changing color in the dawn light.

"Wait, Cassandra, wait for me," I called. I wondered what figure of unhappiness it was that I could see plainly enough in the stiffness of the slender shoulders and forlorn abandonment of the little swathed head. Her feet were describing those sad uncomfortable circles of the young female who runs off with wet eyes or uncommunicative smile or tiny cry clutched, held, in the naked throat, and I wanted to stop her, wanted to walk awhile with my arm about her shoulder and her hand in my hand. But it was no use.

"Jomo, good morning," I heard her say in her best voice, and I saw it all, Cassandra still lightly running and Jomo looking at her from where he was crouched at the gasoline pump and Red watching her from the bow of the *Peter Poor* and Bub buttoning his pants near the overturned skiff and grinning into the wind and watching her. So I put on the steam then and caught up with her.

And leaning over the tin can with the hose in the hole and peering up at me from under the bill of the baseball cap and shielding his mouth with his hand: "How's Papa?" Jomo said, and spit through his teeth.

"OK, Jomo," I said, "I'm OK, thanks." And softly and under my breath, "Viva la Salerno, Jomo," I said to myself.

"A little winded, ain't you?"

"Well, yes, Jomo, I've been running."

But he was returning the nozzle to the pump, spitting between his teeth again, catching the wire handle of the tin can in his hook and lifting it, holding the tin can out to Bub: "Here, Bub, take this fuel to the Captain. On the double. Tide's full."

I thought of offering Bub a hand and then thought better of it. So I stood on the end of Red's jetty—mere crumbling slatted catwalk covered with mollusks and broken pots and splashes of old flaking paint—and watched Cassandra balance herself down the plank to the *Peter Poor,* watched Red take her hand, her elbow, brace one massive palm in the curve of the little sloping rib cage until she had swung her foot, boarded the boat, and I watched Bub lug the gasoline down the plank black with oil and tar and the dawn tide, and wished that he would slip, that he would take a plunge, tin and all. But Bub was steady that morning with chicken feathers sticking to the seat of his pants and the wind in his hair.

And helping her around the anchor and leading her aft: "Sea's rough," I heard Red say, "hope you like a rough sea."

And Cassandra: "I'm a good sailor, Red—Captain Red—really."

March wind, gulls putting the dawn curse on us, cold harsh shadows breaking apart and scattering and the jetty swaying and shaking and the *Peter Poor* yanking at the hawsers and now and again smashing into the side of the jetty and spray and chunks of black water and field mice cowering in the white-haired crab grass—it was a malevolent unpromising scene and it was all I could do to keep my feet. The strongest smell was of gasoline; the next strongest smell was of dead fish.

"You're coming, ain't you?" Jomo said. "We're shoving off," and he indicated with his hook that I was to start down the plank.

"You go first," I said.

"Can't," Jomo said, "the lines."

"Well," I said, "no pushing," and felt the plank bending under me and the black sea beginning to move and just as I found the gunwale with my toe and caught one of the rusted stays in my right hand, I heard the first hawser thundering past my ear and knew the plank was gone. Beneath the floor boards and somewhere toward the stern the engine sounded like an old Model-A with pitted cylinders and water in the exhaust. Rolling, pitching, moody little fishing boat, cold fiery dawn, we left the jetty with a puff of acrid smoke tangled up in the shrouds and the other hawser floating, dragging out behind us on the choppy sea.

"Say, Red," I called, "is there a place for me to sit down back there?"

And from the black and oily cockpit, and holding a full fifth of whiskey in his right hand, easily, lightly, gesturing with it, and smiling at Cassandra and saying something to her under cover of the wind: "Why, sure," he called, "we can make room for you. Sure we can."

"Thanks," I shouted, and managed to reach the cockpit hand over hand.

Lowering sun, wind that socked us counter to the black waves, cockpit full of salt spray, and Bub at the little iron wheel and Jomo crouching on the stern with the bill of his baseball cap level, unruffled, and his hook in the air, and Red, tall, heavyset, bald, early morning reddish whiskers wet on his face, and his pale blue eyes hard and bright in the furnace of his desire, Red knee-deep in yellow oilskins in the unsteady dirty cockpit that revealed the old rotten ribs of the *Peter Poor*.

"Going to be wet when we get out of the cove," Red said. "Wet and rough."

I hung on. I had burned my palm once already on a tin chimney, so I hung on to a convenient but slimy cleat and to a thin inexplicable rusted wire that came down from somewhere overhead. "See all the signs, do you," I said, and let go for a brief moment to wipe my face.

"Yup," he said. "I see the signs all right."

The eye that looked at me then was like a pale translucent grape in a wine-dark sea. Kind. Intelligent. Contemptuous. Then he looked away and the arms and fingers and hands kept moving.

Red among the oilskins. Red getting ready. He pulled on thick loose yellow pants, worked himself slowly into a thick loose shiny yellow coat, fastened a jet-black mountainous sou'wester on his sun-colored head. The captain, the tall stately bulk of the sea-wet man. And then he turned and helped Cassandra into one of the yellow coats—too big, charm of sleeves that covered the hands, all the charm of the perfect small woman's body in the slick ocean-going coat too large—and on her small head and over the kerchief he tied another crinkled black sou'wester, so that she looked like a child, a smiling child, in a captain's rig. She had a little face that should have been on a box of pilot biscuits. Great black protective helmet and soft wet cheeks and shiny eyes. No hands, no breasts, but wet white skin and plaintive eyes.

And then: "Here's yours," he said, and glanced to the wobbling top of the mast and tossed me a bundle, frowned.

"My second skin," I said, because I had gone out once before in oilskins, and I laughed, ducked, took the flying crest of a wave full in the face. "Which way is up?" I laughed, wiped my eyes, held the thick yellow bundle of empty arms and legs in my own fat arms. "How about it, Red?"

"Oilskins," he said clearly, patiently through the wind, the spray, the now billowing sun, "better put them on . . . going to be plenty rough out there."

So I struggled with the monstrous crackling togs, turned them over, turned them around, lost my footing—shoulder smack up against the ironwood edge of the top of the dirty cabin, sudden quick pain in the shoulder—burned my fingers, finally, on the hard wet skins, felt my cheeks puffing out under the ear flaps of the little tight preposterous sou'wester, felt the chin strap digging in.

"It's much too small," I said, but Red was talking.

"That's Crooked Finger Rock over to leeward," he was saying, gripping Cassandra's little shoulder where it was hidden inside the yellow oilskin, gripping her and pointing away with one long red bony finger that was as steady and sure as the big needle of an enormous compass, "and that's the Dog Head Light—she's abandoned—over there to windward. . . ."

"I see," I heard Cassandra say softly in her most interested voice, "I see," as if they were studying an atlas together in Miranda's parlor, and her eyes, I saw, were fixed on the stately wet red features of Captain Red's squinting seagoing face.

"What's that about Crooked Finger Rock?" I said, but Red was telling her about the draft and sailing qualities of the *Peter Poor,* telling her that the *Peter Poor,* fish-smothered little filthy scow, was really a racing craft, a little Bermudian racer which he had only converted to a fishing boat a few years ago for his own amusement. And then he gave an analysis of Bermudian racers and then a discussion of nautical miles and speed at sea and the medal the Coast Guard had given him for heroism on the high seas. Steady deep wind-whipped voice. Rapt attention. Bub doubled over in stitches at the little wheel.

But I, at least, made an effort to see the landmarks he thought worthy of our attention, and twisted to leeward and saw a chip of black rock rising and falling in those black crests and hair-raising plumes of spray, and I twisted to windward and a couple of miles away made out the tiny white spire of the lighthouse.

Waves, bright sun, the bow falling, and suddenly I knew what was on my mind, had been on my mind from the first moment I had seen the *Peter Poor*. "Red," I interrupted him, cupping my hands, insisting, until the big red face swung in my direction and Cassandra stared down at her feet, "Red, there's no dinghy. Is there, Red?"

"Nope."

"But, Red, we've got to have a dinghy. Don't you care about our safety?"

Face sniffing the salt, eyes clear, big legs spread wide in the cockpit: "Dinghy couldn't last in this water. Too rough. Man can't last either. Too cold. Might's well go down the first time when the boat goes down."

"Good God," I said, "what a way to talk in front of Cassandra."

"Candy don't mind. No, sir. She's a sailor. Told me herself."

Tiny face composed under the sou'wester. Water on the eyelashes, flush in the cheeks, eyes down. Modest. No objections. Not a glance for father. Not a smile. So I nodded, felt myself thrown off balance again as Bub laughed and swung the little iron wheel that was clotted now with lengths of bright dark green seaweed. How was it, I wondered, that the others were in league with the helmsman, what signals were they passing back and forth while only I heaved about moment by moment in the hard rotten embrace of that little tub?

"Cassandra gets her sea legs from her mother," I said, but the sea was against me, the Old Man of the Sea was against me, and the waves smelled like salted fish and the engine smelled of raw gasoline and Jomo was still crouching high on the stern and watching me. And all at once I was unable to take my eyes off him: Jomo going up, Jomo going down, up and down, Jomo swaying off to starboard, Jomo swinging back to port, and holding his hook on high where I could see it and aiming the bill of the baseball cap in my direction and fingering his sideburns now and then but keeping his little black eyes on mine and sitting still but sailing all over the place. Without moving his head he spit between his teeth and the long curve of the spittle, as it reached out on the wind, was superimposed against Jomo's unpredictable motion and dark anxious face. And then I heard him.

"You don't look too good," he said. "Don't feel good, do you? Why don't you go below? Always go below if you don't feel good. Here, let me help you down. . . ."

Even as the *Peter Poor* pitched out from under me, Jomo spit one more time and then hopped off the stern, carefully, without effort, and approached me, came my way with his quick black eyes and on his forehead a sympathetic frown. Jomo with his hot advice, his hot concern for my comfort.

"You want to try sleeping," he said. "Try can you get to sleep and see if I'm not right."

It sounded good. I was bruised, hot, wet, sleepy, and my mouth was full of salt. Salt and a little floating bile. My face and fingers were wrinkled, puckered, as if I had spent the morning in a tepid bath. And the red sun had turned to gold and was hot in my eyes.

"Jomo," I murmured, "there's no dinghy, what do you think of that? But the life jackets, Jomo, point them out to me, will you?"

And roughly, stuffing me into the little wooden companionway: "You ain't going to need no dinghy nor no lifejackets neither. . . . Now put your feet on the rungs."

So I went down. I went down heavily, a man of oilskins and battered joints, while Jomo stayed kneeling in the open companionway with his arms folded and his chin on his arms—"I got to see this," I heard him say over his shoulder—watching until my feet touched something solid and I fell around facing the cabin and managed to hold myself upright with one hand still on the ladder.

Pots and pans and beer bottles were rolling around on the floor. Two narrow bunks were heaped high with rough tumbled blankets and a pair of long black rubber hip boots. Little portholes were screwed tightly shut, the exhaust of the gasoline engine was seeping furiously through a leaking bulkhead, and in front of me, directly in front of me and hanging down from a hook and swaying left and right, a large black lace brassiere with enormous cups and broad elasticized band and thin black straps was swaying right and left from a hook screwed into the cabin ceiling.

"Jomo," I said, "what's that?"

"Never you mind what it is. Just leave it alone."

Water on the portholes, stink of the engine, rattle of tin and glass going up and down the floor, long comfortable endless pendulum swinging of her black brassiere and: "But, Jomo, what about the owner?"

"Don't you worry about the owner. She's coming back to get that thing. Don't worry."

And then: "Jomo. I'm going to be sick. . . ."

"Well, hot damn, just hike yourself up here on deck," laughing over his shoulder, gesturing, then scowling down at me again through the dodging companionway, "just drag ass, now, I can't let you puke all over my cabin."

I got my head and shoulders up through the hole and into the open air in time to see Captain Red and Cassandra sitting side by side on the thwart and opening our brown paper bag of sandwiches, got there in time to see the wax paper flying off on the wind and one white sandwich entering the big red mouth and the other white sandwich entering Cassandra's mouth. Then they were smiling and chewing and I was hanging my head into darkness that was like the ocean itself and trying to keep the vomit off the fresh yellow bulging breast of my borrowed oilskin coat.

Third occasion of my adult life when my own pampered stomach tried to cast me out. Third time I threw up the very flux of the man, and for a moment, only a moment in the darkness of a cold ocean, I couldn't help remembering the blonde prostitute on Second Avenue who held my forehead in the middle of the night and shared my spasms, because now I was stuffed into oilskins and slung up in a tight companionway and retching, vomiting, gasping between contractions, and there was no one to hold my forehead now. But it was the sea that had done this to me, only the wide sea, and in the drowsy and then electrified intervals of my seasickness I knew there would be no relief until they carried me ashore at last.

Red was standing in front of Cassandra now, my head was rolling, for some reason Jomo was at the wheel and the sea, the wide dark sea, was covered with little sharp bright pieces of tin and I saw them flashing, heard them clattering, clashing on all sides of the *Peter Poor*. The drops on my chin were tickling me and I couldn't move; I felt as if I had been whacked on the stomach with a rolled-up newspaper soaked in brine.

Then blackness. Clap of pain in the head and blackness. Mishap with the boom? Victim of a falling block? One of the running lights shaken loose or a length of chain? But I knew full well that it was Bub because my eyes returned suddenly to tears and sight returned, settled again into bright images of the yellow oilskin, the hook at the wheel, the stern half-buried and shipping water, and somehow I accounted for them and knew suddenly what had become of Bub, could feel him where he crouched above me on the cabin roof and held upraised the old tire iron which they used as a lever to start the engine with.

But no sooner had I worked it out, that Bub had struck me on the head with the tire iron, than I saw the rock. Red, Cassandra, and then behind them the long low shelf of rock covered with a crust of barnacles and submerged every second or two in the sea, and we were wallowing and drifting and slowly coming abeam of the rock which looked like the overturned black petrified hull of some ocean-going vessel that would never sink.

Had it not been for Crooked Finger Rock I might have done something, might have reached around somehow and caught Bub by the throat and snatched away the tire iron and flung it at Red. Somehow I might have knocked Red down and taken over the *Peter Poor* and sailed us back to safety before the squall could threaten us from another quarter. But I saw the rock and heard the bell and Captain Red and Cassandra were posed against the rock itself, in my eye were already on the rock together, were all that remained of the *Peter Poor* and the rest of us. So I could only measure the rock and measure Red and wait for the end, wait for the worst.

I didn't want to drown with Bub, I didn't want Cassandra to survive with Red, and so I watched the hard black surface of the rock and swarthy bright yellow skin of the man, could only stare at the approach of the rock and at what the old man was doing. Jomo had let go the wheel and was watching too.

Because Cassandra was sitting on the edge of the thwart with her head thrown back and her hands spread wide inside the puffy tight yellow sleeves, and because the rust-colored skirt was billowing and I could see the knees and the whiteness above the knees which until now had never been exposed to sun, spray, or the head-on stance of a Captain Red, and because Red had thrown open the stiff crumpling mass of his yellow skins and was smiling and taking his hands away.

"There 'tis," he said.

And that's when I should have had the tire iron to throw, because there it was and I saw it all while Cassandra, poor Cassandra, saw only Red.

Because she looked at Red, stared at him, and then pulled the string yet gave no sign that she knew the black sou'wester was gone or that she cared—but I did, I watched it sail up, roll over, shudder, actually land for a moment on the rock, slide across the rock, drop from sight-

—and then she pulled at the knot of the pale blue kerchief and held the idle tip of it between two fingers for a moment and then let it go. Drop of blue already a quarter mile astern and the hair a little patch of gold in the wind, the sun, the spray, and the white face exposed to view.

"No, no," I said thickly, because she had reached out her hand—bobbing, swaying, undisturbed—and had drawn it back and was extending it again and Red was waiting for her.

"Cassandra," I mumbled, "Cassandra," but the buoy began to toll and Bub hit me again with the tire iron. So I went down and took her with me, pulled her down into my own small corner of the dark locker that lies under the sea, dragged her to rest in the ruptured center of my own broken head of a dream. Waxed sandwich wrappings, empty brown paper bag, black sou'wester, kerchief—all these whistled above her, and then I was a fat sea dolphin suspended in the painful silence of my green underseas cavern where there was nothing to see except Cassandra's small slick wide-eyed white face lit up with the light of Red's enormous candle against the black bottom, the black tideless root, of Crooked Finger Rock.

The squall came down, I know, because once I opened my eyes and found that I was lying flat on my back in my oilskins on the floor of the cabin, was wedged into the narrow space between the bunks and was staring up at the open companionway which was dark and filled with rain. The rain beat down into the cabin, fell full on my face, and I could hear it spattering on the pots and pans, driving into the piles of blankets thrown into the bunks. The black brassiere was circling above my head and lashing its tail.

We were offshore, three or four miles offshore in a driving squall. We pitched, reeled, rolled in darkness, one of the rubber hip boots fell out of the starboard bunk and down onto my stomach and lay there wet and flapping and undulating on my stomach. At least something, I thought, had saved us from a broadside collision against Crooked Finger Rock.

And later, much later, I awoke and found that they had hoisted me into the port bunk, dumped me into the bunk on top of the uncomfortable wet mass of blankets. I felt the toe of the other rubber boot in the small of my back, the tight sou'wester was still strapped to my head. And awake I saw the low and fading sun on the lip of the wet companionway, felt the tiny hand on my arm and managed to raise my eyes.

"Skipper? Feeling a little better, Skipper? We're coming into port now, aren't you glad?"

Wet, bright. Uncovered. The small white face that had been cupped in the determined hand of unruly nature. Little beads of sea violence in the eyelashes. Wet bright nose. Wet lips. Bareheaded, smooth, drenched, yellow skins open at the little throat, hair still smacking wet with the open sea and sticking tight and revealing the curve of her little sweet pointed skull. And smiling, Cassandra was smiling down at me. But she was not alone.

"Red—Captain Red—has been teaching me how to sail, Skipper."

And moaning and licking my sour lips: "Yes, yes, I'm sure he has, Cassandra. That's fine."

The Old Man of the Sea, timeless hero of the Atlantic fishing fleet, was standing beside her with his pipe sizzling comfortably and the blood running back into the old channels, and I knew that I could not bear to look at him and knew, suddenly, why everything felt so different to me where I lay on the tumbled uncharitable blankets in the wet alien bunk. The sea. The sea was flat, smooth, calm, the wind had died, the engine was chugging so slowly, steadily, that I began to count the strokes.

"Ahoy, *Peter Poor!*" came the far-off sound of Miranda's voice, and I knew that Cassandra was right and that we were heading into port, heading in toward our berth at the rotten jetty. Peace at last.

But then: "Skipper? Are you well enough to show Red what you have on your chest? I'd like him to see it if you don't mind."

Resisting, mumbling, begging off, trying to push her little hand away, but it was no use of course and she peeled away the layers and smoothed out the hairs with her own white fingers until the two of them leaned down together—two heads close together—and looked at me. Their ears were touching.

"That's the name of my husband, Red. Isn't it beautiful?"

He agreed that it was.

"Where's the Salerno kid?" I asked, and it was a thick green whispered question. "Don't you want to show him too?"

But Red was already helping her up the ladder and we were coming in.

And then Miranda was waving from the end of the jetty: "Ahoy, *Peter Poor,* welcome home!" And half a dozen stray young kinky-faced sheep were huddled in front of her on the end of the jetty and calling for mother.

"Boy, oh boy, are you a sight!" Miranda said. And then they kissed, and from where I sat propped on the jetty I looked and saw our skins piled high amidships on the *Peter Poor*. Our wretched skins. And above the pile with the black strap looped over his steel hook and the rest of it hanging down, Jomo was standing there and holding out his arm and grinning.

"Got something of yours, Miranda," he called. "You want it?"

And laughing, and arm in arm with Cassandra: "You bet your life," she cried, "bring it along!"

Silence. Shadows. A moonlit constellation of little hard new blueberries against the picket fence. An early spring. The glider was jerking back and forth beneath me and grinding, squeaking, arguing with itself like a wounded crow. And the bottle of Old Grand Dad lay at my foot and I sat with glass in hand.

"Now go to bed, will you, Skip? My God. She's probably gone to the show with Bub. That's all. What's wrong with that?"

The Labradors came out of their kennel, one head above the other, and looked at us—at me in the painful shadows of the glider and at Miranda sitting on the porch rail with her head against the post and one big knee beneath her chin—and sat down on their black bottoms and began to howl. The Labradors, Miranda's blunt-nosed ugly dogs, were howling for my own vigil and for Miranda's silhouette, because Miranda was wearing her black turtle-neck sweater and a Spanish dancer's short white ruffled skirt which the raised knee had slipped into her solid lap like a pile of fresh white roses.

"Even the dogs know she's not with Bub," I said, cracking the neck of the bottle quickly and gently on the lip of the glass, "nobody can fool those dogs, Miranda. Nobody. They're not howling for the fun of it."

Wasn't she looking at her fingernails in the moonlight? Wasn't she studying the tiny inverted moonlit shields, one hand curved and fluted and turning at arm's length in front of her face, and then the other, peering at her enormous hands and yawning? Of course she was. Because it was May and time for Miranda to appraise her big waxen fingernails by light of the moon. And even in the chill of the late May night I knew there would be no goose flesh on her big waxen silhouetted leg, no hair on the smooth dark calf.

"You're an old maid, Skip. Honest to God."

And staring out at the chestnut tree that was trying to pull itself into leaf once more, I lifted my chin and smiled and drooped the corners of my mouth: "I'm afraid I can't say the same for you. Far from it. But I tell you, Miranda," tasting the iodine taste of the Old Grand Dad on my heavy tongue, sitting on the head of a spring and holding it under, "I'll give her five more minutes, just five, Miranda, and then I'm going to Red's shack and pray to the BVM that I'm still in time."

She laughed.

But I meant it. Yes, I meant still in time, because there had been the rest of March and April with no more mishaps, nothing but Cassandra suddenly light on her feet and fresh and helpful around the house, Cassandra spending all our last days of winter walking from room to room in the old clapboard house with Pixie held tight in her arms and some kind of song just audible in her severe little nose. Now it was May and Cassandra had changed again and as I must have felt and was soon to know, it was the last of my poor daughter's months. So still in time. I needed to be still in time. Because of March and then May and then June and the last thoughts, fragments, highlights of the time that swept us all away.

"Laugh if you want to, Miranda," I said. "You have nothing to lose."

"For God's sake, Skip," looking my way, plucking the ruffles, resting a long dark hand on the angle of the silhouetted thigh, "and what about you, Skip? What about you?"

She must have known what I had to lose since she destroyed it for me. She must have known since she arranged for the destruction, nursed it, brought it about, tormented both herself and myself with its imminence, with the shape of the flesh, the lay of the soul, the curving brawn that was always gliding behind her plan. And what a vision she must have had of the final weeks in May, since the abortive outcome had already been determined, as only she could have known, on a windy day in March.

So I was about to tell her what I had to lose, was sitting forward on the edge of a broken-down glider and collecting myself against the loud irritating pattern of her asthmatic wheeze—she was still propped on the veranda rail with her long heavy legs exposed, but she was wheezing now, staring at me out of her big dark invisible eyes and wheezing— when the black hot rod shot around the corner by the abandoned Poor House and roared toward us down the straightaway of the dark narrow dirt road, honked at us—triple blaring of the musical horn—and disappeared among the fuzzy black trunks of the larches which were tall and young and mysterious in our brimming spring. And I jumped from the glider and reached the rail in time to see the fat anatomical silver tubes on the side of the engine, the silver disks masking the hub caps, the little fat squirrel tail whipping in circles on the tip of the steel aerial, and, behind the low rectangles of window glass, the two figures in the cut-down chariot for midnights under a full moon. It was traveling without lights.

"You see?" I said, "there she goes! And with Jomo—in Jomo's hot rod, Miranda—not with Bub. Who's the old maid now, Miranda?"

Old Grand Dad flat on the floor. Kitchen tumbler sailing out and smashing, splintering, on the roof of the kennel. And I was off the porch and once more running after my destiny which always seemed to be racing ahead of me on black tires.

"Wait a minute, Skip," she cried then, "I'm coming with you!"

So once again with Miranda I entrusted myself to the other hot rod that was still behind her house—orange and white and blue and bearing the number five in a circle on the hood—but this time I myself sat at the wheel and this time, thanks to Bub who had worked on the car as Miranda had said he would, this time that hot rod was a racing vehicle with a full tank of high-octane gasoline, and this time it was spring and the tires were pumped up tight and the fresh paint was bright and tacky.

"Now, Cicisbeo," I muttered, and we swung out onto Poor House Road, took up the chase.

No lights. No muffler. No windshield, no glass in the windows, and I was low in the driver's seat with my foot pushed to the hot floor and my fat hands slick and white on the smooth black steering wheel. Miranda crouched beside me, long hair snapping out on the wind and white skirt bunching and struggling in her powerful arms.

"If they gave us the slip," I shouted, "good-by everything! I hope you're glad. . . ."

Moonlight. Black shadows. Soft silk of the dirt road around the island, and larches, uncut brambles at the side of the road and a dead net hanging down from a luminous branch, and the occasional scent of brine and charcoal smoke on the breakneck wind, and every few hundred feet a water rat leapt from some hollow log or half-buried conduit, dashed under our wheels.

"It's all your doing," I shouted. "I hope you're glad!"

Shaking loose her hair and bunching the white foam of the ruffled skirt up to her breasts, Miranda was larger and whiter and more Venus-like than ever that night, and as we accelerated suddenly onto the silver flats of one of my favorite cow pastures—cows dead and gone, of course, but an open stubbled place in sight of the sea—I knew that in

Miranda's eyes I was not the man to win a hot rod race. So I swerved a couple of times and gunned her, set my jaw. I had taken my chances in this very car before, and Miranda or no Miranda, now I would have my moment of inspired revenge. As we thundered across the bumpy moonlit field I made up my mind: the sea. The black sea. Nothing to do but run the one-handed lecherous Jomo into the black sea.

The road, the wash of stubble, the moonlit mounds of powdered shells, the prow of a beached dory, and off to the right the lighthouse and straight ahead a glimpse of the black-lacquered cut-down car we were chasing. I felt relentless.

"Come on, Skip, do your stuff! Good God!" Somehow she had gotten her enormous legs onto the seat and was kneeling and holding the skirt above her belly with one hand and with the other was clutching me around the shoulders. Her hot breath was in my ear, I heard the rising and falling roar of the beehives that were laboring away inside her enormous chest.

"No!" I cried, "Stop! You'll kill us both, Miranda!"

But she hung on, tightened her grip and snuggled her great black and white head down onto my shoulder. Her hair flew into my eyes and even into my open mouth. And tongue, teeth, hair, I was trying to breathe through my nose and gagging, choking, but somehow keeping my grip on the wheel and driving on. But was she trying to comfort me, encourage me, even love me, at least urge me to great daring after all? Had I been wrong about Miranda?

I knew the answer of course. And yet before I could spare a hand off the wheel or risk a glance in her direction, the other car had come into view again and was heading not for the dunes as I had expected but down toward the hard dark sand of Dog's Head beach which stretched northward about a mile and a half from the abandoned light. I saw him, swung the wheel in time, and followed him, tried to catch him midway between the Poor House Road and the beach. But I had no such luck.

The black car turned northward away from the empty lighthouse on Dog's Head beach, and for a moment we were close enough to see the silver disks on the wheels, the two silhouetted heads, the aerial in its whip position. Hot rod, driver, passenger, they seemed to crawl for a moment in a slow fanning geyser of packed sand, and I stuck my fist out of the window. "Beware, Cicisbeo!" I shouted this time, and stepped on the gas.

Off again, the black car leading up the wide wet stretch of deserted beach, black car racing close to the dark water's edge and filling the air with spray, flecks of foam, exhaust, a screen of burning sand. The aluminum exhaust pipes curving out of the lacquered hood were loud, musical, three or four bright pipes of power. Even Miranda lifted her head, leaned forward now and fought the driving wind to see.

"Faster, Skip!" she shouted, and despite winds, sand, uncertain motion, she bounced up and down on the edge of the seat, whacked me rhythmically on fat arm, knee, shoulder.

Two unlighted hammerheaded cars on a moonlit beach, and three times we raced up and down that beach which had been exposed only hours before by a choppy sea, three times up and down from the north end of low boulders to the south end of tall grass and broken faces of cliff and abandoned lighthouse, and three times he tricked me with his sudden and skillful turns, three times he made his turn and left me driving flat out toward disaster among the sleeping boulders or a crash against the cliff. And wasn't he leading me on? Leading me toward a night-consuming accident on the lonely beach?

But I got the hang of it then, so to speak, and made a short turn and cut him off. A surprise blow. Simple maneuver but effective. Quick action of a dangerous mind.

"Got him now, Miranda," I shouted. "Rapacious devil!"

And we were drifting together, that black hot rod and mine, and I was inching in closer to him and then ahead, fighting for the position from which I would cut him off, sailing out now to the left, now to the right on the treacherous sand and giving her the gun again. Side by side in the sound of speed. Shadows cast by the moon were scudding ahead of us, and there were sharp rocks waiting for us in the cold sea and I could make out the dark slippery festoons of kelp.

"Hold on, Cassandra," I shouted out of the window, "it won't be long!" I smelled the night, the salt, the armies of mussels and clams ground under our wheels and the dense smoke of our high-octane fuel. And the excitement touched the backs of my hands, told me the time was near, and I wondered how he could have been foolish enough to trap himself here on Dog's Head beach, how foolish enough to underestimate my courage, the strength of my love. I was half a radiator length ahead of him and Miranda might have touched that black-lacquered car had she held out her hand.

"Now!" I shouted, "Now!" and swung down on the wheel and smelled the rank sizzling cremation of the brake bands as we stopped short of the moonlit choppy waters—half-spin in the sand but safe, dry, coming to a sudden and miraculous standstill—while the black car went pitching in. It pitched headlong into the rising tide and rocked, floundered, stalled. Smacked one of the rocks.

I fumbled for the ignition and fought the door, using fist, shoulder, heels of both palms. "Get your hook ready," I cried, "I'm coming after you!" And once more I was running until I too hit the shock of the cold water and suddenly found myself knee-deep in it but running in slow motion, still running toward the half-submerged black-lacquered hot rod wrecked on this bitter shore. Already it was bound in kelp, already the cold waters were wallowing above the crankcase, already the thick white salt was sealing up forever those twin silver carburetors which Jomo had buffed, polished, installed, adjusted beside the battered gas pump in front of Red's shack. Half-sunken now, wet and black and pointing out to sea in the moonlight.

"Game's up, Jomo, don't try anything. . . ."

And my two hands went under water and gripped the door handle. My soggy foot was raised high and thrust flat against the side of the car. And then I pulled and there was the suck of the yielding door, the black flood and, baseball cap and all, I dragged him out by the arm and shook him, wrestled with him, until I slipped and we both went under.

And then up again and, "You!" I cried, "It's you!" and I threw him off his feet again and lunged into the car just as Miranda began laughing her breasty deep Old Grand Dad laugh at the edge of the beach. I lunged into the car and reached out my hand and stopped, because it was not Cassandra. Because it was nothing. Nobody at all. A mere device, a laundry bag for a torso, something white rolled up for a head. Oh, it was Bub all right, Bub wearing Jomo's cap and driving Jomo's car. Bub's trick. Bub's decoy. And it had worked. Oh, it had worked all right, and while I was risking my neck in Miranda's blue and white and orange hot rod and making my foolish laps on Dog's Head beach or standing hip-deep in the biting black waters of the Atlantic, my Cassandra was lying after all in the arms I had tried to save her from, and falling, fading, swooning, going fast.

So I plunged both hands down and collared Bub, held him, dragged the streaming and spitting and frothy face up close to mine. He had a nosebleed and a little finger-thick abrasion on his upper lip and terror on the narrow sea-white boyish face beneath the dripping duck bill of the baseball cap.

"Where is she," I said. "Where's Cassandra?"

And choked and high-pitched and faint but still querulous, still mean:

"Him and her is at the lighthouse. Been up there to the lighthouse since sundown. You old fool. . . ."

So for the first and only time in all my lifelong experience with treachery, deception and Death in his nakedness or in his several disguises, I gave way at last to my impulse and put Tremlow's teaching to the test, allowed myself the small brutal pleasure of drawing blood and forcing flesh on flesh, inflicting pain. Yes, I stood in the choppy and freezing darkness of that black water and contemplated the precise spot where I would punch the child. Because I had gone too far. And Bub had gone too far. The long duck bill of the cap, the cruel tone of his island voice and the saliva awash on his thin white face and even the faint suggestion of tender sideburns creeping down the skin in front of each malformed ear, by all this I was moved, not justified but merely moved, to hit Bub then and there in the face with all my strength.

"Hold still," I muttered, and took a better grip with my left hand, "hold still if you know what's good for you," I said and, keeping my eyes on the little bloody beak in the center of his white face I pulled back my arm and made a fist and drove it as hard as I could into Bub's nose. I held him close for a moment and then pushed him away, let him go, left him rolling over in the cold black water where he could fend for himself.

I left him, rinsed my fist, staggered up into the moonlight and shouted, "No, no, Miranda, wait!" Once more I broke into my sloshing dogtrot on Dog's Head beach, because Miranda was in the hot rod and shifting, throwing the blue and white and orange demon into gear, and waving, driving away. So I was alone once more and desperate and running as fast as I could toward the lighthouse. What heavy steps I took in the sand, how deep those footprints that trailed behind me as I took my slow-motion way down that desolate beach toward the lighthouse.

Slow-motion, yes, and a slogging and painful trot, but after a while I could see that the abandoned white tower of Dog's Head lighthouse was coming down the beach to meet me, was moving, black cliff and all, in my direction. And crab grass, pools of slime, the rusted flukes of a lost anchor, and then the rotted wooden stairs up the side of the cliff and a bright empty Orange Crush bottle gleaming on the tenth step and then the railing gave way under my hand on the head of the cliff and the wind caught hold of me and the lighthouse went up and up above my craning head. The lighthouse. The enormous overgrown moonlit base of it. The tower that had fought the storms, the odor of high waves in the empty doorway, the terrible height of the unlighted eye—I wanted nothing more than to turn my back on it and flee.

But I cupped my hands and raised my mouth aloft and shouted: "Cassandra? In the name of God, Cassandra, are you there?"

No answer, of course. Still no word for her father. Only the brittle feet of the luminous crabs, the cough and lap and barest moan of the slick black tide rising now at the bottom of the cliff and working loose the periwinkles, wearing away the stone, only the darkness inside the tower and, outside, the moonlight and the heavy unfaithful wind that was beating me across the shoulders, making my trousers luff. But of course she was there, of course she was. And had she climbed the circular iron staircase knowing she would never set foot on it again? Or, as in the case of my poor father, was I myself the unwitting tinder that started the blaze? Could she really have intended to spend the last six or eight hours of her life with Jomo in Dog's Head light? My own Cassandra? My proud and fastidious Cassandra? I thought she had. Even as I approached the black doorless opening in the base of the tower I was quite certain that she had planned it all, had intended it all, knowing that I would come and call to her and force myself to climb that tower, climb every one of those iron steps on my hands and knees, and for nothing, all for nothing. Even as I thrust one foot into the darkness of Dog's Head light I knew that I could not possibly be in time.

"Cassandra? Don't play games with me, Cassandra. Please. . . ."

Proud and fastidious, yes, but also like a bird, a very small gray bird that could make no sound. And now she was crouching somewhere in Dog's Head light—at the top, it would be at the top if I knew Cassandra—or lying in Jomo's thin brown abrasive arms in the Dog's Head light. What a bad end for time. What a bad end for the BVM.

"Cassandra? In the name of God, answer me now . . . Please. . . ."

Iron steps. All those iron steps and on my hands and knees. Bareheaded, sopping wet, afraid of finding her but afraid too of losing her, I started up then and with each step I found it increasingly difficult to pull my fingers loose from the iron steps and to haul the dead weight of my nerveless feet behind me. Up it went, that tower, straight to the top, and the center was empty, the circular iron steps were narrow, there was no rail. Cracks in the wall, certain vibrations in the rusted iron, it was like climbing up the interior of some monstrous and abandoned boiler, and it was not for me, this misery of the slow ascent, this caterpillar action up the winding iron stairway to the unknown.

But taking deep dark breaths and bracing myself now and again and glancing up and at the moonlight fluttering in the smashed head of the light, I persevered until suddenly, and as if in answer to my clenched jaw and all the sweeping sensations in my poor spine, the whole thing began to shake and sway and ring, and I clenched my fists, tucked in my fingers, bruised my head, hung on.

A long soft cry of the wind—or was it the wind?—and footsteps. Heavy mindless footsteps crashing down, spiraling down from above, heavy shoes trembling and clattering and banging down the iron stairway, and behind the terrible swaying rhythm in the iron and the racket of the shoes I could hear the click, click, click of the flashing mechanical hand as he swung it against the wall with each step he took.

He passed me. He had already passed me—Jomo without his cap, poor Jomo who must have thought Salerno was nothing compared to what he had gotten himself into now—when I heard the breathing beside my ear and then the toneless bellstrokes of catastrophe fading away below in the darkness.

The iron gut of the tower remained intact, and I crawled to the top and crawled back down again without mishap, without a fall. But the damage was done. I knew it was done before I reached the top, and I began to hurry and began to whisper: "Cassandra? He's gone now, Cassandra, it's all right now . . . you'll see. . . ." I heard nothing but the echoing black sky and tiny skin-crawling sounds above me and the small splash, the eternal picking fingers of wave on rock below. "Cassandra?" I whispered, tried to pull myself up the last few shaky steps, tried to fight down dizziness, tried to see, "you're not crying, are you, Cassandra? Please don't. . . ."

But the damage was done and I was only an old bird in an empty nest. I rolled up onto the iron floor in the smashed head of the lighthouse and crawled into the lee of the low wall and pulled myself into a half-sitting position and waited for the moment when Dog's Head light must tremble and topple forward into the black scum of the rising tide far below.

"Gone, Cassandra? Gone so soon?" I whispered. "Gone with Gertrude, Cassandra? Gone to Papa? But you shouldn't have, Cassandra. You should have thought of me. . . ."

The neat pile of clothing was fluttering a little in the moonlight and it was damp to the touch. I could not make myself look down. But I felt that I had seen her already and there was no reason to look down again. So I half-sat, half-lay there in the cold, the moonlight, the wind,

stretched myself out amidst the broken glass and debris and thought
about Cassandra and was unable to distinguish between her small white
oval face—it was up there with me as well as below on the black
rocks—and the small white plastic face of the BVM.

"I won't ask why, Cassandra. Something must have spoken to you,
something must have happened. But I don't want to know, Cassandra.
So I won't ask. . . ."

I clutched a couple of the thin rusted stanchions and in the gray
moonlight stared out to sea. The shoals were miles long and black and
sharp, long serrated tentacles that began at the base of the promontory
and radiated out to sea, mile after square mile of intricate useless channels and breaking waves and sharp-backed lacerating shoals and spiny
reefs. Mile after square mile of ocean cemetery that wasn't even true to
its dead but kept flushing itself out on the flood tide. No wonder the
poor devils wanted a lighthouse here. No wonder.

I turned again, crept back from the edge and started down. I had
climbed to the top of the lighthouse and I was able to climb back down
again, feet first. It was a matter of holding tight and feeling my way
with my feet and dropping down with little terrible free falls through
that tower of darkness. But I managed it. I reached the bottom after all,
and I sat on a concrete block in the empty doorway with my head in
my hands. I sat there with the lighthouse on my shoulders. And somewhere the tide was rising, the moon was going down, the clouds were
scudding. And I sat there while the damp grass sang at my feet and the
white tower listed in the indifferent wind.

Ducks in June. Baby ducks in June. I could hear them, Miranda's brood
of little three-day-old cheese-colored ducklings, hear them waddling behind the house on this bright early dawn in the first week in June, hear
them talking to each other and doing their little Hitler march step as I
stood by the bright black stove and coaxed the coffee to reach its rich
dark aromatic climax so I could sit down to an early breakfast with
Pixie. It was a chilly dawn, but outside the sun was out, and inside
Miranda's kitchen the wood-burning stove was as rosy as a hot brick.

"Hear the ducklings, Pixie? You like the little ducklings, don't you,
Pixie?"

She looked up at me from where she sat on the wide soft boards of
the wooden floor—bright pudding face, bright platinum hair, on her
finger a little tin ring that I had found in a Cracker Jack box—and

opened her mouth for me and kicked her little dirty white calfskin shoes and gave the rolling pin a quick push. I smiled. Pixie always enjoyed the game with the rolling pin.

"Shall we go out and play with the ducklings after breakfast, Pixie? Would you like that?"

Fresh white apron, fresh white shirt, fresh creamy taste of the tooth-paste in my mouth, and Miranda's old tin clock said that it was six o'clock in the morning and already I had ground the coffee in the coffee grinder and put the cereal bowls on the table and finished off Pixie's cold orange juice. And now the sun was shooting golden arrows through the blistered glass in the kitchen window and the stove was warm. The coffee smelled like the new day and was beginning to bubble up into the little myopic eye of the old percolator.

"Where's the corn flakes, Pixie? Go find the corn flakes. . . ."

Big square whitewashed kitchen, sharp golden arrows of the new sun quivering on the white walls and on the table set for two, old tin clock pattering and twisting and clicking in the throes of the hour, little ducks marching around and around outside and the light frost was beginning to disappear. I dangled a quilted pot holder from my fingers and tended the stove and glanced every once in a while at the waiting table. Because instead of the usual unopened fifth of Old Grand Dad on the breakfast table for Miranda, there was a package wrapped in white tissue paper and done up in red, white and blue ribbons and so placed on the table that it could have been meant only for me.

"What do you think is in the package, Pixie? Something for Grandpa? A present for your grandfather, eh, Pixie? Shall we open it after breakfast and then go play with the ducks?"

There was a card tucked under the ribbon and I had already allowed myself a look at the card—*For Skip*—in a bold black handwriting, nothing more—while Pixie was busy with the rolling pin I had slipped it out of the envelope and read it and then put it back where I had found it in such a way that not even Miranda could tell the difference. A quick look at the card was one thing, but the present itself, I knew, would have to wait. Perhaps I could even hold off until I had done the dishes though I suspected not.

Corn flakes and cold milk and the bowl of sugar. And then the usual fight with Pixie until I made her drop the rolling pin and was able to pick her up and strap her into the pink enamel chair and give her the jam jar and little silver spoon to play with. And then the coffee. The heat of the spicy beans. The first heat of the day. Better than bacon.

But just as I was pouring the coffee and sniffing it and watching the sensual brown metamorphosis in my thin cup, just as I was smiling and getting ready to sit down to breakfast with Pixie, I smelled the sudden odor of a lighted cigarette and felt a movement at the door. I waited and then raised my eyes.

"Miranda," I said. "Good morning! Have some coffee?"

At six-fifteen in the morning she was standing in the doorway with her long legs crossed and her shoulder leaning against the jamb. Black eyes and sockets, uncombed hair, white face. And after all these months she was wearing the canary yellow slacks again.

"Come on," I said, "have some coffee. First pot's the best, isn't it, Miranda?"

She puffed on her cigarette, exhaled, shook her head.

"Well, Miranda," and I was stooping, still holding the pot, smiling up at her, "there seems to be some sort of present on the table. We don't have so many presents around here, do we?"

And then: "That one's got your name on it, Skip."

"Really?" I said. "Well, come on, Miranda, tell me. What is it?"

And slowly and keeping the big formless black eyes on mine and sucking the gray smoke back into her nostrils: "Fetus," she said, and the big mouth slid down a little as if it might smile.

I turned, set the coffee pot on the edge of the stove, faced her again, took hold of the back of the chair with both my hands. The arrows were quivering on the walls but she was watching me.

"What did you say, Miranda?"

"Fetus. Two-months-old fetus in a fruit jar, Skip."

I pulled out the chair then, slowly, and sat down. I pushed away the corn flakes, folded my hands. Miranda was smoking more quickly now, was taking deep rapid puffs. And she was wheezing now. There was a little grease on her face but no lipstick, powder, rouge. Only the uncombed hair and spreading black stains of the eyes.

"I don't understand you," I said at last, watching her, smelling the smoke, noticing that under the blouse she was naked. "I really don't know what you mean, Miranda. What kind of fetus?"

"Just a fetus, Skip. Two months old. Human."

Pixie, I saw, was holding the jam jar on its side and had given up the spoon and had thrust her little hand into the neck of the jar. Strawberry jam. Coffee fast cooling off. Baby ducks still marching. And the white tissue and the card and the ribbon. Red, white and blue ribbon. And I wondered, asked myself, if it could possibly be true. How could it possibly be true? Wasn't it only Miranda's whim? Knowing full well that I would never open it, wasn't it only Miranda's cruelest way of tormenting me at six-fifteen on a morning in the first week in June? But why? What was she trying to tell me? And then suddenly I knew the first thing I had to do, and I did it. I simply reached out my hand, picked up the package, put it to my ear and shook it. But there was no sound. And I could tell nothing by the weight. It was a fruit jar, just as she said, but whether it contained anything or was empty, I did not know.

"All right, Miranda," I said, still holding and weighing the jar and looking at her and seeing the mouth slide down deeper, seeing the breasts heave, "all right, Miranda. What is it?"

She waited. The cigarette was a white butt pinched between her two long fingers. Her legs were crossed. And then her lips moved, her mouth became a large quivering lopsided square: "I mean it, Skip. And just as I said, it's got your name on it. And it's hers," throwing the butt on the kitchen floor where it lay burning out and smoking, "Candy's, I tell you. Why do you think she jumped, you old fool?"

I looked at the mouth, the shadows that were her eyes, I looked at the bright package in my hand. Slowly, slowly I shook it again. Nothing. Full or empty, did it matter? There were tiny arrows of sunlight now on the backs of my hands and Pixie had her mouth full of strawberry jam.

"Cassandra's?" I said then. "You mean it was Cassandra's? But surely that was no reason for Cassandra to kill herself?"

And thrusting her head at me and slowly shaking the black tangled hair and with both hands clutching her enormous white throat: "Reason or no reason," she said, "there it is. Good God!" And she was laughing, wheezing, exhaling dead smoke from the rigid lopsided square of her mouth, "Good God, I thought you'd like to have it! Sort of makes you a grandfather for the second time, doesn't it?"

I waited. And then slowly I stood up and unfastened the strap and gathered Pixie into one arm—Pixie covered with strawberry jam—and in my other hand took up the package again and slowly, gently, pushed past Miranda in the doorway.

"I think you're right, Miranda," I said as softly as I could. "I'm sure you're right. But, Miranda," gently, softly, "you better step on the cigarette. Please."

And I knew then exactly what I had to do, and I did it. I went upstairs and took my white officer's cap off the dummy and put it on my head where it belonged and packed up our tattered flight bag. And with my arms loaded—Pixie hanging from one, bag from the other, bright smeared package in my right hand—I went back down to the kitchen and asked Miranda for a serving spoon. I asked Miranda to take a serving spoon out of the drawer and slip it into my pocket.

"Well," she said, "you're leaving."

"Yes, Miranda," I said. "I'm going to the cemetery first, and then Pixie and I are leaving."

"Good riddance," she said and grinned at me, fumbled for the cigarettes, struck a match. "Good riddance, Skip. . . ."

I smiled.

So I carried Pixie and the flight bag and the present from Miranda out to the cemetery, carried them past the sepulchral barn of the Poor House and down the deeply rutted lane and through the grove of pines and onto the yellow promontory where the expressionless old gray lichen-covered monuments rose up together in sight of the sea. Yellow stubble, crumbling iron enclosure, tall white grizzled stones and names and dates creeping with yellow fungus. And the sky was like the stroke of a brush. And of course the wind was only the sun's chariot and the spray was only a veil of mist at the end of land.

I kicked open the gate and let Pixie crawl around in the stubble between the stones while on my hands and knees once more at the side of the fresh mound I dug a little hole at the top of Cassandra's grave with the serving spoon and stuffed the package in, covered it over. Empty or not it was a part of me somehow and belonged with her. Under a last handful of loose black earth I hid the ribbons—red, white and blue ribbons—and stood up, brushed off my pants. Even from here, and standing in the windy glare of that little Atlantic cemetery, I could smell the pines, feel the pine roots working their way down to the things of the sea.

I threw the spoon out onto the black rocks.

Then off we went, Pixie and I, and I smiled at the thought that the night I found Fernandez on Second Avenue was the first night after the day they stopped the war, and that all my casualties, so to speak, were only accidents that came when the wave of wrath was past. But how can I forget what lies out there in that distant part of my kingdom?

THE GOLDEN FLEAS

SO I HAD MY SMALL QUIET VICTORY over Miranda after all, and had my victory over Cassandra too, since there are always faces, strange or familiar, young or old, waiting to kiss me in the dark, and since now there is one more little dark brown face that will soon be waiting like the others. My shades, my children, my memories, my time of no time, and I thank God for wandering islands and invisible shores.

But one more face. Yes, there is one more face because the mountain fell, the flesh went down, they soaked up the blood with coconut fibers, they washed the baby as I told them to, Kate smiled. A big success. And wasn't it the day, the very hour, even the sex I had decided on? And weren't we flourishing together, Kate and I, finishing up our little jobs together on a flourish of love? And didn't Sister Josie and Big Bertha pitch right in and help? Down on their hands and knees with the coconut fibers? And didn't I forbid Kate to have our baby in the swamp, and didn't Kate, young Catalina Kate, bear the baby on the floor of my own room in Plantation House and sleep with the sweat and pleasure of this her first attempt at bearing a baby for me—for Sonny and me —in my own swaying hammock filled with flowers? Didn't Sonny and I wait out in the barn with Oscar until they called us back to the house to see the baby? And didn't I spend the rest of that afternoon—just yesterday, just yesterday afternoon—sitting beside her on a little empty vinegar barrel and giving the hammock a push whenever the wind died down? What more could she ask? What more could I?

But there was last night too, of course, last night when I broke out the French wine and long cigars and took the three of them—Sonny and Kate and little black fuzzy baby in the strip of muslin—down to the cemetery to have a fete with the dead. In the afternoon I rocked Kate and little child in the hammock while the sun hung over us and grew fat and yellow in the leaves and vines outside and the humming-birds sucked their tiny drams of honey at my still window. But with the coming of night and while Josie and Big Bertha softly clapped their black hands and sang to us outside the window, suddenly I felt like taking a long walk and laughing and eating a good meal and drinking the wine and smoking. So I leaned over Kate and shook her gently and told her it was time to get up because the moon was rising and they were already lighting the candles in the graveyard.

"Come on, Kate," I whispered, "time to go." Slumberous. The shadowy color of cinnamon and rouge. Bright and naked and smiling, softly smiling, in my old hammock full of flowers. Her hair was down and hanging in a single black shank over the side of the hammock, was hanging, swaying, brushing the floor. And even in the shadows I could see how full she was and see that already she had regained her shape and that her naked waist was once more like the little belly of the queen bee.

"Time now, Kate," I said, "give me your hand."

So I helped her out of the hammock and helped guide her head and arms through the hole of the dress, garment, rag, whatever it was, and fixed the muslin around the baby, held it out to her. A bunch of homemade candles; the old broken wicker basket filled with blood sausage, pawpaws, the bottle of wine; white cap on my head and baby in Kate's arms, and we were ready to go then and I shouted to Sonny, led the way.

"Go on, Kate," I said, "take one. . . ." And she smiled and did what I told her, and the coals of our three long slim cigars were as bright as the little red eyes of foraging pigs as we puffed away together down the dark path toward our festive hours among the slabs and crosses and shallow mounds in the sunken cemetery. I could smell the three of us in the darkness—rancid smoke, long hair, wet skin, newborn child—smell our invisible lives in the darkness, and I walked with a bounce and swung the basket to and fro and watched for the glow of the candles.

And then: "You hear what I hears, Skipper?"

"I think so, Sonny. Do you mean the birds?"

"That's it, Skipper. Birds. But birds don't sing in the dark. Does they, Skipper?"

"It's a special night, Sonny, a special night. That's all. They're singing for us."

"Oh. I see. Well. So we got the night angels with us, is that it?"

"Sure, Sonny," I said. "That's it. But how's the cigar? Burning OK?"

"She's burning just fine, Skipper, just fine."

Darkness. Shadows. Heavy dissolving moon. And it was the Night of All Saints as I knew it would be, and somewhere ahead I heard the soft voices in the cemetery and smelled the wax. And above us and hopping, fluttering, singing from branch to branch, Sonny's night angels were keeping pace with us toward the heavy uncertain field of light that was hanging, suddenly, about knee-level beyond the vines, trees, velvet silhouettes of the banana leaves. We were the last to arrive, Sonny and Catalina Kate and myself and the baby, and standing together on the lip of that soft bowl and smiling, waiting, peering down at the illuminated graves—candles were already lit and flickering on most of those old graves—and at the shades of soft fat women and squatting men and children who were lighting candles, eating, laughing—the laughter was as soft as the song of the ground doves—it was hard to know whether all those shades were celebrants honoring the dead or the dead themselves preparing a little fete for Kate's new child.

"Look at that grave, there, Sonny," I whispered. "Looks like a birthday cake, doesn't it, Sonny?"

We laughed then, Sonny and I, softly and gently laughed, and then we helped Kate and baby down the steep path into the sunken cemetery and the artificial day that was flickering and shifting in the heavy familiar darkness of our peaceful night. The floor of the cemetery was covered with sand, crushed shells, tall weeds. And all about us were the old graves that had settled long ago at steep angles into the powdery sand. And the homemade candles, the mere waxen stubs and living remnants of dull yellow light—I took a deep breath of tallow, smoke, spice, the wicks going down, and took in the shades and graves and little yellow teeth of light.

"Now, Catalina Kate," I said quietly, "the choice is yours. Do you think you can pick us out a nice grave?"

In the heavy light of the artificial day our birds were crowding around the edge of the bowl, crowding around the lip of the bowl, and were singing, flitting, sighing with their little wings. Our night angels, as Sonny said. Our invisible chorus.

"That's a beauty, Kate," I murmured, "a marvelous choice." And kneeling, shoving the cap to the back of my head, resting a hand on the raw stone: "OK, Sonny? If this one's OK with you, let's have the candles."

It was an out-of-the-way grave at the far edge of the cemetery, a massive untended affair in the shadow of the trees that leaned down from the top of the bowl. No name. No dates. Long and broad and canted into the sandy earth and half-covered with weeds. A bottomless stone box driven into the sand among the little roots of the weeds, great monumental outline of old stone that had survived grief and that had no need of identity. I knelt there in the darkness and quickly swept the little lizards off the rim of it.

"More, Sonny, more," I cried, "let's give him a big light!" And listening to the birds, the women, the soft sound of Kate talking to the baby—Kate was sitting in the crook of an exposed tree root and guarding the baby, guarding the basket—Sonny and I, on hands and knees, inched our way together around the stone perimeter of that old grave, and one by one the gems of the crude diadem took fire, swayed, gave off their yellow light and the long black rising tails of candle smoke. We melted wax and stuck candles everywhere we could on the dark stone, I jammed lighted candles among the weeds in the center of that listing shape. The little flames were popping up all over the grave and suddenly the unknown soul was lighting up Sonny's smile and mine and Kate's, was glowing in Kate's eyes and in the soft sweat on her brow.

So the three of us and the baby sat at the foot of the old dazzling grave, and Catalina Kate tore into the bread and cut the blood sausage into edible lengths while I broke open the French wine. Thick bread. Black blood sausage. White wine. And I propped myself up on Kate's smooth dark rouge-colored young knee and ate, drank, felt the light of the candles on our cheeks. And then I asked Kate for a look at the baby, and there it was, the new face about half the size of her breast and three times as black and squeezed shut in a lovely little grimace of deep sleep.

"Who do you think it looks like, Kate? Sonny or me?"

And smiling down, tangling her shank of hair into the muslin and studying the small candlelit sheen of her first child: "Yes, sir. Him look like the fella in the grave."

"Of course, Kate," I said then, and laughed. "But just think of it. We can start you off on another little baby in a few weeks. Would you like that, Kate? But of course you would," I said. Kate nodded, smiled, held the baby tight. And we finished the wine, packed the basket, waited for the moon to suck the last light of our candles into the new day. When we started back to Plantation House in the morning—this morning—I carried the baby in my own arms. Light as a feather, that baby. Good as gold.

So yesterday the birth, last night the grave, this morning the baby in my arms—I gave Uncle Billy's crucifix to Kate this morning, I thought she deserved it—and this afternoon another trip to the field because Gloria was calling, calling for me. And now? Now I sit at my long table in the middle of my loud wandering night and by the light of a candle— one half-burned candle saved from last night's spectacle—I watch this final flourish of my own hand and muse and blow away the ashes and listen to the breathing among the rubbery leaves and the insects sweating out the night. Because now I am fifty-nine years old and I knew I would be, and now there is the sun in the evening, the moon at dawn, the still voice. That's it. The sun in the evening. The moon at dawn. The still voice.

TRAVESTY

I am imbued with the notion that a Muse is necessarily a dead woman, inaccesible or absent; that the poetic structure—like the canon, which is only a hole surrounded by steel—can be based only on what one does not have; and that ultimately one can write only to fill a void or at the least to situate, in relation to the most lucid part of ourselves, the place where this incommensurable abyss yawns within us.

—Michel Leiris: *Manhood*

You see, a person I knew used to divide human beings into three categories: those who prefer having nothing to hide rather than being obliged to lie, those who prefer lying to having nothing to hide, and finally those who like both lying and the hidden. I'll let you choose the pigeonhole that suits me.

—Albert Camus: *The Fall*

For Three Sophies

No, no, Henri. Hands off the wheel. Please. It is too late. After all, at one hundred and forty-nine kilometers per hour on a country road in the darkest quarter of the night, surely it is obvious that your slightest effort to wrench away the wheel will pitch us into the toneless world of highway tragedy even more quickly than I have planned. And you will not believe it, but we are still accelerating.

As for you, Chantal, you must beware. You must obey your Papa. You must sit back in your seat and fasten your belt and stop crying. And Chantal, no more beating the driver about the shoulders or shaking his arm. Emulate Henri, my poor Chantal, and control yourself.

But see how we fly! And the curves, how sharp and numerous they are! The geometrics of joy!

At least you are in the hands of an expert driver.

So you are going to relax, *cher ami*. You are determined to hide your trembling, achieve a few moments of silence, begin smoking one of your delightful cigarettes, and then after this appropriate expenditure of precious time and in the midst of your composure, then you will attempt to dissuade me, to talk me back to sanity (as you will express the idea), to appeal to my kindness and good sense. I approve. I am listening. The hour is yours. But of course you may use the lighter. Only reach for it slowly and keep in mind my warning. Do not be deceived by my good nature. I am as serious as a sheet of flame.

As for you, Chantal, you must stop that sobbing. I will not say it again. Don't you know that Papa loves you? Not many young women have the opportunity of passing their last minutes in the company of lover and loving Papa both. The black night, the speeding car, the three of us, a glimpse of early snow curled in the roots of a fleeting roadside tree—it is a warm and comfortable way to go, Chantal. You must not be afraid.

And to think that we used to call her the "porno brat." Yes, our own Chantal—no sooner was she able to walk than she was forever stumbling into the erotic lives of her parents. Or perhaps I should say the illusory lives of her young parents. At any rate it was Honorine who began to call our own baby girl the "porno brat." But with a smile. Always with that ingenuous smile so appropriate to the oval and sensual face of the woman who is your mistress, my wife, Chantal's still young and generous mother. And then there was the schoolmate of Chantal's, that boyish jokester, who gave her the optician's chart with its letters diminishing in size and saying TOO MUCH SEX MAKES ONE SHORT-SIGHTED.

But do you know that I have never worn eyeglasses and even now am permitted to drive the fastest cars without anything at all to assist the sight of my naked eyes?

But Chantal and Honorine—what a pair of names. And to think that at this instant the one is white-faced, tear-streaked and clinging to the edge of hysteria in lieu of prayer directly behind us, while the other sleeps in the very chateau we are approaching. But be brave, Chantal. There will be no comforting Honorine when she receives the news.

Murder, Henri? Well, that is precisely the trouble with you poets. In your pessimism you ape the articulation you achieve in written words, you are able to recite your poems as an actor his lines, you consider yourselves quite exempt from all those rules of behavior that constrict us lesser-privileged men in feet, hands, loins, mouths. Yet in the last extremity you cry moral wolf. So you accuse me of planning murder. But with the very use of the word you reveal at last that you are only the most banal and predictable of poets. No libertine, no man of vision and hence suffering, but a banal moralist. Think of the connotations of "murder," that awful word: the loss of emotional control, the hate, the spite, the selfishness, the broken glass, the blood, the cry in the throat, the trembling blindness that results in the irrevocable act, the helpless blow. Murder is the most limited of gestures.

But how different is our own situation. Suspended as you are in time, holding your lighted cigarette between your fingers, bathed in your own sweat and the gentle lights of the dashboard—in all this there is clarity but not morality. Not even ethics. You and Chantal and I are simply traveling in purity and extremity down that road the rest of the world attempts to hide from us by heaping up whole forests of the most confusing road signs, detours, barricades. What does it matter that the choice is mine, not yours? That I am the driver and you the passenger? Can't you see that your morality is no different from Chantal's whim-

pering and that here, now, we are dealing with a question of choice
rather than chaos?

I am no poet. And I am no murderer. But did Chantal ever tell you
about the time she won for herself the title "Queen of Carrots?" No?
But perhaps your sexual knowledge of my daughter has made you short-
sighted after all.

I am not laughing at you. I am the kindest man you will ever meet.

Slow down, you say? But the course of events cannot be regulated by
some sort of perversely wired traffic policeman. We do not argue with
the star, the comet, the locomotive racing almost invisible in the cold
night, the conductor on the empty but moving *autobus*. I am not a child.
I trust you not to demean yourself with mere transparency or pathos.
Our speed is a maximum in a bed of maximums which happen to include: my driving skill, this empty road, the time of night, the capacity
of the car's engine, the immensity of the four seasons lying beyond us
between the trees or in the flat fields. Like schoolboys who have studied
the solar system (I do not mean to be condescending or simpleminded)
you and I know that all the elements of life coerce each other, force
each other instant by instant into that perfect formation which is lofty
and the only one possible. I am aware of a particular distance; these
yellow headlights are the lights of my eyes; my mind is bound inside
my memory of this curving road like a fist in glass.

You cannot know how often I have driven this precise route alone
and at the fastest speed I could achieve. You cannot be aware of those
innumerable late afternoons each of which contained this silent car, the
technician sprawled on his back beneath my car, a bank of chromium
instruments, a silence only faintly smelling of grease and oil, myself as
the patient spectator in one corner of a place that resembled the nearly
empty interior of an aircraft hangar. There, there is your speed. Would
you believe it?

Between the adjustments made by the hand of that white-coated figure lying as if dead on the concrete floor of his vast garage, and the
warm and living pressure of my own two hands on the thick black skin
of this steering wheel—from that time to this, from one hand to a
pair of hands, from the minute adjustments made beneath the car to
the life of the mind that holds the moving car to the road, there is
nothing, nothing at all.

The last time I drove this car to that garage I shook hands with the
technician. On the ramp the waiting automobile gleamed as new. Now

we are traveling as if inside a clock the shape of a bullet, seated as if stationary among tight springs and brilliant gems. And we have a full tank of fuel, and tires hardly a month old.

Do not ask me to slow down. It is impossible.

But you are already loosening your collar while I ramble on about Chantal's childhood, my love of cars, the intimacy we share, our swift progress through the fortress of space. Suddenly you and I are more different than ever, yet closer even than when we were three to a bed. But don't worry, despite all this talk of mine I am concentrating. Never for an instant do I lose sight of the road we follow through our blackest night, though I can hardly see it. Yes, my concentration is like that of a marksman, a tasteful executioner, a child crouching over a bug on a stick. And I understand your frustration, your feelings of incomprehension. It is not easy to discover that your closest friend and husband to one mistress and father of the other is driving at something greater than his customary speed, at a speed that begins to frighten you, and that this same friend is driving by plan, intentionally, and refuses to listen to what for you is reason. What can you do? How in but a few minutes can you adjust yourself successfully to what for me is second nature: a nearly phobic yearning for the truest paradox, a thirst to lie at the center of this paradigm: one moment the car in perfect condition, without so much as a scratch on its curving surface, the next moment impact, sheer impact. Total destruction. In its own way it is a form of ecstasy, this utter harmony between design and debris. But even a poet will find it difficult to share this vision on short notice.

But Chantal, perhaps you would like to remove your shoes. Perhaps you would like to imagine that you are merely one of several hundred airplane passengers preparing themselves to survive if possible a crash landing. And yet we are only three. Only three. A small but soothing number.

Of course I am not joking. How for the briefest pleasure of joking could I risk the lives of my own daughter and a poet acclaimed by the public? I am certainly not the man to take risks or live or for that matter die by chance. I am disappointed. Apparently your need to be spared— your need for relief, for deceleration—is so great that now, after all these years, you are willing to do even the most terrible injustice to my character, merely for the sake of your urgency. You wish only to open your eyes and find us safely parked on the edge of the dark road, the

interior of the automobile filled with our soft and private laughter. I
understand. But I regret that it cannot be that way, *cher ami*.

Why not alone? Or why not the four of us? Well, these are much
more serious and interesting questions. At last you perceive that I am
not merely some sort of suicidal maniac, an aesthetician of death at high
speed. But even to approach these subtle thoughts you must give me
time, more time. And yet doesn't the fact that you've asked the first
question hint at least at its answer?

Please, I beg you. Do not accuse me of being a man without feeling or
a man of unnatural feeling. This moment, for instance, is not disgusting
but decisive. The reason I am feeling a sensation of comfort so intense
as to be almost electrical, while you on the other hand are feeling only
a mixture of disbelief and misery—the reason for this disparity between
us is more, much more, than a matter of temperament, though it is that
too. We have agreed on the surface aspects of trauma: the difficulty of
submission, the problem of surprise, a concept of existence so suddenly
constricted that one feels like a goldfish crazed and yet at the same time
quite paralyzed in his bowl. A mere question of adjustment. But the fact
of the matter is that you do not share my interest in what I have called
"design and debris." For instance, you and I are equally familiar with
our white avenues, our sunlit thoroughfares, our boulevards beautifully
packed with vehicles which even at a standstill are able to career about.
The bright colors, the shouts, the bestial roar of the traffic, the police-
men typically wired for contradictory signals—it is a commonplace, not
worth a thought. And you and I are equally familiar with those occasional large patches of sand which fill half the street, marking the site
of one of our frequent and incomprehensible collisions, and around
which the traffic is forced impatiently to veer—until some courageous
driver falls back on good sense and lunges straight across the patch of
sand, his tires scattering the sand and revealing the fresh blood beneath.
Another commonplace, you say, more everyday life. The triteness of a
nation incapable of understanding highway, motor vehicle, pedestrian.
But here we differ, because I have always been secretly drawn to the
scene of accidents, have always paused beside those patches of sand with
a certain quickening of pulse and hardening of concentration. Mere
sand, mere sand flung down on a city street and already sponging up
the blood beneath. But for me these small islands created out of haste,
pain, death, crudeness, are thoroughly analogous to the symmetry of
the two or even more machines whose crashing results in nothing more

than an aftermath of blood and sand. It is like a skin, this small area of dusty butchery, that might have been peeled from the body of one of the offending cars. I think of the shot tiger and the skin in the hall of the dark chateau. But for you it is worth no more than a shrug. Your poetry lies elsewhere. Whereas I have never failed to pull over, park, alight from my automobile—despite the honking, the insults— and spend my few moments of reverential amazement whenever and wherever I have discovered one of these sacred sites. It is something like a war memorial. The greater the incongruity, the greater the truth.

But what about me, you are asking yourself, what about my life? My safety? And why am I now subjected to foolish philosophy mouthed by a man who has suddenly become an insufferable egotist and who threatens to kill me, maim me, by smashing this car into the trunk of an unmoving tree in ten minutes, or twenty, or thirty?

Now you must listen. The point is that you cannot imagine that I, the head of the household, so to speak, can behave in this fashion; you cannot believe that a life as rich as yours, as sensual as yours, as hon- ored, can suddenly be reduced inexplicably to fear, grief, skid marks, a few shards of broken glass; you simply do not know that as a child I divided my furtive time quite equally between those periodicals depict- ing the most brutal and uncanny destructions of human flesh (the elbow locked inside the mouth, the head half buried inside the chest, the sta- tuary of severed legs, dangling hands) and those other periodicals de- picting the attractions of young living women partially or totally in the nude.

Spare me, you cry. Spare me. But the lack of knowledge and lack of imagination are yours, not mine. And it will not be against a tree. There you are even more grossly mistaken.

Remind me to tell you about little Pascal. He was Chantal's little brother and died around the time Honorine nicknamed Chantal the "porno brat." My son, my own son, who died just at the moment of acquiring character. Even now the white satin hangs in shreds from the arms of the stone cross that marks his grave.

Very well. No radio. Music, no music, it is all the same to me, though had the thought been agreeable to you, I suppose I might have preferred the gentlest background of some score prepared for melodrama. No doubt I am attracted to the sentimentality of flute, drum, orchestra, simply because listening to music is exactly like hurtling through the

night in a warm car: the musical experience, like the automobile, guar-
antees timelessness, or so it appears. The song and road are endless, or
so we think. And yet they are not. The beauty of motion, musical or
otherwise, is precisely this: that the so-called guarantee of timelessness
is in fact the living tongue in the dark mouth of cessation. And cessation
is what we seek, if only because it alone is utterly unbelievable.

But Chantal is not listening. She is preoccupied with an agony even
greater than yours. She cannot care that recently her Papa has begun to
think about our several lives. But of course from you I expect total
attention. We are grown men, after all, and have eaten from the same
bowl often enough. As for me, in this instance I respect your wishes.
My beautiful high-fidelity radio stays dead.

Let us hope that I have not miscalculated and that there is not some
overblown machine now lumbering down upon us, filling the road
ahead, its great belly brimming with thick liquid fire and, in its noisy
cab, a gargantuan young peasant singing to keep himself awake. Disaster. Witless, idiotic disaster. Because what I have in mind is an "accident" so perfectly contrived that it will be unique, spectacular,
instantaneous, a physical counterpart to that vision in which it was in
fact conceived. A clear "accident," so to speak, in which invention quite
defies interpretation.

In the first place I fully intend us to pass the dark chateau where our
own Honorine lies sleeping. We will be traveling at our highest speed,
of course, and already will have reached the top of our arc. But perhaps
for an instant our lights will somehow intrude upon Honorine's interior
life, or perhaps even the sound of our passing—that faint horrifying
expulsion of breath which is the combination of tires and engine racing
together at a great distance—may somehow attract the briefest response
from Honorine's dormant consciousness. She will move an arm, make
a sound, roll over, who knows? Then eight kilometers beyond the chateau and we approach the old Roman viaduct. You remember it, that
narrow dead viaduct that spans the dry gorge and always reminds me
of flaking bone. Of course you remember it. And in the smallest imag-
inable amount of time our demon steel shall fuse its speed with the stasis
of old stone. The sides of our handsome car shall nearly touch the low
balustrades of that high and rarely traversed construction, we shall all
three of us be aware of the roar of stone, the sound of space, our headlights boring across the gorge as in a cheap film. And now, now you
are thinking that here is the spot where it shall all end. Yes, here would

be the natural site of what will be called our "tragic accident." Roman time, modern car, insufficient space between the balustrades, the appalling distance to the rocks in the bottom of the gorge, the uneven surface of the roadway across that viaduct. . . . What could be better? But you are wrong.

Because that is the problem. Precisely. All those "logical" details and all those lofty "symbols" of melodrama speak much too clearly to the professional investigator (and reporter) of such events. No, we shall not be able to crash off the viaduct or even miss it altogether and so sail directly into the wilderness of that deep gorge like some stricken winged demon from the books of childhood. Instead we shall merely continue beyond the viaduct about three kilometers (hardly the twitch of a lid, the snap of a head) where we shall make an impossible turn onto the premises of an abandoned farm and there, with no slackening of pace, run squarely into the windowless wall of an old and now roofless barn built lovingly, long ago, of great stones from the field. That wall is a meter thick. A full meter, or even slightly more.

The car that passes the very chateau that must have been its destination; the unmistakable tire tracks across the viaduct; the turn that is nothing less than incomprehensible; the tremendous speed upon impact; the failure of the autopsy to reveal the slightest trace of alcohol in the corpse of the driver. . . . What can they think? What can they possibly produce as explanation? What will they say about an event as severe and improbable as this one will appear to be, as well as one loud enough to wake the curate in the little nearby village of La Roche?

But that is exactly the point, since what is happening now must be senseless to everyone except possibly the occupants of the demolished car. During the—let me see—next hour and forty minutes by the dashboard clock, it will be up to the three of us to make what we can of this experience. And we will not be able to count on Chantal for any very meaningful contribution.

At any rate the lumbering disruptive oil truck is out of the question. Out of the question. Nothing will destroy the symmetry I have in mind. Don't you agree?

I have never seen the old curate of La Roche, but I know that he coughs a great deal and has a tobacco breath and that his fingers are forever stained with wine. But he is a deep and noisy sleeper, of that I am certain. What an irony that the co-ordinates of space and time have fixed on him to be our Chanticleer, so to speak, and that it will be he who will offer the first cockcrow to the explosion that will inaugurate our silence. Which reminds me, only yesterday I sat in this very automobile and watched an old couple helping each other down a village street (not La Roche, I have never been in La Roche) toward a life-sized and freshly painted wooden Christ-on-the-Cross mounted on a stone block not far from where I sat in my car. The old man, who was holding the woman's elbow, was a thin and obviously bad-tempered captive of marriage. The old woman was bowlegged. Or at least her short legs angled out from where her knees must have been beneath the heavy skirts, and then jutted together sharply at the ankles. This creature depended for locomotion on the lifetime partner inching along at her side. The old man was wearing a white sporting cap and carrying the woman's new leather sack. The old woman, heavily bandaged about the throat in an atrocious violet muffler, was carrying a little freshly picked bouquet of flowers. Well, it's a simple story. This scowling pair progressed beyond my silent automobile (you must imagine the incongruity of the old married couple, the orange roof tiles, the waiting Christ, the beige-colored lacquer of this automobile gleaming impressively in the bright sunlight) until at last the woman deposited the trim little bouquet of flowers at the feet of the Christ.

There you have it. Ours is a country of coughers and worshipers. Between the two I choose the coughers. At least there is something especially attractive about one of our schoolyards of coughing children, don't you agree? The incipient infection is livelier than the health it destroys. Yes, I do appreciate that hacking music and all their little faces so bright and blighted.

But have I never told you I am missing a lung? The war of course. That is another story. Perhaps we shall get to it. At any rate it is probably true that my missing lung determined long ago my choice of a doctor. You see, my poor doctor is missing one leg (the left, I believe) which was amputated only weeks before the poor fellow's wife ran off, finally, with her lover of about twenty years' standing. It was a compounded shock, an unusual circumstance, and as soon as I learned of it I became an additional patient on the diminishing roster of my crippled physician. The affinity is obvious, obvious. But by now you will have perceived the design that underlies all my rambling and which, like a giant snow crystal, permeates all the tissues of existence. But the crystal melts, the tissues dissolve, a doctor's leg is neatly amputated by a team of doctors. Design and debris, as I have said already. Design and debris. I thrive on it. For me the artificial limb is more real, if you will allow the word, than the other and natural limb still inhabited by sensation. But I know you, *cher ami.* You are interested not in the doctor's amputated leg but in his missing wife. Well, each man to his taste. At least I can report that my physician is highly skilled, despite all his cigarettes and his trembling hands. Incidentally, his cough is one of the worst I have ever heard.

But you are groaning. And yet even now we have so far to go that I cannot help but advise you to conserve the sounds in your throat. That's better, much better. But must you wring your hands? Remember, you are setting a firm example for Chantal.

Yes, it seems to me that one of the strongest gratifications of night driving is precisely that you can see so little, and yet at the same time see so very much. The child awakes in us once again when we drive at night, and then all those earliest sensations of fear and security begin shimmering, tingling once again inside ourselves. The car is dark, we hear lost voices, the dials glow, and simultaneously we are moving and not moving, held deep in the comfort of the cushions as once we were on just such a night as this one, yet feeling even in the softness of the beige upholstery all the sickening texture of our actual travel. As children we had absolute confidence in the driver, although there was always the delicious possibility of a wrong turn, some mechanical failure, all the distant unknowns of the night itself. And then there was sight, whatever we could see to the sides of the car or on the road ahead, and it was all so utterly dependent on the headlights, and sight so uncontrollably reduced was of course all the more magnified and pleasing.

It is no different now. Even setting aside our projected destination, which to me is the final blinding piece in a familiar puzzle, the fourth and solid wall in a room of glass, the clear burst of desire that is never entirely out of my mind, while for you it is quite the opposite, since what you know about our particular journey blunts you to the pleasures of this road, this night, this conversation, so that you and I are like two dancers at arm's length, regurgitation locked together with ingestion in a formal, musical embrace. . . . But setting all this aside, as I say, there is still the undeniable world of our night driving, and it is alluring, prohibitive, personal, a mystery that is in fact quite specific, since it is common to child, to lovers, to the lone man driving from one dark town to the next.

Yes, raise your eyes. Look through the clear glass of the windshield while it is still intact. There, do you see how the outer edges of the cone of light shudder against the flanks of darkness? And look at the actual length of our yellow beams, the reach of our headlights. We can see remarkably far ahead, and to the sides as well. Note that clump of wild onions out there in the dark, and that blasted tree, and that jagged boulder stuffed into that trough of moss. And there, that little road marker no larger than a child's stone in a cemetery and which you refused to read.

But I will tell you something. The hour is precisely eighteen minutes past one a.m., and in mere moments, as soon as we are drawn into the gentleness of the long curve that lies just ahead—but of course it is still invisible—there will be on our right a rather small grove of olive trees, a stone hut, a silent but watchful dog. And if you look when I tell you to look, you will see that among the olive trees someone has made a small pile of human possessions: a white wooden chair, a broken trunk, a crude rake for the garden, a heap of clothing that might have been stripped from dead bodies. It is difficult to understand that the life of the stone hut has been emptied into the darkness, and that the olive tree is beautiful only because it is so deformed. Yet these things are true.

It is amusing to think that tonight our speeding car shall frighten the abandoned dog.

But do you know that once Chantal and Honorine together urged me into the arms of a woman of luxury? It is true. Absolutely true. And I complied.

Chantal was only a girl at the time, and we were traveling, the three of us, in a car very like the one we are presently enjoying. We had dined well, after a day of gray clouds, flat road, high speed, and having left behind us connecting rooms with high ceilings, marble fireplaces, wallpaper the elegant color of dry bone, had walked into a moonlit street filled suddenly with the warmth of summer and the smell of flowers. A moving shadow, an open window, a few notes of music, and then we understood that we had stumbled into the very center of the honeyed hive of a city already acclaimed for its women. Down the narrow street we went arm in arm, laughing, Chantal and Honorine both claiming to be well-known residents of that gentle quarter. And I was in the middle, walking between Chantal and Honorine, and somewhere a caged bird was singing and even out there in the street I could smell fat bolsters, feather beds, nude flesh.

It was a night of wine. And the woman, when we found her, was much older than Honorine and might have come fresh from some turn-

of-the-century stage where whiteness of skin and heaviness of flesh and
limb were especially admired. Chantal and Honorine exclaimed their
enchantment; I hesitated; the woman raised her chin and smiled. And
do you know that Honorine proposed with so much good spirit that I
enjoy this woman that I became aroused and agreed to leave Chantal
and Honorine eating chocolates in a little empty parlor while, several
ornate rooms away, I contributed three quarters of an hour of sexual
authenticity to their delightful game? In taking that tall and heavy
woman, who filled her maturity with the exact same elegance with
which she lived in her skin, it was as if I had only found my way again
to Chantal and Honorine, and as if I had accepted from mother and
daughter the same unimaginable gift. So I prepared the way for you.
Don't you agree? And with my two women, who are yours as well, have
I not created a family small in size but rich in sentiment?

The next day we were a close and smiling triad as we continued
driving through the sterile marshlands and past the great brown wind-
mills with their sad faces and broken arms.

But I must tell you that this little romantic story about the complicity
between my wife, my daughter, and the older woman of luxury reminds
me more strongly than ever of a curious emotional reaction of mine—
a reaction I rarely recall and never felt except upon one of those innumerable occasions of Chantal's childhood happiness. That is, Chantal
had only to reveal the slightest sign of personal enjoyment, had only to
pick some leaf or kiss Honorine or show me with evident pleasure some
faintly colored illustration in one of her books, to send me sliding off
into the oddest kind of depression. I was a perfect companion to her
gloom, her anger, her hours of fear, her childhood pantomimes of adult
frustration, her little floods of helplessness in the face of some easy
problem. But let Chantal throw her arms around my neck or grow warm
of cheek or simply give me a clue that she was momentarily alive in one
of those private moments of beatitude all children experience and I was
hopelessly alien from her and depressed, inexplicably downcast.
Throughout all of Chantal's childhood I was sorry for her whenever I
should have been glad. Yes, I was actually sorry for my own child, but
sorry only when she was in one of her states of well-being. And when
she was herself unhappy, why then I was busily content.

I hear your impatience. And in the circumstances my perhaps sentimental recollections must touch you with profound irritation, especially
since you have imagined so much more life than I myself have lived.
And perhaps you have already analyzed my darker, nearly forgotten

parental emotions as fear of mortality, and have thus dismissed them. But I must ask you again to indulge my nostalgia, if only because its source is gone, quite gone, and I am now capable of loving Chantal without putting myself perversely at the center of our relationship, like the fat raisin that becomes the eye and heart of the cookie. No, for years I have been what the rest of the world would call a normal father, feeling only joy for Chantal's joy and pain for her pain. My "perversion" has long since been cauterized. I no longer reverse and then exaggerate what Chantal feels. I still enjoy licking smeared chocolate from my daughter's fingers, and do so with perfect impunity. But I am in no way responsible for maintaining Chantal's life, and long ago gave up anticipating grief for its loss.

Do you know that now I am not even tempted to look into the rearview mirror?

But there, the dashboard settings are now subtly different. You cannot be as aware of them as I am, yet for me the mere climbing or falling of needles, the sometimes monstrous metamorphosis of tiny, precise numbers behind faintly illuminated glass, a droplet traveling too quickly or too slowly through its fragile tube—these for me are the essential signs, the true language, always precious and treacherous at the same time. And now the settings are different. There are the mildest indications that we are beginning to deplete the resources of this superb machine, though in our present context those resources are of course inexhaustible and in fact will probably account for the grandeur of the sound that will wake our poor curate. Nonetheless the life of the car is running out, the end of our journey tonight is not as distant as one might think. Naturally there are steep grades, sudden turns, even abrasive changes in the road's surface, and still time enough to tax us, preoccupy us, demand the utmost from our living selves. And of course you may argue that our experience so far has been constant, virginal, that we have heard no variations in the music that reaches us from beneath the car; that Chantal has not discovered some poor wounded bird imponderably present and expiring on the seat beside her. Yes, things are the same, I am not even beginning to feel the strain of driving at this high speed.

But then our situation is not so very different from my war, as I call it, with Honorine's old-fashioned clock. It is a crude affair that hangs on her wall. Nothing but a few pieces of dark wood, a long cord with iron weights at either end, a circular ratchet, a horizontal pendulum fixed with wooden cubes like a tiny barbell. It is only the bare minimum of a clock, suggesting both the work of a child and the skill of some parsimonious medieval craftsman. Small, simple, dark, naked. And yet this contraption makes the loudest ticking I have ever heard. And slowly, it ticks more slowly, more firmly than any time device created by any of the old, bearded lovers of death in the high mountains. Well, I cannot stand that ticking. It is unbearable. So at every opportunity I stop the clock. But somehow it always starts up again and beats out its relentless unmusical strokes until once again I find it so insufferable that I jam its works.

You know the clock, you say? And you have never bothered to listen to the noise it makes? But of course you are familiar with Honorine's old clock. Of course you are. What a silly oversight. We are not strangers. Far from it. And how like you to be so unconcerned with something that gives me the utmost aural pain. But what I mean to say is this: that I hear that ticking loudest when the clock is stopped. Exactly. Exactly. It is the war I cannot win. But it is a lovely riddle.

The point is this: that our present situation is like my wife's old clock. The greater the silence, the louder the tick. For us the moment remains the same while the hour changes. And isn't it curious that I really know very little about automobiles? I merely drive them well.

Yes, it was a rabbit. You see it is true, as everyone says, that at high speeds you can feel absolutely nothing of the rabbit's death. But next it will rain, I suppose, as if an invisible camera were recording our desperate expressions through the wet glass. Perhaps you should have agreed to the radio after all.

Confession? Confession? But do you really believe that the three of us are sitting here in what I may call our exquisite tension (despite all my own pleasure in this event, I am not insensitive to the fact that we are in a way frozen together inside this warm automobile) merely so that I may indulge in guilty revelations and extract from you a few similar low-voiced scraps of broken narrative? No, *cher ami*, for the term "confession" let us substitute such a term as, say, "animated revery." Or even this phrase: "emotional expression stiffened with the bones of thought."

I do not believe in secrets—withheld or shared. Nor do I believe in guilt. At least let us agree that secrets and so-called guilty deeds are fictions created to enhance the sense of privacy, to feed enjoyment into our isolation, to enlarge the rhythm of what most people need, which is a belief in life. But surely "belief in life" is not for you, not for a poet. Even I have discovered the factitious quality of that idea.

No man is guilty of anything, whatever he does. There you have it. Secrets are for children and egotists and sensualists. Guilt is merely a pain that disappears as soon as we recognize the worst in us all. Absolution is an unnecessary and, further, incomprehensible concept. I am not attempting to justify myself or punish you. You are not guilty. Never for a moment did I think you were. As for me, my "worst" would not fill a crooked spoon.

And yet there are those of us, and I am doing my best to include you among our select few, for whom the most ordinary kind of daily existence partakes of the contradictory sensation we know as shame. For such people everything, everything, is eroticized. Such a man walks through the stalls of a butcher in a kind of inner heat, which accounts for his smile. But if we allow shame to the sensualist and deny guilt to the institutions, it is simply that such words and states serve poetic but not moral functions. In the hands of the true poet they are butterflies congregating high in the heavens, but in the hands of the moralists or the metaphysicians they are gunpowder.

But you are becoming angry, *cher ami*. Be patient.

Another cigarette. I approve. Though you must know that every minute you are growing more and more like my good but crippled doctor, despite the fact that you are in full possession of your four limbs. But it occurs to me that had I not given them up on the very day you entered our household, I would now ask you to reach slowly across the space between us and position your freshly lighted cigarette between my own dry lips. And you would do that for me. I know you would. And your shaking hand would hover there an instant just below my line of vision, sparing my own two hands for their necessary grip on the wheel, until I fished for the end of the cigarette with my parted lips and then found it, held it, inhaled. One of your cold fingers might even have brushed the tip of my nose as I waited and then exhaled, blowing one lungful of smoke against the inner side of the windshield like a silent wave curling along a glassy shore.

Cigarettes always make me think of bars. They remind me of the war, of talkers around a dark table, of wine, of a woman's hand in my lap.

But no, not even that single puff. Not even now. It cannot be. And yet while you are drenched in the aroma of your cigarette, and while

Chantal may be acquiring some slight awareness of the relative newness of this automobile which she cannot help but smell, I myself am breathing in fresh air, dead leaves, ripe grapes. And the windows are closed. Quite closed.

Chantal? Do you hear Papa's voice as through the ether? Whatever you are thinking, *ma cherie*, whatever monsters you may be struggling with, you must believe me that your presence here is not gratuitous. That would be the true humiliation, Chantal: to be as small as you are, to be as young as you are, to be seated behind Henri and me and hence quite alone in the car with no one to comfort you by touch or wordless embrace (precisely as I comforted you at the death of Honorine's Mama, that splendid woman), and then to be conscious of yourself not only as so very different from the two men talking together in the front of this darkened and terribly fast sport touring car, but also to know yourself to be forgotten, only accidentally present, unwanted perhaps. What could be worse? Especially since you are in fact no child, and have spent almost the total store of your youthful sexuality on your own small portion of Henri's poetic vision, and since you have always harbored a special regard for your Papa's love.

But it is not so, Chantal. You are no mere forgotten audience to the final ardent exchange between the two men in your mother's life, men whose faces you cannot even see. Not at all, Chantal. No, I have thought of you with utter faithfulness from the beginning. In my mind there were always three of us, Chantal, never two, and in all the accruing of the elements of this now inevitable event (the month, the day, the night, the route), there you were in the very center of my concern. And during these last hours it has been the same: when I thought of you and Henri finishing your dinner in the restaurant, when I waited for the attendant to go through the motions of pumping the last tankful of gasoline into this silent car, when I noticed on my wristwatch that the time of our rendezvous was approaching, even when I so unexpectedly depressed the accelerator and violently increased our speed and hence interrupted our lively conversation and signaled the true state of things: in all this you were the necessary third person whose importance was quite equal to Henri's and mine.

That the protective parent turns out to be the opposite, that familiar accord turns out to be the basket containing the hidden asp, that it is impossible to weigh the magnitude of what your father is doing as opposed to that of what will soon be happening—this is a disillusionment

I cannot discuss for now. But let me at least reassure you in this other matter: you are here, now, with Henri and me, only because of the strength of my devotion, my poor Chantal. No one can rob you now of your Papa's love.

We are like the crow and the canary, *cher ami*. We are that different. And yet we are both Leos. It is almost enough to engage my interest in astrology. Or at least it is a fact that should help me to suppress more effectively my amusement at the new astrological age of the young. Of course this amusement of mine is more sympathetic than scornful: one cannot merely scoff at the signs of the zodiac sewn to the buttocks of the tight faded pants of our young men and women these days. How like them to believe in the old wizardry and yet sport these portentive signs so innocently, naïvely, on the seats of their pants.

But you and I are Leos. One more unbreakable thread in the web. What does it mean? Is it the crudest irony of all, or does it somehow light the way to our reconciliation? Is it a mockery of our differences or a hint as to the nature of that odd affinity for each other that we appear to share? Perhaps your future biographer will find in this astrological coincidence of ours the essential clue to what will always be known as your "untimely death." Who is to say?

I seem to remember an old adage that the true poet has the face of a criminal. And you have this face. You and I know only too well that you are publicly recognized by your short haircut, the whiteness of your skin, the roughened texture of this white skin, the eyes that are hard and yet at the same time wet and always untrustworthy, as if they have been drained of blueness in a black-and-white photograph. Are you beginning to see yourself, *cher ami*? Yours is the face of the criminal, the lover from the lower classes, the face of someone who has just died on a lumpy sofa in an unfamiliar apartment and who lies there as if alive but already cooling, with one hand touching the bare floor and the grainy head supported in the grip of two cheap sofa cushions. And no matter how you dress, whether conventionally in your dark modest three-piece suit as of this moment, attired in exactly that same absence of flamboyance as myself, as if we had come from separate business offices only to meet on the same outmoded train, or whether you are casually dressed in a somewhat rumpled mauve shirt and loosened tie, as I have often seen you, still for me you are only dressed in one way: in black pants and in a white shirt that is open at the collar, and tieless, and a little soiled. It is the garb of the man about to be executed, the garb of the unsmiling poet whose photograph is so often taken among those festive crowds at the bull ring.

And let us not forget your days as a mental patient. We are all familiar with those red-letter days of yours, *cher ami.*

Yes, I know you well. Only a Leo could cultivate so successfully this *persona* of the man who has emerged alive from the end of the tunnel or who has managed to cross the impossible width of the arena. It is always the same: you are like a man who spends his life in intense sunlight becoming all the while not pinker, darker, but only whiter, as if your existence is a matter of calculated survival, which accounts for your curious corpselike expression, which in turn is so appealing to women. You are plain, you smoke cigarettes, you appear to be the friend of at least half of all those professional *toreros* now working with the majestic bulls, as some people think of them.

And you have spent your days, months, in confinement. We have only to see your name, or better still to see your photograph or even catch a glimpse of you in person, to find ourselves confronting the bright sun, endless vistas of hot, parched sand, the spectacle of a man who always conveys the impression of having been dead and then joylessly resurrected—but resurrected nonetheless. Of course your suffering is your masculinity, or rather it is that illusion of understanding earned through boundless suffering that obtrudes itself in every instance of your being and that inspires such fear of you and admiration. Another way of putting it, is to say that you have done very well with hairy arms and a bad mood. But I am not trying to rouse you with insults. At any rate you will not deny that in yourself you have achieved that brilliant anomaly: the poet as eroticist and pragmatist combined. Though you merely write poems, people admire you for your desperate courage. You are known for having discovered some kind of *mythos* of cruel detachment, which is another way of expressing the lion's courage. And I too am one of your admirers. Just think of it.

Your modesty? Honesty? Humility? Anxiety? I am aware of them all. In you these qualities are made of the same solid silver as that courage of yours. Yes, you are the kind of man who should always be accompanied by a woman who is the wife of a man as privileged as me. Only some such woman could qualify as your Muse and attest to your courage.

Well, I prefer the coward.

Is it possible then that I too am a Leo? I for whom the bull is interesting, if at all, not for his horns but for the disproportion between his large flabby hump and little hooves? I who possess none of those externals of personality which adorn you, *cher ami*, like *banderillas* stuck and swaying in the bull's hump? I who despise the pomp and frivolity of organized expiation? I for whom the window washer on a tall building is more worthy of attention than your *torero* in the moment of his gravest danger? I who must get along without a Muse and for whom poetry is still no match for journalistic exhibitionism? (The poetry of present company excluded, *cher ami*.)

Well, perhaps I am merely the product of an astrological error or, more likely, of some clerical slip in the mayor's office. Perhaps I am only a counterfeit Leo, a person who has lived his life under the wrong sign of the zodiac—the coward to your own man of courage. But then how ironic it is that behind the wheel tonight we find not the poet but only the man who disciplines the child, carves the roast. Perhaps the crow is not so inferior after all to his friend the canary.

It is quite true that I am unable to bear the cold. In all her good humor, Honorine still considers it my severest failing, this inevitable capitulation of mine to the power of the falling thermometer. The shocking whiteness of our bed linen, the touch of approaching winter on the back of my neck, the painful sensation of coldness spreading like water on tiles across the undersides of my thighs, the chill my hand is forever detecting on the surface of my rather bony chest (despite flannel shirt, woolen pullover, tweed jacket), a sudden unpleasant deadening in the end of my nose—here is a sensitivity which even I myself deplore. What could be more cowardly than fear of the cold?

Yes, I fight the drafts. I complain bitterly indeed about the trace of ice on the windowpane, the sound of wind in our vaulted fireplace, the enemy that sets the flame of the candle dancing. Do you know that I suffer acutely because one of my ears is always colder than the other? My feet begin to stiffen inside my thick socks and English shoes, the coldness of my hands defies the most vigorous rubbing, reproachfully I tell Honorine that the walls are cold, that the fire is too small, that someone has left one of our thick oaken doors ajar. But you have heard my complaints. You have even remarked that an old chateau is no place for a man who sniffs out spiteful breezes in all seasons.

And yet you cannot know what it is to have cold elbows. The elbows are the worst. Because in them the little twin fiends of numbness and incapacity appear to sit most easily, comfortably, as if the nearly naked exposure of the bones in the elbows attracts most readily those sensations—those two allegorical envoys—of the ice that is already creeping and hardening across the very surfaces of our last night. Oh yes, Honorine is tolerant of this obsessive susceptibility of mine. She is forebearing, indulgent, good-humored, despite her critical comments and all these years of robes, hot fires, the soft and warming fur of dead rabbits. And yet hours after I have been restored as fully as possible to a condition resembling so-called normal body temperature, it is then that I am most aware of the coldness lingering in my elbows and of the fact that I can never be entirely comfortable while for her part Honorine is never cold. Actually, it is embarrassing to be unable to touch your wife at night without first warming your hands in a sinkful of scalding water. It is not pleasant to feel your wife flinching even in the heat of her always sensible and erotic generosity.

But I hope it is not too warm for you. Surely you can understand that tonight especially the heating regulator is set precisely and, I admit, at the highest possible degree. In this case the discomfort you are being made to feel is simply no match for that which I am avoiding. Don't you agree?

So you think that I am merely deceiving you with words. You think that I am trying to talk away the last of our time together merely in order to destroy the slightest possibility of my change of mind. You think that I am shrouding the last dialogue of our lives in the gauze of unreality, the snow of evasion. You think that euphemism is my citadel, that all my poised sentences are the work of mere self-protection, and that if only you can persuade me to accept head-on the validity of your word—that word—as the simplest and clearest definition of the car accident that is intended and that involves persons other than the driver, then you will have won the very reprieve which, from the start, I have tried to convince you does not exist. Well, beware, *cher ami*. Beware.

But perhaps you are right. Perhaps "murder" is the proper word, though it offends my ear as well as my intentions. However, mine is not a fixed and predictable personality, and you may be right. I too am open to new ideas. So let us agree that "murder" is at least a possibility. Let us hold it in store, so to speak, for the final straightaway. But I ask only that you then find new and more pertinent connotations of that ugly word and make your most objective effort to believe—believe—that there can be no exceptions to the stages, as I've sketched them, of what we may call our private apocalypse. It is like a game: I cannot accept the idea of "murder" unless you are able to refuse the illusory

comfort of "reprieve." After all, how can the two of us talk together
unless you are fully aware that the two of us are leaping together, so
to speak, from the same bridge?

Which reminds me of a singular episode of my early manhood. It occurred when Honorine was hardly more than a seductive silhouette on
my black horizon. And yet it was most instructive, this brief event, and
may well be the clue to the beginning of my romantic liaison with Honorine and even to the lasting strength of my marriage. Certainly it determined or revealed the nature of the life I would lead henceforth as
well as the nature of the man I had just become. It is something of a
travesty, involving a car, an old poet, and a little girl. Perhaps we shall
get to it. Perhaps. For now you must simply believe me when I say that,
thanks to this singular episode, my own early manhood contained its
moment of creativity. In my youth I also had my taste or two of that
"cruel detachment" which was to make you famous. More similarities
between the canary and his friend the crow. But now you must realize
that you have always underestimated the diversity, as we may call it, of
the members of the privileged class.

At least you have always appreciated Honorine. Yet who would not?
In her entire person is she not precisely the incarnation of everything
we least expect to find in the woman who appears to reveal herself
completely, and no matter how attractively, in the first glance? Think
of her now, not sleeping in that massive antique bed of hers, but, say,
outdoors and bending to her roses or better, perhaps, in our great hall
and sitting on her leather divan and wearing her tight plum-colored
velvet slacks and white linen blouse. Only another attractive, youthful-
looking married woman of the privileged class, we assume. Only one of
those conventional women framed, so to speak, by her bankbook and
happy children and a car of her own. We see her against a background
of yellow cloth on which has been imprinted a tasteful arrangement of
tree trunks and little birds; we know that everything in her domain
reflects a pleasing light, a texture of familiar elegance; we recognize that
she is neither large nor small, neither beautiful nor plain, despite her
golden hair cut short and feathery in the mode of the day; we expect
her to be little more than a kindly person, a friend to other women, a
happy mother, a fair athlete, someone who reads books and supervises
the redecoration of an old chateau and secretly tries to imagine a better
life. Large but studious-looking eyeglasses of yellowish shell, shoes that

gleam with the aesthetic richness of the country from which they have been imported, a wedding band excessively studded with rare stones, an agreeable mind that complements the oval face, the willing personality that reflects the hot bath taken only moments before—all these telltale signs we both have scanned too often in the past, have we not? Haven't we here the young middle-aged woman who cannot quite compete with the paid models in the fashion magazine but who yet catches our eye? The young matron not quite distinguished enough to join the striking matriarch on the facing page, yet benign enough to make us think of a drop of honey on a flat square of glass? If this is she—the woman in tennis shorts, the person who smiles, the wife with trim legs in which the veins are beginning to show—then we have seen her kind before and cannot find her especially interesting. Everything about such a person suggests the bearded father, the hand prepared well in advance to tend the sumptuous roses, a certain intelligence in the eyes, but finally the undeniable indications of the female life that is destined, after all, for unfulfillment—which is not interesting. No, we are hardly about to spend time or undertake the risks of seduction for a mere drop of honey on a sheet of glass. Let her remain in her old chateau where she belongs, surrounded as she deserves to be by husband and children and all of her uncertain advantages. At best this woman will give us only pride or pathos, being too long descended, as she appears to be, from that original countess who in ageless vigor maintained who knows what naked dominion in the boudoir.

But how wrong it all is, how very wrong. Superficially correct, and yet totally wrong. Yes, you and I know better, do we not? Together we know that the beauty of our Honorine is that, deserving these various epithets as she surely does, still she contains within herself precisely the discretion and charm and sensual certainty we could not have imagined. On this you will bear me out. I know you will.

Just think of it: you sit beside her on the cream-colored leather divan; you remove the owlish eyeglasses and notice that the eyes are flecked in the corners with anxiety; the great hall is silent, waxen, filled with the residual afterglow of the late sun; you notice that the face turned in your direction is strong but that the smile could be interpreted as timid; your hand grazes the chaste white linen of the blouse which, her eyes still on yours, her body apparently relaxed, she herself begins to unbutton, as if without thinking; with relief you notice an endearing tobacco stain on several of the otherwise conventionally white teeth; and then like a figure from our wealth of erotic literature, you find yourself kneeling on that polished stone floor and holding a firm ankle in one hand and in the other the heel of a shoe that appears to have been molded from dark chocolate. And then she leans forward, leans on your shoulder, frees herself of the shoes you could not remove, and then stands up and, for a moment, experiences girlish difficulty with the zipper of the plum-colored velvet pants. Well, the vision is yours as well as mine: the disappearance of the velvet trousers, the strength and shapeliness of the hands that pull down the underpants, the clear uncertain tone of the voice in which she remarks (quite wrongly, as all of my photographs attest) that she has never been very good at stripping. And there at eye level, for you are still kneeling, there at eye level we find the slight protrusion of the hip bone, the modest appearance of the secret hair which might have been shaven but was not, the smallest off-center appearance of the navel born of the merest touch of a hot iron against that soft and ordinary flesh. But more, much more, as only you and I could know. Because just there, adorning that small area between navel and pubic hair, there you see once again the cluster of pale purple grapes on yellow stems—yellow stems!—that coils down from the navel of our Honorine or, to put it another way, that crowns the erogenous contours of our Honorine as it did even when she was only an unexpectedly eccentric girl. Grapes, *cher ami*, a tattoo of smoky grapes that move when she breathes or whenever there is the slightest spasm or undulation in her abdomen. After seeing them, who would risk any constricting definition of our Honorine?

But you and I have been the foxes to those ripe grapes, have we not? And to think that it is she, this sleeping Honorine, who awaits our passing.

Well, now you can breathe again, as can I. That's a dangerous turn, you saw how much trouble it gave me, for all my knowledge of our route and no matter the perfect timing—or perhaps nearly perfect timing, I should say—with which I prepared once more to meet its treachery. Yes, an extremely difficult turn, a threatening moment indeed, as you could tell by the song of our tires and my silence and the sternness with which I held the wheel. Of course you too felt that sudden inundation of centrifugal force, the nausea that told us that we might in fact be leaving the road. But it's all right, the uncertainty is past, we have emerged from the turn, again we are safely adhering to the earthly path of our trajectory—which on a white road map looks exactly like the head of a dragon outlined by the point of a pen brutally sharpened and dipped in blood. But it is precisely by such small incidents as this one, when all at once the irrationality of the night intrudes upon us, that we inside the car are given to see ourselves as through the eyes of some old sleepless goatherd on a distant hill: to him, we are only the brief inaccessible stab of light that announces impersonally—quite impersonally—the vicious passing of an invisible and even inconsequential automobile through the damp and chilly medium of the black night. Then we are gone.

And so we are. So we are.

Chantal? Can it be? Have you forgotten the injunction of your Papa? Have you, like a poor childish sleepwalker, slipped free of your belt and worked your way down, down to the narrow but thickly carpeted area between the rear seat and two front seats? You, Chantal, burrowing down back there like some little frightened animal or tearful child? But it is a grievous tabloidal gesture. It could hardly be more hurtful to your Papa, who despairs to imagine you now conscious of nothing whatsoever except the burden of your own pure and quite meaningless revulsion. It is not how I thought you would behave, Chantal. Surely you cannot hope to save yourself by lying flat or in the fetal position and bracing yourself with knees and shoulders and covering your distracted face with your beautiful, small hands? Alas, the effort is futile, as you must know. But perhaps you are simply trying to escape your Papa's voice. Could it be that? You prefer the fine soft music of our transmission to the truth of what your Papa is saying? But there is time yet to recover yourself and regain your seat and participate in the assessment, analysis, of our discussion.

After all, you are nearly twenty-five years old. And I confess I found your sobbing more tolerable than this sudden convulsive state of withdrawal. But can't you see that this collapse of yours is, at the very least, an extreme distraction? Think of it, Chantal, we may not be so fortunate on the next turn.

But here it is, *cher ami*: my own dear Chantal lying face down behind us. How much worse it is for my poor child than I imagined. And only a few days ago I watched from our bedroom window as below in the otherwise empty courtyard Chantal, fresh from her riding lesson and dressed in her whipcord britches and black boots, emerged from this very automobile, alone except for her mother's Afghan which she was holding on a leather leash. The cobblestones like loaves of moldy bread, the long beige-colored car, the dog with his silken brown and white coat ruffling in the afternoon's cool breeze, the small and quick-moving woman with her dark hair, olive complexion, black riding boots, and dwarfed by the dog—it was a sight I could not help but admire, safe as I was from the long waves of regret which that same scene would have inspired in me in years past. I was still aware that Chantal's energetic presence below in the courtyard only heightened all the more the abandoned quality I especially appreciate in my wife's chateau, as if one could catch a glimpse of a large modern car left standing empty inside the iron gates of the very castle where the sleeping princess lies in all her pallor. I thought of it from my place at the window. But what most held my attention was the sheer vigor of the young woman below with the dog. How tight she was in her small body, I thought, and in her dark complexion how very different she was from our own fair and slowly sauntering Honorine. Yes, Chantal takes her small size and rose-and-olive beauty from her grandmother, that woman of diminutive regal shape and Roman coloring. How odd that not a trace of the old woman's alluring decadence is to be found in the features of our Honorine.

But now she has collapsed, the "porno brat" who became my child of the Renaissance. A few days ago I watched her crossing the courtyard quickly, happily, somewhat disheveled from her ride. The tall thin dog drifted from view to the clicking of my daughter's boot heels. She abandoned the car, this car, with the door on the driver's side wide open. I smiled. Now Chantal lies behind us, her body crumpled on the floor of the car like the corpse of an abducted socialite. She is a cameo nearly destroyed. And yet need I say that regret is not at all the same as grief?

I have two significant regrets. Only two. The first is that the crash soon to be reported as having occurred near the little village of La Roche must result inevitably in fire; the second is that the remains of the crash must inevitably disappear.

No doubt such considerations are not important. Even now I can hear your argument that these refinements of mine are for you nothing more than trivia elevated to the condition of impossible torment, or that at a time like this my extensive articulation of violent, unseemly details is nothing more than a kind of unfair tugging on the fishhooks already embedded beneath your skin. But of course I would by no means accept the notion of "trivia"; the nature and extent of physical damage can never be trivial, even when measured against the irreplaceable loss of three lives. And surely I need not remind you that I am serious and hence not at all interested in the infliction of minor psychological injury.

On the other hand, if you were in fact thinking, if you were but a little more engaged in our discussion, then you might well retort that for a man who has pre-empted absolute or, we might say, whiplash control over this much immediate last-minute life, all speculative fantasy becomes a mere glut of self-indulgence. What, you ask, is he not satisfied with things as they are, with all the tangible evidence of the terrible blow he is dealing his daughter, his closest friend, himself, but what he must inflate himself still further and so must invent in his own eyes, arrange within his own head, even that context of circumstances in which the three of us will no longer exist? But he goes too far, you say, too far. Well, it would be a pretty speech if you could make it. But even if you did reply to me with some such dubious form of logic, my own reply, prompt and good-natured as it would clearly be, would convince even you that it is this idea precisely that lies at the dead center of our night together: that nothing is more important than the existence of what does not exist; that I would rather see two shadows flickering inside the head than all your flaming sunrises set end to end. There you have it, the theory to which I hold as does the wasp to his dart. Without it, we would have no choice but to diffuse the last of our time together by passing between us the fuming bottle of cognac bought and freshly opened for just this occasion. But thanks to my theory we are spared such an intolerable waste. There shall be no slow maudlin loss of consciousness for you, for me. After all, my theory tells us that ours is the power to invent the very world we are quitting. Yes, the power to invent the very world we are quitting. It is as if the bird could die in flight. And unless we exercise this power of ours we merely slide toward the pit feet first, eyes closed, slack, and smiling in our pathetic submission to an oblivion we still hope to understand. But for us it will be different, *cher ami*. Quite different.

And yet I must say it. I regret the fire. Here even I am helpless. My theory does not apply to exploding gasoline. And I am sure that you will appreciate the fact that my attitude toward the burning of our demolished car has nothing to do with any personal feeling of mine against roadside cremation. On that score I am indifferent. But if I were able to prevent that burst of flame, to obliterate the sparks before their very inception and so stop the hot flame, the sheet of light, the fire that will turn to brightness the entire area of wall, wreckage, gasoline spreading and thus extending still further the circle of this most intense visibility—yes, if I could eliminate the flames I would. Yes, it seems to me that if we preserve this scene in all its magnitude and with all its confounding of disparate substances and with its same volume of sound, but remove from it the convention of fierce heat and unnaturally bright light, so that this very explosion occurs as planned but in darkness, total darkness, there you have the most desirable rendering of our private apocalypse. Announced by violent sound and yet invisible, except for the glass scattered like perfect clear grains across an entire field—what splendor, what a perfect overturning of ordinary expectation. The unseen vision is not to be improved upon.

Well, you will understand that in much the same way I would prefer that the remains of our crash go undiscovered, at least initially. I would prefer that these remains be left unknown to anyone and hence unexplored, untouched. In this case we have at the outset the shattering that occurs in utter darkness, then the first sunrise in which the chaos, the physical disarray, has not yet settled—bits of metal expanding, contracting, tufts of upholstery exposed to the air, an unsocketed dial impossibly squeaking in a clump of thorns—though this same baffling tangle of springs, jagged edges of steel, curves of aluminum, has already received its first coating of white frost. In the course of the first day the gasoline evaporates, the engine oil begins to fade into the earth, the broken lens of a far-flung headlight reflects the progress of the sun from a furrow in what was once a field of corn. The birds do not sing, clouds pass, the wreckage is warmed, the human remains are integral with the remains of rubber, glass, steel. A stone has lodged in the engine block, the process of rusting has begun. And then darkness, a cold wind, a shred of clothing fluttering where it is snagged on one of the doors which, quite unscathed, lies flat in the grass. And then daylight, changing temperature, a night of cold rain, the short-lived presence of a scavenging rodent. And despite all this chemistry of time, nothing has disturbed the essential integrity of our tableau of chaos, the point being that if design inevitably surrenders to debris, debris inevitably reveals its innate design. Until one day two boys stumble upon the incongruity of a once beautiful automobile smashed in the barnyard of an abandoned farm. For them the spectacle yields only delight: a little plastic-coated identity card winking in the sunlight, dead leaves nesting in the wheels which lie on their sides, a green shoot growing from the mouth of the rusty and half-crumpled fuel tank. Indeed, this spectacle now exists merely for them, merely for the pleasure of two boys in ill-fitting trousers and wooden shoes. But who better might we have as witnesses?

Well, it is impossible. It is not to be. Nothing will prevent our sudden incandescence in the night sky. And then we shall have blue lights, motorcycles, radio communications, the arrival of several of our little white ambulances. By dawn they will be hauling apart our wreckage with hooks and chains, and by noon of that first day there will be nothing left but the smell of gasoline and the dark signs of a recently extinguished fire. They will make notes, take photographs, climb through the elbows of hot metal, and then tow it all away with their clumsy trucks.

How sad it is, *cher ami*. What a brutal sport.

Perhaps if you make an effort to remain still, to position your arms so as to allow your chest room enough for its greatest possible expansion, and then breathe in slow conscious cadences through your open mouth, perhaps if you undertake these measures you will be more comfortable. But it is an unfortunate development, this partial suffocation resulting from that dreadful constricting of the bronchial tubes. I can imagine the growing panic of not being able to breathe, *cher ami*. You have my sympathies. Apparently your various nervous and physiological systems are quite determined not to be outdone by all the failures, impairments, of our poor Chantal. Now that the seizure is upon you, so to speak, I do remember your bitter description of yourself as an infrequent but nonetheless violent sufferer of this diabolical chest affliction. Generally it is a childhood illness, is it not? But the unfortunately unavoidable extremity of artificial heat, the closeness of the air around us, the effect of your cigarettes on a chest condition as sensitive as this one is, and of course the severe emotionalism of your present state—no doubt all this is conducive to one of your infrequent attacks, as you call them, of thick and heavily labored breathing. And then the whole thing is circular, is it not? The greater the pain, the greater the weight bearing down on your chest, the louder that dreadful rasping sound (it is indeed a curiously annoying sound, *cher ami*), the greater your own fury which, being directed at the self, of course, only gives still greater impetus to the whole wheezing machine.

Well, you have my sympathies. The onset of this condition of yours, with its promise of facial discoloration and even loss of consciousness so evident in every rattling breath you take, must certainly come as the final outrage, like eczema on top of leprosy. And unless I am mistaken, by now you are quite wet with perspiration. I suppose the body expresses what the mind refuses to tolerate, which probably says something about my own single lung and satisfactory respiratory system. But I would give you relief if it were in my power. Fields of oxygen, the smell of a blue sky. . . . I wish I could give them to you, *cher ami*. As it is, I am certainly going to find it harder to hear your voice, while for you it will be much more difficult to concentrate on anything but these increasing indications of expiring breath. But perhaps you should remember that it is only the rarest person who is not in one sense or another gasping for air.

Our villages carved out of old bone, our forests shimmering with leaves the color of dried tobacco, our village walls over which the dead vines are draped like fishing nets, the weight of the stones that occupy the slopes of our barren hills like sculpted sheep, the smell of wood smoke, the ruby color of wine held to the natural light, the white pigeon drawn to the spit even as he becomes aroused on the rim of the fountain— surely there is no eroticism to match the landscape of spent passion. There is nothing like an empty grave to betray the presence of a dead king in all his lechery. The blasted tree contains its heart of amber, you can smell the wild roses in the sterile crevices of ancient cliffs, suddenly you find the whitened limb of a tree sleeved in green. Yes, ours is a landscape of indifferent hunters and vanished lovers, *cher ami*, so that but to exist on such a terrain, aware of blood and manure, of the little paper sacks of poison placed side by side with bowls of flowers on the window ledges of each village street, or aware of the unshaven faces of our local pharmacists or of the untended pubescence of the girls who work in our markets and confess their fantasies in our darkened churches—yes, simply to exist in such a world is to be filled with a pessimism indistinguishable from the most obvious state of sexual excitation. I am a city person and not without my own form of pragmatism. And yet whenever I have seen from the window of this very car a glimpse of a distant woodland, I have thought of the royal hunting party mounted and in pursuit of a fevered stag, and thought of the sound of the horns, the lovers in that boisterous army, pretty and plumed, flushed and separated on their tossing horses but riding only in wait for the day of the chase to give way to the night of the tryst, when the mouth that took the brazen hunting horn by day will take the elegant and ready flesh by night. Yes, we who are the gourmets and amateur excavators of our cultural heritage know in our cars, our railway trains, our pretentious establishments of business, that we have only to pause an instant in order to unearth the plump bird seasoning on the end of its slender cord tied to a rafter, or a fat white regal chamber pot glazed with the pastel images of decorous lovers, or a cracked and dusty leather boot into which some young lewd and brawny peasant once vomited.

Yes, dead passion is the most satisfying, *cher ami*. You have hinted as much in your verses. But no wonder I have always thought of Honorine as mistress of a small chateau and nude beneath a severe black hunting costume for riding sidesaddle, though she has never been on a horse in her life. And you can imagine my pleasure when Honorine did in fact inherit from her mother, that noble woman, the small chateau which I myself named Tara and which you and I have filled with the deadest of all possible passion. You don't agree? You disclaim anything but vitality and tenderness in your relations with Chantal and Honorine? Then perhaps it is only my own passion that is so very dead, *cher ami*.

But the owl is watching us. And look there. Rain. Just as I expected. Soon the invisible camera will be trained on us through the wet and distorting lens of our windshield.

But I too once had a mistress. You did not know? Well, I hope that despite all you have been told about the power of your sullen allure you do not consider yourself the only person to have received the gift of love as seen through the prism, as I may call it, of another woman, though it is true that my own experience was confined to a single mistress and not to a pair. Never in my lifetime would I have contemplated a pair of mistresses. I am one of those lesser and hence more limited men, as you well know.

But little Monique was quite enough for me at the time. At the beginning of our friendship she was only a few weeks into her twentieth year, which, come to think of it, was exactly Chantal's age when you, in all your mysterious naturalness and unconcern, determined to extend to her the love of the poet, if you will indulge the expression. Then too, Monique was a shade smaller even than Chantal, a fact I take to mean not that I was trying to duplicate my daughter in my mistress but simply that I was lucky enough to win Monique with a single glance and that she was the smallest person with whom I ever shared what she used to call the dialogue of the skin. Her size was important to me not because it mimed specifically the small size of Chantal and Chantal's lovely grandmother, but only because it bore out so perfectly an idea that has obsessed me since earliest manhood: that the smaller the woman one regards the greater one's amazement at the vastness, fierceness, of the human will.

So Monique was remarkable, then, for her startling size, the utter harmony of her physical proportions, the immensity and even dangerous quality of her will. Her self-assertiveness was staggering. Of course she never failed to obey me, and yet even when she conformed to my simplest suggestion (about what to eat, what not to eat, some article of clothing, and so forth) she did so with beautiful vehemence, as if she were acting on her own prideful volition instead of mine. But never fear, she gave as good as she received.

If I loved Monique for her size, I loved her equally for the nature of her skin and its complexion. Tight, painfully and wonderfully tight over the entirety of her little face and limbs and torso, so thin and tight that actually I used to fear the consequences of a slip of the threaded needle. And of course her skin was white, almost glazed, in fact, and whiter even than Honorine's fair skin. And you know that my predilection for whiteness is just as intense as my appreciation of the Mediterranean hues.

Short skirts, short hair, bright blue lacquered shoes, occasionally a blouse tastefully crocheted, and the inevitable silk stockings as if always to confirm her threatened womanhood—I can still see her, one of the most inventive girls and strongest human beings I have ever known. I used to meet her twice a month on a schedule so strict that it did not vary more than several minutes from one occasion to the next. We were equally intolerant of lateness, though the flowers I carried and the luxury of the car I drove always gave me the advantage in these matters of time and demonstrations of anger. But we enjoyed each other's anger, and vied with each other in the creation of embarrassing public displays of bad temper. It was as if we shared between us an unspoken agreement to parody the lovers' quarrel, the domestic disagreement, whenever possible. Yes, even now it gives me oddly pleasurable satisfaction to recall how often I submitted to the insults she shouted at me on the most crowded of street corners (in the sun, in the rain, in the darkness after a splendid meal), and how she in her turn bore with quivering fury the disciplinary blows I so often inflicted with the edge of my heavy fork on her fragile wrist, usually under the eager eyes of an old waiter in the most elegant of restaurants. But as I say, it is a familiar and convenient pattern, this happy ritual of disruption and reconciliation. We relied on it totally, Monique and I.

At any rate Monique was proud, opinionated, hostile, inventive. It never failed to delight me that she could be so cruel of tongue, so vicious, or that a chest as small as hers was capable of such heavy breathing, or that she could become so quickly subdued and smaller than ever once seated in the rich interior of my powerful and highly polished car. But let me tell you that this Monique, whose youth and personality were so impressive, nonetheless and of her own free choice was the living example of all the uninhibited nudes I courted in the pornographic magazines of my own late and isolated boyhood. Not only was she a natural actress in the theater of sex, not only did she become in her mind and body the very flesh and activity of all those distant uncountable images of mine, but on top of everything else she collected in her small overfurnished rooms every conceivable kind of pornographic or erotic book, magazine, photograph that she was able to discover in our museums, kiosks, bookstalls, establishments devoted to the equipment and stimulation of the sexual drive. She lived her very life in unwitting competition with that rare photographic study which I prepared over the years of Honorine's own erotic womanhood. But Monique's performances were cruder, much cruder, than my study of Honorine. And at times they suddenly revealed my young friend's sense of humor, whereas there was no place for humor in my nude or partially nude views of Honorine.

Quick to take offense, quick to become aroused, quick to laugh at herself and at such exaggerated sexual animation in one so small—there we have our tireless Monique, who thrived on her pornography old and new and liked nothing better than to adorn her own little nude figure in the outlandish black lingerie of those ladies of the boas who in another era so incensed our forefathers. Yes, she collected and wore all those belts and harnesses and spangled black stockings as avidly as she immersed herself in her books and magazines. And do you know, *cher ami*, she had a palate that demanded only the finest of white wines. Only the finest.

But then there came at last that warm spring night when, suddenly inspired, I spanked Monique. It was not entirely my fault, and it was the only time in my life when I fell so close to being the sadistic villain lurking everywhere in the stories, photographs and fantasies of my little mistress. You will agree that no one wants to find himself becoming nothing more than a familiar type created by a hasty and untalented pornographer. We do not like to think of ourselves as imaginary, salacious and merely one of the ciphers in the bestial horde, to put it somewhat strongly, *cher ami*. But it was not totally my fault, as I must repeat, since the night was rainy and since the hour was late and since there was provocation, a provocation I did not even think to resist.

Well, you have the picture: spring rain, the city sleeping in its tile and stones, a wash of faint light from a bulb in a rose-colored shade, the warm little room smelling of the new season and of the oil of peach seeds with which Monique had scented her hot douche, and of course the two of us lying nude among the bolsters (except for Monique, who was wearing one of her scanty black harnesses known in the parlance of our grand temptresses as a garter belt). There you have it: the small, young, nearly naked girl on her stomach, the stockings which she had already removed adrift on the floor, the two of us slowly passing between us a set of large new photographs as rich and stimulating as ripened cheese. It was a scene that might have come directly from the writing desk or cold and shabby studio on one of our poor, dull, unshaven pornographers.

But as I have been saying, I had not the slightest thought of causing Monique even a moment of pain that night; I was not unusually aware of her childish, upturned buttocks twitching occasionally in the rose-colored suffusion from the lamp in the corner; I felt no need to exert any special mastery over Monique amidst the muffling softness of so many tasteless (but appropriate) oriental bolsters. And yet when all at once the moment of provocation was upon me, and in fact it was nothing more than a pouting underlip and some sort of pert, injurious remark quite lost now to passing time, it was then that I knew without any hesitation that I wanted to spank Monique—and to spank her in the conventional position, with my bare hand, with conscious determination and as hard and as long as possible. Mind you, until that instant I was absolutely uninitiated into that commonplace practice of familial punishment. And yet I did not hesitate, it did not occur to me to spare Monique one trace of humiliation or one grain of pain: I was not interested in justice or the possible sexual consequences of that event. To the contrary, thought and action were as one and I seized Monique abruptly, joyously, and like a vindictive father of long experience pulled my little startled mistress across my naked lap where I held that sprawled and squirming body in a grip that made escape impossible. The pleasure of the first long, deliberate blow was immense. Simply immense.

Well, the palm of my hand was a cruel and relentless paddle. Monique cried out, I gave not a thought to the sleeping neighbors, I spanked Monique with a lack of restraint astonishing even to myself. It was as if I could not bring the flat of my hand into hurtful contact with the soft, private world of her buttocks often enough or hard enough, so

that I increased my efforts and gave myself total consciousness of touch
and sound and enjoyed to the fullest the agitation of her helplessness.
And then breathless, delighted, feeling the heat in my hand and a sparkling sensation throughout my own nakedness, finally I stopped. Only
then did she cease resisting. Only then did she go limp, roll slowly away
from me, and smother her angry sobs in one of the bolsters. Her weeping was a shameless exploitation of her childlike appearance, but it was
an agreeable addition to the pleasure I was then savoring in my ex-
haustion.

So I myself fell back among the bolsters, surprised at what had happened but smiling, hearing the rain, feeling my own body filled, as it
were, with crystals of vigor. Partially on my side and in a condition of
curious alertness, peacefully I contemplated the body lying in rare qui-
escence and with its back to me. Yes, the buttocks were still pink, and
pinker yet because of the lampshade. Every now and again a tremor
passed down the spine or through one slender leg as if, released from
my grip, she was striving now to relieve the discomfort of her small
derrière by settling her body more deeply into the rolling, Oriental softness. The spare, black, lacy harness was low and loose on her little hips,
one of her hands crept back and of its own accord began to rub and
soothe the afflicted area. I watched her, I smiled. I did not for a moment
think I had done any genuine harm. It even occurred to me, and with
reason, that Monique in her sobbing was actually just as expectant as
I was in my smiling. Of course by now my great bird, if you will allow
the poetic license, was soaring in flight, so that it was only natural that
while I watched Monique's small hand moving to pacify the hurt in her
buttocks, my own firm hand—the very one with which I had performed
what she later called the abomination—became a skilled and willing
communicant with my distended sex.

How long we were held together in that wordless state of sexual
torpor I do not know. Only the movements of our hands, fingers, suggested that even we two nude luxuriating figures lay under the spell of
time. But then Monique herself effected the transition to what would
lead, or so I quite wrongly thought, to our embrace. She turned her
head and looked at me. One moment I was merely the comfortable
voyeur who in actuality sees very little, the next I was looking directly
into the small, handsome face of my Monique and growing suddenly
expansive at the sight of the tears on the cheeks, the wet nose, the
familiar, hard, dark scrutiny which I seemed to detect in the filmy eyes.

Yes, I felt that now I was performing, so to speak, not merely for myself but for Monique's own attentive contemplation. She was watching me, she was waiting, I thought that in a moment she would creep to my arms.

But how wrong I was. Because even now and betraying not the slightest sign of her intention, Monique was already preparing herself to become like nothing so much as a cat in a sack. She smiled, I felt forgiven. In a spasm of her former childish energy she was on all fours, I rose on an expectant elbow. She leapt to her feet on the floor and struck and held a suggestive pose, I responded with more explicit and vigorous manipulation. She stripped off the little black threatening belt, in eager anticipation I sat up and held out one beckoning arm to her. She raised the belt above her head (rather than tossing it away as I thought she would), and even then I merely exposed myself still further to what I thought was going to be some new form of erotic stimulation. Would you believe it?

Even when I beheld and felt the first lash across my thighs, I thought she meant only to whip me lightly to ejaculation, a process, which, at that moment, I imagined as a fulsome and brilliant novelty. But when I received the second lash, this time across the eyes so that instinctively I covered my face with both my arms, and then received full in the lap the pain of the little metal grips affixed to the tips of those four silken straps, of course I realized that she meant quite the opposite.

Yes, with terrible precision and on an ascending scale of strength and tempo, my little mistress thrashed me on face and lap, chest and lap, until I thought the very possibility of sexual discharge was no longer mine. I groaned, I tasted blood, I cowered. My great bird was dead. And yet throughout the ordeal, while attempting hopelessly to protect myself, still I was somehow admiringly aware of the legs apart, the dark flashing eyes, the vindictive, animated dance of that small, nude girl, the black straps that flew from her fist like the snakes from the head of some tiny and gloriously tormented Medusa. She flayed me. She did so with joy. And even that was not the end of it.

Because when at last she stopped, not from fatigue but from an unbearable excess of exhilaration, she flung the now useless garter belt into the very lap she had but a moment before so fiercely beaten. It was a gesture of superb contempt. But as if that gesture of contempt were not enough, for an instant she looked around the room helplessly, trapped in the passion of her distraction and clear purpose, and then in wickedness and exasperation flung herself down beside me among the bolsters and with the furious fingers of both hands brought herself to an orgasm that would have satisfied even a cat in a sack. At least it satisfied Monique. In my defeat and discomfort I too felt a certain relief, a certain happiness for Monique, and if in the midst of helplessness and pain I had nonetheless been able to photograph her benign expression, surely I would have set up the tripod, triggered the blinding light. As it was I merely gave myself to the sound of the rain and finally, on all fours, made my way to my clothes.

Well, it was an instructive night, as you can see. An hour, two hours, and as from nothing a new bond of accord was suddenly drawn between Monique and myself. I learned that I too had a sadistic capacity and that the commiseration of Honorine was even vaster and sweeter than I had thought. But what is still most important about that particular and now long-lost night is that it reveals that I too have suffered and that I am not always in total mastery of the life I create, as I have been accused of being. Furthermore it illustrates that I am indeed a specialist on the subject of dead passion. At any rate, and for better or worse, I abandoned Monique when you entered our household. Somehow your presence made Monique's unnecessary. But of course there are moments, such as this one, when she still dances inside my head with a vividness quite comparable to that of the life enclosed within our own small world which is moving—need I say it?—with the speed and elasticity of the panther in full chase.

I am always moving. I am forever transporting myself somewhere else. I am never exactly where I am. Tonight, for instance, we are traveling one road but also many, as if we cannot take a single step without discovering five of our own footprints already ahead of us. According to Honorine this is my other greatest failing or most dangerous quality, this propensity of mine toward total coherence, which leads me to see in one face the configurations of yet another, or to enter rose-scented rooms three at a time, or to live so closely to the edge of likenesses as to be eating the fruit, so to speak, while growing it. In this sense there is nowhere I have not been, nothing I have not already done, no person I have not known before. But then of course we have the corollary, so that everything known to me remains unknown, so that my own footfalls sound like those of a stranger, while the corridor to the lavatory off my bedroom suddenly becomes the labyrinthine way to a dungeon.

For me the familiar and unfamiliar lie everywhere together, like two enormous faces back to back. I am always seeing the man in the child, the child in the grown man. Winter is my time of flowers, I am a resigned but spirited voyager. Of course the whole thing is only a kind of psychic slippage, an interesting trick of *déjà vu*, although Honorine insists that it is a form of mystical insight. She is inclined to idealize me in her own reasonable and admirable fashion. But then I must add that at certain times she has found my mental disappearances, as she calls them, not merely disconcerting but fearful. And yet I have never given Honorine literal cause for anxiety, I can promise you that. She will be the last to propose any ready answers when she learns what has become of us tonight.

But no doubt I have been meaning to say that every more or less privileged person contains within himself the seed of the poet, so that the wife of each such individual wants nothing more than to be a poet's mistress. In this respect Honorine has been especially fortunate.

Do not be alarmed, *cher ami*. The matter at hand is not necessarily so very important. But we might as well spare ourselves whenever we can. The problem is that there is exactly time enough for me to forewarn you that in a few seconds we will be passing directly through the center of the only village that lies between the beginning of our trip tonight and its conclusion, and that mars an otherwise quite empty road. The little place is known for its ruined abbey, or perhaps it is a ruined mill. But believe me, please. This route was the most fortuitous I could select. I wished only for an unimpeded journey. However, the sore spot of this little village was unavoidable. At any rate, you deserve to know the worst and the best, and should be as clear as I am about our situation and hence be in a position to prepare yourself moment by moment to achieve understanding and avoid merely shocking or destructive surprises. So let me warn you that tonight we will encounter only three genuine points of danger, though unhappily the rain has become a kind of general hazard, albeit one out of your hands and of little interest to me. But back to the three genuine points of danger. The final turnoff to the abandoned farm, the Roman aqueduct, and the village we are rapidly approaching—each of these will present us with grave danger, which I will not attempt to conceal, as I have said. However, I am confident about the aqueduct while our journey itself is preparation for the final turnoff which, hopefully, by that time you will

encounter as something quite beyond danger. So we may discount the
final turnoff. I may even go so far right now as to guarantee you its
serenity.

But to be perfectly honest, the village is something else again. It is
careening toward us this very moment, only a few words or a few
breaths away. Of course the little street through that village is short,
hardly more than several lengths of the car or one of those sylvan paths
that take you from the intersection of two dusty roads to the turnstile
at the edge of the field. So it is a short village street but obstinate, and
unlighted, and extremely narrow, and bordered for its entire length by
a high, sinuous stone wall overtopped by the now wet tile roofs of the
village houses and the limbs of an occasional dead tree. Throughout our
passage through the wretched place the side of the car will be within
touching distance of the heavy stone. If you insist on looking, you will
see an infinite rapid shuffling of rock and wood; iron door handles and
high broken shutters will fly in your face; our way shall consist of impossible angles, a near collision with the fountain in the central square,
a terrible encounter with a low arch. We shall have become a locomotive
in a maze, and the noise will be the worst of all. Our lights will be like
searchlights swiveling in unimaginable confinement, and a forlorn, artificial rose and the granite foot of one of their crucified Christs and a
sudden low chimney will all approach us like a handful of thrown
stones. But the noise will be the worst. It will be as if we ourselves were
a rocket firing in the caves and catacombs of history. Let us hope that
the cats of the village are not as prevalent as the rabbits of our rural
highway. Let us hope that we are not deflected by a shard of tile or
little rusted iron key or the slick, white femur of some recently slaugh-
tered animal. Otherwise we shall brush the stone walls, swerve, bring
down the entire village to a pile of rubble which we shall no doubt drag
after us a hundred meters or more.

There is nothing to be done about the sound. But you may well wish
to close your eyes, or simply lean forward and bury your face in your
hands. The entire deafening passage will last an eternity but also no
time at all. Why see it? Why not leave the seeing as well as the driving
to me? And you might amuse yourself by considering what the peasants
will think when we shake their street and start them shuddering in their
poor beds: that we are only an immoral man and his laughing mistress
roaring through the rainy night on some devilish and frivolous escapade.
Or consider what we shall leave in our wake: only an ominous trembling
and a half dozen falling tiles.

But do you see it? . . . Just there? . . . That huddled darkness of habitation? . . . The stones in the rain? . . . Here it is. . . . Hold on. . . .

Come, come, *cher ami*. It is behind us. But now you know how trustworthy I really am.

Do you realize that among all the admiring readers of your slender and now somewhat rare volumes there are those who, if given even the briefest glimpse into your life and mine, would consider me a silly coward and you a worthless soul? If the invisible camera existed, and if it recorded this adventure of ours from beginning to end, and if the reel of film were salvaged and then late one night its images projected onto a tattered white screen in some movie house smelling of disinfectant and damp clothing and containing almost no audience at all, it is then that your malignant admirers would stand in those cold aisles and dismiss me as a silly coward and condemn you as a worthless soul. As if any coward could be silly, or any soul worthless. But then it is what you at least deserve, since you have spent your life sitting among small audiences in your black trousers and open white shirt and with your cigarette in your mouth and your elbows on your knees and your hands clasped—like a man on a toilet—telling those eager or hostile women that the poet is always a betrayer, a murderer, and that the writing of poetry is like a descent into death. But that was talk, mere talk. Now, if given the chance, you would speak from experience.

As for me, I have said it already and will not hesitate to say it again: I am an avowed coward. I am partial to cowards. If I am unable to detect in a stranger some hint of his weakness, some faint gesture of recognition passed back and forth between us furtively and beneath the table, or at least the briefest glimpse of his particular white flag raised in the empty field that is himself, then I am filled with hopelessness, with a sadness as close to despair as rain to hail. But who is not? Who in the very depths of the dry well of his "worthless" soul does not loathe the stage setting that holds him prisoner? Who does not fear the inexplicable fact of his existence? Who does not dread the unimaginable condition of not existing? It is easy enough to say that tomorrow you are going to turn into a rose or a flower. But this optimism of the believer in the natural world is the cruelest ruse of all, a sentimentality worthy of children. Of course I am overstating the situation grossly. But if you cannot find the rift in your self-confidence or admit to the pale, white roots of your cowardice where it thrives in your own dry well, then you will never ride the dolphin or behave with the tenderness of the true sensualist.

Only a bumpkin would call your cowardly bad-dreamer "silly."

What, *cher ami*, still arguing? Still unable to put aside self-preservation, the survival instinct, the low-level agitation of the practical mind, the whole pack of useless trumps of the ego? (In the deck that represents the ego all the cards are the same and each one of them is a trump. But these are the liars, the worthless trumps.) But why continue wasting your time and mine by inventing false arguments which I will only refute? Your arguments are hardly gifts to the mind. You are not interested in what they mean. It pains me to see you pulling them out of your sleeve—another argument, another trump—and in each one to hear you shout what you have been shouting the whole night: stop talking, stop the car, set me free. That has been your only refrain, through all I have said. But why can't you listen? Tonight of all nights why can't you give me one moment of genuine response? Without it, as I have said, our expedition is as wasteful as everything else.

Let me repeat: you do not want me to take you seriously but only to heed your shouts in the dark, which is why for the first time in your life you are not only wheezing but wheezing on the very brink of savagery. You are strangling in the ill-concealed savagery of your resistance. But you know my position. It will not change. Surely I must be able to strike that one slight blow that will cause all your oppressive defenses to fall, to disappear, leaving you free indeed to share equally in the responsibility I have assumed, short-lived or not.

As it so happens, this particular argument of yours is just as obvious but perhaps a little more interesting than the rest, and I have long ago faced it studiously. Some men, or so goes this line of reasoning, search with uncanny directness for what they most fear to find. We rush off to die precisely because death's terrible contradiction (it will come, we cannot know what it is; it is totally certain, it is totally uncertain) for some of us fills each future moment, like tears of poison, with an anguish finally so great that only the dreaded experience itself provides relief. We are so consumed by what we wish to avoid that we can no longer avoid it. "Now" becomes better than "later." We run to the ax instead of allowing ourselves to be dragged. And so forth. And as one of the few interesting efforts to make sense of suicide (except for the clinical, to which I do not subscribe) this particular argument of yours has its appeal. We have heard it before, we have listened, it has a good ring. We can imagine the shoe fitting. It is possible, it is exactly the kind of paradoxical behavior that engages all but the bumpkins. And who knows? Perhaps it has cut short the lives of a few bumpkins as well.

But this one is not the lever to pry me from my purpose. My clarity is genuine, not false, while my dread, as you in your pathetic hope imagine it, does not exist. What more can I say? I respect your theory; I respect the fear from which you yourself are suffering (though it oppresses me horribly, horribly); perhaps it would be better for all concerned if just this once I could find you in the right and could hear the shell cracking, so to speak, and all at once find myself overcome with fear and so pull to the side of the road, thus ending our journey, and in rain and darkness sit sobbing over the wheel. Then I could take Chantal's place back there on the floor and slowly, slowly, you could drive the three of us to Tara. In that case you would take to your bed for two days, Chantal would return to her riding lessons, I would follow your lead to the asylum that effected your famous cure.

So it would go, if you were in the right. But you are not. If I could discover that my clarity is a sham and that I am afraid of death and have devised the entirety of our glassy web because of that same fear of death, I would give myself happily to sobbing over the wheel and spend the rest of my days (after undertaking the cure) in trying to make restitution to you and Chantal. But I can make no such discovery, because there is no such discovery for me to make. Of course I have my qualms. Who would not? But as for this maniacal dread of death that would explain my planning, my determination, my mounting exhilaration as well as my need for a couple of companions, witnesses, supporters to accompany me in the final flash of panic—well, it is unknown to me, your maniacal dread.

But let me be honest. Let me admit that it was precisely the fear of committing a final and irrevocable act that plagued my childhood, my youth, my early manhood, and that drew me with so much conviction and compassion to those grainy, tabloidal, photographic renderings of bodies uniquely fixed, but nonetheless fixed, in their own deaths. And in those years and as a corollary to my preoccupation with the cut string I could not repair, the step I could not retrieve, I was also plagued by what I defined as the fear of no response. It is true. I have nothing to hide. In those days (needless to say I was then no sensualist) I required recognition from girls behind counters, heroes in stone, stray dogs. Let a policeman dip his stick in the wrong direction and I suffered chills in the spine. The frown was my *bête noire*. If the world did not respond to me totally, immediately, in leaf, street sign, the expression of strangers, then I did not exist—or existed only in the misery of youthful loneliness. But to be recognized in any way was to be given your selfhood on a plate and to be loved, loved, which is what I most demanded. But no more. The heat of those feelings is quite gone. I have long since known what it is to be loved. Now, tonight, I want not relief but purity.

But of course I have just now asked you for "one moment of genuine response." So you see how close you have come to the mark.

I do not know why that figure of speech (the kneeling marksman, the drawn bow, the golden arrow) reminds me so insistently of little Pascal. But so it does, the great naked hunter calling forth the little child like a voice from the shadows. Perhaps little Pascal was destined to become a larger-than-life-size hunter, naked (except for the silver bow, the golden arrow) and stalking his invisible victim among the white boulders beneath a vast sky of unchanging blue. At least I always saw the grown man in little Pascal. By the time he died, when he was not yet three years of age, he had already become a child god, an infant Caesar. Yes, he had already attained his true character by the time he died.

It is a pity that you had no children. So much intimacy with Chantal surely precludes your thinking of her as your own child. But perhaps it is time for you and me to share Pascal—since anything is possible, and since nothing matters, and since he only exists among the white boulders. But it is true: Pascal has been dead for so many years that he might as well be your son as well as mine. What's that? You long ago decided against fathering children? But everything considered, how right you were. Now that you mention it, the thought of a child surviving you is out of the question. But of course little Pascal survives nothing at all.

And yet who can fail to eulogize our infant Caesar?

He was a fat and contrary tyrant, *cher ami*, and in his third year he began each of our days by subjugating Honorine and me, and even Chantal, to the essential paradox of his fatness, his pink skin, the crown of authority with which he masked his sweet nature. Admittedly, Honorine is not small. But neither is she large in her bones, in her flesh. How then did she mother a child so beautiful in his naked weight, so fatly and gently erotic for all his recalcitrance and pretended ferocity? We shall never know. He was his own source, I often thought, and he is gone. But I saw his little fat body on the spit as often as I saw it crowned; in the chubbiness and gleam of his totally sweet and spoiled nature he was that desirable, that strong.

Yes, he came to Honorine and me with every sunrise, bold and bare, having stripped off his white nightshirt and wearing only his buttery skin and disapproving frown and air of infant determination. With every sunrise he pulled away the bedclothes not from me but from Honorine, who was always his happy match for nudity. Perhaps you are not able to visualize those mornings. But I see them still: dawn at the window, sunlight falling across our bed from that window and from the rose and plum-colored tapestry on our bedroom wall, the sound of distant bells, the scent of coffee, and the birds in the air and already the small automobiles congregating somewhere on the cobblestones. And then the entrance of Pascal, the open door, the light winking from the long glass handle, and our little naked son approaching us with his pink cheeks and pouting underlip and little penis which Honorine always used to touch with the tip of her finger, as if that tiny sexual organ belonged not to Pascal but to the winged infant cast in bronze. You must see such a morning as clearly as I do, *cher ami*, if only to know that in fact I am not a person who despises life. Quite the contrary.

But in he would come, pouting, wordless, making his little belly fatter than ever (as might some exotic fish with air) and in my own arousal from sleep I would see his bare plumpness and the light in his fine-spun golden hair. And the lip, the beautiful underlip thrust out and moist in his unmistakable message: that he was the joy of all who saw him, but in return there was nothing in all the world to give him joy. Too ripe, too beautiful, too lordly, pleasing but never pleased—such was the fate and character he had created for himself at that early age. But there he would be, the brown eyes filled with accusation, the sunlight flooding the spot where he stood, the tiny spigot crooked and gleaming in the base of the belly. In that moment the faun in the tapestry would quiver at the sight of him and the silver dove on Honorine's commode would fly.

Well, it was always the same. He would wait until I had had my awesome look at him and until Honorine had begun to smile in her feigned sleep and to make her soft welcoming sound, and then cloaked in all his slow assurance he would march across the carpet and reach out one chubby hand and pull the bedclothes from his mother's nude, youthful body. For a moment the two of us, Pascal and I, would gaze on Honorine, who would continue to conceal her wakefulness and, for our sakes, would incline her cheek toward the pillow and arch her back and stretch out an arm and luxuriate in the aroma of her night's perfume.

Do you see her? Do you see Pascal and me? Are you listening?

Well, after that moment, and as if he had received an invisible and all-important sign of acquiescence from Honorine, little Pascal would begin to climb. Yes, with great deliberation he would climb onto our bed (the very same antiquity in which at present Honorine lies sleeping) and then climb onto his mother's warm and well-shaped body. Yes, with frowning difficulty he would mount that body, straddle the hips, seat himself, position himself, until his rosy and sturdy little buttocks were firmly, squarely in place atop Honorine's cluster of purple grapes. There he would sit. Enthroned. And he was quite aware of how he was sitting and how thoroughly his own baby flesh covered and cushioned the flesh of his mother's grapes. I knew what he knew because there was no mistaking the way he would glance in my direction, settle his weight, and then raise his chin in a perfect gesture of self-satisfied defiance.

Then Honorine would open her eyes, she would laugh, she would seize both his hands in hers, with her hips and stomach she would imitate the gait of a trotting horse. Again and again she would murmur *cheri* and beg for a kiss, which he always refused to give her. As for me, at that moment I would wish my little Pascal a good morning, to which inevitably he replied that it was not a good morning but a bad one.

There he would sit holding us in the power of his princely manner and infant eroticism until at last and rubbing her eyes, poor Chantal would appear obediently to haul him away.

How did Honorine survive his death? How did I? But if he had lived, his little body growing and his infant eroticism maturing into impressive masculinity and his head day by day swelling to the round of the laurels, still he would have fared no better than poor Chantal. Actually, he would have fared much worse.

But I myself cloaked his little stone cross in satin. So it is not as if I have never known what it is to grieve. But perhaps I am the man little Pascal might have become had he lived. Perhaps it is he who inhabits me now in his death. Who knows?

You will not believe it, but only this morning I visited for the last time my one-legged doctor. Yes, only hours ago and on this of all days, I held up my end of our yearly medical rendezvous. But I am attentive to your every nuance, even to the nuances of your stubborn silence, and now despite your misery and against your will you are objecting to yourself that my concern for my health on the day of my premeditated death (and yours, and Chantal's) is worse, much worse, than rabbits, rain, the invisible motion picture camera with its wet distended lens, the emotional orchestration of the radio you refused to hear. At first glance you would appear to be right: illusory circumstances are beginning to justify your horrified contempt for a man who might be engaged in committing drastic actions not from clarity and calculation but merely to satisfy his inmost urge to saw away on the tremulous violin of his self-love. And yet once again you are wrong. Wrong. Because it was not I who was responsible for this morning's appointment with the crippled physician but rather that elderly woman with the girlish body who is the doctor's nurse and secretary combined. It is true: she notified me of today's appointment long after I myself had figuratively torn today's blank page from my appointment book. And what do you think of the fact that the doctor's rooms are situated directly across from the very restaurant which you yourself happened to choose for your dinner this evening with Chantal, the doctor's rooms and the restaurant facing each other on opposite sides of that same little public garden where the lovers sit holding hands on the cold benches? In other words, this morning while waiting for my medical examination to commence, and stripped to the waist in anticipation of needles and the doctor's archaic X-ray machine, I myself stood at a dusty window in shivering contemplation of the exact same suffering old palm tree which you and Chantal regarded this evening over your soup and wine. But you are already familiar with the pleasure I take in these alignments which to me are the lifeblood of form without meaning.

At the appointed hour, then, I touched the bell button, noting as usual the pathetic opulence of the brass nameplate, and climbed the obviously little-used cold stones to the almost empty room where I inhaled the first trace of that antiseptic smell in which in a few moments I would be engulfed. I heard the air stirring in the rest of his chambers, noted in several chipped, white ceramic ash trays the week-old remains of his dead cigarettes. Of course I was well acquainted with his habit of dragging himself to this very room and seating himself and smoking his cigarettes, reading one of the ancient journals, the doctor waiting alone in the room intended for patients who were never there.

Can you understand the peace and satisfaction I felt in that place? The visit was perfectly routine, nothing happened out of the ordinary. And yet from entrance to exit I could not have felt more at home amidst all the paradoxes of this establishment: the unused instruments and archaic machines of medical science located within medieval walls; the sound of birds roosting somewhere amongst surgical knives and old books; the faint smell of cooking food which the antiseptic chemical could not disguise; the doctor himself, who was skilled but thought to be unsavory, and who in his own affliction exemplified the general pomposity and backwardness of our nation's corps of butchering physicians and who in his broken marriage exemplified the soundness of our sexual mores. Then too, I knew for a fact that once every week this poor, ruined man sat entirely alone for precisely two hours in a little nearby movie house devoted only to the showing of so-called indecent films. Understandably, it was this habit rather than the missing leg or absent wife that accounted for his unsavory reputation. No wonder I admired and enjoyed his crippled presence.

As I say, there were no surprises. The doctor, as usual, forced himself to walk the length of the corridor to greet me, thrusting to the side one fat, startled hand for balance and swinging in great arcs from the hip his artificial limb, the use of which typically he had never mastered. We met with effusion; he consulted his files; he enquired about my general health and the health of my wife; unbidden I removed my shirt and undershirt; he disappeared; he returned to his desk; the artificial leg obtruded between us in full and menacing view. Again I welcomed silently the trembling hand, the mucus thick in his throat, the cigarette that was burning his fingers. Again I appraised the awkwardness of the ill-fitting leg, noting as usual that our nation is simply not adept at the crafting of artificial limbs because we are not concerned with the needs and imperfections of the individual human body. Again I realized that in the middle of every night the doctor now puffing and coughing beside me, fumbling over my naked chest with his cold and unsteady hands, must lie awake listening to this same artificial leg walking to and fro on the other side of his bedroom door. He was devoting what remained of his life to this hollow leg which wore a green sock and dusty shoe. But dominated or not by the ugly leg, nonetheless he was listening to the strength of my absolutely reliable heart. I regretted that I had never sat beside him in the old movie house.

I waited, I enjoyed the chilly air on the skin of my chest, shoulders, arms; I surveyed the diseased palm tree below in the public garden; I nodded in pleased recognition when the crippled and perspiring doctor knocked one of his full ash trays to the floor, as he always did. I was pleased with the appearance of the nurse-secretary, whose body had the shape of a girl's and the texture of an old crone's. While she drew as usual a handsome quantity of blood from the thick blue vein in my left arm, I listened to the doctor who was breathing wetly through his nose, his mouth, his nose and mouth together. I listened with pleasure; with pleasure I perceived once more that the old nurse-secretary had dabbed herself not with perfume but with the overpowering antiseptic that killed flowers and defined our circumstances.

Time passed like ivory beads on a black thread. My own blood climbed inside the glass. Again I had my brief affair with the old X-ray machine which, after clanking and groaning, rewarded my patience with its sound like a flock of wounded geese in uncertain flight. And I passed exactly the required amount of urine, watched the doctor himself wrapping up the small warm flask with a string and paper, once again marveled that so much painful incongruity could be assembled so awkwardly into a single person.

Well, once again the doctor pronounced me in perfect health, as you would imagine. And of course he suspected nothing, nothing. In all his discomfort and disproportion he retained his purity. Little did he know that in several days and on the other side of the city a laboratory technician, unshaven and smoking a yellow cigarette, would analyze the blood of a man already dead; or that the hazy image of ribs and single lung on the photographic plate would represent only as much reality as the white organs lubricating each other in one of his weekly films.

But there is no justice in the world, since we may safely say that that poor one-legged creature has finally lost his only patient, and through no fault of his own. But what, you ask, if even this wretched man continues to live, why shouldn't we? Why does your closest friend not have within himself that cripple's determination to remain alive? Well, let me answer you slowly, quietly. The problem is that you are being emotional again, rather than rational. You must remember that both my legs are sound and that my wife is faithful. Do you understand?

Yes, she is vomiting. But you need not have mentioned it. I have perfect hearing and am just as sensitive as you to those faint, terrible noises. Do you think I am not listening? That I have not been listening? After all, there is nothing worse than painful human sounds unattached to words. And the contents of my own daughter's stomach. . . . Even you will concede that my bitterness would be all the more justified. But I am not bitter. And despite all our so-called natural inclinations, why should we not agree that poor Chantal has earned her vomiting? It is the best she can do. And surely it is no worse than your wheezing.

Actually, the music of melodrama (had you allowed us the pleasures of my superb car radio) would not have been a sodden orchestration of wave upon wave of uninteresting feeling but rather a light, sinuous background of muted jazz. The detached and somewhat popular syncopation would have cushioned our every turn while the clear tones of, say, a clarinet would have prevailed and, had he been able to hear them, would have given greater poignancy to the distance between the sleepless goatherd and the momentary, cruel appearance of our headlights in the righthand corner of the wet night. Do you hear that black clarinet? Do you hear the somewhat breezy quality of this dry and sophisticated music? The melody is pleasing, there is even a certain elegance and occasionally a dash of humor in the glassy accompaniment of the invisible piano. How perfect such easy lyricism is for us. What splendid, impersonal sweetness it would have contributed to the tensions of our imaginary and deliberately amateurish film. Well, the radio is already tuned. You have only to extend your arm, reach out with your fingers, touch the knob. But still you are not tempted? Of course you are not. I understand.

A trifle faster? Yes, you are quite right that we are now traveling a breath or two faster than we were. Now is the moment when I must make my ultimate demands. As you can see, my arms are stiffening, my fingers are flexing though I never remove my palms from the wheel, my concentrating face is abnormally white, and now, like many men destined for the pleasures and perils of high-speed driving, now my mouth is working in subtle consort with eyes, hands, feet, so that my silent lips are moving with the car itself, as if I am now talking as well as driving us to our destination. And we are approaching it, that final destination of ours. We are drawing near. Soon we shall be entering the perimeter of Honorine's most puzzling and yet soothing dream. And now beneath the hood of the car our engine is glowing as red as an immense ruby. How unfortunate that to us it is invisible. How unfortunate that the rain is determined to keep pace with our journey.

But while we are on the subject of invalid doctors and vomiting children, and since tonight we seem to be taking our national inventory, so to speak, allow me to say in passing that generally our physical institutions are indeed a match for the inadequacies or eccentricities of our professional personnel. In other words, our buildings of public service are as bad as the people who occupy them. Take the hospital nearest La Roche, for instance. I have not had any firsthand experience with this ominous and in a way amusing place, and in fact have never seen it. But on good authority and thanks to my theory of likenesses, which I have already described to you at length, I know for a certainty that this dark and drafty little place of about twenty beds is not equipped with any separate or special entrance for the reception of emergency cases. None at all. A few lights are burning; several cooks are smoking their stubby pipes in the kitchen; the entire drab interior of the place smells like a field of rotting onions. And there is no emergency entrance. No means of swift and ready access between the narrow cobbled street outside and that small whitewashed room to the right and rear where simple first aid may be administered. No access to this small room for bleeding truck driver or possibly his corpse except through the kitchen. The kitchen. It is a scandal. Even our own remains, such as they may be, will be hurried on rattling litters through the steamy kitchen of the miserable hospital near La Roche, that kitchen in which the cauldrons of soup for the coming day will provide a fitting context for the shoeless foot at dawn. Do you see the humor of it, the outrage? But everywhere it is the same: rooms without doors, sinks without drains, conduits that will never be connected to any water supply, corpses or bleeding victims forever passing through the kitchens of our nation's hospitals.

But why, you ask, why this terrible and at the same time humorous correspondence between physical building and human occupant? The answer is obvious: it is simply that there is no difference between the artist, the architect, the workman, the physician, the bloody victim and the cook slicing his cabbage. One and all they share our national psychological heritage. One and all they are driven by the twin engines of ignorance and willful barbarianism. You nod, you also are familiar with these two powerful components of our national character, ignorance and willful barbarianism. Yes, everywhere you turn, and even among the most gifted of us, the most extensively educated, these two brute forces of motivation will eventually emerge. The essential information is always missing; sensitivity is a mere veil to self-concern. We are all secret encouragers of ignorance, at heart we are all willful barbarians.

But indeed, these qualities also account for our charm, our good humor, our handsome physiques, our arrogance, our explosive servility. We are as we wish to be. We would have it no other way. Our national type is desirable as well as inescapable. You and I? You and I are two perfect examples of our national type.

The reason we make such a perfect pair, such an agreeable match, is that you are a full-fledged Leo, while through the marshes of my own stalwart Leo there flows a little dark rivulet of Scorpio. You were unaware of it? But then naturally you could not have suspected anything of my Scorpio influence since I deliberately though casually concealed even the slightest shade of that all-too-suspect influence from your detection. You see how capable I am of deception, at least of any deception which in my judgment is for our mutual good. But thus we have one more scrap to toss on the heap of our triumphant irony. Because in our case it now appears that the poet is the thick-skinned and simpleminded beast of the ego, while contrary to popular opinion, it is your ordinary privileged man who turns out to reveal in the subtlest of ways all those faint sinister qualities of the artistic mind. Yes, you are the creature who roars in the wind while I am the powerful bug on the wall. But you are not interested? You are not amused? And yet if only you would pause a moment to think, *cher ami,* then you would realize that behind my coldest actions and most jocular manner there lies not hostility but the deepest affection. After all, my Scorpio influence inspires me to unimaginable tenderness.

I applaud the dark night. I love the darkness. Not merely for regressive pleasures: for comfort, security, the peace of the dream. No, I am much too active a person to stop with mere sensual immobility, though I am not at all denying my proclivities in that direction as well. No, it is simply that the night is to my eye as is the pair of goggles to the arc-welder. Through the thick green lens of the night I see only the brightest and most frightening light.

For instance, the cemetery we are about to pass—yes, a cemetery, as luck would have it, along with the rabbit and gentle syncopation of the muted jazz which, at this moment, naturally intensifies and quickens—the cemetery we shall shortly pass is already clear to my eye, brilliant, rock-hard, motionless. You would see nothing even if you looked, so don't bother. I see quite well enough for the two of us. At any rate the cemetery—and now, as a matter of fact, we are abreast of it, just there on the left—the cemetery stands now before my eyes, small, rising in tiers, a very old and typically well-ordered arrangement of crosses and crypts and mausoleums of black marble, white marble, some kind of deep gray stone, and it is quite as if we were staring at that small village of the dead (the likeness is most appropriate, *cher ami*) from a stationary vehicle parked in our empty wind-blown, golden field directly across from that small, excellent example of our morbid artistry. Yes, that is precisely how totally and clearly I see our cemetery, thanks to the night. And there is sunlight but no sun, a quality of deadened daytime colors that could only be perceived in the blackest and, I might add, the wettest of nights. The white vases, the red flowers composed of wax, the sagging ribbons, the tiny photographs that might have been stripped from an album depicting all the participants in the last great war, and the rows of gravel and little barred windows and stone rectangles constructed to the dimensions of the human body, and, thank goodness, not a single mourner to be seen in that entire conglomerate of piety and bad taste —well, now you have an idea of the true reason I so enjoy driving at night. It is not merely because the roads are generally unused at night. Not at all.

But was that cemetery somewhat familiar to you, *cher ami?* It should have been.

Silence. The bird in flight. Silence falling between driver and passenger who find themselves deadlocked on a lonely road, deadlocked in their purposes, deadlocked between love and hatred, memory and imagination. But you need not bother to raise your chin, turn your head, rouse yourself from all your afflictions into unhappy speech. I know what you are thinking. I could not agree more heartily. Silence is what we are after, you and I. Silence. I long for it also. You are not alone.

We will not be denied. After all, we are now on the near edge of recklessness, it is no longer even a question of time to spare, and beyond us the trees are dying, the tiny shoots are turning a bright green, the landmarks are falling to the left and right of us so quickly that their significance is fading in direct proportion to our mounting preoccupation with ourselves, with what is to come. Yes, silence is consuming sight.

The moral of it all is trust me but do not believe me—ever. Why, even as I deny the fleeting landmarks I cannot help but call your attention to that small church set back from the road in that clump of naked trees on our right. Naturally the church has nothing to do with the cemetery. The cemetery is already far, far behind us. It is gone. No, this is the church that is guarded by the old crone who tends the place with her cane and dog. She is an insufferable old creature who tried to frighten me away the very afternoon I stopped and strolled about and committed the landmark of her ugly little church to memory. She has a beautiful cough, I can tell you that. And I knew at once that she was no more taken in by the weedy sanctity of the little church and mutilated calvary than was I. At any rate I had only an objective interest in the steeple, as a point of essential reference, and a personal interest in the fountain which I knew I would discover in the tall grass behind the church.

The fountain was there, as I knew it would be. And just think, according to local legend it was the Fountain of Clarity. You can imagine how pleased I was to stand in the last of the sun with this precise moment of our dark passage fixed in my mind—hearing the rain, the engine, the tires, seeing our lights—and at the same time to lean forward and regard my own face in the little pool of water that lies in the depths of the Fountain of Clarity. Its ancient artisan could not have known that one day a privileged man such as myself would so admire his work. The creators of that ancient legend could not have known that I have never expected anything at all from my life except clarity. I have pursued clarity as relentlessly as the worshipers pursue their Christ. And there I stood, noting the algae in the bottom of the pool, the paleness of the still water, the rough ingenious construction of the fountain hidden in the tall grass. It was a pleasing coincidence. But my own face, our dark night that was as real to me as it is this moment, the automobile that was awaiting me on the dirt road in the shadow of the wretched calvary—it was nothing, nothing at all compared with the intensity with which I was then contemplating the existence of our own Honorine. Your Muse, my clarity, I cannot convey to you my satisfaction as the thought of Honorine filled the silence of an earthly spot which, except for the fountain, was otherwise perhaps a little too picturesque. But if I had ever worn a wedding band, an idea which for me has always been distasteful, certainly I would have removed it then and dropped it as an offering into the cold pool where the cows drank and the old woman filled her jugs and bottles.

No doubt it is just as well that I was not wearing a ring. But tell me, are you feeling better?

Approaching. Yes, we are approaching closer. And once again, you see, I must shift the gears. Shift them from one velvet plateau to the next. And now how directly we are propelled toward Honorine in her mammoth bed. By now she must indeed be smiling in the depths of her sleep.

But of course she has left the old lantern burning for us as usual, burning in our honor and for our protection. If I remember, I will point it out to you—that old lantern swaying on the end of its chain.

Jealousy? Jealousy?

After all I have said . . . after my woman of luxury . . . after Monique . . . after all my fervent protestations of affection . . . after all I have done to clarify our situation and to allay your fears—now, as a last resort, you are finally willing to accuse me of mere jealousy? As if I am only one of those florid money-makers who is afraid to thrust even his fingers into the secret places of his stenographer's attractive body and yet turns green, as they say, whenever he imagines that his lonely wife harbors in her heart of hearts the quivering desire to watch while her husband's best friend climbs nude and dripping from his tubful of hot water? Is it with such implications that you expect to stop me, to bring me to earth, so to speak? As if on this note I will suddenly recognize myself and bow to your judgment, exclaiming that, yes, for all these years I have been an excellent actor outwardly while inwardly nursing the most unpleasant banalities of sexual envy? As if you are the hero and I the villain, the one openly and, I might say, foolishly accepting the favors of the other's honest wife and naïve daughter until the other has finally spent enough years drinking slime (in his toilet, in his monastic bed chamber, in his cold automobile parked side by side with his wife's in what was once the stable) in order to act? But are you then so foolish? And could any man, even me, bear such violent feelings for that length of time? And are you suggesting that Honorine is not sensitive, perceptive? After all, if I had in fact been concealing and suffering all this time the latent frenzy of jealousy, would it not have exposed itself in some faint sign which Honorine, in all her concern for my welfare, would have noted at once? Well, you can see what I think of your last resort. This argument is not your avenue of escape.

Of course it is true that you are not a very good poet. I have always made my opinion plain. And it is true that all your disclaimers (about your worth, the size of your audience, the importance of your prizes, the extent of your creative torment, the unhappiness of your life, and so forth) were always to me offensive. And it is true that you are an emotional parasite. Would you deny it? As for your dreadful and eternal seriousness, it is indeed true that on certain occasions, when you have been brooding alone before the fire, when you have been brooding with

Honorine over some dull line of verse, when after a glass or two of cognac you have converted your brooding into a sullen, pretentious monologue for the benefit of Honorine and Chantal and me, then I have indeed longed to hear you suddenly give voice to a single, extended, piercing shriek of laughter. But no more than that. Never have I wished you pain or discomfort more than that. So please do not accuse me of being jealous. It is a bad idea and a poor ploy.

On the other hand, it is also quite true that even after sharing so many intimate years together, still there is a great deal that you do not know about Honorine and Chantal and me. Witness my discussion to-night. And this discussion is, I assure you, the merest hint of what you do not know about the three of us. Only the clear, white, brutal tip of the iceberg, to borrow a familiar but indispensable figure of speech. But wait. Stop for another moment. Consider everything you do indeed know about your mistress and her only two living blood or legal rela-tives. If you exposed this information in one of your poems you would embarrass the three of us for a lifetime. At least such a revelation would embarrass me if not Chantal and Honorine, who might in fact cherish this permanent form of your devotion.

But have you forgotten it all? Need I remind you of the afternoon and even the hour of day when you wrote your first inscription for Honorine—wrote it, that is, in her copy of your first book of poems? Yes, Honorine's treasured copy of that volume; your earliest and, I later heard, most derivative poems; my own gold-tipped pen which you bor-rowed for that occasion with hardly a word. Don't you remember? There were times when I might have wished that Honorine had chosen to show me that first inscription of yours, but then there were others when I was equally pleased that she had instead chosen to guard it selfishly from any eyes but hers. At least I caught a glimpse of your black, flowery handwriting that afternoon and, to be honest, thereafter kept my gold-tipped fountain pen capped for a week.

But what of all those first days and months and seasons when I retired early to my own sumptuous but monastic room, took unneces-sary business trips, bundled Chantal off to mountain holidays? Have you forgotten how considerate I was, and how discreet, ingenious, flat-tering? Don't you remember Honorine's pleasure when there were two gifts of flowers on the piano in a single day? Or all those winter evenings when, on the white leather divan, the three of us enjoyed together the portfolio of large, clear photographs depicting the charming pornographic poses of a most intelligent woman of good birth? Surely you remember that visual history of the life of Honorine from youth to middle age in which her own appreciation of her piquant autoeroticism becomes increasingly subtle, increasingly bold? Surely you will not have forgotten the night when you remarked that every man hopes for an ordinary wife who will prove a natural actress in the theater of sex? Well, I savored that remark for days. I still do. It was perhaps the only poetic remark you ever made.

I could go on. I could remind you of our disagreements, which were to be expected, or of our "family" celebrations, such as the event of my fiftieth birthday when you decided at last to inscribe one of your precious books for the so-called head of the household. I could remind you of all those physical moments when you managed to convey your awareness of my pleasure, generosity, total absence of perturbation. For instance, I need say no more than "the king drinks!" to recall to you those yearly festive nights when three of us sat around our flower-crowned cake and with shouts of happiness and admiration hailed the fourth. Surely you remember that you were always the king, though I would not remind you of how foolish you looked with your famous cigarette and open white shirt and paper crown. You accepted your royalty begrudgingly, as you did your popularity, but accepted it all the same. Or, for instance, it would be a simple matter for me to say that single word, those several words, which would immediately revive in your memory the sight of your body, of mine, of Honorine removing her nightgown of plum-colored velours before the embers still glowing in the conical recess of her bedroom fireplace.

It so happens that the book you inscribed for me no longer exists. But no matter. You know what I am talking about, and none of it—none of it—can be denied. So you must not accuse me of being jealous. Now is not the time to offer me a wound so deep.

But now I must tell you that once we pass Tara I will say nothing more. And I warn you now that if you make a single movement or utter a single sound once we pass Tara your death will not be an ironic triumph but a prolonged and hapless agony.

And yet I do not mean to adopt that tone of voice. Will you excuse it? To clear the air, I can tell you that whenever anything unusual is about to happen my chest itches. Yes, the skin in the area of my sternum is especially sensitive to unexpected occurrences, changes of scene, threats of impending violence. And now it is itching!

Chez Lulu. That's the place. I remember it well. And how fortunate for me that it is you rather than Lulu who is my companion for tonight's undertaking, since Lulu may have been an agreeable and even seductive giant of a young man but was hardly fit for the mental and emotional rigors of the private apocalypse. He was an excellent host in the establishment that bore his name, but I cannot imagine anyone more frustrating in a discussion such as this one and occurring under these the most difficult of conditions. Actually our charming, dark-haired young brute of a man could not possibly have been your substitute, never fear. And yet both Honorine and Chantal were fond of him. At any rate it was in *Chez Lulu* that Chantal gained her emotional though not legal majority in a spectacle that you especially would have enjoyed. Chantal could not have been more than fifteen years of age at the time.

Well, anyone with a penchant for the ocean and for summers promising a certain harmless decadence will recognize *Chez Lulu* from merely its name. You too must have discovered it in a dozen seaside resorts: the harbor barely large enough for a handful of sailboats and a yacht or two, the summer evening rich with the scent of both the rose and the crab, the couples strolling or arousing each other beneath the aromatic trees, and there, fronted by a few feet of powdered sand, there the bar-restaurant which for its disreputable music and growing adolescents and strings of brightly colored lights is indispensable to any such dark and idyllic cove noted for quietude, natural beauty, safe swimming. With *Chez Lulu* the glorious nighttime summer shore would have offered no champagne vying with spilled beer, no irruption of girlish laughter, no hint of first (or possibly last) romance. Perhaps you are already beginning to smile. I need say no more. The point is that until we concluded that we preferred to spend our summers in an Alpine resort instead of beside the sea in the second and smaller dwelling owned by Honorine's mother, Chantal and Honorine and I were among the most favored patrons of *Chez Lulu*. There, I can tell you, we ate mussels roasted on olive twigs and laughed with appreciation at Lulu himself, who as owner and master of ceremonies was large, handsome, amusing, and the possessor of an unlimited store of sexually aggressive ways. You know his type: one of those tall, strapping young men who would have made an excellent athlete had it not been for his relentlessly dissolute nature.

Well, by now you will have the scene in mind: a warm late night at *Chez Lulu*, Honorine and I seated together at a small wicker table at the edge of the sand; the young accordian player and of course Lulu already making spectacles of themselves on a low, crude, wooden stage facing away from the sea and toward the animated crowd of Lulu's favorite patrons old and young; the protective matting of bamboo strips rustling above our heads; the colored lights strung like a bright fringe about the perimeter of the place; the tide going out beyond us in the sultry darkness; Lulu well-launched into the predictable early stages of his exhibitionism. . . . Yes, everything was conducive to what Lulu had promised us would be a night of surprising and superlative entertainment.

Preliminary to this entertainment, a secret event he had been anticipating for us the entire week, Lulu was in the midst of telling one of his rare, evocative stories which always caused Honorine to smile and settle herself more comfortably into her own special attitude of languor and expectation. The story, as we began to discover, concerned a man who had been sent out by his mistress one rainy afternoon to sell a spray of mimosa on one of the town's busiest thoroughfares. The mistress was a beast of domesticity, the rain was heavy, the street was crowded (mainly with children), the man had a face of amazing scars and was so small and stolid that he was not much better than an impressive dwarf. But most important of all, this maltreated and ridiculous figure was the possessor of a left arm nipped off and drawn to a point at the elbow by one of those familiar accidents of birth that are so prevalent in a nation that still lies under the wing of medievalism.

On he talked, our Lulu, now contributing illustrative gestures to his story, which was punctuated occasionally by a few disrespectful notes of the accordian. Well, the stubborn and resentful lover, such as he was, attempted to sell his enormous branch of mimosa in the rain. He held the mimosa first in his right hand and then in a furious grip in the armpit of his offended partial arm, then in an agony of self-consciousness he shifted the mimosa from armpit to angry hand and back again. The children laughed (as did we of Lulu's audience), the hatless man was wet to the skin, a small but elegant automobile drove past with an enormous heap of gleaming, yellow mimosa covering its entire roof. Well, this story had no ending, of course, but afforded the perspiring Lulu a good many artful strokes along with an increasing number of sour notes to the accordianist. And though Lulu wiped his face and laughed and apologized for being unable to reach the moral of his story, no matter how fast and sonorously he talked, still each and every member of his audience smiled in immediate and pleasurable recognition of that moral, which says in effect that we are a nation of persons not only unashamed of the handicapped but capable, as a matter of fact, of making fun of them.

But now came the moment of the rare entertainment that we were all so primed to receive. The laughter faded, Lulu wiped his partially visible bare chest as well as his face with his handkerchief, the accordianist bestowed upon us a great, gleaming sweep of fanfare music, Lulu made a brief but enticing announcement about the spectacle we were now to see. Then he turned and drew aside an ordinary bed sheet which, throughout the story of the unglorious lover, had concealed the rear portion of the small makeshift stage which, I may now assure you, is all that remains of the long-since abandoned *Chez Lulu*.

But that night, and at that moment, already we saw no signs of impending physical decay. To the contrary, because there before us on that little stage stood three young girls who were delightfully natural, only moderately shy, and appealingly dressed in the most casual of clothing—in undershirts designed for boys, that is, and in tight denim pants. The families of those young girls were in the audience, each member of the audience knew each one of those most reputable young girls by sight. Need I mention the clapping that followed the removal of the sheet? Need I say that the smallest and most attractive of the girls was our own Chantal?

So she was, and barefooted, like the other two, and like them attired to affect simplicity and to erase undesirable differences between the three. As a matter of fact, Honorine and I were pleasantly and simultaneously aware that these three young, innocent girls were already more provocative, more indiscreetly revealed, than most professional seminude girls in a chorus line. You can imagine the activity which this combination (the adolescent amateurs, the public performance) sent rippling through the audience at *Chez Lulu* that night. What, we wondered, had he trained our girls to do? And what were we to make of the three large, orange carrots suspended small end downward approximately a meter apart by lengths of ordinary white twine tied to a slender beam affixed overhead? What "act" could Lulu possibly have in mind?

Well, we had not long to wait. Lulu clapped his hands, the accordianist set aside his great gaudy instrument, we of the audience craned or crowded forward, some of us going so far as to leave our tables and

sit informally in the cool sand at the foot of the stage. And then, while
the two men bustled about, whispering to the girls and positioning them
in an exact giggling line across the impromptu stage, so that each one
stood directly behind the particular dangling carrot which had previ-
ously been designated as her own, suddenly and as if by prearranged
signal, all three girls knelt as one with their faces raised, their knees
apart, and their hands behind their upright backs. The tips of the immense carrots hung barely within reach of the three sets of pretty lips
which, we noticed, had been freshly painted with a glistening red cosmetic for this debut on the stage. There were whistles, random volleys
of clapping, more jockeying for better and closer locations from which
to see. But what now, Honorine and I asked each other with smiles and
raised eyebrows, what now—blindfolds?

Yes, they were indeed blindfolds, and at the first sight of them, and
while Lulu and his grinning assistant were tying them like broad, white
bandages over the eyes of the young trio kneeling as if awaiting the
revolver of some brutal executioner, the audience voiced its approval
and curiosity in a new and sudden spurt of informality. By now we
knew what was coming, of course, and that we were about to witness
some sort of competition or game which would involve the men, the
girls, and the carrots. We could hardly have been more aroused or
appreciative.

Lulu called for silence, and in the next moment one could hear even
the lapping of water against the flanks of an invisible sailboat or the
sound of insects in the bamboo matting overhead. All faces were ad-
mirably attentive. We watched as the three girls, now illuminated in the
bright beam of a single spotlight, shifted nervously in their kneeling
positions and gathered their muscles, so to speak, and raised their pretty,
blinded faces like sniffing rabbits. The girls waited, Lulu raised his thick
right arm, the assistant composed himself behind two of the girls as
might a sprinter. Already the three charming contestants had begun to
perspire. Music from a car radio came to us faintly across the little
midnight harbor.

Then Lulu shouted, flung down his arm, and thereby sent our trio
of sweet girls into an unbelievable flurry of agitation which, we saw
immediately, was all the more pronounced and even feverish because of
the ground rules by which the girls were forbidden to move their spread
knees. In the previous few moments each of us in the audience had made
his firm choice, his loyal commitment, and had fixed upon that particular young girl whose efforts he would champion to the very end. And

now, even at the mere outset of this simple sport, the shouts of encouragement were deafening.

The rest is obvious, as most stories are. And yet there was indeed a
certain mounting excitement, because first it was necessary for each girl
to locate her carrot, a process in which all three initially employed
merely their good will, their innocence, their straining young bodies
(fixed to the rough planks at the knees), the entirety of their groping
faces. But as the game wore on, marked by waves of clapping and held
breaths, one by one the girls began to intuit what was required of them,
began to discover within themselves an abandon which they could not
possibly have known until now. That is, they began to grope for the
tips of the carrots with their open mouths, with their bright, red, girlish
lips now puckered into an oval shape, or at last and skillfully enough
began to fish desperately for the fat carrots with their glistening tongues.
In all this there was a good deal of tension and comedy, as noses buf-
feted carrots or a flushed cheek accidentally knocked one of the great
orange creatures quite beyond reach. The girls swayed and rose and fell
on their spread knees; the carrots swayed in wild circles; the two men
became more pressing as pilots, so to speak, of the now hot and sightless
girls. Yes, Lulu was devoting all his efforts to Chantal while the accordianist, poor fellow, was obliged to divide his attentions between the
other two now frantic girls. Of course it was only too apparent that
Lulu and his assistant were attempting to guide their charges toward
possession of the unobliging carrots not only with whispered words but
with hands that were momentarily visible on a wet and tender shoulder
and then, for long periods, were quite invisible in what could only have
been their impatient grip on the seat of one of the pairs of tight blue
denim pants. The accordianist was not at all in sympathy with his own
two awkward girls while Lulu, on the other hand, appeared to be gaining impressive, delicate control over our remarkably responsive Chantal.
The black, pointed tip of his shoe was visible between her knees, he
crouched behind her like a ventriloquist manipulating an erotic doll.

Well, the admirable young contestants searched in vain, caught the
tips of the carrots between eager lips, screamed joyously, thereby once
again losing the prize. The carrots began to glisten, the denim pants
grew predictably shaded with perspiration, the girls cried out in glee or
in a childish mockery of frustration. We of the audience applauded
whenever a carrot was successfully trapped, we moaned when that same
carrot bobbed away.

You know the rest: the object of the game, which was merely the clever excuse for its existence, was to eat the carrot. And while the two other girls nibbled and tossed themselves about and even shed pretty tears, it was Chantal, of course, who finally understood the game and slowly, sinuously, drew the carrot between her lips and sucked, chewed, reaching always upward with her small lovely face, until the deed was quite beautifully done.

Can you see the hollow cheeks? The tendons in the youthful neck? The traces of smeared lipstick on the now devoured carrot? I am sure you can.

Well, Lulu untied the blindfold and, perspiring himself, lifted our happy Chantal to her bare feet to receive her ovation. And that, of course, is how Chantal became the Queen of Carrots. It was only the next day that she found courage enough to go for the first time bare-breasted to the beach where she spent the morning as well as the after-noon exerting herself in one of the old, white, cumbersome paddleboats. Her companion in the paddleboat was, as you will have guessed, none other than the notorious Lulu. It was plain to Honorine and me that Chantal had quite overcome her shyness and that the gigantic Lulu was enjoying to the full this first day with his little pink and amber Queen.

So you think that my brain is sewn with the sutures of your psychosis. So that's what you think. But how very like you to require not a single last resort but two. And if you will remember, I knew it was coming sooner or later, this double-bladed effort first to persuade me of my own psychological distraction, if that is the term, and second to entice me back to sanity, as only you could express the idea, with promises of repose, forgiveness, your imminent departure, the everlasting adoration of my wife and daughter. Of course I understand that you have no alternative but to lay at my door this your actual last resort. As I have said already, it is my opinion that you publicized and glamorized ex-cessively those few months in which you gave yourself over to the sullen immobility of the mental patient. But I am sympathetic. I am well aware that in that short time they so sutured the lobes of your brain with designs of fear and hopelessness that the threads themselves emerged from within your skull to travel in terrible variety down the very flesh of your face, pinching, pulling, and scoring your hardened skin as if they, your attendants, had been engaged not in psychological but sur-gical disfigurement. I appreciate all this. I regret that you were so abused

and that you took such dreadful pleasure in the line that cracked your
eye, cleft your upper lip, stitched the unwholesome map of your brain
to the mask of your face. But we must remember that we are talking
not about me but you. What I have just been saying applies to you but
not to me. Despite my theory of likenesses, as I have called it, you are
simply not to think that your former derangement has reappeared in me
and, at present, is driving all three of us to what the authorities define
as death by unnatural causes. I believe that if you have been listening
you will have heard in my words the dying breath of your own irrationality, not mine.

Concentrate, *cher ami*. Concentrate. Because I know already that I
am "adored" by wife and daughter. It would never occur to me to wish
for your "imminent departure." After all, *cher ami*, it is I who chose
you to be present with me tonight. But on the last point I am even more
confident: you and I would always shun "repose," even if it in fact
existed and were not merely the phantom of all who refuse to present
themselves to the stillness of the open gate.

But now she is dreaming. Yes, if my calculations are in the least reliable,
we are now approximately seven minutes from Tara where the lady of
the dark chateau lies dreaming. Honorine was always uncomfortable
when, no matter how rarely, I applied to her that romantic epithet. But
of course you are not burdened with her clear integrity and charming
modesty, *cher ami*. So tonight I shall indulge myself for the last time
and speak of Honorine, my wife, as the lady of the dark chateau. And
yet the sleeping rooks; the magnificent shutters drawn closed and only
somewhat in need of repair; the stables long ago converted to a garage
which, this moment, houses one blue automobile instead of the usual
blue car and the beige; the oak tree as bare and formidable as the chateau itself; the stately dog that lies beside the mammoth bed not for
protection but for the sake of elegance and love; the amorous grace of
the sleeper who earlier dined alone and then at a late hour undressed
for bed without fear, without suspicion, and with only a few agreeable
thoughts of us. . . . Doesn't all this justify in a way my romantic epithet?
The glass of water on the nightstand, the slender volume closed but
marked with a ribbon, the sound of breathing, the eyes which, if opened,
would be serene—these at least justify my epithet, *cher ami*. But now I
must tell you that despite our proximity, despite the fact that we have
indeed appeared at the edge of her slumbering consciousness, still

Honorine is not dreaming of our approaching car but of a flock of sheep. Let me explain.

One early afternoon, within hours, it seemed to me, of that moment when I conceived of the journey you and Chantal and I were shortly to take—I am being as honest as I possibly can—Honorine and I were walking in one of the distant, rocky fields adjoining Tara. You, I believe, had accompanied Chantal to her riding lesson. The afternoon was fair, the sun was warm, Honorine and I were walking so closely together among the rocks that we brushed shoulders, touched each other hip to hip or hand to hand, pleasantly and unintentionally. A tree far to the west was as small and bright as a golden toy. The rocks were like pre-historic signs to our suede boots. And then Honorine stopped us short and pointed. Because there, just ahead of us, the rocks appeared to be moving while the air was suddenly filled with a music of bells which Honorine, under her breath, described as a kind of heavenly *Glockenspiel,* though in fact she has always been quite as irreligious as her head of the household.

Well, it was a flock of sheep, of course, and we were caught in its midst. Honorine smiled; the tinkling and caroling of the bells increased; a thrush was in flight; for no reason at all the two of us turned and looked back at Tara which, in that soft light was far away and empty and both majestic and shabby, exactly as it had always been and as we wanted it to be. A place of comfort, mystery, privacy, as you surely know. But it was then while the sheep were rippling and purling about our legs (I noted that Honorine was not much interested in the baby lambs, being her typically unsentimental self), it was then and for no reason that I could discern, that Honorine ran her fingers through her short, blonde hair streaked with gray and, keeping a slight distance apart from me, smiled up at my face and began to speak. Without preliminaries and in her clear, quiet way she said that she thought you and I were both a little out of our heads. She said that we were selfish, that we were hurtful, and that she did not trust either one of us. But then she laughed and said that she loved us both, however, and was willing and capable of paying whatever price the gods, in return, might eventually demand of her for loving us both.

You will know how I felt. But may I point out that not once have you raised the question of cruelty or advanced the argument that my insistence on suicide and murder—at this juncture let us be honest—may reflect nothing more than my secret desire to punish eternally the lady of the dark chateau, as I may now call her without impunity? Well, allow me to advance precisely that neglected argument of yours and provide an answer as well.

It is cruel. Could anyone know better than I how cruel it is? Yes, what I am doing is cruel, but it is not motivated by cruelty. There is a difference. And who better than I should know that it is in fact motivated by quite the opposite? These are my reasons: first, Honorine is now more "real" to you, to me, than she has ever been; second, when she recovers, at last, she will exercise her mind in order to experience in her own way what we have known; but third and most important, months and years beyond her recovery, Honorine will know with special certainty that just as she was the source of your poems, so too was she the source of my private apocalypse. It was all for her. And such intimate knowledge is worth whatever price the gods may demand, as she herself said. No, *cher ami*, Honorine is a person of great strength. Sooner or later she will understand.

So you see the importance of a woman's dream and a flock of belled sheep.

But I have promised you a glimpse of the formative event of my early manhood. It was nothing, really, though I suppose that in retrospect all of the formative or most highly prized events of our days fade until they no longer have any shape or consequence. At any rate this particular event was the simplest of that entire store which at one time or another defined me, thrilled me, convinced me of the validity of the fiction of living, but which I have now forgotten. I will be brief. A few lines and you will have it.

The automobile, a bright green, was large enough only for two, and I was alone. The street was wide but the hour was such that the crowds, composed mostly of children, were jostling each other from the curbs. I was driving quickly, too quickly, in my desire to visit Honorine, whom I hardly knew. The old man, bewhiskered and wearing a bright silk cravat and carrying a furled umbrella, though the sun was such that it could not possibly have rained that day, was unmistakably one of your kind, which is to say an old poet. From the first instant I saw him he irritated me immensely, holding by the hand, as he surely was, a child more astounding than any I had ever seen.

I remember the car, which was powerful despite its size; I remember the street precisely because I was so uninterested in it; I remember the old poet because at the very moment I noticed him I saw that he was gripping the child's hand in lofty possessiveness and was already staring directly into my eyes with shocking anger. But most of all I remember the child. She was a waif with dark hair, dark eyes, an ingenuous little heart-shaped face filled with uncanny trustfulness and simple beauty. She was wearing a crudely knitted stocking cap with a tassel and a small once-discarded leather coat so old that it was scarred with white cracks. I marveled at the child and yet detested the old man who was already raising his brows, opening his mouth in fury, drawing back the child as if he could read in my face the character of a young man who would regard such a poor and sacred child, as the old man would think of her, with indifference or even disrespect.

I accelerated. I saw the tassel flying. The old poet's face was a mass of rage and his umbrella was raised threateningly above his head. I felt nothing, not so much as a hair against the fender, exactly as if the child had been one of tonight's rabbits. I did not turn around or even glance in the rear-view mirror. I merely accelerated and went my way.

I do not believe I struck that little girl. In retrospect it does not seem likely. And yet I will never know. Perhaps the privileged man is an even greater criminal than the poet. At any rate I shall never forget the face of the child.

What's that? What's that you say? Can I have heard you correctly? *Imagined life is more exhilarating than remembered life.* . . . Is that what you said? *Imagined life is more exhilarating than remembered life.* Can it be true?

But then you agree, you understand, you have submitted after all, Henri! And listen, even your wheezing has died away.

But now I must tell you, Henri, that if you reached your hand inside my jacket pocket nearest to you—an action I would not advise you to attempt despite a moment's gift of agreement—your fingers would discover there a scrap of paper on which, if removed from the pocket and held low to the lights of our dashboard, you would find in my own handwriting these two lines:

> Somewhere there still must be
> Her face not seen, her voice not heard.

Do you recognize them? They are yours, naturally, and give us the true measure of your poetry. And I may say it now, Henri, I am extremely fond of these two lines. I might even have written them myself.

But look there. We have passed Tara. And we failed to note the lantern. And now it is gone.

Chantal. . . . Papa has not forgotten you, Chantal!

But now I make you this promise, Henri: there shall be no survivors. None.

FOR THE BEST IN PAPERBACKS, LOOK FOR THE

In every corner of the world, on every subject under the sun, Penguin represents quality and variety—the very best in publishing today.

For complete information about books available from Penguin—including Puffins, Penguin Classics, and Arkana—and how to order them, write to us at the appropriate address below. Please note that for copyright reasons the selection of books varies from country to country.

In the United Kingdom: Please write to *Dept. JC, Penguin Books Ltd, FREEPOST, West Drayton, Middlesex UB7 0BR.*

If you have any difficulty in obtaining a title, please send your order with the correct money, plus ten percent for postage and packaging, to *P.O. Box No. 11, West Drayton, Middlesex UB7 0BR*

In the United States: Please write to *Consumer Sales, Penguin USA, P.O. Box 999, Dept. 17109, Bergenfield, New Jersey 07621-0120.* VISA and MasterCard holders call 1-800-253-6476 to order all Penguin titles

In Canada: Please write to *Penguin Books Canada Ltd, 10 Alcorn Avenue, Suite 300, Toronto, Ontario M4V 3B2*

In Australia: Please write to *Penguin Books Australia Ltd, P.O. Box 257, Ringwood, Victoria 3134*

In New Zealand: Please write to *Penguin Books (NZ) Ltd, Private Bag 102902, North Shore Mail Centre, Auckland 10*

In India: Please write to *Penguin Books India Pvt Ltd, 706 Eros Apartments, 56 Nehru Place, New Delhi 110 019*

In the Netherlands: Please write to *Penguin Books Netherlands bv, Postbus 3507, NL-1001 AH Amsterdam*

In Germany: Please write to *Penguin Books Deutschland GmbH, Metzlerstrasse 26, 60594 Frankfurt am Main*

In Spain: Please write to *Penguin Books S. A., Bravo Murillo 19, 1° B, 28015 Madrid*

In Italy: Please write to *Penguin Italia s.r.l., Via Felice Casati 20, I-20124 Milano*

In France: Please write to *Penguin France S. A., 17 rue Lejeune, F–31000 Toulouse*

In Japan: Please write to *Penguin Books Japan, Ishikiribashi Building, 2–5–4, Suido, Bunkyo-ku, Tokyo 112*

In Greece: Please write to *Penguin Hellas Ltd, Dimocritou 3, GR–106 71 Athens*

In South Africa: Please write to *Longman Penguin Southern Africa (Pty) Ltd, Private Bag X08, Bertsham 2013*